Chip in the Madrasa

Chip in the Madrasa

A Novel

Vivek Sinha

ISBN: 978-1-54994-979-1

for my father,
who gave away his present for my better tomorrow

SECTIONS

ACKNOWLEDGEMENTS

I wish to thank Shahid Hussain, a Social Worker and an Islamic Scholar, for all the help in conducting extensive research about Islam and Islamic scriptures. I am also thankful to several other Muslims and Islamic Scholars who have chosen to remain faceless and yet have extended every possible help during my research that helped me understand the issues tormenting Muslims around the globe. I am also grateful to my Guruji, my brothers and my family for their support.

I. Seizure

1.

Ambulance took a sharp turn at the roundabout. It was late in the night and trucks were all over on the Delhi roads. The sirens blared in full volume and blue light shimmered atop the ambulance's roof as it waded through the traffic in India's capital city. Heavy traffic had slowed it down and it was now crawling in the massive jam.

Inside the ambulance, lay a young man on the stretcher battling for his life and braving the two bullet shots that were pumped into his torso. Blood had now stopped oozing from his wounds, probably the thick clots over his wounds had arrested the blood loss, or it was the effect of paramedic's medication, or....

"No, Never, Absolutely Not...nothing will happen to my Abdul," Maulvi *sahab* mumbled as felt for his pulse. Abdul's blood had smeared up to his arms, his palms and on to the white *kurta,* and there were big blood stains all around. His eyes were red, the reddishness competing with the red blood clots on Abdul's chest. Abdul was his son, his beloved, his dream, his aspiration, and his world.

Maulvi *sahab* blamed himself for Abdul's present condition. "These bullets had my name inscribed on them," he wailed. If he could, he would have dug out bullets from Abdul's body, swap places with him and lie down on the stretcher. But Maulvi *sahab* knew this was just wishful thinking.

Abdul's pulse was weak but palpitations were present. His mother was gently massaging his feet and wife Sakina lovingly caressed his head. Their lips quivering in unison as they continued to recite the verses of the Holy Quran, invoking Allah to save Abdul.

"How long will it take to reach the hospital?" Maulvi *sahab* asked, worriedly looking at the slow moving traffic from the ambulance's window.

"We are almost there…just five more minutes," said Arjun, who was sitting on the front seat along with the driver. "….Yes, this is an Emergency. My friend has been shot in his chest…yes they were pistol shots…oh please…the police has been informed and you only need to prepare for the surgery….," Arjun was constantly on phone with the hospital's staff.

A convoy of cars and motorbikes had been following Abdul's ambulance, they had been driving for over two hundred kilometres, worried and concerned for Abdul. A few of the men hurriedly got off their cars and bikes, cut through the nasty traffic and made way for the ambulance.

The ambulance careened at the hospital's ranch, its tyres made a screeching noise and it came to a grinding halt. The paramedics rushed through the emergency gateway to attend to the patient.

"Gently please," Maulvi *sahab* pleaded with the paramedics as they dragged Abdul through the ambulance doors to make him lie on the hospital stretcher. The medicos did not hear Maulvi *sahab's* pleas to be gentle. They knew their job and the protocol. The moment Abdul was on stretcher they rolled and pushed it inside the hospital. More than a dozen people from Abdul's village were running ahead of the stretcher, shoving and pushing other people on the corridors to make way for the stretcher. Maulvi *sahab*, his wife Begum *sahiba* and Abdul's wife Sakina were running behind the stretcher wailing and sobbing with tears flowing through their eyes.

Everybody was abruptly halted at the big white door. The paramedics slid through this door with Abdul on the stretcher.

"Nobody is allowed in the operation room. Please wait in the lounge," the attendant was polite but firm.

Maulvi *sahab* lifted his head to look at the lounge's wall clock. It was a giant clock and each swipe of the seconds arm was distinctly palpable. Probably, these giant clocks have a purpose in the hospital. They help the people waiting in the lounge to keep track of each second spent by their loved ones in the operation theatre.

'It has been more than three hours since the medics took away Abdul on that stretcher,' Maulvi *sahab* thought.

'Have they been able to extract the bullet from his chest?'
'What if the bullet had pierced through his heart?'
'What if his rib cage has been fractured?'
'What if....'

Maulvi *sahab's* mind was racing fast. He tried to connect dots to the sequence of events and the frenzy that had led to Abdul being shot.

'How can a petty Maulvi of some madrasa in a far off small village become such a big threat to the Wahhabis of Saudi Arabia?'

'What did I do to invite the wrath of these fanatic Wahhabis and their stooges in India? And if I was the threat, why not shoot me? Why did they have to fire at my innocent son?' Maulvi *sahab* was relentlessly questioning himself. He looked up at the giant wall clock again. It had been four hours.

Next moment, the doctor emerged. He walked up to Maulvi *sahab* and other anxious faces in the waiting lounge. There was an eerie silence and the doctor stood still.

Maulvi *sahab* opened his mouth but words refused to come out. All others stood still in stunned silence.

"Well," the doctor said breaking the uncomfortable silence, "...Abdul is still alive but his condition remains critical. He was lucky that the bullet did not pierce through his heart, but it brushed past his left lung... The next twenty four hours are quite critical for him."

"Doctor *Sahib*,… my Abdul… will he be alright? Will he be able to walk and run?" Begum *sahiba* asked earnestly. Her eyes wide open, the saliva in her mouth had dried up due to some unknown fear.

"We have done whatever best we could do with surgery and medicines…Pray to God," the doctor said with a solemn face and walked away.

Tears welled down from Sakina's eyes and Begum *sahiba*. They held each other's hands. Sakina slumped on the chair, almost pulling Begum *sahiba* along with her.

Anxiety and nervousness had given way to despair and helplessness in the waiting lounge.

Arjun was taking deep breaths as he made strenuous efforts to stop himself from breaking into loud sobs. He was Abdul's childhood friend and the two had grown up together.

The duty nurse announced that Abdul has been shifted into the intensive care unit, the ICU.

Maulvi *sahab* peeped inside the glass door of the ICU. Abdul lay motionless on the ICU's electric bed, pipes and wires were attached to his body, monitors beeped at regular intervals with the nurse keeping a close eye on his vital signs. He had been staring at his son with tears in his eyes when someone tapped his shoulder. Maulvi *sahab* turned around. It was the duty nurse.

She ushered everyone to the in-patient waiting lounge.

The waiting lounge was a plush room with grand reclining chairs, a big television screen, tea-vending machine and a snacks bar. Older people settled on the soft cushioned sofas while younger ones spread around the room to sit on chairs, some walked up to the snacks bar and ordered tea.

A few youngsters were busy watching football match on the flat television screen, hung from the wall. The match was between Europe's elite soccer clubs and the teenagers were completely engrossed in it, they had taken sides and were cheering for their respective teams, completely oblivious of the fact that they were in a hospital. Thankfully, the match ended and the raucous adolescents stepped out.

An elderly gentleman stood up and changed the channel. Being a news buff, he had flipped over to a news channel. A pretty news anchor emerged on the television screen along with a panel of experts who discussed something that was of no interest to people in the waiting lounge.

Arjun's father had ordered tea for everyone and everybody was busy sipping tea. Maulvi *sahab* had lifted his head, he appeared to hear the television discussion, but his mind was still in the ICU worried about his Abdul.

Several minutes later, the television anchor introduced another topic of discussion, *"Marginalisation of Muslims in today's mainstream society"* and introduced her panelists. "...so on my immediate left is a revered Islamic cleric, *Maulana* Kamran and to my far left is Aakash Kumar, General Secretary of FPI, one of India's largest political outfit and I will be joined by....," she went on with other introductions.

Maulvi *sahab* went numb as he saw the two men on television screen. The tea cup slipped from his hands and he walked nearer to the screen.

The news anchor opened the discussion with *Maulana* Kamran and asked as to why Muslims continue to remain on the margins of the society.

"A Muslim has come to this planet with a mission. His whole life must be devoted to serve this purpose. The life on this planet is just a transit stay and for a Muslim the actual life begins only after his martyrdom....The issue is not with Muslims, rather the actual problems lie with nation states that continue to create hurdles in a Muslim's life. The country's political set up and administration need to understand about the purpose and value of a Muslim's life... They must facilitate, make amends and provide Muslims with all necessary resources to help them accomplish their goals," Kamran said with a smug look on his face.

Maulvi *sahab,* turned sideways, rubbed his hands in exasperation as he stood in front of the television screen. Several people who had come from his village along with Abdul's ambulance had, by now, converged along with Maulvi *sahab* in front of the television screen.

"Okay let me bring in the politician here," the news anchor said as she turned towards Aakash. "What role have politics and politicians played in to deny the Muslims their rightful place in the Indian society?" the anchor asked with a smile, her beaming smile was slightly out of place for a news discussion and seemed apt for a toothpaste advertisement.

Aakash straightened up. And he began with his explanation, "Well, this is an extremely complex situation. We need to understand that a Muslim is discriminated against right from his childhood. A Muslim child is not able to secure admission in good schools and so he is forced to study in sub-standard schools where there aren't any good teachers or books and look at the condition of the madrasas, most of them are in shambles or in a dilapidated condition... also when a Muslim youth walks up to some multi-national or to any government department he is denied the job because of his religion...and all this happens because there are no policies to safeguard the interests of Muslims. The political parties who have been in power need to answer... why followers of Islam are discriminated at every step....and you need to understand that these things are the cause for growing dissent among Muslims... and this dissatisfaction manifests itself in a Muslim picking up arms, which the world calls terrorism."

"Bloody hypocrite. This man is a fraud. Bloody filthy....," Anjali screeched, she had controlled herself from blurting out expletives. Anjali was a member of the FPI till a day ago, and had worked with the men who were now discussing about the plight of Muslims on national television.

Maulvi *sahab* merely shook his head in disgust and disbelief. His eyes drooping due to anxiety and tiredness had now drooped further due to repulsion. He looked towards Aftab *sahab,* his friend, and said: "*Ya* Allah, how can a person stoop so low."

A rude shock awaited him the next moment. Sakina was running towards him. Her unkempt hair swung wildly as she shoved past people in the waiting room.

"There's an emergency. Please come over. The nurse has made an emergency call for the doctors," Sakina was panting as she spoke. Her eyes were full of tears. Maulvi *sahab's* heart started pounding as he rushed towards the ICU.

Outside the intensive care unit Abdul was being taken away to the operation room. A distraught Begun *sahiba* was weeping inconsolably. The doctors had informed that due to internal bleeding Abdul will have to be operated upon yet again.

Maulvi *sahab* could feel his world crashing down. He collapsed on his knees and started weeping.

The surgery went on for an hour. A little later the team of doctors arrived. They informed that Abdul's condition continued to be critical. His blood pressure has nosedived and he has been kept on heavy medication. The internal bleeding had stopped but his heartbeat was erratic.

"We have tried everything that we could possibly do. If his condition deteriorates further then…," the doctor paused.

"Then what?… Yes, my husband will live on, say this, please..," Sakina was pleading with folded hands. She held Begum *sahiba,* her mother-in-law, tightly and burst into tears.

Maulvi *sahab* was ash-faced. He was at loss with words. The doctor gently pressed his shoulders and walked away silently, his head down.

Maulvi *sahab* slumped on the ground. His vision blurred. He had not known that things would come to this.

He had simply wanted to revamp his village's madrasa such that he could teach modern subjects along with Islamic scriptures. He had introduced at his madrasa, the *duniyawi taleem*--the modern education, along with *deenee taleem*--the Islamic religious knowledge.

It all started almost a decade ago.

II. Genesis

2.

Tears continued to roll down from Maulvi *sahab's* eyes, blurring his vision. People and objects in the hospital looked like shadows, and yet he evoked the events of yesteryears to make sense of the current situation around him. His eyelids slithered over his eyeballs and he went into a trance. It was several years ago when he undertook that bus journey, which led to a flurry of events at his village and in his life. It was the most memorable bus ride he had had in his life. Laying slump on the hospital chair he reminisced about that bus ride from Delhi till his village.

Maulvi *sahab* stepped out from the bus. He was the only passenger who hopped out. He had been standing at the bus's exit door for over fifteen minutes as the bus raced through the national highway, waiting anxiously to get down. His eyes were fixated on the road so that he did not miss out on the narrow culvert. He held a big brown packet in his left hand and held the iron bar with the other hand. The packet was heavy and Maulvi *sahab* had to frequently shift it from one hand to another. He oscillated between rusty bars at the exit door, and yet deftly maintained his balance. The gentleness with which he changed hands, shifting the packet from one arm to another suggested that he carried something delicate. His gentle smile and the contentment with which he looked at the packet alluded there was something precious in that brown packet.

The bus' tyres skidded on the gravel and it stopped with a screeching sound in front of the culvert. This culvert led him to his world—the village Basera.

A thick smog of black smoke and dust rose up as the bus accelerated and sped off. From a distance Maulvi *sahab* looked like the military commando who has just vanquished his enemy and was walking amidst dust and smoke in the background to felicitations and a much deserved rest. But, Maulvi *sahab's* similarity with the commando ended here. His battle, rather the war, had just begun.

Maulvi *sahab* had a lean built with an average height. He sported a beard and a moustache that were neatly trimmed. His jawline was narrow, eyes were big and black but his gaze was gentle. When at the village he wore *kurta* and pyjama but when going out he dressed up in shirts and trousers. Today he wore an off-white coloured shirt with a matching grey pant which replete with the black shoes and black belt gave Maulvi *sahab* the look of a corporate executive.

He continued to walk on the narrow unpaved path that had thick bushes on either sides. The wiry sling, which wrapped around the large brown packet, sliced through his fingers causing sharp pain if he held the packet for more than a minute, thus forcing him to constantly switch the packet between his hands. Unmindful of this discomfort, he wiped the tiny beads of sweat on his forehead and walked briskly.

As he paced ahead, Maulvi *sahab* thought of the events that had unravelled over the last few days. He was the teacher at Basera village's Islamic school—madrasa. He had proposed that apart from religious books and Islamic scriptures the madrasa children need to be taught other subjects, as well. He had been informally teaching other subjects to madrasa children but had long felt the need to formally introduce modern academic subjects such as science, mathematics, economics, history and social sciences to the children. Contrary to his expectations the youngest member in the madrasa management committee had opposed his proposition. Those in his age bracket and the much older members had been more receptive to the idea of teaching other subjects to madrasa children.

Afroz, the relatively youngest member, was against the idea of introduction of mathematics, science, economics and social sciences for madrasa students. Afroz's attitude had surprised Maulvi *sahab*. He was educated in supposedly the best schools of India and had completed his college from European Universities. A year earlier, after his father's demise, he had come on board of the madrasa management committee. Initially, he remained a passive listener during the management meetings but had become quite vocal in the recent months.

Maulvi *sahab* did not think much of his opposition. He was happy that all other committee members had acceded to his request to formally introduce and teach mathematics, science, economics, history and social sciences at the madrasa. A small sum was sanctioned to get books for the children. The amount was insufficient and Maulvi *sahab* had taken it upon himself to go to Delhi to buy the books. He felt happy and contended that he could bring in the books and workbooks for his students. The distributor at Delhi offered him concession and had neatly packed the books in a brown sheet. The bundle of books was bigger than Maulvi *sahab* could have carried but he did not mind the extra weight.

It had almost been thirty minutes since Maulvi *sahab* de-boarded the bus and had been walking towards his village. A grubby green coloured board mounted on short rusty iron poles had 'Basera' inscribed in Hindi, Urdu and English, one below another in a sequence. This board announced to the visitors that they have entered the village—'Basera'.

"*Salam-walekum* Maulvi *sahab*," Nazir greeted as he piloted a herd of buffaloes to the nearby pond. The bare chested Nazir was sitting atop one of the buffaloes and shooed the herd with a long narrow stick.

"*Walekum-salam* Nazir *bhai*," Maulvi *sahab* acknowledged his greetings with a smile as he walked on.

His house was still a few furlongs away. It lay in the middle of the village across *Khidmat-ul-Islam,* the madrasa, where he was the teacher. A big lane separated his house from the madrasa, and the madrasa was an extension of

"*Abbu,* you know today morning I was playing with Arjun in the fields. I felt hungry and plucked guavas from the tree to eat. Do trees also feel hungry? Who gives them their food?" Abdul asked, his fingers caressing the image of guava tree in the book.

"Oh yes trees do feel hungry and they prepare their own food"

"How?"

"Trees derive nutrients through their roots and their leaves prepare food with the help of sunshine. Just the way your mother prepares food for us. And this process is known as photosynthesis," Maulvi sahab explained, impressed by the curiosity of his son.

"Photosyn…." Abdul struggled to pronounce the word.

"Photo – synthesis," Maulvi sahab said, breaking the word to make pronunciation easy for Abdul.

"*Salam-walekum* Maulvi *sahab.*" Arjun's father greeted as he pulled a chair to sit beside them in the courtyard. Arjun was Abdul's best buddy in the village and the two spent most of their time together.

"*Walekum--assalam* Pundit *ji,*" Maulvi *sahab* replied as he coughed.

"*Salam-walekum* uncle," Abdul greeted Pundit *ji* as he ran inside the house to get a glass of water for him.

"I was passing by, so came in. You've got cough. Have some warm water."

"Ah it's just a simple cough and nothing to worry about"

Begum *sahiba,* Maulvi sahab's wife, overheard her husband dismissing his cough as something trivial and came out of the kitchen with the spatula in her hand. She felt irritated that her husband, Maulvi *sahab,* does not take due care of his health.

"It's been more than a week and still you are dismissing it as some ordinary cough. *Bhai-jaan* please make your friend see a doctor. He just doesn't listen to me anymore," Begum *sahiba* complained, waving the spatula in her hand.

"*Bhabhi ji* is right. You must see a doctor," Arjun's father said and then turning towards Begum *sahiba* added, "…okay *Bhabhi ji* so I have convinced my friend to visit the doctor and you can now keep the spatula back in the kitchen."

Begum *sahiba* embarrassed by the way she still held the spatula in her hands pulled back her hands behind her back as Maulvi *sahab* and Arjun's father burst into laughter.

Arjun's father asked about his Delhi visit to the book distributor.

"I got some of the books that were immediately required by the students. The remaining books will come through courier. But…" Maulvi *sahab* paused.

"What happened? Is everything okay? Did the distributor say something about money," Arjun's father asked. The distributor was one of his friends and he had referred Maulvi *sahab* to him.

"Oh no it's not about the distributor. I am worried about Afroz's attitude. That day during the meeting of madrasa management committee…you could have seen his attitude. He himself is educated in some of the famous colleges and universities and the way he was opposing my proposal to teach science and mathematics…this does not augur well," Maulvi *sahab* sighed as he sipped warm water.

"Don't worry these are just teething troubles that come up whenever something new is begun"

"So, I wish. Amen"

Begum *sahiba* had served tea and biscuits. Arjun's father promised to come next morning to take Maulvi *sahab* to the doctor.

3.

Mornings at Basera village were serene. Large farm fields spread afar, touching the boundaries of adjoining village, bunds demarcating boundaries of the farm of one owner with another appeared like creases on a vast green carpet. Apart from farming, almost every household in the village reared buffaloes, cows, goats and hen. The relatively well-off people had buffaloes or cows and the poorer had goats and hen. Those who owned farm lands sought help from the landless for their gamut of agricultural operations, the landless in return received grains apart from the cash as a payback of their labour. Very few households had tractors and most relied on bullocks to till their land. People began their days at dawn and by twilight, retired to their homes.

Maulvi *sahab* had laid the mat to offer day's first *namaz*. Abdul and his mother finished off their daily ablutions and hurried towards Maulvi *sahab*. Abdul adjusted his white coloured skullcap, on his head and stood alongside his father to offer the prayers. After the morning *namaz*, Maulvi *sahab* went over to the shed to tend to his buffaloes. He washed the wide mouthed pot, mixed hay with green fodder and bathed the buffaloes, his hands gently caressing their coarse black skin. Maulvi *sahab's* buffaloes looked neat and clean unlike most other buffaloes in the village that almost always had mud smeared on them. Most villagers never bothered to wash off the mud that stuck to their buffaloes after they came out from a dip in the village pond. A few, like Maulvi *sahab*, diligently removed specks of dirt from their skin and applied oil on their horns. During late afternoons when the herd of buffaloes returned after grazing from the pastures, Maulvi *sahab's* buffaloes could be easily spotted due to their shining black horns and much cleaner skins. Every morning Maulvi *sahab* milked the buffaloes, cleaned the cattle shed with a broom and then headed to the madrasa.

Basera's madrasa, the *Khidmat-ul-Islam,* looked quaint. Maulvi *sahab's* father along with some village elders had conceptualized the need to have a madrasa within the village that would cater to the education of poor village children. Afroz's father had donated his plot besides the mosque, someone paid for the bricks and mortar while others helped with copies of the Holy Quran and other books. Maulvi *sahab's* father, a retired college professor, had agreed to devote his time to teach the students at Basera madrasa. He became the Maulvi. When he passed away his son Haider took over the job of a teacher at *Khidmat-ul-Islam.* The entire Basera village held Maulvi *sahab* in high regard for his decision to continue in his father's footsteps. Maulvi *sahab* had qualified for a job at a government bank in Delhi but the untimely demise of his father and the dire need for a Maulvi at the Basera madrasa forced him to rethink his proposition.

Teachers were not willing to stay back in a small village like Basera, they were more interested in taking up a job in the Middle East to make a quick buck. Those who turned up for the job were not up to the mark. Student attendance at the madrasa had fell sharply during those days. It was then that Abdul's father, Haider decided to take up the job of a teacher at the madrasa. And he never held any grudges that he had to forego his government job, rather he way happy that he was able to contribute towards education of young kids at his village who would otherwise have been bereft of education.

One day Haider was discussing interpretation of the verses of the Holy Quran at a gathering, which was attended by a village elderly who was also a member of the madrasa's management committee. Impressed by young Haider's knowledge of Quran and the Hadith he had called him 'Maulvi *sahab'*. It was he who suffixed *sahab* to Maulvi Haider and from then onwards Haider became Maulvi *sahab*. The name struck such a chord with the villagers that now hardly anyone remembered Maulvi *sahab's* original name. And Maulvi *sahab* had lived up to his reputation ever since, dedicating his life for the betterment of students at the *Khidmat-ul-Islam*.

Praising Maulvi *sahab* for his commitment towards education of Basera's children the village *hakim* (doctor) offered to marry his daughter Mehrunisa with him. Entire Basera had come to attend their nikah and yet nobody wanted to be the guest, everyone was keen to be the host. It was a grand get-together for Basera denizens. Maulvi *sahab* was twenty four years old at the time of his marriage. He lovingly called his wife, Begum *sahiba*.

Mehrunisa suffered two unfortunate miscarriages and Abdul was born to the couple only after they sought blessings at the *Dargah* of Nizamuddin Auliya in Delhi.

"Abbu come on, let's go," Abdul urged his father as he flung the cloth bag on his shoulder. The green coloured cloth bag was hand-sewn by his mother for him. This elegant bag replete with sequins on its borders was his school bag.

Each morning Abdul was the first to get ready for the madrasa and nagged his father to hurry up. Maulvi *sahab* got a delightful satisfaction to see his son rush for the classes. Sometimes he deliberately stayed a bit longer in his room to let Abdul get restless for the classes. He felt pleased to see Abdul's thirst for knowledge increase with each passing day.

The paint on the walls of *Khidmat-ul-Islam* madrasa had peeled off at several places revealing the brownish black mortar of its walls. The repair work with cement were carried off and on, but without fresh painting the outside walls bore a patchy look. The black rusted iron gates reminded that the madrasa had held its ground for several years. Yet, the old and patchy looks on the madrasa's façade were in sharp contrast to its spick and span inside. The interiors did not wear any branded paint but the walls were periodically brushed with white lime water. There were no teak wood furniture but the

19

few tables and chairs and the clean carpets spread across the classrooms served the students well. There were no costly books but the ones that were available were neatly stacked inside the cupboard. The madrasa's ambience whispered that it was built with sweat and passion of the villagers, rather than with packets of cash.

"Salaam-walekum Maulvi *sahab,"* the chowkidar greeted.

"Walekum-assalam," Maulvi *sahab* replied as he proceeded towards the main porch of the madrasa. Abdul joined ranks with the other children and reached the classroom.

The children kept their bags and put on their skull caps for the morning recitation of Quranic verses. Maulvi *sahab* and other madrasa teachers had arrived. They gathered in the central hall for the recitation of *Surah Ar-Rahman.*

After the recitation, Maulvi *sahab* stood up. He announced to the students that he will discuss about the Allah's creation of this universe.

"So one day Allah called his angels and said that he will create living beings…," Maulvi *sahab* began. "…hearing Allah's words, the devil who is also one of the angels of Allah was surprised and asked Allah… Why O' Almighty what is the need for living beings on earth. We angels are willing to do anything and everything at your command. We follow each of your instructions every time every day…"

Abdul's eyes had widened as he listened intently to Maulvi *sahab's* explanation about the origins and reasons for life's creation.

"…Now, see how Allah answers to the devil's argument.…"

"Allah says: Listen O devil, all these angels live with me in heaven and do exactly what I tell them but these living beings whom I wish to create will live on the earth and they will have the option to perform good deeds or commit sins and whosoever carries on with the good deeds will reach the Heaven…"

"…but then the devil was devil indeed. He continued with his arguments and said: O' Allah, I will pollute the minds of these humans and compel them to commit sins. I will ensure that men and women deviate from the path of goodness and commit sins such that they are not able to come to heaven…," Maulvi *sahab* explained.

"And then Allah said whenever this happens I will send a Prophet to earth who will show the path of righteousness to every man and woman. My Prophet will be the guiding light for people on the earth….," he elaborated to the spellbound children.

Soon the bell rang and everybody stood up to offer *namaz*.

After *namaz* was the mathematics class. Maulvi *sahab* distributed the new math books and workbooks that he had brought from Delhi for the students. The children were still busy flipping through the book's pages to see numbers, images and sentences when Maulvi *sahab* walked up to the black board and with the white chalk wrote a big and lengthy calculation on the board. The arithmetical calculation required all four mathematical operations of addition, subtraction, division and multiplication to be conducted to arrive at the answer.

"Okay so this is today's question and we need to find the answer to this question. So, Taufeek tell me how are you going to solve this question," he asked Taufeek, the blacksmith's son.

Taufeek said that he would first do the addition, then subtraction, after that he would multiply and then finally divide.

"Okay, so Taufeek will do the addition first. Rukhsana what will you do?"

"I will multiply first," said Rukhsana, Rashid's daughter. Rashid was a roadside barber and had a wobbly wooden chair and a mirror under the neem tree, which he called his salon.

"Abbu…a..mm Maulvi *sahab,* I will divide first," Abdul responded.

"So everybody has a different method to solve this problem. But whose method is right?" asked Maulvi *sahab*.

The children start murmuring among themselves.

Maulvi *sahab* wrote 'BODMAS' in big and bold on the board. He went on to explain how each alphabet of *'bodmas'* meant following a pre-defined sequencing to conduct mathematical operations.

Maulvi *sahab* had a modest upbringing and he needed bare minimal material comforts for himself. He cycled his way through the village. Though motorbikes were now common in Basera and he could have easily afforded one, he never felt the need to buy one.

Cycling keeps me healthy and fit, he would say whenever he was asked to get a motorbike. A teacher needs to be healthy so that he never misses his classes and should be mentally agile to be able to impart quality education to his students, he told his *begum* whenever she insisted that he get a motorbike for himself.

Begum *sahiba* never complained. She was happy and content. Her day started with *namaz* that was followed by washing and cleaning the home. Thereafter she prepared food on the mud stove by burning firewood. After seeing off Maulvi *sahab* and Abdul to the madrasa she busied herself in other household chores. This was her daily routine.

Maulvi *sahab* was in his late thirties yet he commanded respect from everybody in the village. He was known by several people in the adjoining villages as well, and everyone vouched for his kindness, goodness and integrity. On every nook and corner of Basera, Maulvi *sahab* was greeted by the young and old, men and women, children and elderly, Muslims and Hindus alike.

Maulvi *sahab* turned his cycle around the big banyan tree. He saw Abdul, Arjun and other children of the village playing cricket. The young boys had improvised with the tree trunk and with a black charcoal piece drew three vertical lines like the cricket stumps on the trunk of banyan tree.

"Uncle come play with us," Arjun urged Maulvi *sahab*, and he happily obliged.

"Okay I will bowl"

Maulvi *sahab* bowled a couple of balls and the children were happy that he played with them.

"Is your father at home?"

"Yes," said Arjun. Maulvi *sahab* cycled towards Arjun's home. Arjun lived across the canal that brought water to Basera and several other villages. During rainy seasons when it rained incessantly it was this canal that carried the excess water away. Village elders said before this canal, floods across the entire region were a regular affair and hundreds of villages were inundated during the rainy season. The canal quenched their thirst during summers and when rains arrived, its belly swelled like the big serpentine dragon. This canal was their lifeline.

"*Namaskar bhaisahab.* How are you?" Maulvi *sahab* waved at Arjun's father as he parked his cycle alongside the concrete veranda. The Delhi distributor had sent in the remaining books to madrasa and Maulvi *sahab* had come in to personally thank Pundit *ji* for all the help.

"*Namaskar* Maulvi *sahab*, what a pleasant surprise. We were discussing about you and see you have come over," said Pundit *ji* as he pulled a chair for Maulvi *sahab*.

Arjun's father was relatively richer. He owned a sugar mill. He bought sugarcane from the famers and produced sugar in his mills. His house was one of the few bungalows in Basera.

"Maulvi *sahab* he is Sharma *ji*," Arjun's father introduced the well-dressed gentleman sitting alongside him. "….Sharma *ji* is from Delhi where he runs his business and is a very good friend. I was discussing about Arjun's education in this Delhi school," he said pushing the school's prospectus into Maulvi *sahab's* lap. "…I feel Abdul is a very talented boy and he too should go to this school for further studies," Arjun's father said.

Maulvi *sahab* flipped through the prospectus. "Well it's a good idea there's no doubt about it, but for Abdul it seems rather difficult," Maulvi *sahab* said, turning the pages rather wistfully. "You know all about me. I am an ordinary Maulvi in the village madrasa. Yes Allah has given me enough to comfortably sustain my family but I feel sending my son to this big school in Delhi will entail huge recurring expenses which I may not be able to bear."

"Oh you need not worry about the expenses at all," Sharma *ji* retorted even before Arjun's father could react. "This school belongs to a trust and every year the trust awards full scholarship to meritorious students whose parents' income is low. Pundit *ji* has been praising Abdul, he says Abdul is an extremely bright student who will clear the school's scholarship examination."

"Oh okay. Can any child appear in this scholarship exam?"

"Yes, any child whose parents' income is low can appear in this scholarship exam," Sharma *ji* explained handing out the school's form to Maulvi *sahab*.

"Please will you do me a favour?"

"Yes, Maulvi *sahab*. Tell me what else you want me to do"

"Get me a few more of these forms. I will hand them to other meritorious students at my madrasa to appear in this exam. Allah willing if they clear the exams they too can study in this prestigious school."

Sharma *ji* did not speak for about a minute. He was stupefied by Maulvi *sahab's* demand. His hands froze during those moments and he continued to hold the tea cup in front of his lips. Maulvi *sahab* thought probably he had been too demanding. He kept his cup of tea on the table and its sound broke Sharma *ji's* stupor.

"Wonderful Maulvi *sahab*. Wonderful. You are a real gem. These days when people are overtly selfish and think only of themselves, their sons and daughters, you still think of other poor children," Sharma *ji* broke into fulsome praise for him. Arjun's father smiled. He then went on to explain that it was for these reasons that people from this village and other adjoining villages revere Maulvi *sahab* and swear by his name. Sharma *ji* smiled in admiration and promised to get more scholarship forms of the prestigious Delhi school.

4.

It was a bright sunny morning, students at the madrasa had finished their daily *namaz* and Quranic recitals, and were studying science. The madrasa attendant knocked at the classroom door and handed over a packet to Maulvi *sahab*. The papers inside the brown envelope brightened up his face.

"These are the admission forms of a very prestigious school in Delhi. This school offers scholarship to meritorious students such that it takes care of all your educational expenses. There will be an exam… tell your parents about it. I will help you prepare for the exams and Allah willing you will be able to get admission to this school," Maulvi *sahab* explained as the eager children looked on.

"I will appear for this exam," Abdul announced, his eyes gleaming with excitement.

"Other children should also talk to their parents. I will paste the school's information leaflet on the madrasa walls so that everybody from the village can get information about this Delhi school," Maulvi *sahab* said waving the school's admission forms.

He then carefully tucked the bunch of scholarship forms and school prospectus into the brown envelope and carried on with the science class.

Later in the afternoon, he called the madrasa attendant to get a big white paper. In chaste Urdu he wrote about admission process of the Delhi school and its scholarship scheme for meritorious and poor children.

The madrasa attendant smeared glue on the white sheets and Maulvi *sahab* stood on a wooden chair to paste the information sheets on madrasa walls. The white paper stood out on the green coloured walls of the madrasa. Maulvi *sahab* had picked up a black marker to darken the words written on the sheets, when Rashid passed by.

"*Salam-walekum* Maulvi *sahab*," Rashid greeted with a big wide grin. He had stopped over as he saw Maulvi *sahab* sticking big white sheets with something written in Urdu.

Rashid was the village barber. He had a heavy built up, was around six feet tall and sported a thick moustache with beard. The black kohl in his eyes replete with the long hair gave him a menacing look. He was famous in the village for his short-temper. Once, while shaving the beard of his customer he got into an argument with him on a petty issue. He immediately put down his shaving knife and wiped off the foam from his face, refusing to shave it further. The customer ultimately had to walk over with his half-shaven beard to Basera's another barber Fazlu.

Rashid could barely read or write and showed no inclination towards knowledgeable pursuits. After much insistence from Maulvi *sahab* he had agreed to send his daughter Rukhsana to study at the madrasa. He had relegated Rukhsana to assist her mother in household chores and other odd jobs that she picked up from relatively well-off homes, such as cutting hay for buffaloes or getting grass for their goats.

Maulvi *sahab* had to waive off Rukhsana's fees so that Rashid sent her to study at the madrasa.

"What is it that you are pasting on the madrasa walls?" Rashid was curious to know.

Maulvi *sahab* was elated over Rashid's curiosity and informed him about the Delhi school. He thought Rashid was keen to send his daughter for higher studies.

He was mistaken, though.

"Does this school offer Islamic knowledge?"

"No, this school teaches other subjects such as science, mathematics, computers, history, economics, and social sciences among several other modern subjects"

"And what about the Islamic knowledge? How will the children get to know about our great religion Islam, its teachings and our beliefs," Rashid retorted.

"Well, we have already imparted the basic knowledge about Islam, children regularly recite verses of Quran and if a child wants to gain further knowledge about Islam—the *Deeni taleem,* then the parents could teach them at home, get them religious books and literature...they can visit any local mosque...,"

"This means you are pushing our children towards apostasy—*kufr,*" Rashid blurted out cutting short Maulvi *sahab's* explanation. He was livid at the idea of his children studying modern subjects which he believed led towards heresy.

"Not apostasy my brother, rather I wish to see that our children progress and become prosperous," Maulvi *sahab* said, turning towards him to explain further. The madrasa attendant stood smiling at Rashid's arguments.

"You consider worldly progress as true progress. Is this what you teach our children at the madrasa? We are Muslims and it is the duty of a true Muslim to...."

"It is the duty of a true Muslim to tread on the path of righteousness as laid down by Allah, love his brethren, help establish peace and harmony in the world and to seek knowledge from all sources. And you must know that our Prophet had said that it is the duty of a Muslim to seek knowledge from all possible sources. It is the duty of a true Muslim to read, learn, know, seek education in as many disciplines as possible and tread on the righteous path as shown by the Holy Quran."

It had been several minutes since Rashid accosted Maulvi *sahab* and got into a verbal duel with him. A small crowd had now gathered around them, amused to see Rashid quarrelling on a non-issue with Maulvi *sahab*. None of the villager took sides as they knew that Rashid must be arguing on something worthless. Yet they stood around to witness Rashid make a fool of himself. They looked upon Rashid as an entertainer who picked up fights with anybody on any issue. A few of them tried telling Maulvi *sahab* that he is unnecessarily wasting his time on a dumb-witted moron like Rashid.

They were right. Maulvi *sahab's* explanation could hardly impact Rashid's closed mind. He just refused to acknowledge Maulvi *sahab's* point of view.

Rashid seldom interacted with knowledgeable or wise people and his customers who came to his makeshift rickety saloon under the neem tree weren't good, either. Almost always his days were spent talking and dreaming about making a quick buck or about seeking women. He had hung provocative photographs of women and girls in skimpy outfits on big placards that hung on the trunk of neem tree. While he cut hair or trimmed and shaved beards, his clients ogled on those pictures of scantily clad women. His education and background notwithstanding, Rashid was stubborn in his convictions. He considered himself qualified enough to talk about Islam and the duties of a true Muslim.

Pointing his finger towards Maulvi *sahab* he said, "Just because you have read a few books you think you can twist around your arguments and I will be convinced. I am not convinced. You have befriended *kafirs* and you are planning to push our children to seek non-Islamic knowledge and become apostates. I am not going to meekly surrender. I will tell other villagers about your impish designs." Rashid's face twitched, the unkempt beard dithered and his kohl rimmed eyes widened as he spoke. He thought his body language were injecting seriousness into his arguments. The villagers thought otherwise. They giggled, albeit surreptitiously, lest Rashid would direct his anger towards them.

The next minute, the mosque's muezzin gave a call for *namaz*. Maulvi *sahab* put his arm around Rashid's shoulder and gestured him to come and offer the *namaz* and that their discussions can continue later on. Rashid jerked his hand and walked away.

His action stunned Maulvi *sahab*. This was the first time anybody in the village rebuffed him so blatantly and that too when he had prodded Rashid to come over for *namaz* and when he was discussing about Islamic beliefs. Maulvi *sahab* and the other people walked inside the mosque to offer *namaz*.

Apart from Rashid there was another person in this crowd who walked away without offering *namaz* at the mosque. He had been intently listening and observing Rashid. While all others went along with Maulvi *sahab* to offer *namaz*, he quietly slipped over. His name was Jamil.

Nobody in the village actually knew what Jamil's vocation was. In the mornings he was never in a hurry to rush to the fields like other farmers in the village, nor did he own any workshop like others. No one in the village could say it with certainty where exactly did he come from. He was not a native of Basera as his ancestors were not from this village. Yet, he was never short of money. He frequented Chacha's tea shack and never failed to pay for the tea or snacks. Interestingly, most of the times he offered to pay for others. The poor villagers of Basera were more than happy to get their tea bills paid by a Samaritan. Once at the Chacha's tea shack someone asked Jamil about his source of earnings and he had told that he used to work in the Gulf nations of Middle East and has earned millions of dinars. It's that money and the returns on the investments made thereafter which helps him sustain now. No one, after this, ever asked Jamil about his source of income.

The sane old men of Basera, however, were not convinced. They used to talk that this man was not what he appeared to be. They dismissed him as an irritant and advised, in hushed tones though, the village youngsters to stay away from him.

5 .

Overnight drizzle had washed the dust and dirt from the leaves of guava tree that stood in a corner in the courtyard of Maulvi *sahab's* home. Abdul lay perched on the tree, eating guavas. The ground below was wet and there was nip in the air.

Maulvi *sahab* had donned a light shawl and a cap at the insistence of his wife. He had been coughing since last night and Begum *sahiba* asked him to take a day off from the madrasa. Maulvi *sahab* insisted to go. A few children had shown interest to appear for the scholarship exam of the Delhi school and he wanted to prepare these students thoroughly. Abdul jumped from the guava tree, picked up his green sequined bag and rushed to the madrasa.

Maulvi *sahab* pulled up a chair, the cough syrup had a dizzying effect on him. He braved the drowsiness and continued his classes. "Allah insists that we feel the pain of others and work towards assuaging that pain. Prophet Muhammad (*Peace Be Upon Him*) had clearly stated that a true Muslim should not get wayward and also not let others get wayward. Apart from offering *namaz*, as true and good Muslims we need to cleanse our soul and thoughts before we point fingers towards others. A true Muslim should feel the pain of others and should think about the well-being of people in his neighbourhood without discriminating on religious or racial lines. If our neighbours are sleeping hungry and we sleep with full stomach then we are faltering in our duties as a Muslim. It is our duty to ensure that our neighbours have something to eat...," the children listened intently as Maulvi *sahab* went on elaborating the duties of a true Muslim.

After a while, he asked the attendant for some warm water.

"Take out your science books. It's time for some science lessons," he said sipping the warm water.

At the far end of banyan tree, towards the other extreme of Basera, a tea shack had sprung up overnight. A stout man in his mid-forties with sparse hair had put up a tarpaulin sheet outside an old and decrepit warehouse. He wore clothes in a weird manner and his appearance was bizarre. His pajamas were above his ankles but his *kurta* flowed below the knees. His beard was thick with a few strands of grey hair in between, but minus the moustache this beard made him look like a giant buck goat. Unlike others in the village he did not seek help from anyone in the village to set up the tea shack. He was not from Basera.

Beneath the tarpaulin sheet, outside the warehouse, he assembled bricks to create a makeshift platform and put up a kerosene stove over it. A couple of grubby canisters were kept alongside. One was for milk and another had water.

The dilapidated warehouse belonged to Aaqib who used it to store animal hides. Aaqib had four sons and all were now settled in Saudi Arabia. When Aaqib was alive they occasionally came to meet him. But after his death none of the sons or anyone from his family turned up. The mosques' *imam*, with help from some villagers, buried Aaqib at the village cemetery. It had been a year since Aaqib passed away. The warehouse had been closed ever since.

A day back villagers spotted this man sweeping the floors of Aaqib's warehouse. He claimed to be Aaqib's nephew and was sent by his eldest son to take care of the warehouse.

Over the next few days he converted this makeshift tea shack into a roadside tea stall and offered free tea to the children playing nearby and to the daily wage labourers. After the tea a child had said, 'thank you Chacha.'

Chacha is uncle in Urdu and in Hindi, but since that day he became famous in the village as "Chacha". Nobody asked his real name and he never told anyone. He became Basera's Chacha.

Over the next few weeks Chacha gradually upgraded his tea stall. The tarpaulin sheet gave way to the tin roof and wooden benches replaced brick seats. Chacha had now employed a kid to wash soiled utensils and serve tea to his customers. Strings of pouches containing tobacco, *beetel* nuts, toffees, sugar balls, lolly pops dangled from the overhead sling. Chacha's tea stall had now become the favourite hangout place for vagabonds and strollers. Instead of sleeping on torn rugs on the floor, he now slept on the cot placed inside the warehouse. And there were still several days to go before Chacha could boast of completing a month at the warehouse.

One fine morning Chacha was mopping the wooden benches, when a large car with black tinted glasses stopped at his tea stall.

Draped in white suit, a man with neatly trimmed beard got down from the car and walked towards his tea stall. He was well built, around five feet ten inches tall, had a squarish jawline and a thick crop of black hair. A thick gold chain stuck around his neck. He was flanked by two burly men.

"*Aslaam-walekum* Chacha *jaan* how are you?" he said dusting the wooden bench with his kerchief that was cleaned by Chacha just minutes ago. He sat down on the bench's edges, conscious to avoid his dress getting soiled. He ran his fingers on his beard and the moustache as he looked around. A couple of daily wage labourers sipping tea felt intimidated by his demeanour.

"Salaam. My name in Jamil," he told the labourers, enjoying their discomfort.

"Oh I am so happy that a person like you has come over to my shanty. Look I don't even have a decent chair to offer you," Chacha said, exalting in surprise and excitement that a person like Jamil had himself come over to his place.

"Ah c'mon Chacha. Don't worry about my suit and my car, just prepare a cup of tea. Anwar and Bilal have been talking very high about your shop's tea," he said as he looked towards the two burly men standing beside him, waving them to sit down. Anwar and Bilal looked bewildered. They multi-tasked for Jamil as his cook, watchman, driver and bodyguards. They were his trusted lieutenants. But they had never talked about Chacha's tea stall to Jamil.

It was Jamil who while speaking over phone in the morning had suddenly asked them to sit in the car and drove up to the Chacha's shack.

"Yes..yes… I will quickly prepare the tea," Chacha said, bowing before Jamil.

It was still early morning and Chacha had no time to light up a coal fire under the earthen stove. He quickly poured kerosene into the rusty stove and hurriedly prepared tea.

The strong odour of kerosene seeped into the tea and Jamil would have vomited at the first sip. But he held it back and somehow gulped it.

"Wonderful. You have magic in your hands, the tea is really good," he said. His face convulsed as he suppressed the vomiting sensation.

Anwar and Bilal were confused further. They knew the tea was terrible and yet Jamil was all praise for it. They kept quiet, nonetheless.

"So Chacha *jaan* I am expecting some guests tomorrow evening. Will you come to my bungalow and cook for them… and of course, prepare this awesome tea for them as well," Jamil said in a slightly louder voice as he gulped down the last sip. His face red as he tried not to throw up. He looked at the two labourers who were watching him with awe. They now looked towards Chacha with admiration.

"Sure I will. It's an honour for me," Chacha said smiling, revealing his blackish brown teeth.

"Let us meet tomorrow evening"

"Yeah Sure, I will come over," Chacha said with a wide grin.

By evening the word had spread that Chacha had been invited in the big bungalow to cook for the guests. The labourers, masons, artisans, carpenters and barbers, among others felt it an honour to be able to hang out with Chacha who had been personally invited by Jamil *bhai*.

Jamil had, last year, purchased the farm land at Basera from Wajid, the carpenter. His wife had suffered a spinal injury and he was in dire need of money. Incidentally Jamil was looking to buy out land and the deal was struck. Jamil was not from Basera and he never stayed in the village for more than a few days. Villagers looked at his grand bungalow with awe but not many people had been inside. Jamil's bungalow had a big imposing gate that opened into a lush green garden inside. At the margins of the garden, alongside the long walls were several exotic flower plants. Ornamental plants in big brown pots adorned the sideways of the porch that led into the big living room. The bungalow was double-storied with a total fourteen rooms inside it. Villagers knew about Jamil's bungalow only through the people who had been to work inside, such as the gardener, carpenter and mason. Yet these were hired and dealt with by Jamil's men, Anwar and Bilal. It had been just three months since the bungalow was completed and Jamil had been coming here on and off.

It was for the first time that he had personally invited someone to come over. Chacha's stature had surely increased in the eyes of his customers.

The next evening, Chacha spent several hours at Jamil's bungalow. Jamil introduced him to Bilal and Anwar.

"He is our *bhai*." Jamil said about Chacha to Anwar and Bilal. He then left for Delhi to attend to a business meeting. Chacha had spent rest of the evening drinking with Bilal and Anwar.

But the next morning Chacha had grand stories to share, about his culinary skills, with his customers at the tea stall.

As days passed, the flow of men to Chacha's tea stall increased steadily. So the labourers, cycle rickshaw pullers, masons, artisans, plumbers, carpenters and all other kinds of manual labours had discovered a favourite hang-out point for themselves. Sipping tea and while chewing tobacco they exchanged contacts for different kinds of work, such that a mason would pass on leads to the carpenter or the plumber about a possible contract who in turn would offer leads about a construction activity. Chacha's tea stall had become famous in Basera. On several days people from adjoining villages could also be seen enjoying tea at Chacha's place. Chacha's business was growing and with it the stature of Chacha in the eyes of villagers.

A fortnight later, a hatchback stopped at Chacha's tea stall.

It was evening and Chacha's stall was buzzing with people. The labourers were back from their daily grind and had stopped over to this new perch for a cuppa. Some smoked *bidi,* and others chewed tobacco as they shared the day's experience and discussed other worldly matters.

The driver had jumped out of his seat and pulled open the car's door. Jamil stepped out. He was immaculately dressed, beard neatly trimmed, gelled hair shinning in the golden streak of evening sunlight, thick gold chain stuck around his neck and gold rings adorned his fingers. Jamil's pupils were constricted as he looked around the shack making efforts to focus on the people present there. His gait was confident as he walked towards the bunch of labourers, sipping tea and smoking *bidi*. The labours stood up in reverence. Those smoking, hid the hand holding the *bidi* behind their backs.

"*Assalam-o-Walekum*. I am Jamil. I live in the white bungalow along the canal. My brothers, you know that the pious month of *Ramadan* is beginning from the next week. And during the entire period of *Ramadan* I will host *iftaar* for *Musalmaan* brothers who are on fast during this holy month of *Ramadan. Musalmaan* brothers will be welcome to my bungalow to break their fast," Jamil announced. He asked to spread the word about his *iftaar* party around the village so that all Muslim brothers can come in. He then turned around and drove away in his hatchback.

Jamil's car created a whirlwind of dust as it sped away from Chacha's shack, leaving behind wide-eyed men who were still dazed by his announcement. They looked at each other, unable to believe what Jamil had just said.

Chacha was unfazed. All this while he had continued to boil tea and scrap the pockets of brownish cream that lay stuck on the sides of sauté pan. Jamil had not bothered to take note of him and he too returned the favour. He was busy preparing tea. His customers, whom Jamil had invited for the *iftaar* at his bungalow could not notice these subtleties.

"Did he invite us for the *iftar* at his bungalow? Is this what he meant?" Zafar, the carpenter asked, his eyes were wide and mouth open.

"Yes, I think so. He asked us to come and break our fast at his bungalow. But why does he invite us?" Hashim was thinking aloud. Being a mason it was his job to stick together the bricks and build walls, yet he struggled to stick the bricks of his thoughts on this issue. Ditto with all others.

"Go get your eye sights examined." It was Chacha, still busy wiping the tea stains on the concrete slab. The men were confused. They could not understand why Chacha would ask them to get their eye sights examined. He could understand their quandary.

"Can't you see that Allah has been quite generous on Jamil *bhai*? He has a flourishing export business and is endowed with all the material comforts one can ask for. Still being a true Muslim that he is, he did not forget to help his Muslim brethren. And so he came over to personally invite you all for the *iftaar* at his bungalow. This shows his generosity. He is a live example of how a true Muslim should behave. We should emulate his dedication for Islam and the believers…," Chacha explained, singing paeans about Jamil as the wide eyed labourers listened in rapt attention.

There was no counter question as Chacha's lecture had left everyone in a daze. Nobody asked for any explanation and no one bothered to explain further. *Ramzan* was still a week away but the word had spread about Jamil *bhai's* invitation for *iftaar.*

Jamil was true to his word. He had opened the bungalow gates for anybody to come in for *iftaar* during *Ramzan.* Every evening before *iftaar* the courtyard was washed and a large green mattress spread at the entrance. Large wooden tables were placed in a line across the lawn. Several varieties of fruits, dates, fig, sweet sherbet, roasted chicken, kebabs, mutton and rice adorned these wooden tables. Jamil had deputed Bilal and Anwar, his two trusted lieutenants, to usher in all those who came for the *iftaar.* Initially the labourers, their children and women were reluctant and in awe of the imposing façade of the bungalow and the opulence inside but Bilal, Anwar and Chacha made active efforts to break the ice and let the labourers feel comfortable inside the bungalow.

The news about Jamil's generosity of hosting lavish *iftaar* for the underprivileged and deprived had spread to adjoining villages as well. Over the next few days almost everybody from Basera had been to the bungalow for *iftaar*. There were many who brought small plastic bags with them to carry the eatables to their homes. Jamil received fulsome praise from everyone for being a true Mohammedan who uses his wealth for pious purposes. Jamil's *iftaar* party was a hit and was being talked about in adjoining villages as well.

6.

A week had passed since the start of holy month of *Ramzan*. It was dusk and Maulvi *sahab* walked with brisk steps towards the mosque to offer *namaz* before the *iftaar*. After *namaz*, the mosque's *imam* asked Maulvi *sahab* if he had been to Jamil's place for the *iftaar*. Maulvi *sahab* said he had heard a lot about it but had been unable to go because the madrasa works had kept him busy.

The mosque's *imam* was a frail octogenarian who walked with the help of a stick. He was all praise for Jamil's efforts during *Ramzan*. The imam was keen to see the humanitarian Jamil and convinced Maulvi *sahab* to meet this pious man. Maulvi *sahab* said he would finish off errands at home and come over later in the evening. He too wanted to personally meet Jamil and thank him for all his noble efforts.

At home, Maulvi *sahab* fed his buffaloes and milked them. He then sat down to teach the neighbourhood kids, who had come over to his home, to prepare for their lessons for scholarship exams of the Delhi school. It had started to drizzle when he remembered his promise to *imam sahab* for a visit to Jamil's place. He hurriedly put on his slippers and told Begum *sahiba* that he would be back in an hour.

Basera did not have any concrete roads and the narrow muddy pathways and lanes became slippery during rains. Begum *sahiba* asked her husband to shelve his plans but Maulvi *sahab* was insistent. He said he would take an umbrella. "Imam *sahab* must be waiting for me," he said and stepped out promising that he would not remain out till late.

'Thank you Allah for creating good humans like Jamil who make efforts so that the poor, deprived and underprivileged do not go hungry,' Maulvi *sahab* said a silent prayer in his heart as he walked together with *imam* towards Jamil's bungalow.

It was past nine that night, and there wasn't any soul near the bungalow. They knocked at the big black iron-gate but no one replied back. The gate was ajar and a gentle push flung it open. Maulvi *sahab* and *imam* entered inside. They stood at the gate for a couple of minutes as they knocked again, waiting for someone to come over, but there was no reply. The heavy noise of electricity generator had subdued their knocks and calls. The bungalow was well lit with incandescent bulbs and tube lights. The manicured hedges, ornamental plants and numerous flower plants spoke about the affluence of its owner. A thick black smoke of the electricity generator hung over the garden and over the main porch in an omen of things to come.

But for the noise of the electricity generator, the bungalow appeared quaint. Yet there was something eerie about this silence, Maulvi *sahab* could feel it and the discomfort showed on his face. He could hear a voice within him say that this place was not what it is being made to believe and advertised. Maulvi *sahab* turned around to leave but the *imam* said, "...now that we have come this far let us at least say *salaam* to Jamil." The drizzle had graduated into a downpour, Maulvi *sahab* looked towards the raining sky and gave in, albeit reluctantly.

They walked across the porch along the narrow alley that led inside the bungalow. The rains' intensity had increased as Maulvi *sahab* and *imam* hurriedly walked through the porch. The window panes of the living room opened towards the porch, the lights were on but there was nobody inside. The porch led to the alleyway which was covered by the roof above. Large wooden boxes were lined on one side of this alleyway, piled along the bungalow's boundary wall, while walls of living room defined another margin of this alleyway. The two men walked slowly across the alleyway that opened into a gallery inside the bungalow. Walking across the gallery they crossed a brightly-lit room.

Maulvi *sahab's* jaw dropped and his face turned white. He looked towards *imam* who was equally bewildered.

There was this room on to their left, its door open. On the big sofa was Jamil, surrounded by three women in itsy-bitsy lingerie. Jamil's hand had cupped the bosom of one of them who sat on his thighs. The other two were busy smoking weed and smiled suggestively at the unsolicited guests.

Jamil was too busy with the women to notice Maulvi *sahab* and *imam* standing just outside the room at its door in the gallery. The woman he was playing with pointed towards the intruders at the doorsteps. Jamil casually turned his head towards the door, his eyelids battled the effects of weed smoke to remain open. And then he was stunned. Jamil was dumbfounded to see Basera's two revered men standing inside his bungalow looking towards him playing with escort women. His mind raced at a lightning speed, he regained his composure and let off an impish smile. His beard twirled and face smirked to reveal the yellowish teeth inside his mouth.

"*Marhaba* Maulvi *sahab*… *marhaba imam sahab*," Jamil said pushing aside the woman on his lap. She was hardly perturbed and curled towards the other end of the couch. She spread her legs and made no efforts to cover her bare chest.

"You have come in at just the right time. Please take your pick and break your fast. Consider this as the special *iftaar* for your good services to the illiterate mendicants of Basera," Jamil looked towards Maulvi *sahab* and the *imam* as he waved towards the three women, still smiling slyly.

"J a m i l… How Dare You…?" Maulvi *sahab's* face was red with anger as he snapped back on top of his voice. "How dare…, how dare you offer me this sin. And then you have the audacity to say that this is special *iftaar* during the holy and pious month of *Ramzan*. Is this what you had been offering to villagers during this pious month?" Maulvi *sahab* thundered.

Maulvi *sahab* probably had never raised his voice to a pitch this high. His eyes had widened and pupils dilated, his hands trembled with anger and voice crocked as he spoke. *Imam* stood there frozen, the stick in his hand stuttered on the ground as his hands trembled. He felt weak in his knees and gently sat on the stool kept in the gallery.

Anwar and Bilal were in the side room smoking weed. Hearing the commotion and loud shouts they rushed to Jamil's room. The three hustlers casually collected on the corner couch in this commotion. They continued to smoke weed and looked towards the men in the room to sort it out among themselves.

"Maulvi *sahab* must be hungry. Please come over to the dining room. We have all the dishes neatly laid out on the table. Have some food, all these can wait. We have these women for the whole night." It was Anwar who tried to calm down the volatile nerves of Maulvi *sahab*.

"You people are disgusting. You are no Muslims. You are rascals. You are devil. I will go right now and let the entire village know of your real face," Maulvi *sahab* exploded. His voice still loud and firm but he meant what he said. Jamil could sense this.

"Yes Maulvi *sahab* let us go. The whole village should know about these people," the *imam* said, standing up slowly from the stool taking support of his stick. His hands were still trembling and he could not muster courage to look up. In his heart he felt guilty to have asked Maulvi *sahab* to come over to Jamil's place that had put them in such an embarrassing situation. He tapped his stick to turn around. Maulvi *sahab* stepped back to leave.

They had barely turned around that Jamil flung from the couch and fell at Maulvi *sahab's* feet. He had skid almost fifteen feet to fall on Maulvi *sahab's* feet.

"Please Maulvi *sahab* forgive me. We are like your son. We promise. We will mend our ways," Jamil said as he turned towards Anwar and Bilal and winked at them.

The next moment, Anwar and Bilal were prostrating along with Jamil. The three escort women smiled in bewildered amusement.

Maulvi *sahab* and *imam* looked at each other. Neither of them could fathom what to say. They stood frozen in bewilderment.

"There was no one to castigate us. Now that we have found true teachers we promise that we will mend our ways and become a true Muslim," Jamil pleaded, still lying down on the floor at their feet. "We will never smoke weed, quit alcohol and shoo these escort women away from our lives," he went on. "Hey you sinners dress up and leave my house immediately," he turned around and told the women in a firm voice. The women, on their part, looked confused. They were still smiling.

"Don't you understand? Dress up and leave immediately or else I will throw you out of my house," Jamil thundered as he got up to button his shirt. The hustlers shrugged and started dressing up.

Jamil turned around towards Maulvi *sahab* and sat on his feet, again. "It's because of you Maulvi *sahab* that we were saved from committing this sin during the holy month of *Ramzan*. Please, please, please forgive me. I am like your son, please forgive me," Jamil begged Maulvi *sahab* and *imam* for pardon.

"Okay since you are realising your mistakes so we will forgive you," *imam* said, his voice quivering.

"Yes *imam sahab* I accept this is a grave sin. I wow to purge myself of all evil thoughts. I will repent and pray to Allah. But please promise me that you will not say anything about our sins to the villagers or else my reputation will be doomed forever. I promise *imam sahab*, I promise Maulvi *sahab* that I will tread on the path of goodness. You will see the change in me from this very moment. Please forgive," Jamil begged with folded hands. Tears had welled up in his eyes and he shook his hands gently and sought forgiveness.

"Okay we will not say anything but you should also stick to your promise to give up all your sinful activities. And the holy month of *Ramzan* is the best time to give up your vices and turn towards the path of Allah," *imam* said, his eyes down and fingers still trembling.

"Allah-*hu*-Akbar," Jamil said.

"Allah-*hu*-Akbar," Bilal and Anwar repeated.

Maulvi *sahab* held *imam's* hands and quickly walked out of Jamil's bungalow. He walked briskly holding *imam's* hands firmly. The rains had stopped and the ground was slippery. Yet, Maulvi *sahab* did not slack his pace. Somewhere in his heart he knew that Jamil and his cohorts Anwar and Bilal were lying through their teeth and have only bought time to re-think their nefarious designs. While walking out of the bungalow he had a premonition about the impending gloom approaching his beloved Basera.

"This does not augur well for our village," he gave out a sigh as he walked through the rain soaked roads. "Oh Allah please save our village Basera from these devils," he prayed silently as he continued to walk on the slippery village lanes holding firmly *imam's* hands.

He vowed never to set his foot anywhere near Jamil's bungalow again.

"Bastards how many times I have to remind you to lock the main gate and bolt the doors. Just look at the situation you guys have put me in due to your laziness," Jamil reprimanded Bilal and Anwar, grinding his teeth.

The three escort women had dressed up and picked up their hand bags to leave. Jamil held the hands of two and winked at the third one to follow him. The women were bewildered, but smiled and followed him. He led them to the bungalow's first floor corner room and bolted the door from inside.

It was wee hours and Basera was bustling with activity. Muslim families who had to fast had woken up for *sehri*, the eating before dawn, to help them fast through the day.

Anwar sat on the driving seat of the car with tinted windows. The three escort women lay bundled on the rear seats. They were extremely tired after a rocking night with three men and were now headed to Delhi. Anwar sped off the moment the hookers came inside the car. Jamil had instructed him to get back to the village by early morning.

It was nine in the morning. Jamil woke up bleary eyed. Last night's precarious situation still hammered in his head. Maulvi *sahab* and the local mosque's *imam* had got to know about his shenanigans. He had managed to save the situation from turning ugly last night, but it was far from fixed.

Anwar was back from Delhi after dropping the escort women and Bilal was preparing tea at the kitchen. Though both were his trusted men but he was cross at their laziness of letting the main gates unlocked and doors unbolted. Anwar and Bilal admitted to being at fault and said they would be extra cautious from now on.

"There is absolutely no room for error in our game. I just ask you to be cautious, extra-cautions and that's it. And in return I give you the best food to eat, best wine to drink and the best girls to screw. Yesterday night should the first and last blunder of your lives," Jamil said as he sipped the hot tea to fight off his hangover. Anwar and Bilal hung their heads, listening intently to Jamil.

Jamil felt happy that he could still save the day for himself by his presence of mind. He, however, was convinced that the storm was not over yet. He knew there was no quick fix solution as he thought of the various options available before him. He lay still below the bathroom shower as water trickled down from his head to his beard down to the bare torso and below.

An hour later, Jamil emerged from the bathroom rubbing his hair with the towel. He called Anwar and Bilal. "You need to spread the word across Basera that I have lost a close relative who lived in Saudi Arabia. And now I have to rush urgently for his funeral. Cancel all *iftaar* plans for the remaining month of *Ramzan*," he said. Anwar and Bilal looked at each other. Jamil turned around and said, "Do as I say, and do it now. Immediately." The next moment, Bilal was out to Chacha's tea stall and Anwar started packing Jamil's bags.

7 .

Chacha's tea stall was bustling with activity. It was the *Ramzan* month and almost all the labourers were on fast, but to hang out at Chacha's tea stall had come into their habit now. Every day before they headed for work the daily wagers sat at Chacha's place lazing around and discussing their lives.

Today was no different, they were discussing about how the timely rains this year would yield good crops when Bilal came running in. He broke the news about the mishap in Jamil's family at Saudi Arabia. He panted as he spoke. On deliberate purpose he had come running to the shack, to show urgency and gravity of things at Jamil's home in Saudi Arabia.

Hashim and Maajid, the two daily wagers were up on their feet hearing about the catastrophe at 'their' Jamil *bhai's* home.

"Jamil *bhai* is a pious man. But Allah is all supreme. We bow before Allah-the Almighty. We need to be besides him at this critical juncture. Let's go to his bungalow and pray for the deceased," Maajid said putting on his slippers. Hashim also straightened up his rugged tool bag to go. Bilal looked towards Chacha, maintaining his gaze for a moment.

Chacha turned towards Maajid. "Sit down my brother. Don't get over-anxious. Let us offer our *namaz*, pray for Jamil *bhai* and the deceased person over here. Jamil *bhai* has to travel a long distance to the Saudi." Chacha's words were polite but his tone was commanding. He had stressed upon the word 'here' to emphasize that he disapproved anyone's going to Jamil's bungalow. Chacha's easier access to Jamil had risen his stature in the eyes of all and so his words carried weight.

The next moment everyone was spreading the mat to offer *namaz*, as Bilal briskly walked away.

It had been almost two months and there was no news about Jamil. Bilal and Anwar were seen in Basera, intermittently though. Villagers talked that Jamil had bagged a big order in the Gulf and was busy raking mullah. Some said Jamil's deceased relative owned an oil well and after his passing away Jamil was the owner of this oil well. Some said he dealt in leather, others said he was into construction business. A few said in hushed tones that he was a narcotics smuggler who supplied opium and marijuana which he sourced from Afghanistan and exported it to the European countries.

Even Anwar and Bilal never gave a clear answer to Jamil's business. Once at the Chacha's tea stall when a villager had confronted them about Jamil's narcotics business Anwar had slapped him so hard that he almost fell on the ground. "Jamil *bhai* is a respectable man in the Gulf. Never dare to say anything bad about him again."

After this incident no one ever talked about Jamil's business in the open.

A week later, Jamil arrived at his bungalow in a black car with tinted glasses. It was late afternoon and Jamil looked carefully at the fields around his bungalow, he craned his head to look far inside Basera, turned his head towards the bungalow's façade and then slipped inside through the black iron-gate. Anwar and Bilal hurriedly followed. Jamil's bungalow stood on the edges of Basera. Large fields in its front and the canal towards its rear cut if off from the main settlements rendering it as an island of sorts. A narrow pathway in front of the bungalow that led up to Basera's grand banyan tree bore testimony that Jamil's bungalow was a part of the village.

Else, the bungalow and its occupants were still struggling to be a part of Basera.

"There was this fellow Rashid who that day was arguing with that madrasa's Maulvi. Find out about him. And call this grumpy Chacha tomorrow evening, feed him with some good food and wine, and ask him to come again after a couple of days," Jamil instructed Bilal and Anwar. He then dug out a pen drive from his bag and inserted in the laptop to download videos. Anwar and Bilal had left and Jamil was busy watching the newly downloaded porn.

Bilal came after a couple of hours loaded with information about Rashid. He described Rashid in great detail, his vocation, his family, temper and his inclination towards *Wahhabism*. He also described about a few others in the village. Jamil picked up his phone when Bilal had finished. The person on phone's other end heard intently as Jamil described about Rashid and others.

Next morning Anwar was readying to drop the escort women who had arrived late last night, when Jamil called for Bilal. Bilal was supposed to cook and do the cleanings at the bungalow, and like a dedicated cook who eats only after the owner of house and his guests have finished, Bilal was always the last man to get time with escort girls. He had just finished off the business when Jamil called him. He came running, hurriedly zipping up his pants.

"Afroz. His name is Afroz that you had mentioned last evening. And he is in the management committee of the madrasa, right?" Jamil asked Bilal, running his fingers through his beard.

"Yes, after his father's death he got into the management committee," Bilal said sitting on the wooden stool near the sofa.

"Hmm okay. Ask him to come and meet me"

It was late afternoon when Afroz came over to meet Jamil at the bungalow. It was a closed door meeting and no one was allowed inside, not even Anwar and Bilal.

Maulvi *sahab* was mixing dry bran with the green fodder for his buffaloes. He woke up late today and was in a hurry to reach madrasa on time. He affectionately caressed the buffaloes on their back as they slurped the mix of fodder and bran. Maulvi *sahab* was milking the buffalo when the main gate opened with a heavy click sound.

It was the madrasa attendant. He announced that an emergency meeting of madrasa management committee has been called today. Maulvi *sahab* was pleasantly surprised. He thought about the reasons of emergency meet and felt a gush of excitement. It has been a year since he had been asking for madrasa's whitewash, new furniture and cupboards, which the madrasa committee had been shelving for want of funds.

'Maybe the funds have come in or a devout philanthropist has reached out to the management committee to help in madrasa's renovation.' Maulvi *sahab* exulted at the joyous thoughts. He quickly finished off his errands and went ahead to take bath.

"Begum *sahiba* I have to rush to the madrasa," he called out rushing to take bath and get ready for the meet.

"I have readied your breakfast. Don't go without eating," Begum *sahiba* said roasting the chapattis.

Maulvi *sahab* was out of the bathroom in a jiffy. He could hardly eat, brimming as he was with excitement.

"You have enough time. Have one more chapatti," Begum *sahiba* said as she turned around to place a chapatti in Maulvi *sahab's* plate, only to find the empty chair. Maulvi *sahab* had already finished his breakfast and was washing his hands.

"Nothing can stop you when it comes to your madrasa. The meeting is still a couple of hours away. At least you should eat properly. You should take care of your health...look at your health it has been deteriorating. You have time for everything in this world except having proper food...." Begum *sahiba* continued with her repartee. Her words sounded more from a caring wife who was unsatisfied over her husband's eating habits, rather than that of a nagging spouse.

"I have to prepare a list of things that we need to do at our madrasa. Books, notebooks, library, repair works, whitewash, new chairs, new desks. I need to prepare a proper list of works that needs to be done urgently. What else is this meeting for? I have been waiting for these things for several months..." Maulvi *sahab* babbled as he pulled the *sherwani* over his head.

"*Abbu* we also need new tables. Many tables are broken and have holes. It becomes difficult to keep our notebooks on them and write," Abdul said as he quickly put on his slippers to accompany his father to the madrasa.

"Yes my son we will get new tables, as well"

Maulvi *sahab* entered the madrasa and called for the accountant at his office. Abdul went ahead to the main lobby along with other children. Maulvi *sahab* and the accountant prepared a detailed list of things 'to do' and the estimated funds required. Maulvi *sahab* then arranged each one of the items on their priority basis. So books, notebooks, pens and pencils figured at the top, followed by necessary repair works and new furniture, whitewash and paintings came at the bottom.

There was spring in his steps as he walked towards the meeting. He read and re-read the diligently prepared list and was yet thinking hard if he had missed out on something. His priority was to have a good collection of books and a refurbished library. '...if funds fall short of the need then I will ask to get books and a refurbished library, but then some repair works are also important and yes the whitewash....' Maulvi *sahab* was thinking as he entered the large hall of the madrasa for the meeting.

"*Assalam-o-walekum*" Afroz's greeting broke Maulvi *sahab's* chain of thoughts.

"*Walekum-assalam*" Maulvi *sahab* replied as he settled down on the wooden chair.

"It's good to see young men take active part in charitable activities," Maulvi *sahab* praised Afroz as they waited for other members to come in. He seemed to have forgiven and forgotten objections raised by Afroz during their earlier meeting when Afroz had opposed formal introduction of modern subjects in the madrasa.

Response to the formal introduction of modern subjects had been very good and parents were quite excited that their children now studied mathematics, science and social sciences at the madrasa. 'Seeing is believing and Afroz has seen that villagers want their children to study modern subjects as well…' he thought about Afroz.

He sat attentively on the chair, his body leaned forward in excitement.

"I am here only to render selfless service in the name of Allah, whatever His will, whatever His wish I am always ready for it," Afroz gave a cliché reply. He sat in a sloppy posture, his back rested on the chair and head rolled over to a side. His fingers twitched as he fidgeted with them while speaking.

"*Insha-Allah* may Allah give you strength and power to carry on the good work," Maulvi *sahab* heaped praises on Afroz. A worthy son of a worthy father, he thought nodding his head.

Over the next few minutes all other members of the management committee came in and exchanged pleasantries. Aftab *sahab*, the oldest of all said Afroz had called this meeting so he should take charge and explain what he had in mind for the madrasa.

Everyone turned towards Afroz as he spoke. Maulvi *sahab's* face brightened in anticipation that a young man educated in some of the best institutions of India and Europe would indeed bring in the much needed fresh breath of energy to the administration and functioning of Basera's madrasa.

"As you all are well aware that my father was a true *Musalmaan* and all through his life he worked towards the cause of Islam. As his son it is my duty to further his good work and make efforts to propagate the teachings of Islam. Whenever and wherever I see that Islam and Islamic teachings are being sidelined I will flag that issue. And charity begins at home so I need to first fix the issues at our home. The first and foremost place where I see Islamic teachings being tossed through the window is our madrasa. I have been receiving several complaints from worried parents that the teachings at madrasa are not up to the mark and if this continued then Islam might be into danger…and.."

"Are you out of your mind Afroz? Do you even understand what kind of allegations you are making on the madrasa and especially on me?" Maulvi *sahab* snapped back, almost involuntarily, his happy and beaming face was now pale. He had slipped towards the edge of the chair and his lips quivered as he spoke.

"Please Maulvi *sahab* calm down, let me talk," Aftab *sahab* tried to calm him.

"Afroz," Aftab *sahab* said in his tender voice, "...son what exactly are the issues at our madrasa which 'You' feel are not according to the teachings of Islam?" he was polite but firm. He had deliberately stressed upon the word 'you' to emphasise that rest of the committee members were not in agreement with him.

"Madrasa is the place to know about Islam and learn about Islamic teachings...'

"And what do you know about Islam and what are Islamic teachings?" Naseem *bhai* cut short Afroz. Naseem *bhai* was in his late forties. He had a tailoring shop in Basera but was an avid reader. Often times he frequented Maulvi *sahab's* home to discuss *Hadith* and its interpretations.

"Well, I mean Islamic teachings and by Islamic teachings I mean about our Holy Quran," Afroz stammered at the sudden questioning. He had been anticipating that his words would be taken on face value. He was not prepared for this cross examination.

"So you mean to say that Maulvi *sahab* does not teach Holy Quran at the madrasa?" Naseem *bhai* retorted. He held Maulvi *sahab* in high esteem for his knowledge and understanding of Islam.

"No I don't say this but then Naseem *bhai* we need to understand that proper teachings of the Holy Quran is an obligation on us Muslims"

"That's what I want to understand. Will you please elaborate what do you mean by proper teachings of the Quran? Do you even know that Maulvi *sahab* could have been a Mufti?" Naseem *bhai* spoke, his voice calm and composed.

"Mufti?" Afroz's eyes constricted and jaws dropped, probably he did not understand the purport and the context.

"Mufti is the one who's considered an authority on Holy Quran and its interpretations," Naseem *bhai* sighed, and slumped back on his chair.

"You need to first study about Islam and the Holy Quran, only then you will be able to understand the good works being done by Maulvi *sahab*." This time it was Maqbool *bhai* who spoke in favour of Maulvi *sahab*. Maqbool *bhai* was a businessman who purchased food grains from the village farmers and supplied it in the wholesale markets of Delhi.

The management committee had five members and no one supported Afroz when he pointed fingers towards Maulvi *sahab*. Afroz was the wealthiest of the five members and he had thought the weight of his wealth would help him sail through. But he was grossly mistaken. The management committee members were men of character and the Basera madrasa was a dream project for all of them. They saw madrasa as a temple of learning that could shape the future of Basera's poor children. Everyone's children had studied, at least for a few years, at the madrasa and they had full faith in Maulvi *sahab's* integrity, abilities and knowledge.

"Afroz… my son, you are a young man. Your father was an erudite person. You should follow his footsteps. I feel it will be good if you learn about Islam from Maulvi *sahab*, there is no age to learn Islamic teachings and develop understandings about Allah. I am sure Maulvi *sahab* will be pleased to help you," Aftab *sahab* said in his soft voice looking towards Maulvi *sahab* for his approval.

Maulvi *sahab* just nodded his head in approval. He was deeply hurt by Afroz's allegations but maintained his composure.

Afroz's father and Aftab *sahab* were good friends and both of them shared the vision to have a good educational school for village children. Afroz was the youngest of the three siblings. He had two elder sisters who got married when Afroz was still very young. One of his sisters was married off to a rich businessman in Mumbai and the other was settled with a property broker in Delhi. Afroz being a kid spent a lot of his time in Delhi at his sister's place. His brother-in-law, being a property broker, had befriended all types of people for his business dealings. And that included radical Islamic *mullahs* and *maulvis* who preached virulent interpretation of Islam. Afroz's brother-in-law sought help from these radical elements to instigate a mob of Muslims whenever he had to encroach upon government land. Of course, these *mullahs* and *maulvis* extracted their pound of flesh in cash or kind. But these business dealings apart, Afroz got a chance to see from very close quarters how religious fanaticism can be used as a weapon. His mother insisted that Afroz stay at his sister's place and study at a Delhi school rather than at the dilapidated madrasa of Basera. Afroz's father respected his wife's wishes and never vetoed her decision to let Afroz stay in Delhi with his sister.

This was probably the biggest mistake of his life. He guided and taught several poor kids of Basera and other adjoining villages but his own son got into the company of radical Islamists. Though a healthy man he could not survive a sudden and massive heart attack. Being his only son, Afroz took his place in the madrasa's management committee. This was a year ago.

With Aftab *sahab's* intervention, when he asked Afroz to learn about Islamic scriptures, the meeting of madrasa committee was formally over. Biscuits and tea were being served and discussions wandered about general issues of the village, home affairs, children and their future etcetera.

Maulvi *sahab's* mind wandered as he sipped tea. It was the first time in his life that someone had pointed fingers towards him and his efforts were questioned. He was hurt by Afroz's allegations and his injury showed in his mannerisms. He kept responding in monosyllables or in very short sentences to the general discussion by other committee members.

Later during the day at madrasa, he could barely concentrate on his teaching and somehow ended the day's schooling by giving assignments to the students.

"What happened, you look very worried, what has happened at the meeting?" Begum *sahiba* asked, gently touching his shoulder. The gentle caress of his wife helped Maulvi *sahab* regain his composure.

"Umm okay," he mumbled.

"What okay? You don't seem to be okay"

"Begum tell me how am I as a teacher? Do I impart proper Islamic teachings at the madrasa?"

Begum *sahiba* looked intently into her husband's eyes.

"Why do you ask this question? Your whole time is devoted to the madrasa and you hardly have any time for our home or for me? And you still feel this is not enough?" she said in a lovingly complaining tone. Her voice was laced more with love and less with anger.

Maulvi *sahab's* mind was still stuck at the morning meeting and Afroz's words continued to echo in his mind. Yes, he looked at his wife and could hear her speaking but his mind could not register her words. It continued to echo Afroz's words.

"Some people in the village think that I am not giving proper Islamic teachings at the madrasa; that I am a bad teacher; that I am thrusting the madrasa students towards *kufra*..."

"Who said these things?" Begum *sahiba* abruptly countered her husband. Her facial expression had changed, the eyebrows curled together, pupils constricted and lips curled with anger. "Every member of the madrasa management committee knows about your commitment as a teacher and your dedication for students. What do they expect from you now? Are these people blind? Can't they see for themselves how you have dedicated your whole life to the betterment of madrasa students......," Begum *sahiba* was livid. She could not fathom how the management committee made baseless allegations on her husband. It was only when Maulvi *sahab* interrupted her and said that it was Afroz who made wild accusations on him that Begum *sahiba* calmed down.

Maulvi *sahab* went on to explain how Afroz had made allegations at the management committee meeting. He also explained that all other members of the committee Aftab *sahab*, Naseem *bhai* and Maqbool *bhai* had vociferously defended him and that Afroz was tongue-tied and could not put any counter points.

Begum *sahiba* relaxed upon hearing this. She heaved a sigh of relief. "When everybody was in your favour then why are you worried? And moreover this Afroz... he is just a kid. Does he know anything about Islam? I have heard that while in Delhi he spent his entire day loitering around girl's colleges on his bike and he has the audacity to talk about Islamic teachings. Worthless son of a worthy father. His father was such a learned man and he has turned out to be a true rascal. He should not have been allowed to be a part of the madrasa's management committee in the first place....," she went on with her tirade as she continued with the household chores. Maulvi *sahab* continued to stare blankly.

Begum *sahiba's* monologue and Maulvi *sahab's* chain of thoughts were interrupted by the loud bang at the iron-gate. They rushed towards the gate to find Abdul lying down at the gate. He wriggled in pain and yet, was grinning.

He had been running madly towards his home and in a zest to hastily enter inside he had slipped upon and banged with the iron gate of his home. Arjun who was on his heels running behind him, was trying to lift up Abdul from the ground. The two friends were panting and giggling. Finally, Arjun and Maulvi *sahab* held Abdul by his armpits and made him stand on his feet.

Abdul was chuckling as he stood up taking support from Arjun and his father. His face twitched with pain and yet he sported a broad grin.

"*Abbu* I have cleared the entrance test of the Delhi School," Abdul said as he hugged his father.

"Yes Uncle, Abdul has also bagged a full scholarship from the school," Arjun said and added that three students from Basera had cleared the test. Apart from Abdul and Arjun, Rukhsana had also passed the test and secured a full scholarship.

For almost a minute Maulvi *sahab* could barely speak. He hugged his son, his eyes gleaming with the unshed tear formed after hearing his son's success.

Begum *sahiba* ran inside the house to get *jaggery* and offered everyone as a mouth sweetener. Tears rolled down her eyes as she hugged Abdul and Arjun.

The boys were ecstatic. They refused to sit at one place and were jumping around and across the courtyard. They ran around Maulvi *sahab* and Begum *sahiba*, they jumped on the table, stood on the chair, even the buffaloes were not spared. Both Arjun and Abdul picked up the bundle of green fodder and sprayed them in the large pot for the buffaloes. The buffaloes mooed loudly at the unexpected feast.

Maulvi *sahab* and Begum *sahiba* cried in joy. These were blissful moments and they made no efforts to hold back their tears, the tears of joy.

"*Abbu* let's inform Rukhsana. She'll also jump with joy on hearing that she has bagged a full scholarship at the Delhi school," Abdul said jumping across the courtyard.

Rukhsana was Rashid's daughter.

8.

Rukhsana was a nine year old studious child, quite fond of books. When she heard about the big school of Delhi and about its scholarship exam she urged Maulvi *sahab* to help her appear in the tests. At first Maulvi *sahab* was somewhat reluctant due to Rashid's invectives against the Delhi school and his diatribe against the need for modern education, but Rukhsana was persistent. Her family was extremely poor and she could see how her father, Rashid, slogged every day from dawn till dusk to earn money. On several days due to lack of work at his rickety salon, Rashid worked as a daily wage labourer at farms, at construction sites, pulled cycle rickshaw, lifted gunny sacks or did anything to earn some money.

Rukhsana's mother picked up odd jobs in the village neighbourhood. Helping the village women in their household chores she too tried to make some money. The relatively better off village women paid her in grains, food or a few rupees. One such day when Begum *sahiba* needed help for de-husking and cleaning the freshly harvested wheat she had called Rukhsana's mother. She happily came over. Rukhsana was then barely four years old and she tagged along with her mother.

While the women were busy cleaning wheat, young Rukhsana played in the big courtyard.

At the other end of the courtyard Maulvi *sahab* was on a chair reading books. Besides him sat Abdul on the cloth mat reading his books. From the corner of his eyes Maulvi *sahab* could see Rukhsana looking wistfully at the colourful books of Abdul. Probably she was too afraid and did not dare to come closer. Maulvi *sahab* promptly called her and asked Abdul to give her a book. Abdul was kind enough. She sat on the cloth mat and within seconds seemed completely engrossed in the books. Her eyes were gleaming with happiness and as she turned the book's pages and was completely oblivious of the surroundings. Maulvi *sahab* was pleasantly surprised to see such fondness for books in a four-year old child. Being a teacher he instantly recognised that Rukhsana was a bright child.

"Why don't you send her to study?" he had asked Rukhsana's mother.

"We barely are able to earn enough to be able to eat, how can we afford the fees and other costs of education. And moreover in a year or two she will help me in my work so that I will be able to earn a bit more," her mother had replied, rather nonchalantly.

Maulvi *sahab* felt bad at this callous attitude towards a child's education. He was a firm believer that each one should learn, read and gain knowledge. And moreover his madrasa's fees was quite nominal.

"I will waive whatever little fee we charge for Rukhsana. You must send her to the madrasa."

"Yes, yes *Ammi*. I will go to study. I will also read and write," Rukhsana had started jumping with joy and hugged her mother even before she could react any other way.

From the very next day Rukhsana was enrolled as a student at the madrasa and true to Maulvi *sahab's* expectations she turned out to be a very bright student.

Rashid was never in favour of letting his daughter study. He was himself an illiterate man and showed no inclination towards education. His wife, though, had studied for a couple of years and could somehow read, and write a little. He reluctantly agreed to send Rukhsana to Maulvi *sahab's* madrasa thinking that she would learn the prayers and that would free her mother to take up more jobs in the village neighbourhood. Years trickled by and Rukhsana was now nine years old.

Rashid was livid when he heard Rukhsana talk about the Delhi school, its scholarship exam and her desire to appear for the same. In a fit of rage he threw a metallic pot on Rukhsana that had barely missed her head. Rukhsana cowed and snuggled herself into a corner of the house sobbing inconsolably.

"Maulvi *sahab* may have gone insane, not me. I am a true *Musalmaan,*" Rashid had boasted about himself. Earlier in the afternoon that day, he had been into an altercation with Maulvi *sahab* when he saw him pasting information posters about the Delhi school on the madrasa walls.

The next morning Rukhsana gathered courage to ask her mother about the possibility to sit for the scholarship exams of the Delhi school. Her mother only cried and hugged her tightly.

"*Ammi* is it wrong to study. Do you think Allah is very happy with people who never seek knowledge?" the nine year old Rukhsana had asked her mother.

'Umm…aaa..ah' her mother could not say anything beyond heavy sighs. Deep in her heart she knew her daughter was right. Years back she too was pulled out of the madrasa when her father had refused to send her to the madrasa. She had meekly surrendered to her father's wish and never questioned his decision, not in her actions and not in her thoughts, either.

She was happy that her daughter, Rukhsana, had at least raised objections. Yet, she knew this was too little, too late to make any difference. There was no point convincing Rashid. She spent the next two days thinking about how to help Rukhsana realise her dream and help her study further. After Rashid's rebuke Rukhsana hardly ate. She was on a silent protest. Rashid, on his part, was completely oblivious of the tensions at his home. He cared too hoots about the aspirations of his children and education was the last thing on his mind.

Next morning Rashid's wife reached Maulvi *sahab's* home. Maulvi *sahab* was at the madrasa. She sat beside Begum *sahiba* and narrated her predicament.

"*Bhabhi jan* please help my daughter. She is not asking for the moon she simply wants to study," Rashid's wife said wiping away her tears with the *dupatta*. Begum *sahiba* assured to help her in all possible ways.

Begum *sahiba* broached the topic that evening when Maulvi *sahab* came home. His lips curled as he thought through. A couple of days earlier Rashid had created a ruckus at the madrasa when Maulvi *sahab* was pasting the advert of Delhi school on the madrasa walls. Maulvi *sahab* knew Rashid was an obstinate man who simply refused to listen to any logic. He was under the spell of selfish Muslim clerics who had fed in his illiterate and uneducated mind that pursuit of knowledge is forbidden in Islam. There was hardly anything that could be done to reason out with Rashid. And yet his daughter was a bright child who had this strong desire to learn. Maulvi *sahab* quietly had his tea, got up and went to pray.

'If people like Rashid are determined to push children towards ignorance and darkness then he must make efforts to light up the lamps of knowledge,' he thought.

He kept pacing in his courtyard for almost an hour, his mind racing as to how can he help Rukhsana appear in the exams. An hour later the idea blinked in his mind.

"Begum, exams for the Delhi school are on Sunday," Maulvi *sahab* said as he picked up the wooden stool to sit beside Begum *sahiba* in the kitchen.

"So?"

"Well, the big monthly fair is also on that day and several children from the village go with their parents to that fair...," Maulvi *sahab* paused, deliberately.

And so did Begum *sahiba*, as she looked at her husband's face, holding the uncooked and raw chapatti in her hand a wee bit longer before hurling it on the hot flat iron pad above the mud stove.

"I get your point," she let out a mischievous smile, adjusting the burning wooden sticks under the mud stove, surprised that her usually suave and gentle husband can think of such a stratagem. Maulvi *sahab's* facial muscles had relaxed after his wife approved of the plan.

"You must have been very naughty in your youth? Isn't it?"

Maulvi *sahab* turned around and said, "You know me very well. I am just trying to help a child who has this burning desire to study and seek knowledge, and…"

"Oh come on, I am just pulling your leg," Begum *sahiba* winked and added, "…sometimes it helps to have a naughty mind."

Maulvi *sahab* smiled. "I am in Abdul's room to help him prepare for the scholarship exams," he said walking away from the kitchen. The tension on his face had melted away and there was a sense of satisfaction. There was spring in his steps as he walked towards Abdul's room.

That Sunday when other village children were talking about which ride to take and what to buy at the fair, Rukhsana was silently revising her lessons at the corner of her hut. She woke up quite early in the morning, helped her mother finish household chores, prepare food and then readied herself for the 'mega-fair'.

"Come on time and cook my dinner. Don't be late," Rashid gave terse instructions to his wife. "Yes we will," his wife said as she wiped the freshly formed sweat beads on her forehead trying hard not to be nervous. Even a speck of suspicion could have invited Rashid's wrath thereby instigating him to simply pronounce that the family stay at home, that nobody would go for the mega-fair and they will stay back within the village. If that happened Rukhsana would miss her exams and her dreams of carving out a better life would come crashing down. The humble scholarship exams carried on its shoulders a bunch of big dreams for Rukhsana and her mother.

Rukhsana tidied the clothes of her two year old sister. She was excited to go to the mega-fair and was jumping with joy. She was too young to understand the 'other plans' made by their mother and elder sister

Rukhsana.

After Rashid left, Rukhsana helped her mother quickly wind up things at home and left for the bus stand. In the bus while other children were busy talking about what to expect at the fair, Rukhsana parked herself on the rear window seat and quietly opened her book. She desperately wanted to pass this exam. Her mother thought that if Rukhsana cleared the scholarship exams then with help from village elders Rashid could be persuaded to let her daughter study at the prestigious Delhi school. Rukhsana could possibly go on to become an engineer, doctor, a lawyer or make any other career for herself. She would be a role model for her younger sister who would then follow her footsteps and study towards a better future. This was the only way to pull out the family from abject poverty that they were in at the moment.

During the entire bus's journey Rukhsana did not lift her head and remained glued to the books she was reading. Her mother was engrossed in her own reverie and occasionally burst into smiles as she dreamt of a bright future for the family.

Getting down from the bus, Rukhsana's mother held her two-year old daughter in her lap. Rukhsana followed closely on her heels. The family walked briskly.

Pundit *ji's* big car was waiting at far end of the bus stand. Inside it were Maulvi *sahab*, Begum *sahiba*, Abdul, Arjun, Arjun's father and his mother. They were all waiting eagerly for Rukhsana to come in. Maulvi *sahab* got down and gestured Rukhsana to get inside the car. Rukhsana's mother hugged her daughter and wished her luck for the exams, then quietly slipped over for the mega-fair with her two-year old daughter.

The car raced towards Delhi. It was hardly an hour's drive to Delhi from the bus stand. The kids reached on time for the two-hour exam at Delhi. After the exams, Pundit *ji's* car dropped Rukhsana at the bus stop and she joined her mother and younger sister late that afternoon for the mega-fair. She was upbeat as her exams went off very well. Rukhsana's mother had ample time to return back to Basera well on time and prepare Rashid's dinner. It was a hectic day but neither Rukhsana nor her mother complained. They were extremely happy.

Everybody had expected that once Rukhsana clears the scholarship test at the prestigious school, Rashid would be convinced that it was indeed a gateway to a decent and prosperous life for his daughter.

The big day had finally arrived. All three kids had cleared the exams and Arjun and Abdul were running towards Rukhsana's home to give her this wonderful news. They reached Rashid's home only to find an ugly lock dangling from the rusty iron-gate to welcome them.

"Where have they gone?" Abdul asked the kid playing in the lane.

The kid pointed towards Afroz's house.

Wearing a grubby and oversized frock that reached her ankles Rukhsana was busy washing a pile of soiled dishes under the mango tree in the courtyard at Afroz's house. Her mother did the same besides her.

Rukhsana's two year old sister was crawling in the mud nearby. A few meters away Rashid was busy stacking the unkempt pile of chairs into neat columns. There had been a big gathering at Afroz's house last night and Rashid was called over to clean up the mess. He brought in his wife and children to help him earn some extra bucks.

"Rukhsana, all of us have qualified for the prestigious Delhi school. We will now study in Delhi...we will get scholarship and all our expenses will be taken care of," Abdul blurted out the good news to Rukhsana. He and Arjun had come running and they both skidded to a stop near the pile of utensils. His voice was relatively muted yet his enthusiasm was intact. Arjun nodded as he chuckled.

Rukhsana broke into a big broad smile as she looked towards her mother. Tears of joy flowed from her eyes that were dull and morose a moment ago. Those sorrow laden eyes were now gleaming with elation. She hugged her mother tight and they remained in an ecstatic embrace for several moments. Those were the blissful moments for Rukhsana and during those minutes, a million dreams flashed in her mind. She could see herself wearing a smart school uniform, reading books and writing in crisp white notebooks, passing out from school, graduating from a college, getting a job, bring gifts for her *Ammi, Abbu* and her younger sister Tabassum. They would now eat good food, have a beautiful house, wear good clothes....Rukhsana just could not stop dreaming. Those were blissful moments for her and she continued to bask in that heavenly sunshine.

The hapless girl was unable to foresee what lay for her in the next moment. Both mother and daughter were naïve to be able to understand what was brewing inside Rashid's head. They remained in a tight embrace shedding tears.

Minutes later when Rukhsana opened her eyes she saw her father, Rashid, right in front of her.

Rukhsana smiled at him and made no effort to wipe off the tears that were still flowing down her cheeks. Even before she could utter a word, Rashid burst out with dirtiest expletives he could think of. Rukhsana was confused. Rashid's tone and visage made him look like a stranger to her. Yes, he never used kind words for his daughter and would often thrash her, but today was even different. She looked at her mother, who quickly wiped away her tears to explain, "Your daughter..."

"Your daughter is a slut. She's a whore," Rashid had cut short his wife and shouted in a shrill tone.

"How dare you conspire against me and make this slut appear for the wretched exams when I had ordered her not to fall for this wicked plan," Rashid raised his finger and waved it vigorously on his wife's face. His eyeballs widened, facial muscles twitched and nostrils had expanded with anger. He was not willing to listen to her and continued to glare at her face.

"...and look at these rascals, first they swayed you to fall for their wicked plan and now they have the nerve to come to my home and announce that my daughter will dance on their tunes," Rashid said waving towards Abdul and Arjun.

Abdul and Arjun were stunned. Not even in their wildest of dreams they had imagined that they would have to confront such a situation. They looked at each other in utter bewilderment.

"Your home? Do you think this is your home? You and your whole family are mere servants working here for a few rupees," Rashid's wife had mustered some courage as she countered her husband.

"Just Shut Up...you wayward woman," Rashid was livid. "...any true Muslim's home is our home and Afroz *bhai* is a true Muslim. Not like the wretched father of this boy," Rashid said flinching his teeth, and pointing towards Abdul.

"Rashid *chacha* why do you call my father wretched. He just wants Rukhsana to study..."

"Rukhsana, how dare you take my daughter's name...just wait...," Rashid took out the dirty slippers from his feet and darted towards Abdul.

Arjun held Abdul's arm and pulled him back.

Rashid's wife held his arm as Rukhsana clung on to her mother. She was too terrified to even open her mouth. Rashid paused for a moment. Arjun dragged Abdul out of Afroz's house.

All this while, Afroz along with his cronies was watching from the first floor window of their house. No one, including Afroz, made any attempts to intervene. Afroz's demeanour suggested contempt for Rashid and his family and yet he was smiling, thinking and making plans about him.

Rukhsana's two-year old sister had begun eating leftovers from the dirty utensils, oblivious of the surrounding tensions.

Abdul and Arjun had left but Rashid's temper showed no signs of cooling down.

"Finish off quickly," Rashid thundered pointing towards the heap of soiled utensils.

With Rashid refusing to be cowed down Rukhsana and her mother had no other option but to clean up the mess at Afroz's home. They sat on their hunches to clean the utensils. The toddler continued to fish into the heap of dirty utensils to find any leftover food to eat.

Rashid hopped and sat on the heap of chairs. Perched on the chair's heap he felt a sense of accomplishment that he could browbeat his family into submission and bring them to, what he thought was, a righteous path. He crisscrossed his legs and watched his wife and Rukhsana wash utensils, while the younger Tabassum continued to eat leftover food.

Rashid was still staring at his wife and Rukhsana when he heard someone call his name. He turned around to see Afroz waving his hands from the first floor window. He jumped down immediately, from the heap of chairs.

"Come inside," Afroz said in a polite yet firm tone.

Rashid meekly obeyed and walked inside his house. An hour later when he came out of the room he saw Rukhsana and his mother washing the last heap of utensils while the two year old Tabassum was sleeping on the muddy courtyard.

"Go home after you clean up everything," he commanded in a terse voice.

Rukhsana and her mother maintained a stoic silence as they continued with their job. Rashid walked away.

Abdul and Arjun walked away with a heavy heart. They reached Arjun's house. Maulvi *sahab*, Begum *sahiba*, Arjun's father, his mother and a couple of other relatives and friends had gathered to celebrate the occasion. The mood was ebullient.

Arjun narrated the entire incident at Afroz's home and Rashid's subsequent behaviour. Everyone was perturbed for they had collectively believed that once Rukhsana cleared the entrance test, Rashid would be pacified. Yes, everyone knew that Rashid was stubborn but that he would behave in such a manner was something which was beyond everyone's expectations.

"Don't worry Maulvi *sahab*, we will talk to Rashid and convince him. If need be we will also ask village elders who can reason out with him. After all nobody is asking for a personal favour. If Rukhsana studies further then it is for her own good and their entire family including Rashid stands to benefit," Arjun's father said.

Maulvi *sahab* merely nodded. He understood that Arjun's father was suggesting the right approach but he also knew that reasoning out with Rashid will be extremely difficult. Yet the idea to involve village elders looked promising and he could see a ray of hope. This helped dissolve the despondency, at least for now.

The families were now discussing the Delhi school, yet again. Mothers were worried about the quality of food that would be served at the school's mess and how to ensure that Abdul and Arjun eat properly while they are away from their homes. They discussed what food items to send with the boys that could stay fresh for a longer time in jars within their hostel rooms. They tutored the boys to avoid being fussy over food at the hostel.

Arjun's father and Maulvi sahab were discussing the paperwork and other formalities, certificates to be taken to complete the admission process. Arjun and Abdul discussed what new dresses they would take and how their life would be in a hostel, away from their parents.

A couple of days back Jamil had entrusted Afroz with an important task. This task was to somehow overtake the day-to-day workings of Basera's madrasa and then the adjoining mosque. It was precisely for this reason that Afroz had called for an emergency meeting of the madrasa management committee.

Earlier in the morning that day Afroz had tried to push his agenda at the madrasa management committee meeting. He was under the impression that since his father had taken the initiative to build the Basera madrasa other committee members will not go against him. But his efforts to corner Maulvi *sahab* had failed as all committee members sided with Maulvi *sahab*. He was rather worried that his inability to execute a simple task entrusted by Jamil will, in effect, put his nascent political career in doldrums.

He was in a pensive mood after the light lunch and was staring at the courtyard through the living room window. Rashid and his family were cleaning up the mess that had been left behind after yesterday night's get-together at his bungalow. Afroz sniffed an opportunity when he saw Rashid create a ruckus at the news of Rukhsana clearing the exams for admission at

Delhi. He carefully observed Rashid's behavior and broke into a wide grin when Rashid took out his slippers to hit Abdul, Maulvi *sahab's* son. All was not lost for him and there still was a ray of hope. Rashid was this hope.

'I'd been trying to light up fire in a pile of wet logs when dry wood is readily available in my own courtyard,' Afroz said to himself as he sneered at Rashid who was admonishing his wife and daughter. 'Just a little spark and this man will turn into a rolling inferno,' Afroz scoffed as he looked towards Rashid. He had then promptly asked for Rashid.

"*Salam-Walekum* Afroz *bhai*," Rashid greeted Afroz. His torso was bent as he greeted Afroz, almost parallel to the ground.

"Rashid, come in my brother. Come and sit here," Afroz said pointing towards the sofa with a big soft cushion.

Rashid hunched on the sides of the big sofa.

"Oh come on…sit on the sofa, you are my brother," Afroz said as he held Rashid's hands and guided him to the sofa. He was careful to touch only the fingertips of Rashid's hands, conscious of the fact that Rashid had been cleaning up the mess in his courtyard and his hands wore a black layer of dust and dirt. Afroz did not want to soil his hands.

Rashid was mesmerised by Afroz *bhai's* generosity. Very reluctantly he sat on the edges of the grand sofa and leaned forward to listen to his 'Afroz *bhai*'.

"Rashid my brother, I am very proud of you. Your actions and behaviour were like a true Muslim. This is exactly a true Muslim should and would do. Only a true soldier of Islam can ward off the evil temptations of this impure world. You know my father used to tell me that *Shaitaan*--the devil, will attack your family if he is unable to persuade you. And look at how it was able to persuade your wife and daughter to walk on the path of *kufr*. Yet you held your fort like a true *Musalmaan*…," Afroz doled out his sugar talk. Rashid was spellbound, he listened with his eyes wide open, focusing on Afroz *bhai's* each and every word.

"Do you know Jamil *bhai*?" Afroz asked.

"J…j…Jamil *bhai*?" Rashid stammered hearing Jamil's name. "Of course I know him." "Who would not know a big man like him?"

"I will talk to him about you. Come to his house today evening, I will introduce you to him," Afroz said.

Rashid smiled. He could not believe his ears that he will get an opportunity to meet Jamil *bhai* that evening. During *Ramzan* when the gates of Jamil's bungalow were open for *iftar,* Jamil himself had never come out to meet any of the villagers. All arrangements were made in the bungalow's big lawn with Bilal, Anwar and other helpers arranging the eatables on large tables. The ambience never felt homely, it was not meant to be, and the entire arrangement appeared like a large buffet that was arranged free and as some kind of a throw away. Though the focus was on free food yet Jamil was portrayed as a larger-than-life benefactor who never sought publicity for his pious deeds, akin to a true Muslim.

Rashid felt honoured at Afroz's suggestion that he was chosen above all others who would be able to meet Jamil *bhai* in person. He bowed his head and came out of the living room. The next moment, his demeanour changed when he saw his wife and children. He gave them a flurry of instructions. They were supposed to quickly finish off the cleanings, reach home on time and prepare dinner.

Rashid's wife looked towards him. There was hardly anything at their shanty to be cooked. That morning Rashid had brought them at Afroz's place in the hope that after finishing off the odd jobs at his bungalow they would earn some money with which they will buy food and milk. Now Rashid was walking away ordering her to prepare dinner.

"What kind of a man is he? Does he even remember that except *bajra*, there's hardly anything at their hut. Their daughter had qualified for a prestigious school in Delhi and yet all he could do is shout and abuse her publicly. And now he has walked away without even bothering to find out what will his family eat…," Rashid's wife murmured in a very soft voice that was barely audible. She displaced her anger on the heap of utensils. The vigour with which she rinsed utensils was increasing, every passing minute.

It was still late afternoon when Rashid reached Chacha's tea shack. He asked for a cup of tea. Chacha happily obliged him with a packet of biscuits along with the tea. Rashid looked at him anxiously. He had no money not even for the tea. Chacha pressed his hand gently, in assurance.

Rashid sipped tea and munched biscuits as Chacha sang paeans about Jamil *bhai's* deeds for other customers at the tea stall.

"Only Jamil *bhai* is truly concerned about poor Muslims like us. All these people who roam around with big fat books just use poor *Musalmaans* as their door mat," Chacha said as he poured tea into small glass tumblers. His comment on men with big fat books was an obvious jibe towards Maulvi *sahab,* who very often could be seen with books in his hand.

Rashid did not speak much. He smiled at his good fortune. He looked around the shack and saw masons, carpenters, blacksmith and labourers sipping tea as they listened to Chacha eulogizing Jamil *bhai*. He smiled again. The likes of Chacha and others can only talk about Jamil *bhai* but only true *Musalmaans* like him get a chance to meet Jamil *bhai* in person, he said to himself. And his luck favoured him only because he is actually walking on the path of Islam like a true Muslim, not like others who may talk of Allah and Islam but falter at the first instance. Rashid felt proud of himself, he smirked as he sipped the third cup of tea. He did not realise that all these while, Chacha had been closely observing him from the corner of his eyes.

9 .

It had been more than two hours and Rashid was still sitting at Chacha's tea stall. People walked in, had tea and left, but Rashid kept sitting. He already had three cups of tea since he came in and yet showed no inclination to leave.

"What happened Rashid *bhai*, today you are not in a mood to go home?" Chacha asked him, his tone suggesting that he was in the know of a few things. Rashid ignored Chacha's question. Giving explanations was futile, he thought. Rather than waste his energy in answering futile questions of a tea maker he thought of making use of his time to think through of the ways to impress Jamil *bhai* during the meeting. During those couple of hours he had dreamt of having a car, a big house and the company of beautiful women.

"Rashid *bhai* its time"

Rashid woke up from his sweet reverie to the soft words. Chacha was sitting beside him and had whispered in his ears.

"Ahh yes," Rashid said as he started to walk away. He thought he had been sitting for long and Chacha wanted him to go so that his other customers may get a seat.

"This way, Jamil *bhai's* bungalow is this way," Chacha said with a mischievous smile.

Rashid's eyebrows converged as he gave a surprised look.

"Yes, I know that you have to meet Jamil *bhai*. Go meet him and then we will talk," Chacha said softly before Rashid could ask any other question. He then got up and walked towards the concrete pavement and lit up the stove to prepare tea.

Rashid walked away.

There was no one at Jamil's bungalow when Rashid reached. Usually his car and a couple of motorbikes were parked on the outside but today there was nothing. Rashid stood motionless in front of the black gate for several minutes, still unable to decide if he should knock. The large expanse of sugarcane fields lay behind him. He could hear the gurgling sound of water running through the canal that flowed behind the bungalow. Despite the cool breeze swishing past him he was sweating and had to constantly rub off the forehead with his palm to wipe off the sweat beads.

'What if Jamil *bhai* is into an important meeting; what if he were disturbed by the knocks; after all he is just a labourer who can wait for his turn; probably he should come some other day with Afroz *bhai*....' an array of thoughts raced through Rashid's head as he stood there motionless.

After several minutes when he could not muster enough courage to knock at the gate he decided to go back. Just as he turned around, the big black gate opened slowly with a creaking sound and Anwar popped out. All this while, he had been watching Rashid from the cat's eye.

"Yes, tell me?" Anwar asked.

"I am Rashid. Afroz *bhai* had asked me to come here and meet Jamil *bhai*," he spoke in a quivering voice.

"Okay, come inside"

Anwar was careful to close the gate behind them. Rashid walked past the porch and the long and dark alley to reach the brightly lit living room.

Jamil and Afroz were sitting on the big sofa.

"*Salaam-o-Walekum*," Rashid greeted in a soft voice.

"*Walekum-o-Assalam*," Afroz replied, gesturing Rashid to sit on the carpeted floor. Rashid happily hunched down in the corner. He was attentive and looked eagerly towards Jamil *bhai* to listen to his diktat.

"Jamil *bhai* he is the one I was talking about. His name is Rashid," Afroz said turning towards Jamil. Jamil continued to stare at Rashid. His eyes scanned Rashid from top till bottom. Rashid wore a grubby black shirt and baggy pants. The white sweat-patches were distinctly visible on his black shirt. His feet were dirty, the heel cracks were wide and held several ounce of mud in between. There was dust on his unkempt beard and moustache which coupled with the disheveled hair gave a brownish hue to his face. Jamil's continuous gaze made Rashid nervous. He hung down his head in submission.

It was then that Jamil decided to speak.

"Hmmm. I saw you arguing with Maulvi *sahab* that day at the madrasa. You seem to be a true soldier of Islam," Jamil spoke slowly but authoritatively. He then briefly narrated to Afroz how Rashid had publicly challenged Maulvi *sahab* when he was using the madrasa premises to advertise about the Satan's Delhi school.

"Oh that was very well done. And Jamil *bhai* do you know what happened today?" Afroz turned towards Jamil and then went on to describe in detail how Rashid was able to control his wayward wife and daughter who had defied him and appeared for the exams of this Satan's school in Delhi. Jamil smiled, fondling his moustache and beard with his index finger and thumb.

"That's what is expected from true soldiers of Islam. This Maulvi and others like him have made the lives of *Musalmaans* a living hell in this Basera village. It is only because we have some true followers of Islam like Rashid *bhai* that *Musalmaans* are able to breathe in this village otherwise this Maulvi will strangle every Muslim to death," Jamil said leaning forward, looking intently towards Rashid.

Rashid had settled by now and was sitting cross-legged on the carpet. He was listening attentively as Jamil spoke. Afroz, Anwar and Bilal had also leaned forward as they too listened to their 'Jamil *bhai*' in rapt attention.

"...this Maulvi is actually a characterless man. He has a bad eye on every woman. In the garb of teaching children he casts his spell on every woman of Basera. He eyes every girl of our village and fancies his chances with all ladies, whether young or old. He talks of the need of teaching the girls and look at its after effects...none of the woman in our village puts on a *burqa* or even the hijab. Tomorrow when they start working they will no longer cook for their husbands and who knows they might as well sleep around with other men...," Jamil went on.

"I will cut this Maulvi into pieces. How dare he eye my wife," Rashid burst out abruptly cutting Jamil's speech. He stood up grinding his teeth and with clenched fists.

Jamil smiled.

"We empathise with you and we share the same resentment," Jamil added, "...look how this wicked Maulvi hypnotized your wife and daughter to appear for the scholarship exams of this wretched Delhi school even after you strictly forbade them for this. And do you know what this Maulvi's real intentions are?"

Rashid leaned forward, his pupils dilated that made his big eyes look even bigger.

"He has been fancying your wife for a while and maybe even your nine year old daughter. It was Afroz who first got the wind of Maulvi's real intentions," Jamil said in a slow voice and leaned back after he finished off his sentence.

Rashid stood up in a jiffy and turned around. "I will finish off this Maulvi today itself," he said and turned around to leave.

"Ohh wait...," Jamil almost shouted. He asked Rashid to come and sit on the sofa besides him.

"Listen Rashid *bhai* don't do anything foolish else you will surely land up in jail. Think about the safety of your wife and daughters. This Maulvi is a very clever man so we need to be extremely careful"

"But I can't just sit idle and…"

"Who is asking you to sit idle? Bilal give a glass of cold water to our Rashid *bhai*"

"You are a true soldier of Islam--a *Ghazi*, but then we have to be level headed and think through our strategy. Understood?"

"Okay Jamil *bhai* I will do as you say and do whatever you say," Rashid had stepped forward, held Jamil's hand in his hands and bowed his head in abject surrender to his wishes.

Jamil smiled and looked towards Afroz. This was exactly what they had wanted from Rashid. He smiled back and so too Anwar and Bilal. Rashid was in their clasp.

Afroz stood up. "Welcome…'Rashid *bhai*--the *Ghazi*'…welcome into our family…our family of true Muslims," he said as he stepped forward and hugged Rashid. As he came closer to Rashid, he held his breath to stop breathing in the reeking smell of sweat emanating from Rashid's body. Even while hugging he made sure to have minimal contact with Rashid's shoulder.

"This is not done Afroz *bhai*. This is not the way you welcome a *Ghazi* into our family of believers," Jamil chided.

Afroz was bemused. Before he could say anything, Jamil winked. Afroz let out a broad grin. "Rashid *bhai* you are a valuable member of our family and to celebrate your induction, Jamil *bhai* wants to offer you a very special gift," he said and waved his hands towards Bilal.

Bilal came ahead, held Rashid's hand and started to walk towards the other side of the living room. Jamil and Afroz nodded their head, and let out a wicked smile.

Rashid walked across the living room into the gallery. They walked towards the room at the other side of the gallery. It was dimly lit. Bilal stopped a step before the room's entrance and lifted his eyebrows in a signal for Rashid to go ahead and get inside the room. Rashid curled his eyebrows, looking confused. Bilal insisted that Rashid go inside the room.

Rashid's jaw dropped and he felt a gush of blood rushing below his abdomen, the moment he stepped inside the room. A woman, smoking cigarette was lying on the big grand couch. A towel lay on her that barely covered her naked thighs and shoulders. She saw Rashid from the corner of her eyes and continued to smoke making no attempts to cover herself.

"Rashid *bhai* this is a small gift from us. Enjoy your moments," Afroz shouted from the living room.

Rashid could barely move or speak. He was stunned. Bilal came forward to close the door.

The woman suddenly jumped out from the couch, the cigarette dangling from her fingers while she clutched the towel with another hand. As she stepped out, the towel slipped from her behind exposing her derriere to Rashid. The intensity inside him was now becoming unbearable.

She darted out of the room and shouted. "How many more?"

"He is the last one for today," Jamil shouted back.

"I will charge extra."

"Okay," said Jamil.

The next moment Rashid pulled her inside the room, shut the doors with his legs and pounced upon her like an animal.

He came out of the room an hour later. Jamil, Afroz and Anwar had left. Bilal was speaking over phone. He paused for a moment and handed over fifty rupees to Rashid and asked him to go home and come over tomorrow evening.

Rashid ambled towards his home thinking about the pleasure moments spent with the escort woman. 'Jami *bhai* really feels for poor people of this village otherwise why would he induct an impoverished person like him into his troupe, call me a *Ghazi* and give a grand welcome,' he kept thinking as he walked. He felt that after years of struggle he could find true mentors who will now transform his otherwise worthless life. He was still engrossed in thoughts about the escort woman and the time spent with her. 'I am barely able to make my ends meet and no way could have I been able to afford such a costly escort woman,' he told himself. 'This Jamil *bhai* is a real messiah sent by Allah to transform my life. Jamil *bhai* knew that I do not have money and so he gave me fifty rupees as well. He is going to transform my life. I will do whatever Jamil *bhai* and Afroz *bhai* tell me to do,' Rashid thought as he walked on the muddy pathway. The swishing sound of air that rubbed past the sugarcane plants created the background music to the movie that was playing in his mind.

"So how was she?" Chacha's voice had jolted Rashid from his sweet reverie. His voice sounded like a bell that stopped the movie playing inside Rashid's head which was going on beyond its scheduled run time.

"She was marvellous" "…umm.. wait a minute… who she?… what are you talking about?" Rashid tried to defend himself after subconsciously blurting out the truth to Chacha.

"Don't worry. Count me as one of your brother. Just like you I am a *Ghazi* too. And from now on we are all brothers of Afroz *bhai* and Jamil *bhai*"

"I did not understand"

"I will make you understand. Come with me," Chacha led Rashid to the local liquor shop. He bought a bottle of cheap whiskey. Chacha pulled the *kafiyah* scarf from his shoulders and laid it on the ground under a neem tree. The two men sat on it, there being nothing around in the vicinity except for the vast expanse of sugarcane fields.

Over drinks Chacha revealed how Jamil *bhai* and Afroz *bhai* aimed to improve the condition of Muslims in the village. "You need to understand that we Muslims are a part of the *Ummah* and so we need to think for all our brethren across this village, city, state, country and elsewhere. This is exactly what Jamil *bhai* and Afroz *bhai* are doing. Their patrons are very powerful and pious people who continue to guide our Jamil *bhai*. And it's not that Jamil *bhai* inducts anybody and everybody to be a *Ghazi*. You should feel happy that he has chosen you for this pious role….," Chacha went on with his glib talk as they gulped whiskey pegs one after another. By the time whiskey bottle turned empty Rashid was beaming with pride. He thanked his stars for the luck bestowed upon him such that Jamil *bhai* chose him to be a part of the big Islamic movement. Rashid looked towards the sugarcane fields, but he could not see any sugarcane plant. He saw a huge green carpet that was flying in the air, he called Chacha to catch hold of the green carpet before it flies away. Chacha understood Rashid was completely drunk and he changed the topic.

"Today's girl was heaven. Isn't it?" Chacha tossed the question, revealing his brownish black teeth as he grinned.

"I am still unable to understand how could you know about her, when you were not present in the bungalow?" Rashid said flinging his head sideways, sozzled under the influence of the cheap whiskey.

"Oh man. I was the one who got her from Delhi. I was driving the vehicle. She came in the afternoon and we had our "lunch" with her. You were the last one," Chacha winked. "Now listen carefully," he whispered, "… these type of girls come on a regular basis to Jamil *bhai's* house and if you want to be in 'heaven' then you too have to begin your work at the earliest," Chacha explained, leaning forward.

"And what is the work?" Rashid asked as he attempted to shake off the alcohol's affect.

"Our job will be to do as and what Jamil *bhai* says. At the moment it is to identify the potential warriors of Islam and bring them to Jamil *bhai*. That's it. And in return you get 'heaven' along with the money," Chacha winked yet again, leaning back as he rested on his elbows.

Rashid smiled back. This should be an easy task for him, he thought. He looked at the bottle. It was empty. He kicked the empty bottle into the sugarcane fields.

Rashid reached home completely drunk. He was unable to keep his steps straight and swayed sideways as he walked.

Rashid and his family lived in abject poverty. Their hut's roof was thatched with palm tree leaves and walls were made up of mud. Often after heavy rains the hut had to be re-erected. They had two goats and half a dozen hens. The goats had to be sold last year to raise money for Rashid's treatment when he was diagnosed with tuberculosis. The hen's egg brought them some money but that was grossly inadequate to run the entire family. Rashid's barber salon was not a reliable source of income either. Often he would continue to wait for a customer and then pick up some odd work at a construction site as a labourer or plied cycle rickshaw.

All those months when Rashid remained bed-ridden, his wife picked up odd jobs in the village neighbourhood like cutting fodder for buffaloes, cleaning grains or washing utensils. Rukhsana remained at home to tend to her father while the younger infant daughter went along with her mother. Quite often people in the village gave milk to the infant girl but on several occasions when milk was not available, her mother had to feed her with boiled barley water. Rashid's wife never complained about the penury in which they lived. She was a deeply religious woman who offered her *namaz* to Allah and then got on with the drudgeries of livelihood.

Rashid himself came from a very poor family. His father was a barber, had two wives and ten children. The family lived in a shanty and there was hardly any space for everyone. Food was always in a short supply and the family relied on alms and *zakat* from richer Muslims to survive. None of Rashid's siblings had ever been to school or to a madrasa. Education could never be the focus of family since they were always grappling with shortage of food. When Rashid was barely eight years old his father succumbed to malaria leaving behind his two wives and their ten children. Within a year, both women re-married. Strangely, even though the women married within their extended families they were reluctant to take along their own children sired by Rashid's father. After much squabbling, only three of Rashid's siblings could find a new home with their mothers. The rest of seven kids, including Rashid were tossed among relatives, friends and road side shops. A couple of years later four of them died due to consumption. Of the three that survived, two were girls and the third was Rashid. The two girls were married off to their uncles before they were fifteen and Rashid never heard about them ever again. Rashid started working as a barber and to supplement his income he also started plying cycle-rickshaw. He was still a teenager with an impressionable mind.

At the rickshaw stand, while waiting for passengers, the talks centred on making a quick buck and improving lifestyles. A few men talked about saving money and buying their own cycle-rickshaw to save on the daily rentals on their rickshaw, others talked about going back to farming while a few said they should get a passport and work as labourers in gulf nations, rake in mullah and start their own business. A few bearded men amidst them blamed their faith for all ills. These men started their day with reading a few Urdu newspapers and internalised whatever was written as gospel of truth. It was here where Rashid first became conscious of his Muslim identity. With every passing day his conviction of being a victim due to his religion grew stronger. There was no one to remind him that he was illiterate who could not be employed for any of the white-collared jobs. Nobody asked him to take any specific training so that he could join the organised labour force. Those who could have explained, never bothered to waste their time on him while the remaining fed into his victimhood and accentuated his identity as a Muslim. Gradually Rashid started believing that the world is difficult for Muslims but if he continued on the righteous path to Islam then things would turn brighter. But, a fundamental loophole remained in Rashid's conviction. What was this righteous path to Islam? Rashid never bothered to ask and nobody explained him.

The mood was sombre at Rashid's home. His wife, Rukhsana and the two year old daughter had returned home after washing utensils at Afroz's home. They had expected to get some money so that they could have bought the day's ration but Afroz had left early and his henchmen drove them out saying whatever money need to be given will be given to Rashid.

Rukhsana was morose after Rashid's severe reprimand earlier in the day about the Delhi school. She was feeding boiled barley water to her two year old sister while her mother sifted through the plastic boxes to find something to cook. The boxes were empty. After much effort she found some *bajra*. She lit up the wood sticks underneath the mud-stove to prepare *bajra* chapattis.

"Don't be so sad. I will talk to your father. I am sure I will be able to convince him. I will reason out with him, don't worry. After all if you study and get a good job then all of us will benefit. Even your father's life will improve. You can get him a motorbike when you start earning. Don't worry things will be okay," Rukhsana's mother tried to lift her spirits.

Rukhsana did not say a word. All she could muster was a blank smile, after much effort. She was eating *bajra* chapattis when she heard some hustle-bustle outside. Her mother stood up and peeked through the short mud wall that separated their make-shift kitchen with the remaining portion of their hut. Almost involuntarily she grinned.

Maulvi *sahab*, Begum *sahiba*, Arjun's father, his mother, Abdul and Arjun had come over.

"We have come to congratulate you on the success of your daughter," Arjun's mother said, offering her a bag full of sweets.

"Yes, yes, thank you…thank you," Rukhsana's mother said sheepishly as she glanced sideways in a futile attempt to find something where the guests could be seated. "Rukhsana get the mat," she said.

Rukhsana quickly came out with a mat that was falling apart with countless threads dangling all around its edges. Begum *sahiba* and Arjun's mother promptly helped Rukhsana lay down the mat. Begum *sahiba* put some sweets into Rukhsana's mouth.

"This is a good opportunity for your entire family," Maulvi *sahab* said folding his legs as he sat on the mat. "Rukhsana is a bright kid and if she gets higher education then her life will transform and with her all of you will prosper."

Rukhsana's mother nodded in agreement.

"I heard about Rashid's behaviour this afternoon. And so all of us have come here to talk to him about Rukhsana. He has certain misconceptions about Islamic teachings. The basic tenet of Islamic belief is to seek knowledge from all sources…. I firmly believe that deep inside Rashid is a good man but he needs to be educated about Islam and about the importance of education in a person's life…," Maulvi *sahab* explained.

The two families waited almost an hour for Rashid to return.

By then, Rukhsana's sister who was sleeping aside started crying as she woke up. In her lisped voice she asked for something to eat. Rukhsana quickly got the *bajra* chapatti and made small bits of it to feed her.

"Give her some milk. The *bajra* chapatti is quite coarse for a toddler," Begum *sahiba* told Rukhsana.

"There is no milk. But I will get some barley water," Rukhsana said in a low voice, feeling rather embarrassed. Arjun's mother took some sweets and broke it into small bits to feed the young girl. "I will get some milk from my house," Begum *sahiba* said as she stood up. Their house was hardly fifty metres away.

Others stood up too. It was decided that since Rashid was not at home and it was late in the night so they will come tomorrow morning to discuss Rukhsana's admission to Delhi school with Rashid.

Maulvi *sahab* bid goodbye to Arjun's family who stayed on other side of the village and they hurriedly rushed to their home.

At their home, Begum *sahiba* quickly filled a jar with buffalo milk and handed over to Maulvi *sahab*.

A few minutes after Abdul and Arjun's family had left, Rukhsana heard a thud sound outside their hut. She came out of her hut to see Rashid holding the mud wall, his torso swayed wildly and he was unable to lift up his head. His body had banged against the mud wall as he sought its support and a big mud block from wall had fallen on the ground causing the thud sound. The next moment Rashid tried to enter his hut but continued to sway wildly. He would have fell on his face in the hut's courtyard, had he not clutched the mud wall. A bigger portion of the mud wall broke this time.

"*Ammi*, come quickly," Rukhsana shrieked. Her mother came out and they both held Rashid. With their support Rashid dangled forward and sat on the rickety cot kept in the courtyard.

A few minutes later Maulvi *sahab* came riding on his bicycle with the milk jar in his hand. Rukhsana's mother saw Maulvi *sahab* holding the milk jar and went ahead to take it from him. Rashid was sitting with his head down yet from the corner of his eyes he could see that Maulvi *sahab* had come to his hut. His face turned red with anger at the sight of Maulvi *sahab* at his hut.

Slowly he lifted his head. "M A U L V I...," he shouted on top of his voice. He tried to stand up but collapsed on the cot.

Maulvi *sahab* understood that Rashid was heavily drunk. He quietly handed over the milk jar to Rukhsana's mother and left.

Next morning Maulvi sahab woke up early to the chirping of birds. He was always amongst the first to reach neighbourhood mosque to offer the morning *namaz*.

That morning was no different, he woke up to the pleasant sounds of cuckoo singing and sparrows squeaking. He was busy with the daily ablutions when he heard a din, its pitch indicated that it was emanating from somewhere nearby. Maulvi *sahab* ignored and carried on with his routine. The hullabaloo grew louder as he took bath. He came out of the bathroom to see Begum *sahiba* peeking from the gate in the direction of the noise.

Maulvi *sahab* opened the main gate and came out. The din was growing louder by the minute. He asked for his *kurta* and started walking towards the source of noise. He walked at a brisk pace realising that something was terribly wrong somewhere in the village.

On other days, the moment he stepped out of his house he was showered by greetings, young and old, men and women greeted and bowed before him with love and respect. Something was amiss today, and he could sense that. Yes, the greetings flowed thick and fast but through sideways glance he could see people murmuring behind his back. A few turned their heads away after seeing him, probably a first of its kind in Maulvi *sahab's* lifetime.

Nevertheless, Maulvi *sahab* continued to walk past the narrow lanes. The noise had turned into a commotion and almost everybody was outside their homes on the pathway. As he walked, Maulvi *sahab* saw that the nucleus of this clamour was outside Rashid's hut and that he had been creating this ruckus.

"….Ask her why she fell for that Maulvi," Rashid shouted at the top of his voice, addressing the villagers who had collected in front of his hut. He had held his wife's hands and was dragging her outside the house. She was on her knees, begging for his mercy. Rukhsana had held her two year old sister and the girls cried loudly. Around fifty people, mostly from the neighbourhood, had gathered outside Rashid's hut.

Maulvi *sahab* made his way to confront Rashid, shoving aside people who had assembled outside the hut.

Rashid was livid as he saw Maulvi *sahab* walk towards him.

"What happened Rashid? Why are you so worked up?" Maulvi *sahab* asked undeterred.

Rashid left his wife's hands and almost jumped towards Maulvi *sahab* and held his *kurta* by its collar. Maulvi *sahab* was stunned, but he also knew that Rashid was short-tempered and quite often he lost his cool for silly things. He held Rashid's hand and wrapping his arm over his shoulders, asked what this whole matter was about. Rashid released Maulvi *sahab's kurta* with a jerk.

"Now look at this my friends. This man who claims himself to be a Maulvi silently sneaks into my house at night with evil intentions on my wife. He even fancies my little girl who is his daughter's age. He took my daughter and my wife to Delhi on a pleasure trip without my permission. And last night…"

"*Yaa* Allah, please have some fear of the Almighty," Maulvi *sahab* shrieked at Rashid's wild aspersions.

"Fear of Allah? Huh! It's you and not me who should have the fear of Allah. I am a *Ghazi*. I am righteous. I can do no wrong. I am a true soldier of Islam."

The crowd outside Rashid's hut was swelling by the minute. He turned towards the bystanders, raised his arms up in the air and urged them to ask why this Maulvi should come to his house at night to meet his wife and daughters when he was not at home.

"Your daughter was hungry. There was no milk in your home and she was crying…"

"…And how did you know that there was no milk in my home. This means you had come over earlier as well. See my friends this is what I had been saying. This man had come to see my wife inside my hut. He is such a characterless man that his evil eyes have not spared even my daughters. He very well knew that I was not at home, yet under the pretext of giving milk to my toddler he came to my hut last night…."

"Yes we had come over to your hut in the evening. Our wives were there with us," Arjun's father thundered as he made his way through the crowd outside Rashid's hut. He was accompanied by his wife. Begum *sahiba* had also came running in from other corner of the street. The news about Rashid's allegations over Maulvi *sahab* had spread thick and fast across Basera. A neighbour told Arjun's father about the fracas and he had immediately rushed to Rashid's hut on his motorbike. The crowd now included village's elderly people as well.

With Arjun's mother and Begum *sahiba* walking in, Rashid's wife came running from inside. She fell down at Begum *sahiba's* feet, wailing. Rukhsana and her two year old sister were weeping inconsolably as they huddled around their mother.

Arjun's father explained everything to the elderly who had come over. Very soon it dawned upon everybody that Maulvi *sahab* was not at fault and that Rashid was heavily drunk last night and he is making baseless allegations on a revered person of Basera village, Maulvi *sahab*.

The melee had now started to melt away with people slowly walking away realising that they were already late for their work.

Amongst all this clamour where allegations, counter-allegations and explanations flew thick and fast nobody noticed the car with tinted glasses parked leisurely under a far off neem tree. As the crowd thinned, the tinted window panes of the car rolled down. Inside were Afroz and Jamil. They gave a cursory glance towards Rashid's home, rolled up the car's windows again and slowly drove away.

Afroz looked a bit tense but Jamil was smiling. He had curled his upper lips and was whistling gently as he drove off the dusty lanes of the village. He knew that he may have lost the battle but the seeds of war had been sown.

10 .

This day marked a turning point for the village Basera. On surface, things looked calm yet there were sharp undercurrents that flowed through underneath. After this day, Maulvi *sahab* drastically cut down on his philanthropic activities and confined himself to teachings at the madrasa. He just could not forget the unfound and baseless allegations of Rashid that he was after his wife and his daughter Rukhsana. Nobody had ever cast aspersions on his character, in fact villagers vouched for his integrity and selflessness but Rashid made an attempt to sully his image, albeit unsuccessful yet it was enough to push Maulvi sahab into a self-created shell from where he remained reserved in his interactions with villagers.

'What if Arjun's family had not accompanied him to Rashid's home and had not known the truth? All his good work and repute as a man of character would have been washed out. It will take just one mad man like Rashid to stand up and scream falsities about him and the villagers would believe.....' Maulvi *sahab* often got nightmares about the dire consequences of that ominous incident. It had left an indelible mark on his psyche.

He often woke up at night thinking about what could happen if a similar incident with him happened at the village again. Begum *sahiba*, other village elders and Arjun's father often tried to allay his fears urging him to forget the episode as a one off incident but for Maulvi *sahab* it was easier said than done.

No, Maulvi *sahab* was not over-reacting. That day while returning back from Rashid's hut he could overhear some villagers taking sides with Rashid. They did not dare to confront Maulvi *sahab* on his face but that a few people talked behind his back was enough to hold him back.

In fact, he had extremely progressive views about women and openly advocated their right to seek knowledge.

Once, after the Friday prayers at the local mosque he spoke about the concept of veil in Islam. "If you want to put a veil, put it on your larger-than-life egos and be humble. It should be practiced by both men and women. Confining our women in black tents known as a *burqa* defeats the basic concept of veil in Islam. A true Muslim is one who never boasts of good deeds rather covers them under a veil and continues with goodness," Maulvi *sahab* had explained in response to a question about the essentiality of *burqa* for Muslim women.

On another occasion he spoke about *jihad* and explained that it refers to slaying the evil within oneself. "Slay your evil thoughts whenever they arise. Have no mercy on evil within you. Wage a *jihad* to purge yourself of the wicked and immoral thoughts," he would say.

Maulvi *sahab's* interpretations often got him into heated verbal duels with other orthodox *mullahs* and *maulvis*. Everyone respected his viewpoints even though they agreed to disagree with him.

All this had changed now.

Rukhsana had stopped coming to the madrasa from that day onwards. It never bothered Rashid that now her daughter cleaned utensils in the village neighbourhood. As long as Rukhsana and her mother earned money he was least concerned.

One such day she was washing utensils under the big banyan tree. A few meters away old women lay sitting on the charpoy gossiping, a few children were playing on the makeshift swing that hung from the big strong branch of the banyan tree. They had been calling Rukhsana to come and play with them on the swings but she was too busy scrubbing the oil from pots. It was then that she saw Maulvi *sahab* on the bicycle. She wanted to drop the utensils, run towards Maulvi *sahab* and urge him to free her from this slavery, this drudgery, and take her to the world of books at the madrasa or to Delhi or anywhere but unshackle the chains that her own father had put on her feet, on her dreams and on her soul. She wanted to run to Maulvi *sahab* and tell him how badly she wanted to get out of this netherworld.

Maulvi *sahab* saw Rukhsana sitting under the tree, scrubbing the heap of utensils. His impulse was to rush towards her, and ask her to drop those dirty utensils and go home. Her delicate hands were not meant to scour those aluminium pots and pans. It pained him to see her childhood wither away. He wanted to gift back her childhood. He had almost turned around his cycle towards her but then Rashid's words and his allegations echoed in his head, piercing both his body and soul. He slammed the brakes of his bicycle. Maulvi *sahab* looked towards Rukhsana from the distance, her eyes resembled the doe being chased by a fox, eagerly looking towards some cover to save her life. Rukhsana earnestly felt that Maulvi *sahab* was indeed that cover who could save her from the clutches of foxes and wolves all around her.

Tears rolled down from Maulvi *sahab's* eyes, wetting his beard and moustache as he stood there, frozen. How much he wanted to pedal his cycle towards Rukhsana, take her to Rashid and explain it to him how he was ruining the child's life. Maulvi *sahab* tried hard to fight the rationality in his head with the affection in his heart for Rukhsana. His head was constantly reminding him to mind his own business and not meddle into Rashid's affairs.

'What if Rashid made the same allegations once again? Will the villagers believe you this time too? What will happen to your reputation? How will you justify your interference? There is no one around to vouch for your innocence this time. You should leave this place as early as possible.' Maulvi *sahab's* brain advised him.

His heart was not willing to give up so soon.

'But it's the matter of a child's life. You cannot let Rashid ruin her life, just because of the fear of some false allegations. You cannot and you should not run away like a coward. You should call all the village elders and put this mater in front of the *panchayat*. The poor girl, she is not asking for the moon, all she has asked is to get back her childhood. She wants to study,' Maulvi *sahab's* heart argued passionately against his head.

He was still in the middle of his predicament listening to the arguments of both his head and heart, and just when his heart seemed to have scored over his head, a gruff shout broke his chain of thoughts.

It was Rashid.

"Move your hands a bit faster and finish it quickly. The guests will arrive by evening so finish off everything before that," he commanded Rukhsana, his daughter. Rashid was accompanied by Afroz and two other men.

Maulvi *sahab* could not recognise the two men with Rashid and Afroz, they were not from Basera. The men walked past the banyan tree, smirking at Maulvi *sahab* as they crossed him.

Rukhsana stooped her head and silently begun her drudgery. It did not concern Rashid that the pile of utensils was too huge for a nine-year old to clean. He had no time to read her face or feel the sadness hidden in her eyes. He was on a bigger mission in his life, or so he thought.

"…thanks to Afroz *bhai* and Jamil *bhai* that I could keep my family together. Otherwise a wretched Maulvi had almost wooed my daughter and wife," Rashid told the two men as a beaming Afroz looked on. "The Maulvi wooed your wife and daughter? How did that happen," one of the bearded man asked Rashid as they walked past Maulvi *sahab*.

Maulvi *sahab* could not hear the rest of conversation. He was not interested in it. He had hoped against hope that probably Rashid would have had a change of heart and that he could be able to convince him about the need for Rukhsana's education. But this was not to happen. With a heavy heart he pulled up his leg to pedal his bicycle. His eyes were red, he was breathing hard as he tried desperately to fight back the tears.

Rukhsana's tears disappeared in the water that washed the dirty utensils. The large aluminium pots and the utensils sparkled, but her face had turned ash-grey with salt of the copious tears that flowed through her eyes down to the cheeks.

Maulvi *sahab* reached home in a sullen mood. Abdul was jovially jumping around the home, busy setting up things for his stay at the Delhi school's hostel. He was unmindful and unconcerned about the happenings elsewhere in the village. Begum *sahiba* had neatly arranged his clothes in a bag. A couple of neighbourhood women had come over to help her. One of them roasted groundnuts. Another packed cashew nuts into a glass bottle. Begum *sahiba* was constantly instructing Abdul to eat well and to eat on time.

"I will not be there to run after you and remind you to eat so you have to be careful with your eating habits else you will fall sick," she said fighting hard to hold back the tears that had welled up in her eyes. These tears did not upset Maulvi *sahab*, he knew they were tears of joy.

The next morning, Abdul and Arjun had reached the Delhi school with their parents. The mothers went over to hostel room with their sons, while their fathers were busy interacting with school authorities knowing and understanding about the school's curriculum and other extra-curricular activities at the school.

III. Context

11 .

A storm was brewing in Basera. Afroz and Jamil were now emboldened that Maulvi *sahab* had been sorted out. They had found a dedicated *sepoy* in Rashid, who was more than willing to implement their dirty tricks. Then there was Chacha who served as an informer of all that was happening in the village. Rashid was in awe of his Jamil *bhai* and looked upon as him as his mentor and a warrior of Islam. He did not know that Jamil in reality was a crook who was merely using Islam as a vehicle to further his political ambitions.

Jamil was readying himself for the bigger battle. His plan was to contest the parliamentary elections while Afroz was eyeing the state assembly elections. Both knew that if Muslims vote en bloc in their favour then they can easily sail through. But this was not going to be an easy task. Jamil was a member of a fledgling political outfit Modern Muslim Party (MMP) which was in alliance with the Federal Party of India (FPI), a much bigger political party that had its support base across India. For years the FPI had been winning elections by talking about the rights of labours, peasants and farmers. During each elections their leaders promised to create employment, build roads, get electricity into each home and remove poverty but after elections they simply vanished, only to surface when the next elections were announced. FPI's support base had eroded and the party's think tank knew about it. A very large portion of funds and donations to FPI came from the Wahhabi clerics of Saudi Arabia. In return of the petrodollars that came in, the Wahhabi fanatics had their own people in the political and policy apparatus of India who made policies that were sympathetic and acceptable to the Wahhabi outlook of Islam. The legislators and parliamentarians turned a blind eye when a few propped up Islamists presented Wahhabism as the puritanical Islam. They openly advocated persecution of other Islamic sects such as the Shias, Ahmadiyas, Ismailis, Bohras, Hanafi Sunnis and several others, and none of the policymaker protested. All this was part of Wahhabis' game plan to conquer the world and bring it under one umbrella, which they thought was puritanical.

FPI was an important player in helping them realise this dream. But with the FPI's support base shrinking at a very fast pace the Wahhabi's grandiose plan was under threat. It was then that the idea to form a new political party that would unite Muslims and seek their votes en masse was thought of. Jamil was merely a puppet into their hands whose strings were being pulled by those in Saudi Arabia and their proxies in India. The sudden coming in of Chacha to the now defunct warehouse of Aaqib and his setting up a chai shop was a part of this gambit. Jamil's walking up to Chacha' tea shack, asking him to come over to his bungalow for a meeting was all scripted. That evening at Jamil's bungalow Jamil and Chacha were formally introduced to each other.

The game plan was simple but brilliant. Muslims constituted close to forty five percent of the electorate in that region and if they could be brought together under one umbrella then it could be replicated elsewhere in the country too.

Yet, despite the money and muscle these were easier said and planned than could actually be executed on ground.

These Wahhabi strategists had got a taste of their ideas and plans when during subsequent *panchayat* elections most of their propped up candidates were routed. Several villages had rejected the Wahhabi's virulent interpretation of Islam and voted on the lines of development. Learned men of the villages had been asking pointed questions and had turned the tables against the candidates backed by the Modern Muslim Party. Smarting under their insulting defeat the Wahhabi ideologists had now decided to double up their efforts to use Islam as the unifying force for electoral victory. The Village Basera was one of the laboratories in this power tussle.

In order to realise this ambition their puppet Jamil was to try whatever it takes to win people on his side. So in his effort to accentuate the Muslim identity of the villagers he was willing to bribe, cajole or fool to make them cross over to his side. Maulvi *sahab* had stood like a wall who challenged him and his ideas. Jamil never had any answers to hard hitting questions of Maulvi *sahab* and his group of learned men. These were men of character who could not be bribed or cajoled or be fooled.

The only way left was to discredit them.

Jamil tested waters with Rashid as a pawn to discredit Maulvi *sahab*, and was successful. He was now emboldened. He was now ready to wage the bigger war. And he had been gaining ground.

In the recent years a slow and steady change had begun to unfold at Basera and adjoining villages. The younger men were becoming increasingly assertive while the older ones confined their activities. Aftab *sahab*, the ageing chairman of Basera's madrasa, now seldom ventured out of his home and devoted most of his time to prayers and recitation of Holy Quran inside his home. His friends were also senile and withdrew themselves away from the social activities of the village. Maqbool *bhai* and Naseem *bhai*, the two other members of Basera madrasa's management committee busied themselves with their own businesses. A couple of times when Maqbool *bhai* intervened and questioned the relevance of certain social practices being introduced in the village he was booed down by the new evangelists of Islam. He was questioned about his understandings of Islamic teachings.

Maulvi *sahab* had also relegated himself only to teaching of students at the madrasa. He consciously made efforts not to interfere in the household matters of others. Earlier he had arbitrated over petty disputes and offered unsolicited advice to villagers and his words carried weight. He was quite pro-active in his social outlook. But the baseless allegation that Rashid levelled against him, changed an outspoken and social man into a recluse.

Whatever time was left after teaching madrasa students, Maulvi *sahab* now spent in reading and tendering to the fields and the cattle. He visited only his very close friends such as Aftab *sahab*, Arjun's father, Maqbool *bhai* and a couple of neighbours with whom he felt on the same mental plane.

On their part, Jamil and Afroz had increased their influence. They had been pumping money into Basera and adjoining villages. So, Chacha's tea shop now had a fridge and the makeshift shanty had been replaced with a well laid out concrete structure. Chacha now sold branded food packets, had four boys as helpers and had bought moulded plastic chairs for the customers.

Rashid had replaced his rusty old bicycle with a motorbike. He had also bought a new buffalo at his home, but his wife and daughters continued to do petty work in neighbouring houses for daily sustenance. Jamil had resumed his *iftar* parties at his bungalow and Afroz threw some crumbs for labourers brought in by Chacha and Rashid in the name of their Muslim brethren. Despite this, not a single soul in Basera could claim that their lives had transformed due to Jamil or Afroz's initiatives. In fact, it was never meant to be that way.

This was a well thought over strategy. Keep the Muslims ignorant and keep them deprived. When there's a dire need, give some scrap here and a speck there to make Jamil look like the saviour, and constantly harp on the victimisation of Muslims in the country.

Rashid was busy with the 'bigger purpose' in his life. He had quit as a barber and most of the times ran errands for Chacha, Jamil and Afroz. Whatever little he earned, he would spend it upon himself and seldom had any money for household expenses. It was left to his wife and Rukhsana to think about arranging the next course of meal and to keep the kitchen running. Whenever his wife confronted him to think about household affairs Rashid curtly told her not to nag him with petty things as he had a bigger purpose in life, and that was to spread the light of Islam and fight for the rights of Muslims.

Islam for Rashid was to do whatever Jamil and Afroz asked him to do. And that was to sing paeans about their commitment to Islam and how Jamil *bhai* and Afroz *bhai* had dedicated their lives to fight for the rights of Muslim brethren in this country.

Initially there were no takers for Rashid and Chacha's brand of Islam but gradually through the lure of money they built a loyal fan base among the people who were at the lowest rung of social strata. They would often pay for the cuppa or buy a bottle of cheap rum for the daily wage labourers, occasionally they also paid for their food at road side eatery joints. Bit by bit and step by step these acts had helped them win friends over their side.

The educated and rational Muslims like Maulvi *sahab*, Aftab *sahab*, Maqbool and Naseem *bhai* were strategically side-lined in this narrative so there was hardly anyone left to question this vicious but well thought-out propaganda.

Middle class is the conscience keeper of any society and Basera was no exception. It's the educated and rational mind of middle class members in a society that has the potential to analyse the finer nuances of the rich and powerful elite. Basera's middle class, led by Maulvi *sahab* that had successfully staved off devious designs of the likes of Jamil had now withdrawn itself into a shell.

The lower strata, which is too engrossed in earning and fending for themselves and their family, are mentally ill-equipped to see through these deceitful stratagems. These are the most vulnerable groups to fall for the glib talks of politicians. Jamil, rather his handlers in Saudi Arabia, were smart enough to exploit this.

Gradually, the daily wage earners, masons, carpenters, blacksmith and butchers started to buy the argument put forth by Jamil and Afroz that they had to toil hard only because the entire system was anti-Muslim. They had begun to accept that all miseries of their life was a result of the systematic atrocities being committed on them due to their religious beliefs as a Muslim. The Muslim identity was gradually evolving. An increasing number of villagers were identifying themselves with the 'Muslim as the victim' notion and buying into the arguments put forth by Jamil & Co.

Rashid was an over-enthusiastic foot soldier of this game. His mandate was to bring these vulnerable Muslims within the network and thereafter the likes of Chacha, Bilal, Anwar and others took the indoctrination process forward. Almost always the discussions focussed about atrocities on Muslims in the name of Islam. Oftentimes they obliged this 'vulnerable Muslim' with some money or helped him bag some petty work, which the beneficiary looked upon as a help from his Muslim brethren whereas Jamil looked upon this as an investment that would offer rewards at the time of elections.

In return, they were expected to take active part in spreading the word about brutality on Muslims and how only a true Muslim like Jamil *bhai* helped them.

Over the next phase these new recruits were instilled about the need and importance of following Sharia law, and how their ills were present only because the villagers did not follow Islamic rule of law. In proverbial terms, while the left hand created artificial scarcity of food the right hand threw some morsels and the mouth sang paeans about the right hand, hailing it as the benefactor.

A few weeks later these new Islamic recruits were taken over to Jamil *bhai's* weekly durbar on Fridays after the *juma namaz*. Often Jamil and Afroz would take turns to explain about how Muslims were being subjugated and what needs to be done to extricate them from the existing quagmire.

The likes of Maulvi *sahab* and other knowledgeable Muslims in the village came in for heavy criticism. Chacha most often used fictitious stories to boost his claims and discredit Maulvi *sahab* and Aftab *sahab*.

Maulvi *sahab* and his group of learned Muslims found this new ambience quite suffocating. They often discussed these issues during their evening gatherings and whenever they could confront fellow villagers they reasoned out with them. It was due to their silent yet persistent efforts that over the next one decade Jamil and Afroz remained deprived of any major electoral victory. Jamil lost two consecutive Parliamentary elections while Afroz had lost the Legislative elections.

Yet, Maulvi *sahab*, Afroz *sahab* and other village elders were well aware of the rising influence of these nefarious forces. Jamil and Afroz may have had lost two consecutive elections but their vote share had increased dramatically over the last decade. In the last *Panchayat* elections the candidate with the backing of Jamil had won, albeit with a small margin. In his victory speech he had clearly said that his aim was to run the village strictly according to the tenets of Islam. When a person in the crowd asked as to what those Islamic tenets were, he openly declared the person as a heretic and his supporters booed him amidst loud cheers from other villagers.

This new *Panchayat* member had started meddling in people's lives from the very first day he took charge. The first diktat came in the form of making *burqa* compulsory for all women. Any women without a *burqa* or the hijab is inviting trouble, explained the new *Sarpanch* at his first public meeting.

That these diktats were being issued was of no surprise to Maulvi *sahab* and other sane Muslims of the village. What surprised and worried them was that the villagers had slowly begun to embrace these instructions and begun to believe that this indeed was true Islam. The people who believed in this version of Islam were still fewer but they were gaining ground, steadily.

Maulvi *sahab* was worried about these aspects and it's far reaching consequences for the village but he felt helpless. He could foresee the consequences of these issues and quite often discussed them with his close friends. His instincts would tell him that Jamil and his cohorts were trying to replicate the Kashmir model in his village.

During the late eighties and nineties these Wahhabis had started sending imams from Uttar Pradesh and Bihar to the madrasas of Kashmir Valley. These imams slowly started preaching the Wahhabi hatred and accentuating the Islamic identity of Kashmir. They denounced the composite culture of Kashmir and preached a culture of guns and stones such that a very large section of the Kashmir's society started dancing to the tunes of these rental imams and subsequently ruined the state's peace and prosperity.

Everybody shared Maulvi *sahab's* concerns and they often tried to set up another narrative but after a point felt helpless as the forces backing Jamil were just too powerful for them.

Often when Maulvi *sahab* seemed morose and helpless at the state of affairs in Basera, Begum *sahiba* would talk about Abdul and his achievements at the Delhi school. She would cheer up Maulvi *sahab* by saying that their son was all set to be on the path of building a good life for himself. Abdul's achievements used to lift up Maulvi *sahab's* spirits and he would break into a smile.

Rukhsana and his mother continued to eke out a living through doing household chores. Rashid had pulled out Rukhsana from Maulvi *sahab's* madrasa and he never bothered to put her sister Tabassum into the madrasa at all. A few years later when Rashid's wife was pregnant with his third child it was Rukhsana who took upon herself to finish off all household chores and earn a living for the family. Rashid never bothered to know if there was anything to eat at his house or whether his wife and children have had food. He considered himself too important a person who was fighting for larger interests of Muslims who should not be bothered about these petty issues. The day when his wife was writhing in labour pains he was nowhere to be found. It was Rukhsana who begged her neighbours for help and called a midwife for the delivery. Late that night when Rashid returned home, he was ebullient to see that his wife had delivered a boy. His first words upon seeing his new born son was that the boy was Islam's youngest soldier who would lay down his life for Islam.

Rashid's indoctrination was complete and his thinking had reached a different plane altogether, which was unfathomable for his family.

It had been almost three years since Jamil's proxy candidate managed to win the *panchayat* elections. Since then several candidates propped up by Jamil and Afroz had managed to win *panchayat* and municipal elections. In every election there was only one winning formula, which was to harp about Muslim victimisation. Yet, despite these successes major victory still eluded them. Both Jamil and Afroz had been losing Parliamentary and Legislative elections. Jamil's financers in Saudi Arabia and in India were getting impatient. They needed their people within the policy making apparatus and this was not possible till Jamil and Afroz win parliamentary elections. The next major elections were still a couple of years away but there was a growing sense of restlessness within the handlers sitting in Middle East that they need to do something fast and quick. A thought was developing that if need be then Jamil should be replaced with somebody more effective.

12 .

One morning Jamil received a call from Saudi Arabia. The caller informed him in a terse tone that his uncle was unwell. Jamil understood the purport. He was asked to come immediately to Saudi Arabia.

A flurry of meetings took place in the hot desert lands of Riyadh, the capital city of Saudi Arabia. The likes of Jamil had been summoned from several parts of the world who were told in clear terms to step up their efforts and push for the Wahhabi ideology in their respective regions.

In the past, Jamil had participated in similar such meetings wherein each attendee detailed the progress in their regions and their areas of work. Earlier the meetings used to be laidback, everyone was relatively relaxed, future strategies were drawn amidst gala feasts, wine flowed freely and women were made available in plenty. It was different this time.

"We need results, and we need them quick," thundered the burly man in the crisp white dishdasha. His moustacheless thick beard oscillated softly as he spoke. He never smiled, never raised his voice but when he spoke everyone sat on the edge of their seats and remained overtly attentive.

Jamil could not understand the sudden urgency for this impetus. During lunch he confided in one of the attendees. He was told, in hushed tones though, that the continuous fall in oil prices has made the Wahhabi captains jittery and they want to quickly cement their place within the governance apparatus of as many countries as possible.

"Without the monetary push it will be difficult to establish that Islam means Wahhabism," the man whispered into Jamil's ears, as he tore down a large lump of camel meat in his plate. Jamil could not make much of the relation between oil prices and Wahhabism but could sniff the urgency in air.

Over the next couple of days Aakash and Nadeem came over for the meetings in Riyadh.

Nadeem Khan was a leather exporter to the Gulf nations. He was one of the main conduits through which the Wahhabi strategists in Saudi Arabia pumped in money within India. He was also the brain behind the newly formed political outfit Modern Muslim Party, the MMP. Aakash Kumar was the General Secretary of Federal Party of India (FPI), one of the largest national political party in India.

Nadeem and Aakash held several closed door meetings with the Wahhabi chieftains. Jamil remained out of all these closed door meets and was tersely told to follow the 'advice' of Nadeem and Aakash. "We do not want anyone questioning our beliefs. We don't give answers. We do not rule over nation states, we rule over the Muslim mind," the burly man in white dishdasha pronounced, his hands swayed gradually in a swipe from right to left as he spoke. His looked intently towards Jamil, unnerving him for the moment. Jamil understood that his task was cut out, all his doubts had now vanished. Later on, he discussed future strategies in greater detail with Aakash and Nadeem.

A month later, a big white car stopped in front of Jamil's bungalow.

"*Assalam-o-Walekum*"

"*Ya* Allah. Jamil *bhai* it's you. Sorry I didn't immediately recognise you because of your thick beard. But you look dashing as always," Bilal shrieked with excitement as he picked up Jamil's suitcase. As they walked across the porch, Bilal shouted for Anwar, who came running from the first floor room of the bungalow.

"We need to have a grand celebration tonight in honour of our Jamil *bhai*," Anwar winked at Bilal. Taking the cue from Anwar, Bilal curled and cusped his lips in a corner and broke into a wicked smile. He was just about to dial the escort girl's number when Jamil snatched the phone from him. Castigating them he said all these can wait.

"Call Afroz *bhai*," he thundered as he briskly walked through the alley inside his room. In an hour, a couple of other bearded men had arrived from Delhi at the bungalow.

Rest of the day was spent in meetings and devising future strategies for the upcoming elections. The intent and Jamil's gaze as he spoke during the meetings left Afroz, Bilal and Anwar perplexed. Elections were still a couple of years away and yet Jamil's tone and urgency suggested as if they were round the corner. The meetings were business like, crisp and to the point, unlike the earlier similar meetings that were informal and discussions happened over booze and ended up with the arrival of escort girls.

"Think through and we will meet tomorrow to discuss finer details," Jamil said as he winded up. He hugged the two bearded men before they left.

"Jamil *bhai* you must be tired after a long day. We deserve to relax a bit. What do you say?" Afroz winked, breaking into that mischievous smile.

"The arrangements have been made and 'they' will come here any moment," Jamil said smiling for the first time in the day. As he finished a car stopped at the bungalow and Jamil craned his neck sideways in a signal to Afroz.

There was a faint knock at the gate. Jamil asked Bilal and Anwar to get the visitors.

Minutes later, they returned with two teenaged girls.

Afroz looked at the girls swinging his head up and down. He could not believe his eyes. He looked towards Bilal and Anwar who simply shrugged their shoulders and twirled their eyebrows towards Jamil in an indication to say that this is what had come in. Afroz leaned back in sheer frustration.

Escort girls came on a regular basis to Jamil's bungalow, most of the times they were foreigners. Jamil had a distinct liking for fair girls and on one instance he had sent away a girl for not being fair enough for his liking.

The girls who came today were dusky and were shabbily dressed.

Women and girls were just lumps of meat in the worldview of Afroz and Jamil. They were simple commodities meant for entertaining men. So, whenever they bought their 'commodity' they demanded them to be fair skinned. The ones that arrived today were nowhere close to their 'standards' and this is what perplexed them. They were waiting for Jamil to end his call. Jamil was merely listening to whatever the speaker on the other end said. All the time, while he was on call he kept his eyes glued to the two women who stood midway in the room amidst those hungry men.

Finally, the call ended and Jamil sat on the couch leaning backwards.

"Jamil *bhai* what has happened to your taste. Why did you get this rusty stuff?" Afroz questioned giving a disgusting look at the girls. The already frightened girls were further terrified.

"Relax Afroz *bhai*. Since morning we have been strategizing about the upcoming elections," Jamil said as he gave a hard look towards Afroz. The next moment he stood up, held Afroz's hands and pulled him to the adjoining room.

While Jamil and Afroz talked inside a separate room, Bilal went inside the kitchen to chop mutton to prepare kebabs. Anwar busied himself in eating the left-over chicken pieces kept on the table. He continued to ogle at the girls while he ate. An unwritten rule at Jamil's bungalow mandated that Jamil had the first right over escort girls, followed by Afroz and others. The two girls stood motionless inside the room waiting for the four hungry men to lay their hands upon them.

Anwar continued to devour the roasted chicken in front of the girls. Neither did he offer them to eat nor did he ask them to sit. They stood with their heads down, petrified over what lay for them in the next minute and in the coming days.

Jamil and Afroz came out of the room after about an hour. Jamil walked briskly towards the girls, scanned them for about a minute, picked the relatively fairer one and walked with her inside his room. Afroz lifted his middle finger and curled it towards his fist as a gesture for the other girl to follow him into another room.

Bilal and Anwar waited outside for their turn.

The girls were sisters, Heena and Fawzia. Heena was two years older to Fawzia. They were from Bangladesh. A year ago a spice exporter from Kerala had been to Dhaka on a business trip. He had married the sisters at a private function. Convincing the family for this marriage was not difficult. The family lived in abject poverty, their father was a carpenter and had seven other children apart from Heena and Fawzia. The local *Qazi* had introduced Malik as a suitor from Kerala to the family who offered twenty thousand rupees to the girl's father in return for their nikah with him. The father had happily obliged. It took less than four hours to seal the deal and nikah to be solemnised.

After nikah the girls stayed at a Dhaka hotel for a week. After their visa to India came in, the sisters reached Delhi to a guesthouse along with Malik. They had no inkling as to what fate had in store for them. Malik spoke very little and remained out during the day for work. He returned only at night to sleep with his two 'wives'.

The guesthouse was located on a busy Delhi street, yet it was an island of sorts. The street outside was bustling with activity but inside the boundary walls, guesthouse remained in an eerie silence. There was a caretaker who doubled up as the watchman. His thick beard minus the moustache along with the kohl-rimmed large eyes made him look like an ape. He seldom spoke but kept a very close eye on Heena and Fawzia. One evening when the sisters had wanted to step out for a stroll in the market outside, this ape-man had tersely asked them to get back to their rooms. He had stood like a wall before the girls.

Heena and Fawzia were confined to their room in the guesthouse citing security hassles and were strictly forbidden to step out. Barely three days later, since they arrived at the Delhi guesthouse, Malik announced that he will be away for an important meeting and would return in a day. He did return the next day.

The sisters never forgot that afternoon that changed their lives forever. Malik barged inside the room and asked them to get ready for luncheon at his friends' place. The sisters happily dressed up in bright clothes, elated to step out with their husband after days of solitary confinement.

It was late afternoon, and the sisters had been waiting in their sequined clothes for their husband, Malik, to arrive for the luncheon party. Malik did come but he came in with two people whom he referred to as his friends. Malik ordered for lunch at their guesthouse room. He reasoned that his friends had come over to the guest house to meet his new wives.

After the sumptuous lunch Malik stood up yawning lazily and then ordered his wives Heena and Fawzia to 'please' his friends in every possible way. He then turned around to leave.

'Please' your friends? What does that mean? Heena had asked. Malik turned around and said that they needed to sleep with his friends, without batting an eyelid. It was Fawzia who had jumped and held Malik's hand asking him how he could demean his wives in front of strangers. Malik then pronounced *talaq* three times to both his wives, and laughed away. He smirked, turned around and left. Heena and Fawzia could hear him whistling as he walked away.

The men had then raped Heena and Fawzia. When they left, the ape-faced caretaker came over and raped them. Over the next one month the sisters stayed at the guesthouse and were repeatedly raped by different men. A month later they were driven in to a bungalow. The name plate outside the bungalow read Nadeem Khan.

Nadeem gave a hard look to girls and said they had been chosen by Allah to wage jihad on non-believers and that they should feel happy about it. "Your training will start soon," he had said. The sisters had been badly bruised and shattered to speak or to resist.

Heena and Fawzia were then driven around the narrow by-lanes of Delhi to a two room flat of an imam. It was late evening when they reached imam's place. Imam was in the mosque when the sisters arrived at his apartment. It was a Friday and imam came back after the sermons. He was pleased to have the two girls as his guest.

"You are on the righteous path. This path has been chosen for you by Allah himself. In this path of jihad every individual has a role to play. Our Muslim brothers are picking up guns or blowing themselves up so the all benevolent Allah has ordained and chosen you to provide comfort to these martyrs. You are doing a great service by sleeping with the soldiers of Islam…." This sermonizing went on for almost an hour. At night he forced himself on them.

Over the next several months Nadeem made Heena and Fawzia meet dozens of imams, maulvis and muftis. Everyone whom they met, talked about rescuing Islam from the pitfalls and then assaulted them. The girls had now understood that their husband Malik had sold them to these sex-hungry maniacs, who now use them to satisfy their carnal desires. Several times these maniacs had video-recorded their 'acts' and had issued veiled threats about their family in Bangladesh.

One day when Fawzia created a fuss and vehemently resisted the assaults, Nadeem had walked inside her room. In a calm, cold and calculated voice he had said that he can get Fawzia's teenage sisters from Bangladesh for these work if she did not want to continue. Nadeem's tone and his mannerisms had sent shivers down her spine. She had three younger sisters aged nine, twelve and fourteen years, back in Bangladesh. The fiery Fawzia was cowed down, at least for now.

This continued for almost a year. It was when Nadeem was convinced that he was in full control of the sisters' mind, body and soul, he sent Heena and Fawzia to Basera. His plan was to make them settle somewhere in the village, engage them as domestic help and make them work as informers during the day, at night the foot soldiers of MMP could visit them to satiate their carnal desires.

Nadeem was explaining Jamil over phone when Heena and Fawzia had arrived at the bungalow. Jamil, in turn, elaborated Afroz about Nadeem *bhai's* gambit. Nadeem was their financier and Afroz's only option was to meekly accept his commands.

Rashid and Chacha came to know that their Jamil *bhai* was back in the village. They waited for the sun to set down and then rushed to the bungalow for 'celebrations'.

The sisters were distraught when Rashid and Chacha reached the bungalow. Every bone of their body was aching after the long day with Jamil and his men. They had just dressed up and laid down for some rest when Rashid and Chacha knocked at the doors.

Chacha pounced on Heena. Rashid leapt towards Fawzia. He looked towards her and vacillated for a moment. Fawzia was her daughter Rukhsana's age and her resemblance with Rukhsana was striking. For a moment when Rashid thought of Fawzia as Rukhsana he was stupefied. The next moment he cursed the cheap whiskey for his confusion and went ahead to tear away Fawzia's soul.

It was past midnight when Rashid reached home. He was heavily drunk and his body swayed rapidly. Leaning on Rukhsana's shoulder he came inside his hut. After a while he threw up on the floor, turned around and dozed off. Over the next hour Rukhsana painstakingly cleaned his vomit without any protest. She had become used to this grind.

13 .

Maulvi *sahab* was pacing up and down restlessly in his courtyard. Every minute he would look at his wrist watch and then towards the gate. Begum *sahiba* smiled at her husband's fidgety behaviour. She had been busy preparing an array of different sweets since morning.

"Why don't you sit? It's still some time before they arrive," Begum *sahiba* asked her husband. Maulvi *sahab* did not seem to hear his wife's words, his eyes remained glued to the gate and he continued to pace across the courtyard. He, after all, was waiting for his son. Abdul had graduated from college and was finally coming back home to his village to stay with his parents.

Maulvi *sahab* had to cancel his plans to go along with Arjun's father to Delhi as examinations were scheduled at his madrasa. The two families had then decided that Arjun's father and mother will go to Delhi to receive the boys and Begum *sahiba* will prepare a lavish dinner for everybody to celebrate the occasion of their homecoming.

As Begum *sahiba* prepared the favourite dishes of Abdul and Arjun, kebabs, *sewiyan*, mutton curry and *paneer*, Maulvi *sahab* busied himself in tidying up the house.

There was yet another reason that had perked up the excitement of Begum *sahiba* and Maulvi *sahab*.

The next morning Sakina's parents were to visit their home. Her parents had proposed Sakina's marriage with Abdul. Maulvi *sahab* was busy thinking through the marriage of Abdul when the car stopped by the gate. Maulvi *sahab* almost leapt out. He welcomed Abdul with a wide grin and open arms. The father and son entered into a tight embrace and tears flowed freely.

"Wouldn't you let everyone in?" Begum *sahiba* chastised her husband, her eyes glittering with that unshed tear. Maulvi *sahab* realised that as he embraced his son he had blocked the way for others to step inside. He hugged Arjun, and with Abdul and Arjun tucked under his arms he walked inside.

A small crowd had gathered at Maulvi *sahab's* house to welcome the kids back. Abdul and Arjun had completed their graduation in commerce from the prestigious University of Delhi. This in itself was a big achievement for a village like Basera where women were mostly illiterates and most of the men were school dropouts. Arjun was all set to join his father's sugar mill business.

At night Abdul broached his future career plans with his father. He wanted to set up a tomato ketchup plant in the village. During his graduation days he had interacted with several entrepreneurs who were now running successful business ventures. Abdul had hence been bitten by the entrepreneurial bug.

"Tomato ketchup, what's that?" Begum *sahiba* asked Abdul, placing the sweet sherbet on the table.

"*Ammi* that's the sweet tomato syrup you prepare for us... when it's processed and packaged in a bottle it's known as ketchup. You know there is a huge demand for tomato ketchups in big cities like Delhi. There are several canteens, eateries that consume several bottles of ketchup every day. This is a very good business and plus we can provide employment to people in our village as well. Abba, I can begin the unit from our land behind the mosque..."

"The idea, no doubt is very good. But where will we get the money from. You know our financial status…," Maulvi sahab interrupted Abdul.

"Oh I will take care of the finances. There are several schemes wherein banks provide support to budding entrepreneurs. I had already met one of the bankers at a seminar in Delhi. And he had asked me to meet him to discuss the necessary formalities," Abdul went on, excited about his business venture.

Maulvi *sahab* smiled. He was proud that his son was now mature enough to understand issues and take decisions about his future.

"Okay I have understood about your tomato factory. Now listen carefully to what I am saying…." Begum *sahiba* pulled up the small stool and sat beside his cot. Abdul turned towards her mother.

"Tomorrow evening Ameena *bi* and her husband are coming to meet us. Her husband was in the Army and has now retired…"

Abdul kept nodding, still wondering why his mother had asked him to listen carefully. 'Ameena *chachi* and Raheem *chacha* visit their home off and on what is so special this time that *Ammi* is asking me to listen carefully,' he said to himself. But the next sentence cleared all his doubts.

"Their youngest daughter is Sakina and tomorrow they are coming with her marriage proposal for you…"

"*Ammi*, m..m …my marriage…." Abdul almost jumped out from his cot and ran outside the room into the courtyard.

"I have seen Sakina she will be a perfect match for you…," Begum *sahiba* yelled to Abdul. "…her parents are coming tomorrow to meet you so be ready and be at home when they come," Begum *sahiba* had pronounced her diktat as she got up to finish off the remaining household chores.

Abdul was perplexed. Seeing her mother vanish into the kitchen he turned towards his father with a questionable look. Maulvi *sahab* only shrugged his shoulders.

"*Abba* why don't you say something. I am yet to start earning. I have to set up my ketchup plant…"

"So you mean to say that you are not confident about your plan?" Maulvi *sahab* raised his eyebrows.

"No I am not saying that. But all this will take some time and…"

"Okay so we will fix the nikah's date after a few weeks. Don't worry," Maulvi *sahab* shrugged, bursting into a smile.

Abdul knew he had no other option. Both *Ammi* and *Abbu* were for his marriage. Lying down on the cot he thought about Sakina. He had met her long back when they were small children. He didn't even remember her face. He thought that if his mother had said that she is a perfect match for him then she must be good. He didn't know when his lips curled into a smile. He turned around to sleep.

Begum *sahiba* and Maulvi *sahab* watched the impromptu smile on their son's face from the kitchen. They looked at each other and smiled back.

Abdul and Sakina's marriage was a gala gathering for villagers. Maulvi *sahab* was a revered soul across Basera and in several adjoining villages. The villagers felt it was their duty to lend a helping hand in the arrangements and attend Abdul's marriage. Everything worked on auto-pilot. The tents were erected, a make-shift kitchen was in place, eatables brought in, table-chairs were arranged, flowers came in, and decorations were being taken care of. Arjun's father had taken upon himself to welcome each of the guests personally. Everybody was busy with some work, except Maulvi *sahab* and Begum *sahiba*. Naseem *bhai* had made them sit in the courtyard and asked them to supervise everything. He wouldn't let them do anything. The enthusiasm of villagers and the revelry turned it into a fairy-tale wedding.

It had been a fortnight since Abdul and Sakina were married. The relatives, friends and other guests were gone.

That morning Abdul was readying the papers and certificates that the bank official had asked for to be able to process the loan requirements. Sakina was neatly placing all the papers into a file according to the list of documents required. The next minute a motorbike honked at the gate. It was Arjun. He had come over to accompany Abdul to the bank. Sakina wished luck to her husband as he left for the bank.

The bank manager was known to both Maulvi *sahab* and Sakina's father. Abdul had diligently prepared his project's business plan and was pretty confident of his loan application being accepted. The meeting with bank manager and other bank officials went off well. The bank manager was impressed with Abdul's business acumen. His business plans were appreciated by all the officials at the bank. Abdul and Arjun were bubbling with enthusiasm as they stepped out of the bank. Abdul had a million dreams in his eyes. Arjun promised Abdul every possible help to market the ketchup brand.

"Have you thought of any name for the ketchup's brand?" Arjun asked Abdul as he pulled up his motorbike at the Chacha's tea stall.

"Basera. *Abbu's* lifetime dream has been to bring prosperity to our Basera village, so if I start something in this village then it has to carry the name of the village," Abdul said as he sat on the moulded plastic chair of Chacha's tea stall.

"Chacha *jaan*...two tea and some biscuits," Abdul waived at Chacha. He turned around to look at the affluence at the stall, and was impressed that the rickety tea shack had now transformed beyond recognition. The broken wooden chairs had given way to moulded plastic chairs, the paint at tea stall wore a fresh look, the biscuits were neatly stacked in clean glass jars and packets of fried chips and other eatables dangled from the slings.

"Chacha *jaan's* customers have ample choice of snacks with their tea," Arjun said eyeing the entire assortment of eating options available at Chacha's stall. "It's so nice to see our village progress," Arjun said as he looked around. Abdul was glued to the papers that had details of his business plan.

Chacha gave out a sly smile as he poured tea into glass tumblers. He had been intently watching them from the moment they walked inside his tea stall. There were other customers at his tea stall but his attention was focussed on Abdul and Arjun.

Abdul and Arjun were unaware of Chacha's unfound interest in them. They sipped the hot tea and were engrossed in their discussions when a sharp thud sound caught their attention. Somebody had kicked the wooden table and it fell down after hitting the wall. Abdul and Arjun looked over their shoulders. It was Rashid. He had kicked the table and was standing with hands on his waist. His lips were curled, eyebrows raised and there were frowns on his face as he wore an irritated look. The two labourers who had accompanied him stepped ahead to tidy the furniture. They goaded Rashid to sit after putting the table and chairs in order.

At any other eating joint the owner would have kicked out such a customer or at least would have had strongly objected to this rowdy behaviour, but then this was Chacha's tea stall. He merely smiled. Abdul and Arjun found Chacha's behaviour strange but chose to shrug it off. They knew about Rashid's temperament and thought that probably Chacha was trying to avoid an unnecessary controversy.

But Abdul and Arjun were wrong. They knew little about the new stratagems at Basera being played in the name of Islam. They had no idea that what they considered bubbling business and prosperity behind Chacha's refurbished tea shack was actually a well-planned strategy and an investment to spread the Wahhabi tentacles across the region. Chacha and Rashid were mere pawns in this larger scheme and it were the Wahhabi players sitting in Saudi Arabia who made the moves.

Abdul and Arjun had long forgotten that fateful night when Rashid had alleged motives to their families for taking his daughter Rukhsana for the scholarship exam at Delhi. Abdul had forgiven Rashid's wild aspersions on his father as some kind of an aberration from a man who goes out of his senses when heavily drunk. The kids while studying in Delhi did visit their village during vacations but were completely out of sync with the subtle developments at Basera and adjoining villages. Over last decade the definitions, outlook and worldview of villagers had changed drastically. Abdul and Arjun were still innocent kids.

Rashid kept blurting expletives, harping angrily about the atrocities being committed on Muslims and their exploitation at the hands of *kafirs*—the unbelievers.

"There is only one solution to this problem. We need to convert this land, this country into *Darool Islam*. Till the time we implement Islamic Sharia, Muslims will continue to remain slaves. It is time to put an end to all this atrocities….," Rashid went on with his tirade as others at the tea stall listened in rapt attention.

"Rashid *chacha* why are you so angry? What happened? Who has made you a slave?" Abdul said, interrupting his rant. He had a broad smile on his face. He still looked upon Rashid as the father of his childhood friend Rukhsana. He had anticipated that his Rashid *'chacha'* will reciprocate with same warmth.

Instead, Rashid frowned. His eyebrows curled, eyes narrowed as he bore a questionable look towards Chacha.

"Abdul. Maulvi *sahab's* son. He has recently returned from Delhi," Chacha said while stirring the boiling tea in the pan. He did not look up, rather answered with his face down.

Rashid took a deep breath and leaned back on his chair. He placed his hands behind his head locking his fingers behind and looked askance. Almost every day at the Chacha's tea stall, Rashid would howl and shout about the atrocities on Muslims, tell stories about Muslims being victimised, most of which were cooked up. Almost every day the customers present, would either endorse or listen passively to Rashid's drivel. Chacha kept a close eye on his customers and all those who concurred with Rashid's tirade would be treated with free biscuits and an extra tea at a discounted price as an encouragement. This was the first layer of inducement that was followed by more sophisticated forms of bribery.

A mental note was made about these potential volunteers and information about them was quietly passed on to Bilal and Anwar who would further work upon these potential recruits.

Nobody ever challenged Rashid's narrative that Muslims were being exploited due to their religious belief. It was primarily because most of those who frequented Chacha's tea stall were largely illiterate or semi-literate labourers who were never in a position to reason out. The educated customers who came once in a while thought they had better things to do than get into an argument with this rustic Rashid. They thought it was better to ignore somebody like Rashid and carry on with their daily routine.

It, therefore, came as a rude shock to Rashid that of everyone it was still the Maulvi *sahab's* son who could dare to question him in full public view.

"Rashid *chacha* what happened?" Abdul had pulled his chair closer to Rashid and was waiving his hand in front of Rashid's face to seek his attention. Rashid was grinding his teeth and had placed his clenched fists on the table in a bid to control his anger. He saw Abdul as the son of a man who had almost abducted his wife and daughter.

Abdul, on his part, looked upon Rashid as Rukhsana's father. He had expected him to hug and feel happy that the little Abdul is now a grown up man.

Rashid did not respond. He still could not fathom how to respond to questions from a young and inquisitive mind.

"Rashid *chacha*? What happened? Where were you these days? Why did you not come for my wedding? And what is this that you are angry about? Who is committing atrocities on Muslims?" Abdul was not ready to give up. He had fired a volley of questions as he looked towards Rashid with an innocent smile.

"Just go and ask your wretched father about who is committing atrocities on Muslims. Have courage to question that Maulvi and get answers," Rashid thundered. His outburst was sudden and pitch extremely high. Rashid had jumped up from his chair as he blurted out, almost knocking off Abdul.

The masons sitting on the adjacent table were stunned at Rashid's tone and demeanour. One of them spilled tea on his hands in dismay. Arjun who had been fiddling with his smartphone rushed towards Abdul. He was still at his wit's end trying to fathom what the issue was that had made Rashid screech. Other labourers who till now were listening passively to Rashid's monologue were petrified and curled their legs inside and under the chair.

Abdul maintained his composure. He was not hassled and Rashid's attitude could not intimidate him.

"Rashid *chacha* why do you call my father wretched? What wrong has he done to you and to this village? Despite his high qualifications he continued to teach at the village madrasa so that poor children of Basera could be educated...."

"And in the garb of education he has been pushing Muslim children towards *kufra*. Did he tell you about how he has been in cahoots with the enemies of Islam and teaches the *kafir* subjects at the madrasa? The innocent villagers send their children to the madrasa to learn about Quran, Hadith, Sharia and what does this Maulvi teach? He sends them on the path of *kufra*,"

"So what's wrong in teaching and learning of subjects other than religious texts? Unless a person learns about modern subjects such as science, mathematics, computers, history and economics how will he get a job? Who will employ them? Reading, learning and knowing the Holy Quran and Hadith is a must but learning about other modern subjects and gaining skills is also much required in today's times…"

"See did I not say that this Maulvi is a wretched person. And look at the language that his son is speaking. They are out to make the lives of poor Muslims a living hell…"

"Rashid *chacha,* why are you making baseless allegations. Let me explain it to you," Abdul came closer making genuine efforts to explain to Rashid about the needs of modern education, "…see I recite the Holy Quran but I also studied economics which can now help me get a job or start my own business…"

"Now a bloody pimp will teach me about Islam. You and your father that Maulvi, are cheap pimps who sell innocent villagers for their personal gains," Rashid thundered, as he stood up. He had kicked the table in front of him, forcing the labourers to further curl themselves up.

Abdul leaned forward to explain, he was just not ready to give up. But Arjun gently tapped on his shoulder indicating him to stay quiet. He pulled Abdul's hand, paid for their tea and quietly left Chacha's tea stall.

Chacha broke into an impish smile as he saw Abdul and Arjun leave the tea stall.

Maulvi *sahab* was home when Abdul and Arjun came in. He asked about their meeting with the bank officials. Abdul replied in a bland 'yes' sipping the cold water. He looked visibly disturbed. Maulvi *sahab* gave a hard look, his probing eyes moving back and forth on Abdul and Arjun's face. Not satisfied with Abdul's answer he asked if the bank officials had imposed any stringent conditions to sanction the loan.

"No, nothing *Abbu*," Abdul replied, staring at the water jug on the table.

Maulvi *sahab* was still not convinced with his reply.

"Arjun is there something which you both are hiding from me? Tell me honestly what's the matter? I know there's something that is worrying you both."

"*Umm*... no nothing uncle...nothing from the bank or about the business plans...but...," Arjun fumbled when confronted by Maulvi *sahab*.

Arjun and Abdul then went on to explain in detail about their chance meeting with Rashid at the Chacha's tea stall and their heated exchange over there.

Maulvi *sahab* listened intently as Abdul and Arjun spoke. He stood up after they finished. He was pacing inside the room and was disturbed at Rashid's fresh round of allegations. After several minutes he spoke.

"Do you know why this averseness to learning and teaching at the madrasa?" Maulvi *sahab* asked, and after a moment's pause answered. "...it is only because of the fear of a thinking mind...."

"...A thinking mind asks questions for which these people have no answer, the thinking mind is rational and refuses to accept their illogical arguments. A thinking mind is able to see through the dirty game plan being woven around in the name of Islam. It is for this reason that a Maulvi... a petty Maulvi of a madrasa has become a bone of contention for them. I teach the madrasa children to question, to be rational in their outlook, to rise through merit in their life. But what do these Wahhabis want? They want people to remain ignorant, only because an ignorant person can be fed with all kinds of information-garbage and he will readily accept it. But an enlightened person, a person with knowledge will be difficult to convince because he will ask tough questions. A knowledgeable person's question is unsettling for these power-hungry wolves and this is why they fear books and the knowledge which the books impart…," Maulvi *sahab* went on with his explanation as Abdul and Arjun listened intently. Sakina and Begum *sahiba* had come from the kitchen, hearing Maulvi *sahab's* emotional outburst as they laid lunch on the table.

"Uncle who are these Wahhabis? Aren't they too Muslims?" Arjun asked. His childlike curiosity stumped Maulvi *sahab*.

Maulvi *sahab* stood still, staring at the guava tree in the courtyard. He took deep breaths to calm down. Arjun had raised a valid point. The Wahhabis have indeed convinced the world that they represent a truer form of Islam and whatever they say is 'Islam'. Yet this was not true. Maulvi *sahab* understood that he needs to clear the air about Wahhabism.

"My sons Arjun and Abdul," he said sitting down on the chair. "…you need to first understand where has this name Wahhabism come from…"

"…there was this person called Muhammad Ibn Abdul Wahab, a self-proclaimed preacher of Islam who lived in the eighteenth century. This Ibn Wahab allied with Muhammad Ibn Saud, a tribal chief of a very small town of Saudi Arabia. The two formed an alliance to use Islam for expansion of their territorial rule across Arabian Peninsula. Very soon Muhammad Saud anointed himself as the Emir of Nejd and Ibn Wahab took upon the title of Sheikh-ul-Islam. Wahab had an extremely narrow view of Islamic teachings and he preached the same. Any Muslim who refused to accept Wahab's parochial Islamic teachings was declared as an apostate, which justified Saud's invasion of neighbouring tribes and provinces. Wahab termed Saud's blatant and unjust invasions as Jihad, thus giving Islamic sanction to naked imperialist designs of Ibn Saud. This entire movement was known as Wahhabism and their followers were known as Wahhabis. Unfortunately, Wahhabism and Wahhabis have travelled all across the world. These are the ones who indulge in all kinds of nefarious activities and give a bad name to all Muslims. So technically Wahhabis may call themselves as Muslims, but their actions bring a bad name to Muslims all across the world. They may justify their actions in the name of Islam but in reality they have nothing to do with Islam," Maulvi *sahab* explained.

Abdul and Arjun did not speak much and quietly finished off their lunch. Later on, while Arjun left for his home, Abdul silently retired in his room. He did not speak to Sakina. Even during dinner at night, he kept quiet. Rashid's screeches and his father's explanations were echoing in his mind. At night he kept tossing on the bed and could not sleep at all. The more he tried to forget the day's incident the more was the intensity with which the echoes came back to haunt him. Unable to sleep he started pacing in his room. He looked at Sakina. She was fast asleep, unaware of the intense hurricane blowing inside his heart and mind. Abdul stared at Sakina for a minute and then, he woke her up. He said he wanted to talk about something important.

It was early morning and Maulvi sahab was milking the buffaloes. Abdul went over to him and said he wanted to discuss about an idea. He was so impatient to discuss about his plan that he almost dragged his father towards the living room.

"Are you sure you want to do this?" Maulvi *sahab* asked Abdul, looking straight into his eyes.

"Yes *Abbu*. I have been thinking about this since yesterday. And I have decided about it," Abdul said in a confident voice. His mother walked up hearing the early morning discussions.

Abdul went on to explain to his mother that he intends to expand the gamut of subjects being taught at the madrasa. And so he wanted to introduce computers, history and economics for madrasa students. Maulvi *sahab* was already teaching science and mathematics so with introduction of newer subjects the students will get holistic education, Abdul reasoned.

"It has been *Abbu's* dream to have a well-equipped library at the madrasa so we will get all modern books on science, mathematics and computers such that the village children have access to quality education. I will put some of my savings to buy a couple of computers and to set up the library. Sakina knows about computers and she has agreed to teach basic computers. I will also take out time every day to take classes at the madrasa. If Rashid and company are hell bent upon propagating ignorance and illiteracy then we should strive to impart education among the Muslims."

"This is indeed a noble idea my son. But what about your business venture and your plans to set up that tomato ketchup plant?" Begum *sahiba* quizzed her son.

"*Ammi* the ketchup plant will also come up. I have talked to Sakina about it. She will lend a helping hand and I'll handle both things simultaneously. The ketchup plant will be set up but before that happens computers will arrive in the Basera madrasa," Abdul was beaming with confidence as he looked towards his father.

Maulvi *sahab's* eyes were moist with tears. He stepped ahead and hugged his son.

Abdul hurriedly finished off his breakfast and took off on his motorbike to Arjun's home to discuss about his plan. Arjun was excited about Abdul's plan. He offered support in all possible ways. The two friends immediately got down to calculate the funds required to execute their plans.

Maulvi *sahab*, on his part, called upon the management committee members to press upon Abdul's idea to introduce computer education at the madrasa. As expected, barring Afroz all others in the committee were happy about the idea to introduce computers at the Basera madrasa. Aftab *sahab* was particularly pleased that Abdul had taken upon himself to introduce computers at the madrasa. Maqbool *bhai* said he had been thinking about it for a long time and it was good that young Abdul had taken that initiative. Naseem *bhai* was also in the favour of computers. Afroz was isolated, yet again. He had opposed the move saying it was un-Islamic to teach computers and other subjects such as history and economics at the madrasa.

"Why did you to Europe?" Aftab *sahab* bluntly asked Afroz after a couple of minutes. "What...what do you mean? Why did I go to Europe? I was there to complete my university degree?" Afroz stammered at the sudden questioning.

"And your subjects were...?" Aftab *sahab* countered. He was in no mood to relent today.

"I was there to study engineering. I am a qualified computer engineer," Afroz burst out. A moment later he realised the purport of the question and his almost involuntary answer.

"Computer engineer! I think this rests your case." Aftab *sahab* was curt. Over the next hour while everyone discussed the finer details of new course schemes Afroz sat completely mum. And nobody missed him. He knew he had no chance at this madrasa, not least with these members of the management committee.

IV. Firestorm

14 .

It was early evening and Afroz was waiting for Jamil at his bungalow. Jamil had been to Hyderabad for some meetings and was due to return a day earlier but got caught up with some work.

Afroz looked at his wrist watch. He was restlessly pacing in the porch outside, desperately waiting for Jamil. He should have come at least an hour ago. He was cursing under his breath as he marched up and down, occasionally punching the air with his fist.

It was late when Jamil came in. He straightaway walked into the first floor corner room and asked Afroz to come over. He had to discuss the developments at the Hyderabad meeting.

"Afroz *bhai* things are fast moving out of our hands. If we lose the elections this time then...," Jamil did not finish the sentence and instead kept staring at the knob of the closed door.

"Then what, Jamil *bhai*?" Afroz prodded. He was worried too.

Jamil kept staring and appeared blank. He just shrugged. After a while he said that he has been given clear instructions that if they are unable to win the parliamentary and legislative elections this time then their funding will be stopped and other possible candidates will be groomed for this constituency.

"These Hyderabadi *muftis* have all gone nuts. How quickly they forget what all we have been doing through these years. Why don't you talk to our financiers in the Saudi? Probably they would understand our efforts…"

"All these instructions are coming in from the Saudi. It is being said that the larger game plan has been delayed due to electoral reverses and they have taken a serious note of it. They had conveyed it in very clear terms and that is why I was called for a meeting at Hyderabad," Jamil paused and added, "They want results."

"There's more bad news from the village. That Maulvi is introducing computers at the Basera madrasa. A new library is also being made…"

"And what were you doing when all this was being discussed at the management committee meeting?" Jamil stood up shouting at Afroz.

"What can I do? Everybody in the committee is in favour of introducing computers, nobody even asked for my opinion. That old lunatic Aftab even announced that since I am a computer engineer myself so I had no right to oppose computers at the Basera madrasa," Afroz said in exasperation. He leaned back, taking a long deep breath.

"If this thing succeeds at Basera then it will definitely have a domino effect on other madrasas of the region. They will all introduce computers and modern subjects. And then who will buy our narrative of victimisation. This needs to be nipped in the bud. Right here right now," Jamil murmured. "…and why don't we get a heads-up of all these plans. What are these sluts Heena and Fawzia doing in Basera? Isn't it their job to get a whiff of these stuff and inform us on time…?

"This Maulvi planned everything in a jiffy. All within a day, I believe," Afroz said, defending the sisters.

Jamil knew time was running short and that he needed to act fast and act now.

Afroz had never seen Jamil so disturbed in all these years. He knew that things risked running out of their hands and they could well end up losing all political ground in the region and across their constituency.

It had been an hour since the two came inside the corner room for discussions. They had finished a bottle of whiskey and cigarette stubs were strewn all across the room. The stench of cigarette smoke and alcohol had now stretched to the alley downstairs. They were yet to zero down upon any idea. Jamil had asked Bilal to get another bottle of whiskey as he lit up a cigarette and swallowed the smoke, refusing to let it escape through his mouth. After a minute, the cigarette smoke flowed through his nostrils and ears in a manifestation, albeit symbolic, of the fire raging within him.

"Jamil *bhai* we need to do something. This Maulvi has become a gangrene for us," Afroz said, pouring whiskey into the glass.

Jamil just chugged the whiskey down his throat. His face contoured as the neat alcohol burned his wind pipe. "Wait. Yes wait a minute. There is hope. I know what to do next," Jamil's eyes brightened at the sudden insight. He stood up and shouted for Bilal.

"Tomorrow early morning I am going to Delhi. Wake me up early in the morning," Jamil ordered Bilal. He nodded and slipped back.

Jamil was now relaxed. He turned around, slumped on the couch and reclined back. He turned towards Afroz. "I am going to meet Aakash *bhai*. He is sharp and intelligent. He will definitely help us out," Jamil explained.

Afroz's eyebrows curled inside as he bore a confused look.

"Now, what can Aakash *bhai* do in this situation? And what will he do for us?" he murmured, his head slumped sideways.

"Aakash *bhai* will be our saviour. He has the brains to pull us out of this dire situation," Jamil said as he gulped another peg of whiskey.

Jamil knew that FPI's Aakash was one of the trusted lieutenants of the

Wahhabi Sheikhs in Saudi Arabia. Aakash's sharp mind and political acumen had floored him during their meeting in Riyadh. Jamil had detailed discussions with him about the political landscape in the region and Aakash had promised to lend all possible help.

Office of the Federal Party of India (FPI) was located in the heart of Delhi. The red-coloured double storey building boasted of a huge and dedicated parking space in its front, a luxury in Delhi. Huge posters of FPI revolutionaries adorned the alley that led to the main hall in the building. Behind this main hall was the canteen that served American colas, burgers and chicken that were relished by FPI members, even though they raised anti-America slogans at the drop of a hat. The party cadres were found sipping imported European wine and whiskeys at the city's five star clubs and hotels at night, while they cursed Western imperialism during the day. They talked of women's rights but happily advocated black cloaks for Muslim women in the name of freedom of choice. They spoke impeccable English and their sympathisers were evenly spread across powerful positions in the administrative and societal set up.

During recent years FPI had suffered huge electoral losses. FPI's traditional financiers had backed off and the party faced a massive fund crunch. It even had to mortgage some of its properties to stay afloat. Youth found no connect with FPI's ideology and its support base was dwindling at a fast pace. At several places the restless party cadres had quit to join rival parties, which had left FPI's leadership worried. Senior FPI leaders were aware of the problem but were at their wit's end to find a credible solution. Despite its sympathisers and supporters within the fields of media, art, culture, cinema, literature and academics who constantly doled out matter eulogising FPI's ideology, the party's downslide continued at a steady pace. Part of this problem was FPI itself. The party's leaders were corrupt who in the garb of simplicity, were neck deep in nefarious activities. So, wherever the party was in power, murders, extortions, pilferage of resources, opaque dealings were the norm. The masses had begun to realise that FPI preached a definite set of standards for the people but its own leaders and cadres practiced something that was diagonally opposite to those ideals. In the changed world order, FPI was fast losing its appeal among the younger population and that had worried Aakash and other senior FPI ideologues. Their leaders were nervous and were grappling for answers.

The party was desperate to retain its appeal and was willing to own up any issue as long as it guaranteed votes. It was in this desperation that they had owned up the Wahhabi school of thought that had a virulent interpretation of Islamic scriptures.

The radical Wahhabis who propagated a noxious version and interpretation of Islam had their own challenges. They had used the cover of Islam to further their own political ambitions since the eighteenth century and through their network of radical *maulvis, imams* and *muftis* created an ignorant mass of Muslims across the world. The descendants of erstwhile tribal chiefs now owned numerous oil wells and thus had packets of money to splurge and propagate the Wahhabi ideology. However, the ongoing glut in crude oil production had depressed global oil prices and squeezed their profits. Technological advancements in oil production techniques and proliferation of alternate sources of energy meant that the days of making billions of dollars from sale of crude oil were now over.

The Wahhabi Sheikhs knew they would face a cash crunch sooner or later. It was due to this that they wanted to step up their efforts to proliferate the Wahhabi interpretation of Islam across all corners of the globe. But then they lacked finesse and marketing. It was here that a Left-leaning political party like FPI came into fray. Their sympathisers were sitting pretty at media groups and other cultural organisations. It was a win-win situation for both. Owning up of Wahhabism brought windfalls for FPI. The political party got people behind its back and in return they had to package and brand radical Wahhabism as the only pious version of Islam in the world.

So, on the one hand a steady flow of petrodollars was ensured, while on the other, local propped-up Muslim leaders ensured bulk support to the dwindling fortunes of FPI. Yes the Wahhabi Sheikhs felt a squeeze in their profit margins yet they still had more than enough to fund their political and expansionist activities.

The adherents of Wahhabi thoughts, in return, got the services of suave and genteel faces to argue their case in the public domain. A political alliance between FPI and the Modern Muslim Party had meant that the Wahhabi ideology had found an entry into the state legislatures and parliament of India. This nexus helped establish Wahhabi ideology as the only authentic version of Islam and any Muslim who disagreed was branded as an apostate and heretic.

Jamil, and several others like him, were small cogs in this grand design who were being propped in their constituency by the Wahhabi handlers of Saudi Arabia. Jamil had been thinking that he would be able to control things in his constituency owing to lower literacy levels. But the restlessness among Wahhabi Sheikhs due to falling oil prices had made them impatient about the extent of their gains in all regions where they had been pumping millions of petrodollars. They were now unwilling to tolerate electoral reverses and wanted their men to reach policy making apparatus at the earliest. This message was read out in clear terms to Jamil, Aakash and Nadeem when they were called for the meeting in Riyadh.

The plans to modernize Basera madrasa had the potential to spill over to other villages, which could further upset Jamil's electoral calculus. This made him reach Aakash's door at the FPI.

15 .

It was a bright sunny morning and Aakash had called for a meeting of his senior cadres at the party office. They were discussing about an event that had virtually gone unattended. Despite best efforts by the FPI cadres they could not muster enough people to attend the function and empty chairs at the big hall had forced Aakash to hurriedly wind up his speech. They were discussing about ways to call people to their events when Jamil walked in.

"*Assalam-o-Walekum* Aakash *bhai*, we can fill up those empty chairs. You just have to inform us," Jamil greeted Aakash, grinning broadly as he walked inside the conference room at the FPI office.

"Ah ha Jamil *bhai* what a pleasant surprise. You could have informed me that you are in Delhi and I would have sent someone to receive you," Aakash said as the two shook hands and hugged.

Aakash introduced Jamil to his cadre as the politician with a huge support base among Indian Muslims. Aakash quickly wound up the meeting and led Jamil to his room for private talks.

"Aakash *bhai* we need to join hands and work together if we have to survive, else things might go out of our hands," Jamil told Aakash, sipping the hot coffee.

"Oh yeah, we are already together. And yes I know that you are facing some headwinds in your constituency," Aakash said, sifting through the papers on his table.

"Aakash *bhai* we need to douse the fire before it becomes an inferno," Jamil sighed. He then went on to reiterate about the concerns being raised by Nadeem *bhai* and the growing impatience of Wahhabi Sheikhs in Saudi Arabia. Aakash was listening intently, his eyes were still fixed on reading the papers on his desk. "Yes, yes we should and we must. I agree," Aakash nodded, his head still down as he sipped coffee from the mug.

"Aakash *bhai* we need to do something. These are crucial elections and it is a do-or-die situation for us. We have to win this time," Jamil sounded desperate, and added, "…there's a Maulvi in our village who is bringing computers at the village madrasa. His college educated son wants to teach computers, economics, mathematics…"

"What? What did you say? Come again," Aakash burst out, he had jerked up his head and looked towards Jamil, his mouth wide open.

Jamil then went about explaining how a Maulvi had been teaching mathematics and science at Basera's madrasa and now along with his son wanted to introduce computers. He added that the management committee members of Basera's madrasa were backing the Maulvi in his efforts and their plans were to make madrasa students capable enough to find admission in any of the big colleges of India for further education.

Aakash nodded. He put his arm at his nape, twirled his lips and swung his head sideways. He eyes closed his eyes and remained motionless as if in deep sleep. A minute later he opened his eyes. He gazed intently at Jamil unnerving him for a moment.

"Hi Aakash how are you?" a girl had walked inside the meeting room interrupting Aakash's thoughts and gaze. She had barged in unannounced and uncaring. She bent over to pick up a dossier kept behind Aakash's chair. Jamil felt an instant rush of adrenaline at the chance glimpse of her cleavage as she bent over. His mouth was wide open as he unabashedly stared at her bosom.

"Meet Anjali. She is the youngest and most energetic party member," Aakash said, introducing Anjali.

"Hi," Anjali said in her soft silky voice.

Jamil could not say a word. His eyes were wandering through Anjali's curves as he mentally undressed her.

"Huh, another creep," Anjali murmured barging out of the room, slamming the door behind her.

Aakash smiled as he saw her go away. Jamil shamelessly turned around to see her walk away through the glass window. His eyes were still stuck to her gait as she walked across the big corridor of the party office.

"Jamil *bhai*...Jamil *bhai*," Aakash had to raise his voice to make Jamil come back to his senses.

"Aakash *bhai* you virtually live in a heaven. Such beautiful girls are your mistresses...,"

"Ah come on. Anjali is not my mistress. She is a hard working political activist..."

"But she is damn hot," Jamil burst out. He just could not shake-off Anjali from his mind.

"Jamil... *bhai*, we can discuss women after the elections." Aakash was polite but curt. Jamil could only nod to Aakash's jibe.

"So you were telling me about your concerns. And the trouble mongers of Basera..."

"Yes...yes," Jamil nodded.

"This is serious. If they introduce computers and other modern subjects in one madrasa then it will surely have a spin-off effect on other villages of the constituency and then on the entire region. This will definitely spoil our electoral chances," Aakash said, leaning back on the chair. He then asked several questions to Jamil.

He sat motionless for a couple of minutes. And then closed his eyes. He remained in that state for several minutes. Jamil leaned forward to see if Aakash had dozed off. Aakash was unconcerned. He kept thinking hard to find a credible solution. After few minutes he opened his eyes and jumped on his feet.

"Yes, this is going to work. We will use an iron knife to slit through this iron sheet," he said smiling.

Aakash explained his plan to Jamil. He jumped from his chair to hug him. "Aakash *bhai* you are a genius. This simple idea...such a simple idea...why did it not come to me?"

"It's because you are still a political rookie," Aakash winked at Jamil.

Aakash picked up his phone and dialled a number.

"You have just one week for preparations," he told Jamil putting the phone down.

It was dusk when Jamil reached Basera. He did not stay overnight at Delhi. The plan had to be executed.

Bilal was loitering outside the bungalow when Jamil's car pulled over. Jamil rolled down car's shade and ordered Bilal to summon Afroz and all others.

"Now?" Bilal asked.

"Yes. Right Now," Jamil ordered, as he briskly walked inside. There was spring in his steps.

Over the next hour Afroz, Anwar, Chacha, Bilal, Rashid along with a few others assembled in the big living room of Jamil's bungalow. Jamil came out of the bathroom violently rubbing his hair with the thick white towel. Pulling down a tee over his head he sat down on the big sofa.

"Allah has sent Aakash *bhai* as our saviour. He is planning everything for us. We just need to execute his plan seamlessly. And mind you there is no scope for any glitch," Jamil wound up the short meeting with a terse message. Everyone nodded. There were no questions asked and everybody got down to business. Work was distributed.

This day was a Friday and the mega-event was on next Friday, exactly a week later when *Maulana* Kamran was scheduled to visit Basera.

Jamil and Afroz had to crisscross the entire constituency urging people to come over for the big *majlis* of *Maulana* Kamran. Rashid and Chacha busied themselves with infrastructure issues sourcing out mattresses, fixing of loud speakers, getting the dais ready etcetera. Bilal and Anwar were busy pasting posters on the walls of mosques, madrasas and houses.

Even Jamil was on his toes. He was constantly on the move in his car explaining to all that *Maulana* Kamran was a great Islamic scholar and listening to him will indeed be a great service to Allah. Afroz called upon his men and they were personally visiting the homes urging people to come to *Maulana* Kamran's *majlis*.

Heena and Fawzia were now settled in a shanty near Chacha's tea stall. Chacha had spread the word that the two sisters were his distant relatives whose parents had died in an accident and so the two had come over to him. Afroz had helped them pick up odd jobs in a few homes wherein they helped women in their household chores. The sisters had been categorically told to keep mum about their real identity to ensure their family's safety in Bangladesh. The household work was to be their cover and the 'real work' was to be assigned to them as and when required.

Maulana Kamran's congregation was their first major assignment. Jamil gave strict instructions to the sisters that they should sing paeans about *Maulana* Kamran's *majlis* and help build hype around it. Heena and Fawzia, already terrified at the turn of events in their life, were working overtime talking about the Islamic congregation being held for the first time in their city.

Aakash was constantly in touch with Jamil and took frequent updates, advising in-between. His instruction to Jamil was crystal clear. *Maulana* Kamran's visit and his *majlis* should be branded and marketed as a religious Islamic congregation. It should not be turned into a political rally. So no political symbols or flags were being used anywhere. All cars, vehicles, and clothes worn by Jamil's team or even the stage at the venue were bereft of political symbols.

The event was being marketed as 'Jamil *bhai's*' philanthropic initiative. It was being sold in a manner that portrayed Jamil as a deeply religious man who had first heard *Maulana* Kamran in the pious lands of Saudi Arabia and had since wanted all Muslims around his neighbourhood to benefit from *Maulana* Kamran's knowledge of Islamic scriptures. Villagers were being told that *Maulana* Kamran had recently come over to India from Saudi Arabia and on Jamil *bhai's* request had agreed to conduct a *majlis* here.

All of this was a blatant lie.

In fact, Jamil had never met *Maulana* Kamran. He did not even know who this *Maulana* Kamran was, and what does he look like. Everything was being planned by Aakash in Delhi. Jamil and his ilk were blindly executing this plan. The story about Jamil meeting up with *Maulana* Kamran in the pious lands of Saudi Arabia was cooked up by Aakash. He knew that mere mention of the holy lands of Saudi Arabia will give Kamran the credibility amongst Muslims to talk about Islam and its teachings.

That afternoon Jamil had accompanied Bilal for the door-to-door invitations in Basera. Bilal was busy pasting posters on the walls about *Maulana* Kamran's discourse and Jamil was urging people to come in large numbers at the pious Islamic congregation. Maulvi *sahab* had just stepped out of his madrasa *Khidmat-ul-Islam,* when he saw Bilal pasting Kamran's poster on the madrasa wall. Maulvi *sahab* looked towards Bilal and without saying a word turned around to walk away.

"Maulvi *sahab*, please do you have a minute?"

Maulvi *sahab* turned around to see Jamil walking towards him. "I know you have not forgiven me for that day's fault, but trust me, now I am a changed man. I now want to do something for the community, for our own Muslim community. And this is why I have invited *Maulana* Kamran to come over to our area for this discourse and the congregation on Islam. He is a great Islamic scholar and when he speaks he mesmerizes the audience. Maulvi *sahab* may I request you to please come over to this gathering?" Jamil pleaded.

Maulvi *sahab* simply nodded and walked away. He still could not trust Jamil, and his mere presence gave him an eerie feeling. Yet, Maulvi *sahab* was curious to know about *Maulana* Kamran. Jamil & Co. had branded Kamran's Islamic credentials quite well and there was a very strong buzz across city about the grand Islamic congregation. Discussions were rife that *Maulana* Kamran had spent several years learning about Islamic scriptures in the pious Saudi Arabian lands and so he too felt that *Maulana* deserved a chance to hear, at least once.

The reality was completely different though.

Kamran was a school dropout. He came from a very poor family and yet was highly ambitious. He was barely fourteen years old when while working on the roadside eatery he was first spotted by a Wahhabi preacher, who had stopped for a cuppa and was highly impressed by Kamran's oratory skills. This preacher was a large man with broad shoulders and a broader face. He had grown thick bush of hair on his cheeks that he said was his beard but without the moustache he resembled an ape.

Kamran was enthusiastic and lively in his interaction with each of the customers present at the eatery. Kamran's voice, the way he spoke, the words he chose, and his pronunciation had that zing, that mojo which attracted customers towards him. Kamran's liveliness had enthralled the Wahhabi preacher. He asked about him and his ambitions in life. Kamran said he wanted to be a big man, earn loads of money, enjoy the company of women and lead a lavish life. The preacher had smiled and asked how he would achieve all these things in his life while working at a roadside eating joint.

"Oh this is just a stop gap arrangement. *Abbu* forces me to work here," the young Kamran had said with a tinge of sadness in his voice.

"What if I take you on the path where you can lead a lavish life?" the Wahhabi preacher asked.

"Oh will you? Please, please, please tell me how to earn big money. I will do whatever you say," the young Kamran was almost on his knees, pleading with the preacher to take him in his fold.

The preacher had smiled and promised that he will come over to meet him again over the next few days.

"Do not discuss about our meeting with anyone. Not even with your *Abbu* or anybody else in your family."

"Yes, yes I will do as you say." There was spring in young Kamran's steps, and he was bubbling with enthusiasm.

The Wahhabi preacher had returned after a fortnight. He was accompanied by other men who sported thick beards without the moustache. They asked young Kamran to come over to their madrasa on Friday and left. Their madrasa was some fifteen kilometres away and was located on outskirts of the city, adjacent to a mosque. Kamran found his way and reached the madrasa. He had walked bare foot and was quickly escorted to the preacher's room.

"Come on in. You are the future of Islam. Allah has sent you to save Muslims," the Wahhabi preacher had said. The preacher sat on floor on the embroidered green carpet. Other men too sat with their legs crossed, on the edges of the room. Every man in the room sported thick beards but without the moustaches they looked menacing. No one smiled, rather they had an angry look on their faces. Kamran could feel a dozen eyes scanning him as he entered the preacher's room. He smiled, yet nobody returned the smile of a young fourteen year old boy, rather they kept on continuously gazing at him. Their piercing eyes had unsettled Kamran. He sat on the edge of the room, the vast green embroidered carpet lay in front of him.

The preacher could sense his uneasiness and asked him to have a glass of water. He then went on to explain about Kamran's oratory skills to others present in the room, quickly adding that Kamran should be mentored to become a good *imam*.

"Oh no. Absolutely not. I don't want to become an *imam*. I want to earn money and lead a lavish life. You said that I will earn big money and that is why I am here," Kamran blurted without a pause. At fourteen years of age, he was quite fearless, and this was his strength. All the men in the room liked Kamran's forceful, fearless attitude.

The preacher smiled for the first time. The other men maintained stoic silence but did not move their gaze away from Kamran.

"Okay, so you want to earn money and lead a lavish life. So be it," the preacher had said. Kamran merely nodded.

The preacher then asked his help to usher Kamran to the 'guest room' on the top floor.

Kamran was amazed at the upkeep of the guest room. The bed was soft as silk, the chairs were grand, an attached bath, mirror that almost extended till the roof, bed covers and pillows with bright embroidery and towels with sequined edges, even the smallest paraphernalia in the room smacked of luxury.

The food served to him was delicious and sumptuous. There was mutton korma, kebabs, biryani, desserts and cold drinks. Kamran was hungry and ate to his heart's delight. He never had such delicious food in his life. He soon fell asleep on the soft and silky bed.

When he woke it was dark outside, but his room was glowing in dim light. He turned around to get up, but was left startled. On the big chair there was a beautiful girl, smiling suggestively.

"Who are you and how did you get inside? What do you want? Did anybody see you coming inside....," Kamran had fired a volley of questions on her.

The girl kept smiling. She stood up rolling her tongue on her upper lips and walked towards Kamran. "You ask too many questions," she said and bent over him.

An hour later, Kamran still lay on the bed, unable to fathom whether all this was for real or just a dream. The girl was gone but he was still engrossed in her thoughts. Never in his wildest of dreams had he imagined that his first experience with a woman would be this picture perfect. A loud knock at the door broke his trance.

The Wahhabi preacher stood at the door, smiling. The broad grin made his wide face look even broader.

"So, how was your experience?"

"I..t..it..was good," Kamran stammered, suddenly realizing that he was still under the wings of the preacher and inside his madrasa.

"How if I tell you that you can enjoy these things for the rest of your life?" the preacher said softly as he sat down besides Kamran on the soft and silky bed.

Kamran's eyes widened as he listened intently to the preacher.

He never went back to his home from the madrasa, his family never bothered to find about his whereabouts nor did he make any efforts to reach out to his family ever since.

Over the next three years, Kamran was indoctrinated with the most lethal Wahhabi ideology. He learnt the most virulent and narrow definition of Islamic verses and mastered the art of public speaking. After his training in India he was sent over to Saudi Arabia for final injection of the Wahhabi ideology. He stayed there for the next couple of years.

Years later when Kamran came back to India he had grown a thick black beard minus the moustache. He was presented as a Hafiz before a select gathering of Islamic students who were being trained to become Muslim clerics.

Being a glib speaker Kamran was able to enthral the gullible audience with his interpretation of Holy Quran and Hadith. It was a carefully crafted event. None of the Islamic scholars were allowed to ask questions or challenge Kamran's narrow interpretation of Quranic verses. A long monologue by Hafiz Kamran was followed by extensive coverage by the Urdu newspapers on how an ascetic Kamran had devoted his life for the path of Allah and has spent his youth in the holy land of Saudi Arabia to seek knowledge about Islam.

In reality, what Kamran preached and what he practiced in real life were diagonally opposite. While he preached abstinence before marriage he needed a woman every night. He advocated that Islam demands its followers to be a teetotaller while he got drunk every night. Of course, all these were arranged for Kamran in a discreet manner and nobody would dare talk about it.

Kamran was introduced to Aakash at the gathering of *Ulemas* in Hyderabad. He was impressed by Kamran's speaking skills. A thick flowing beard and his youth would make him appealing for the gullible Muslim youth, Aakash had thought. Gradually he started inviting him to small lectures to speak about atrocities on Muslims and the American hegemony.

This was five years ago and Kamran was now a brand in himself. He was now known as *Maulana* Kamran. His words were marketed as an authority on Islamic interpretation. Nobody questioned *Maulana* Kamran, everybody listened, rather was supposed to listen passively. Free thinking was never allowed so that a narrow and dubious interpretation of Islamic scriptures were passed upon as the final word.

When Jamil had discussed about problems in his constituency and the presence of free thinking Muslims such as Maulvi *sahab*, Aftab *sahab*, Maqbool *bhai* and others at Basera village, Aakash had immediately got down thinking that he needed somebody of that stature to stand up to these free thinking men. Aakash's impish mind zeroed upon *Maulana* Kamran who he thought had the stature to match up to these free-thinking rational Muslims of Basera who were standing tall between mass-radicalisation of the entire area and subsequent easy electoral victories.

Aakash's game plan was simple. Establish *Maulana* Kamran as an authoritative voice on Islam in the region and discredit anything and everything being told by rational free thinkers within Muslims. Any other interpretation of Islam except Wahhabism was to be branded as apostasy and their proponents as heretics. Once this was done Jamil would establish the narrative about Muslim victimisation. This would help stir passions and Muslims could be herded to vote en masse on the basis of their religion.

16 .

Jamil and his team were doing the ground work at Basera and adjoining villages. Aakash was constantly monitoring the situation from Delhi. He knew that this initiative was bound to give rich electoral dividends. Muslim population comprised almost half of the total electorate and if groomed properly it could be translated into parliamentary seats in the upcoming elections.

Aakash had given clear instructions that branding and marketing of Kamran should be such that every Muslim man across the region is forced to come over for his *majlis*. Kamran was an ace up Aakash's sleeves and he told Jamil in clear terms that all needs of Kamran had to be met with.

"Keep *Maulana* Kamran happy and he will make us all very happy," Aakash chuckled, as he described Kamran's 'needs' to Jamil.

Kamran arrived a day before the congregation at Jamil's bungalow. His arrival was not made public and only a few among Jamil's coterie knew about Kamran's arrival. And the reason for this secrecy was Kamran's carnal desires. The man had a very high libido and Jamil had been told to make 'adequate arrangements' for him. Jamil had contacted one of the best escort services in Mumbai and had called beautiful models. The models had flown to Delhi and had come in big cars with tinted glasses and were hurriedly escorted to the rooms reserved for them at the bungalow. Kamran was already briefed that 'arrangements' had been made for him and he could feel the gush of blood.

So where's the "arrangement"? Kamran had bluntly asked Jamil as soon as he got down from his car. There was no usual *'Assalam-o-Walekum'* as could have been expected from a *Maulana* who was supposed to be an Islamic scholar.

Jamil merely smiled and ushered him to his room. He showed him the mini bar with several exotic brands of whiskey, wine, rum and vodka arranged neatly into a line. Kamran opened a bottle, poured whiskey into the glass and chugged it down his throat. He turned around to Jamil and gestured him to get the girl. Kamran's restiveness to sleep with the girl was just too much. Jamil promptly escorted in the model like a professional pimp. Over the next couple of hours he personally stood as a guard outside the doorway lest Kamran ask for anything. Afroz and Anwar were downstairs and Bilal was in the kitchen. Everyone was on their toes to promptly respond of Kamran's demands.

Saudi Arabia is the birth place of Islam and anything even remotely related to this country is deeply revered by Muslims across the world. Shrewd politicians know this and have always played upon Muslim psyche disguising all their wily plans under the guise of Saudi Arabia. A party in this treacherous gambit are the half-baked Islamic clerics who join hands with crafty politicians and play along. This is a win-win game both for the politicians and Muslim clerics. The politicians win seats with the help of Muslim votes and clerics get political patronage and easy funding. The only loser in this game is the ordinary Muslim who has no idea that by playing upon their fear psychosis they are being misused and are being further pushed into a dark well of ignorance.

This strategy was, in fact, perfected in the eighteenth century when Muhammad ibn Wahab teamed up with Muhammad Ibn Saud, a petty tribal chief in Saudi Arabia, and gave an Islamic sanction to Saud's blatant expansionist pursuits. Saud returned the favour by allowing Wahab to re-interpret Islamic teachings as the only pure form of Islam. It was this nexus that led the Saud family to capture entire Saudi Arabia and thrust upon its people a newly packaged version of Islam that got its name from Mohammad Wahab and was called Wahhabism.

That Friday, Maulvi *sahab* and Abdul went to the village mosque to offer prayers. There was buzz about the learned *Maulana* who was coming from Saudi Arabia to the Basera village. Everybody was talking about the renowned scholar that *Maulana* Kamran was. Even Maulvi *sahab* was curious to know and listen to him. He asked Abdul that he too should come over to listen to *Maulana* Kamran.

"*Salam-Walekum* Aftab *sahab*," Maulvi *sahab* greeted.

"*Walekum-Assalam* Haider," he replied.

After exchanging pleasantries, Maulvi *sahab* asked about the *Maulana* Kamran's *majlis* that was scheduled later in the day. Aftab *sahab* was on the same page as Maulvi sahab. He too was curious about the *majlis,* but at the same time he was sceptical.

"I am curious about its timing. Why is this *majlis* being organised now? Why this sudden change of heart by the organisers?" Aftab *sahab* asked, putting on his shoes after the prayers.

Maulvi *sahab* shrugged. He too had been trying to find answers to these questions. They decided that they will listen to *Maulana* Kamran and then form an opinion.

The *majlis* venue was bustling with activity. Scores of men had gathered from the Basera village and several other adjoining villages to listen to the 'Islamic scholar' *Maulana* Kamran.

The marketing blitzkrieg had ensured a huge turnout and several people could be seen jostling for space. Jamil and Afroz had made travel arrangements for villagers that lived far-off from the venue. Huge green tents had been erected on the open farms. Sugarcane had been harvested and the next crop was still a few weeks away. Several village farmers had willingly offered their farm lands to be used for the pious congregation. The large green tent stood on upright bamboo poles that were draped in green cloth, even the side pegs to which ropes were tied were green in colour. The colour hues were chosen in a manner that gave an impression that organisers had strictly ordered that anything and everything at the venue has to be in shades of green. So the roof was dark green while the tent's wall were in the lighter shades of green. The carpet laid across the floor was parrot green and the table cloth on the dais was a very dark shade of green. Even the back rest of chairs were green.

Green as the theme colour was strategically thought out. Nadeem had specifically instructed Jamil to use green as much as possible so as to give a semblance of Islamic piousness to the congregation. Jamil had understood Nadeem *bhai's* purport. Green is indeed a pious colour in Islam and Jamil had procured almost everything for the *majlis* in green colour. The wrapping paper of food packet was green and the sweets were green in colour.

Abdul accompanied Maulvi *sahab* and Aftab *sahab* to the venue. They reached well on time for the *majlis* and took their seats.

Sitting on the dais were Jamil, Afroz, and several other local leaders who were probable candidates in the upcoming elections. Afroz introduced people on the dais and then called upon Jamil to give details about the learned Islamic scholar *Maulana* Kamran. During his thirty minute speech Jamil kept on emphasizing and underlining the point that Kamran had come from the holy lands of Saudi Arabia where he had spent years reading and learning about Islamic scriptures. He hailed *Maulana* Kamran as the truest Muslim present across the region, to loud cheers.

And then the moment came when *Maulana* Kamran got up to speak. The already attentive crowd became extra-attentive, so people straightened their backs and craned their necks to look up to *Maulana* Kamran.

"*Bismillah-hirRahman-nirRaheem…*," Kamran began his speech.

Over the next hour he kept harping about his stay in Saudi Arabia and how he had been to the holy land and learnt about the correct practices of 'real' and 'purer' form of Islam. When he felt that he had reiterated about his knowledge of the purer forms of Islam he began to untangle the nefarious Wahhabi ideology. He said that Islam means following the righteous path as has been laid down for Muslims all over the world.

"And what is that path… is something which I will tell you. This path is not so easy to decipher. The *kafirs* and the false practicing Muslims are there to deviate you from this chosen path." "…the aim of Islam is to establish Sharia rule across the world. A true Muslim cannot sit idle till the time he sees through that Sharia is established. Many people do not understand what is Sharia? Sharia is the law ordained by Allah himself. And if a Muslim follows Sharia then he need not follow any man-made laws. Anyone who equates man-made laws above Sharia is committing heresy."

"It is the duty of every Muslim to wage jihad in his lifetime…."

Kamran's tirade went on, and with each passing minute Maulvi *sahab* was getting restless. He was now convinced that this man who claims to be true and pious Muslim has only a narrow view of Islamic teachings and the Holy Quran. Instead of advocating and teaching that an individual submit to Allah by indulging in noble deeds, Kamran's idea of Islam was to completely forbid critical thinking amongst Muslims.

"His aim is to close the Muslim mind. This is not Islam. I wonder if he has actually read the Holy Quran or has any understanding of the context of any of the Hadiths," Maulvi *sahab* whispered to Aftab *sahab*, who nodded in agreement. Aftab *sahab* asked Maulvi *sahab* to challenge this man right here in the *majlis* so that the large mass of people can understand that what this man is saying is not real Islam.

Maulvi *sahab* agreed. He stood up and shouted for a mike so that he could be heard.

Everybody on the dais were stunned. This, probably, was the first time in several years that somebody had dared to interrupt Kamran's monologue. Over the years he had simply said whatever he had to say with people listening in abject silence and then leaving quietly after his speech.

Jamil and his coterie had thought the same about this *majlis*. A large majority of the attendees were poor and illiterate, yet there was a difference. Basera village had some real learned men such as Maulvi *sahab*, Aftab *sahab*, Maqbool *bhai* and others. They followed Islam in real spirit and were strong votaries of the same. These were men of character and were courageous.

Jamil knew this. He was well acquainted of the fact that Maulvi *sahab* and Aftab *sahab* had good knowledge of Islamic scriptures and that Kamran was absolutely no match to them. He got jittery when Maulvi *sahab* got up to speak. He was at his wit's end as to how to stop the juggernaut.

Kamran was jittery too, as he had never entered into a dialogue at any of his discussions. He had simply given a monologue of whatever he thought was the interpretation of Islamic verses, which in fact was the Wahhabi ideology. Most of this were a narrow and distorted way of interpreting the text written centuries ago for a specific set of people under specific circumstances.

Jamil and Kamran looked at each other. Both understood that they were on a sticky wicket and should not get into any kind of a debate on Islam lest the tenuous sling with which they held Kamran's superman façade would break and expose the horrid interiors.

But then the Wahhabis have an uncanny ability to slither out of uncomfortable situations. Every time they are challenged, they take refuge that they come from Saudi Arabia, the holy land of Islam. This day was the same.

When challenged by Maulvi *sahab* at the congregation 'Maulana' Kamran did exactly the same.

"I have come from Saudi Arabia. How dare you challenge me on Islamic knowledge? How can any Islamic scholar from Saudi Arabia be challenged? This man does not have the decency to listen to a scholar from Saudi Arabia....look at his audacity he has interrupted a learned scholar from delivering his sermons..." Kamran had played the Saudi Arabia card in the most devious manner. Loud murmurs could now be heard from the crowd.

Jamil immediately seized the opportunity. He took upon the mike and said in a harsher tone that it is inglorious for an ordinary maulvi of a village madrasa to challenge a revered Islamic scholar who has spent his entire life in Saudi Arabia reading the Islamic texts. Afroz and other wannabe local leaders sitting on the dais also sprang on their feet and started harping about Kamran's Saudi Arabian credentials.

Maulvi *sahab* was aghast and looked towards Aftab *sahab*. He too felt stumped. The only argument that came from Kamran was about his Saudi Arabian credentials and nothing was being said about the Wahhabi interpretation of Islamic texts. There was no talk about interpretation and meaning of *jihad* or the origins and sanctions of Islamic Sharia law. The whole argument revolved around the fact that an ordinary village maulvi cannot challenge a scholar from Saudi Arabia.

Aftab *sahab* tried to intervene but he too was shouted down. Abdul who had been listening intently to Kamran's speech gestured his father and Aftab *sahab* to quietly sit down. They preferred to leave the congregation. As the three left, Kamran announced in a much harsher tone that Muslims need to be aware of such *kafirs*.

"I have come from Saudi Arabia and only I have the authority to tell you what is Islam and what is right for Muslims in Islam," Kamran thundered. He went on to prescribe the most regressive interpretation of Islamic scriptures as the gateway to heaven.

His interpretation, though faulty, was perfect to use Islam as a political tool. Jamil couldn't have asked for more. By the time *majlis* ended he was certain that the coming elections will herald good fortune for him. Kamran had showed the way how to use Islam as a political tool. After the *majlis* a large majority were talking about the Kamran model of Islam and how they were being led astray and not doing enough as a Muslim.

Yet there were a few who had found fault with Kamran's arguments and wanted him to discuss Islamic interpretations with Maulvi *sahab*. But they chose to keep mum. The overwhelming support for Kamran model was just too much for them to even register their dissent.

Maulvi *sahab*, Aftab *sahab* and Abdul left the *majlis* with a heavy heart. They were disgusted and disturbed at the turn of events. The three were quietly sipping tea at Maulvi *sahab's* house. While Maulvi *sahab* and Aftab *sahab* were relatively relaxed, Abdul was tense. He was sitting on the chair's edge with Kamran's words still echoing in his mind.

"Whatever *Maulana* Kamran said… is it right *Abbu*?" Abdul asked his father putting down his cup of tea as he broke the silence in the room.

"Don't call him a *'Maulana'*. He is a crook who is simply using the name of Islam to further his interests," Aftab *sahab* said even before Maulvi *sahab* could respond.

"I agree. I was sceptical about this person from the beginning when I first heard that it was Jamil who had organised all this. But since this Kamran was said to have learnt about Islamic scriptures in the holy land of Saudi Arabia I thought maybe he is a learned man. But I agree, this man is a crook," Maulvi *sahab* answered putting the cup on table.

"But *Abbu* isn't he quoting from the Holy Quran? How can we deny that?"

"Yes he is quoting from the Holy Quran. But look at the interpretation he's giving to those pious verses. All his interpretations are narrow, extremist and lopsided. He is not following the spirit of our Holy Quran," Maulvi *sahab* explained.

"…son, the Holy Quran and Prophet Muhammad's (PBUH) sayings--the *Hadith* ordain that each Muslim should be on the path of *Ijtehad*, which is personal enlightenment. It is the duty of each Muslim to read and reflect what Allah expects from him," Aftab *sahab* added.

"But then this is what Kamran was telling us at the *majlis*," Abdul was still not convinced.

"My son he was giving his own narrow interpretation and asking everyone to become a copycat. This is not what Allah expects from a true Muslim," Maulvi *sahab* explained. "…the situation, aspirations, desires and challenges are not the same for everybody. Yet everyone needs to do good to be able to reach heaven after their life. So Allah has ordained that we do well, we pray to him and continue our good deeds amidst all kinds of obstacles only then we become a good Muslim," Maulvi *sahab* added.

"...and this what these people like Jamil and Kamran do not want us Muslims to do. A thinking Muslim is their worst enemy. Any Muslim who can think critically is an antidote to the poison that these enemies of Islam are spreading all across," Aftab *sahab* promptly added.

Begum *sahiba* and Sakina were keenly hearing the interesting conversation among Maulvi *sahab*, Aftab *sahab* and Abdul from behind the curtains of their room.

"...it is the foremost duty of a Muslim to purify his own soul by good thoughts and deeds. This is the basic concept of jihad. Sadly a few power hungry people have misrepresented every Islamic concept for their own good," Maulvi *sahab* said.

"Did you hear what this Kamran was saying about women?" Aftab *sahab* asked, his eyes wide open with surprise. Before Abdul could say a word, Aftab *sahab* himself answered, "...he was advocating that according to Islamic tenets women need to cover themselves up from head to toe because if they do not do so then their sight instigates carnal desires in a man and if such men indulge in wrong doing then the blame lies with women. In other words he was justifying rape."

"Yes I agree this Kamran was justifying rape. Nowhere in the Quran has it been explicitly mentioned that women need to be covered in black tents or have to essentially cover their hair and face. If they do so fine, but if they don't wear a *burqa* or even the hijab then too it's a matter of their choice, it's not mandatory. Decency lies in the eyes of beholder. Islam does not permit a man to hurt, abuse or offend any woman regardless of her attire. It's these devious *Maulanas* and *Maulvis* who have given fabricated interpretations to Islamic teachings and used Islam to oppress women," Maulvi *sahab* added, endorsing Aftab *sahab's* words.

Abdul was unable to sleep that night. *Maulana* Kamran's words and his subsequent chat with Aftab *sahab* and his *Abbu* echoed in his ears. He restlessly tossed around in his bed, unable to sleep. After a while he stood at the window. Standing at the window of his bedroom he was staring at the darkness outside. The vast darkness spread across his village seemed in sync with the darkness in the lives of Muslims, he thought.

A soft touch on his shoulder woke him up from the trance. Sakina had silently tip-toed by his side and cusped his hand with her hands. Gently, she asked if everything was okay. Abdul seemed not to hear her and ignored her presence. He stood that way for several minutes gathering courage to say to his wife, what he had been thinking and planning and had wanted to do. Over the next several minutes he described his plan in detail to Sakina, his wife. She stood there motionless, attentive as her husband spoke. Abdul did not face his wife as he spoke. He stared outside the window, in the dark expanse.

Probably, he feared that his wife would consider his thoughts and plans too radical. Or, perhaps he drew inspiration from the darkness outside the window. Sakina did not speak for several minutes after Abdul had finished. She stood there staring at Abdul, her husband. There was silence.

Abdul turned around to his wife. He saw tears rolling down her cheeks. She came closer and hugged her husband tightly.

17 .

It was late in the morning when Abdul woke up. Sakina was busy with the household chores, Begum *sahiba* was preparing breakfast and Maulvi *sahab* was cutting fodder for their buffaloes. The local newspaper lay on the table. *Maulana* Kamran's *majlis* was covered in great detail. The eight-column photograph splashed across the paper showed Jamil, Afroz and other electoral candidates along with Kamran on the dais. The news report had termed the *majlis* a 'religious event' and hailed the efforts of a revered 'Islamic scholar' from Saudi Arabia who had explained true and pious Islamic values and their correct interpretation to the huge mass of 'ignorant Muslims' who till now were unaware about real Islam.

Abdul browsed through the newspaper and dumped it on the table. He picked it up yet again, kept staring at it and dropped it back. He walked briskly towards Maulvi *sahab*.

"*Abbu* have you read today's newspaper?" he asked.

"Yes, I have." Maulvi *sahab* replied with a tinge of sadness, as he mixed the green fodder with the dry bran for buffaloes.

"We cannot sit idle we have to do something. I have thought of something and I want to implement it as soon as possible. I have been thinking about it the whole night and I want to discuss this with you," Abdul said. He then held his father's hand and literally dragged him from the buffalo's shed to the main courtyard. Small shreds of fodder and bran were still stuck across Maulvi *sahab's* arm.

He called his mother and wife. The family gathered around the large table in courtyard.

Abdul announced that he had become slightly more ambitious. "I have added wings to my earlier plan. It's time to fly high," he said and went on to explain that instead of introducing computers only at the Basera's madrasa he wants to start dedicated computer labs at all the madrasas in the region. "Each madrasa student will be given technical training so as to equip them with necessary skills that will help them get jobs. During evenings students will be coached to appear for competitive examinations so that they can get admission to professional colleges like engineering, medical, finance, law and others."

"And," Abdul paused for a moment to stress upon the next part of his plan. "...On these computers we will also play videos of the lectures about 'correct interpretation' of Islamic scriptures. Our audience will be young students, madrasa teachers, support staff and any other villager who may wish to listen to genuine talk about Islamic thoughts. I will record videos of lectures and discussions about various facets of Islam by Maulvi *sahab*—my *Abbu*, Aftab *sahab*, Maqbool *sahab*, Naseem *sahab* and other such learned men. We will use one of the rooms in our madrasa to record the videos and these recordings will then be provided to all other madrasas."

"If evil men like Jamil and Kamran are working with a devious agenda and polluting the minds of Muslims then we cannot sit back in our homes doing nothing. We need to take this scourge head on," a determined Abdul announced.

Maulvi *sahab's* eyes were wide open, he had leaned forward as he listened intently. After Abdul detailed his plan, he rose slowly from the wooden chair and came closer to his son. He hugged him tightly. "I am proud of you my son. I am proud of you."

Begum *sahiba* wiped tears with her *dupatta* yet those joyous droplets kept rolling down her cheeks. Sakina was smiling sheepishly. She was happy and content that she indeed had married the right man.

The family quickly finished off their breakfast and set off to give wings to their thoughts. Maulvi *sahab's* life was a mission in itself and Abdul, his son, had added a fresh whiff of air into it. The family had their breakfast together where finer details of the plan were discussed and work distributed amongst themselves.

So, Maulvi *sahab* was to muster support from his own madrasa management committee. He would rope in Aftab *sahab* and together they would convince other madrasas across the region to implement their plan. Aftab *sahab* and Maulvi *sahab* would together reach out to philanthropic Muslims to donate funds for buying computers, books and hiring of qualified teachers.

Abdul would take care of the logistics, so he would prepare a detailed plan about the number of computers to be bought, camera set-up, purchase books and enrol teachers. Begum *sahiba* would take care of the accounting and maintain a ledger record. Sakina would help develop the course content. She had already informed her father in the neighbouring village who had agreed to offer all possible help in this noble mission.

Abdul reached out to Arjun and sought his help. Arjun's father said he will help them get computers at a discounted price. Arjun and Abdul spoke to their school and college friends requesting them to come over and teach specialised subjects at the madrasas.

Maulvi *sahab* reached Aftab *sahab's* home and apprised him of his thoughts. Aftab *sahab* immediately liked the idea. He sent for Maqbool *bhai* and Naseem *bhai*. Maqbool was also a member of the management committee of another madrasa at the adjoining village. Naseem had friends who were members of other madrasas' management committees. Both of them liked the concept and promised to help in all possible ways. Aftab *sahab* phoned his friends describing them of the idea. Afroz was kept out of these discussions, on purpose. His views were known plus discussions were still premature and no one wanted Afroz to come and put a spanner at the incubation stage itself.

Over the next couple of days Aftab *sahab* and Maulvi *sahab* kept detailing their plan to village elders convincing them about the need for modernizing madrasa syllabi and roping them for video recording of sermons and lectures on Islam. The reaction was mixed. There were a few who were totally convinced about the need to teach computers, science, economics, history and other subjects and also to play video recording of the discussions about Islamic issues on the newly brought computers for the madrasas. There were a few who concurred on the teaching of modern subjects but had strong reservations about video recordings of the likes of Maulvi *sahab* and Aftab *sahab* discussing Islamic teachings being played on the madrasa computers.

A few were totally opposed to any changes in the madrasa syllabus and were against the idea of videos. This group felt that Muslim children need not be weaned away from Islam and if they read books other than the Holy Quran or Islamic scriptures they would fall into Satan's trap.

A large majority were confused as to what was right and what comprised the wrongs. It was here that Maulvi *sahab* saw a ray of light. 'These fence-sitters are the ones whom we should win over and put on the righteous path,' he said to himself.

"I have been saying this all through the years that a large majority of Muslims aspire to have a good life, they want to get into decent jobs, and they seek security of their children without compromising on the Islamic values. Unfortunately it's this large majority that falls prey to the vicious propaganda from the likes of *Maulana* Kamran who scare them in the name of Islam thereby silently gnawing away their progressive thoughts. Our battle is to occupy their mind space else they would continue to fall prey to the vicious agenda of the likes of Kamrans and Jamils," Maulvi *sahab* told Aftab *sahab* as the two men discussed the feedback received from all quarters.

Aftab *sahab* said the matter was delicate and grave that required elaborate deliberations. He called upon a meeting of elders and the management committee members of all the madrasas in their region. A date was fixed, and was announced. The word spread like wild fire that plans were afoot to bring drastic changes in the workings of madrasas.

This news reached Jamil and Afroz, as well. Jamil's initial reaction was to shrug it off as a plan that was doomed to fail but after he briefed Aakash about these developments he was asked to keep a close tab. Aakash personally asked Afroz to be a part of the meetings and take detailed notes. Afroz, being a member of the Basera madrasa's management committee, was formally invited for the meeting.

"Reach on time. Apart from the formal proceedings let me know the general buzz. Listen to what people say in hushed tones, in small private discussions. Try to gauge the general sentiment of the meet," Aakash had instructed Afroz. Aakash had briefed Nadeem about this grand meeting, who in turn informed the Wahhabi financiers sitting in Saudi Arabia.

Everyone was keeping a close eye on the developments.

Basera's neighbouring village had a large central mosque with a very big hall. This mosque was chosen as the meeting's venue.

There were intense debates and discussions during the larger meeting of madrasa management committee members. One side was led by soft, gentle and learned men of the likes of Maulvi *sahab* and Aftab *sahab* while the other side had crooks such as Afroz who saw madrasas as their laboratory where they could inject the virulent interpretation of Islamic teachings into the impressionable minds of young children and turn them into lethal tools to be used at their free will.

Afroz had found support in several others committee members from other madrasas whom he had won over these years by bribing them with wealth, women and wine. The progressives supporting Maulvi *sahab's* ideas and ideals lacked wealth but were rich in their thoughts and outlook. And today they were in no mood to relent. They were quite assertive. Sandwiched between the two sides were the fence-sitters who remained perplexed, unable to take sides and decide as to who was right. They were still not able to grapple as to which side represented truer and pious form of Islam. These were the people who did not want to invest much of their time interpreting and analysing religious scriptures and holy texts and yet were not willing to compromise on their Islamic identity. This segment was the most vulnerable to lethal toxins emanating from *Maulana* Kamran. They were in a majority and it was this segment whom Aakash and Jamil were looking to exploit.

At stake was the policy decision for over ten dozen madrasas that were spread across three parliamentary constituencies and thirteen legislative council seats.

Education has a spin off effect that goes beyond the boundary walls of a madrasa. Oftentimes when a madrasa's *maulvi, imam* or the teacher unleashes virulent interpretation of Islamic texts as the 'only pious version of Islam' it somehow percolates to the student's parents who face a social pressure to practice that version of Islam. This is taken a step further when Wahhabis give incendiary speeches at the behest of scheming politicians and tighten the vice-like grip on the Muslim mind. When this happens, an ordinary Muslim faces immense social pressure to conform and accept this virulent interpretation of Islam as 'true Islam'. Wily politicians like Jamil bring in the likes of *Maulana* Kamrans to give out a narrow interpretation of Quran and Hadith which is then propagated as the one and the only version of Islam and anyone deviating from this prototype is branded as a heretic. This helps the use of Islam as a political tool. In reality this is poles apart from the state of Islam where a Muslim is required to submit to Allah and interpret Quran and Hadith according to his or her own specific conditions.

The ordinary Muslim, before he could realise, cedes his mind space to these crooks who are now able to remote control his thoughts and actions for their own selfish needs. As this takes shape, a mass hysteria envelops the Muslim sub-conscious. Hordes of people wear Muslim identity on their sleeves, behave like zombies and remain devoid of any critical thinking. Amidst this if anyone dares to question the existing set of beliefs and insists on a rational and logical explanation is promptly labelled as a heretic and an apostate. Social sanctions are almost immediately imposed and killing of this deviant person is sanctioned citing some ossified but dubious instances in the Islamic Sharia law. The beginning of critical thinking is thus nipped in the bud.

It was precisely for these reasons that the Wahhabis and their stooges

Aakash and Jamil were vehemently opposed to introduction of contemporary modern subjects and computers at the Basera madrasa. A thinking Muslim mind will never vote on religious lines and could mean the end of Islamic politics based on Muslim identity and knell death bells for MMP and for the FPI. In order to prevent this they needed to stall Maulvi *sahab's* initiative at all costs.

There were fiery exchange of words during the meeting of madrasa representatives. To everyone's surprise, Aftab *sahab* despite his old age was extremely vocal and vehemently supported the introduction of computers and study of other subjects such as science, economics and history along with the Islamic teachings. He was ably supported by Maulvi *sahab*, Maqbool *bhai* and few others who had deep understanding of the Islamic scriptures. Their arguments were logical and rational.

Afroz and his bunch consisted of people who had half-baked information about Islam but were harping on the need to preserve a true and pious Islam. None among this group was willing to define or debate what this 'pious Islam' was. They did not speak rather kept on shouting and their only claim to fame was that they had the support of *Maulana* Kamran who had learned about Islamic scriptures during his stay in Saudi Arabia. Every time Aftab *sahab* or Maulvi *sahab* countered their points by logic, they retorted quickly saying no interpretation would be acceptable other than those detailed by *Maulana* Kamran. They waved Kamran's writings in support of their point.

The fence-sitters sat there confused. They intently listened to each side's arguments but were unable to take sides. They were in a large majority and were the passive listeners.

The meeting went on for about five hours and yet consensus eluded them. Both sides were unwilling to budge.

"Okay I have a solution to this stalemate...," Maulvi *sahab* gradually stood up. His body was tired, his legs ached and back went stiff yet his mind was agile. All eyes now turned towards him, eager to know what could be the possible solution in Maulvi *sahab's* mind.

Afroz curled his eyebrows, swung his head sideways and twirled his lips. His eyes shrunk and nostrils dilated, his face resembled a fox waiting to pounce upon a prey.

"…since we all have issues about the introduction of contemporary subjects at madrasas and there seems to be no consensus…our brothers are vociferously opposed to the idea of using madrasa computers to play video series about discussion on Islamic scriptures as well….so instead of a mass scale changes across all madrasas in the region I propose to use the Basera's *Khidmat-ul-Islam* madrasa as a pilot project. We have already been teaching a few of the modern subjects at our madrasa, let us take the initiative and introduce computers. The video series on discussions about Islamic scriptures will also be first run in the Basera madrasa. Our management committee members are already in favour of the introduction of these subjects so let us first begin at the Basera madrasa and over the next few months committee members from other madrasas may come over to review our progress and…"

"How can this happen at the Basera madrasa? No absolutely not. I am not in this favour," Afroz jumped on his feet abruptly cutting short Maulvi *sahab*.

"Why what's your problem? Maulvi *sahab* is absolutely right. We will begin from the Basera madrasa. I am sure nobody from our committee has any issue," Maqbool had stood up to counter Afroz, and looked towards Aftab *sahab* and Naseem *bhai*, the other committee members of Basera madrasa.

"I have an issue. I do not agree," Afroz was unwilling to give up.

"Your consent is not mandatory for the Basera madrasa. All other committee members are in favour of Maulvi *sahab's* proposal," Aftab *sahab* said as he looked towards other committee members of the Basera madrasa who nodded their heads in support of Maulvi *sahab's* proposal.

Afroz was left grinding his teeth. He did have support from the committee members of several other madrasas but he still had no hold over the madrasa committee in his own village, Basera. He still was the lone member in the madrasa management committee who was not on the same page as Maulvi *sahab* and Aftab *sahab*.

Just when the meeting was about to end, the mosque's imam, where this meeting was being held, stood up. He was opposed to the idea of running video series on Basera computers. "Let us take one step at a time. Get the computers first, the video series can wait," he said in a polite tone. The *imam* had spoken for the first time since morning.

Aftab *sahab* looked towards Maulvi *sahab*.

"Okay we respect imam *sahab's* request. The video series will be implemented some time later," Maulvi *sahab* announced.

So, after the day-long intense debates and discussions the marathon meeting ended on a rather cordial note. Everybody seemed happy and both sides claimed victory. Afroz was happy that through his proxy, the mosque's *imam*, he could stall the video series plan. Maulvi *sahab* was happy that at least he will now be able to initiate teaching of modern subjects and computers at the Basera madrasa. He was confident that once villagers see the success at Basera madrasa the model would be replicated across all the madrasas.

The fence-sitters who were confused about their next course of action quite liked the idea that Basera's madrasa takes the lead in implementing all the plans. They can always come over to take stock of the progress and if things go wrong at Basera they will never implement the changes at their villages but if it were right they could replicate the model. They saw Basera as their safety valve.

Afroz gave detailed descriptive account of this meeting to Jamil, and hare-brained as he was, he could not figure out if this was a victory for them or a defeat. He was perplexed.

Jamil called up Aakash and explained it to him about the new developments in the region. Aakash spoke after a long silence.

"Jamil *bhai* this is a serious issue. It could have far reaching consequences. This could affect our chances very badly in the upcoming elections. I am coming to your village tomorrow," Aakash said as he hung up.

"I think Aakash *bhai* is over-reacting. Basera has just one madrasa and even if they do start teaching computers or any damn subject how can it have an impact on the elections?" Afroz said as he poured whisky into the goblet for Jamil.

Jamil maintained a stoic silence. He too was unable to fathom whether this was a victory for him or for Maulvi *sahab*. He spent the rest of evening, drinking and thinking.

18 .

The next morning Jamil and Afroz woke up to the loud blaring of a car's horn. Aakash and Nadeem had arrived. They barged inside the living room. Jamil and Afroz were sleeping on the couch after getting drunk last night when they had walked in. Bilal was himself bleary eyed when he ran out to open the gate after the loud blaring of car's horn. He vigorously shook Jamil and Afroz to wake them up.

Jamil turned around rubbing his eyes, trying to shake off last night's hangover.

"Where is this Maulvi's home?" Aakash asked, in a terse tone.

"Ammm..mm...yes this Maulvi's home...," Jamil yawned, rotating his head, his eyes still half closed and knees bent when he saw Nadeem standing to the other side of room.

The mere sight of Nadeem gave him an intense electric shock and almost immediately he sprang up on his feet. He kicked Afroz on his bums who was still asleep. Afroz opened his eyes uttering his choicest expletives but went mum at the sight of Aakash. He did not recognise the other gentleman in the room.

"*Salam-o-Walekum*. My name is Nadeem Khan," Nadeem said sitting on the chair, sensing Afroz's curiosity about him.

"*As..as..asalam-o-walekum* Nadeem *bhai*," Afroz stammered. He had only heard about Nadeem *bhai* and had desperately wanted to meet him but he never knew the meeting would be so dramatic.

"Okay so we are getting late. Please help us with the location of Maulvi's home," Aakash said, picking up the apple from the fruit bowl on the table.

"What's the hurry Aakash *bhai* ?...just settle down. Let's have breakfast and then we can discuss our strategy," Jamil said, making a desperate attempt to smile.

"I know my strategy. You need not worry about it. It has been approved by both Nadeem *bhai* and Usman *bhai*...and you can see for yourself that Nadeem *bhai* himself is here. Just tell me about the location of Maulvi's home...and then you guys may carry on with your lazy sleep," Aakash was curt. He meant business.

Usman *bhai's* name struck like a lightning bolt to both Jamil and Afroz. They sprang on their feet, literally, and looked at each other. Usman was the main financier of MMP. His business interests were spread across Saudi Arabia and he headed an Islamic think tank in Mumbai that funded several dubious activities across India. He had been funding MMP over the last several years, but of late his patience had run dry. He had clearly mentioned to Jamil during the recent Hyderabad meeting that he needed to win elections and enter the policy making organs of the government so as to be able to push for Wahhabi Islamic thoughts in government policies. Usman was answerable to his business associates and the Wahhabi Sheikhs in Saudi Arabia who were growing impatient with the slow progress of Wahhabism's spread in India.

"Give me an hour to get ready. I will come with you," Jamil said.

"Get into the habit of starting your day early," Aakash said turning around his shoulder. He did not wait to hear an answer and swiftly walked out with Nadeem.

Maulvi *sahab* and Abdul were at home having their breakfast in the courtyard when they heard the sound of a car stop in the narrow by-lane.

"*Assalam-o-walekum* Maulvi *sahab*. May I come inside?" Aakash asked peering over the black gate.

"*Walekum-assalam*," Maulvi *sahab* said with a puzzled look on his face as he tried to recognise the uninvited guests. Aakash's face seemed familiar to him but Maulvi *sahab* could not immediately recognise him.

"I am Aakash, General Secretary of FPI...the Federal Party of India. FPI is a political party and I am its general secretary," Aakash said with a charming smile as he stepped in. "...and he is Nadeem *bhai*, my very good friend. Nadeem *bhai* is a businessman and he lives in Delhi."

"Oh yes. I remember now. I have seen your photographs in newspapers. How may I help you?" Maulvi *sahab* asked, still puzzled by the arrival of a person of the stature of Aakash, a well-known politician and Nadeem a businessman from Delhi.

"If you permit and if you don't mind may I please come inside? Can we sit and talk?" Aakash talked in a glib tone.

"Oh yes. I am so sorry. Please come in," Maulvi *sahab* stepped aside feeling embarrassed about not asking the uninvited guests to come inside his house. Abdul ushered Aakash to the wooden chairs in their courtyard.

Aakash and Nadeem gave furtive glances around Maulvi *sahab's* house as they walked along Abdul to the chairs placed in the middle of courtyard. Abdul promptly cleaned up the table of used plates.

"Village life and village homes are such delight. It's calm and serene in direct contrast to the maddening city life," Aakash began his slick talk, looking towards Nadeem.

"The air, the ambience everything in a village is heaven," Nadeem smiled, sitting on the wooden chair.

"I feel it's a question of our mind set, rather than about village or the city life. Anybody who feels content with whatever Allah has given feels happy in either a city or a village," Maulvi *sahab* said. He asked Abdul to get breakfast for the guests. Abdul brought dal, chapatti, curd and a glass of buttermilk.

"Hmm it's delicious. Wonderful. Wow. Fantastic." Aakash kept praising the food with every bite, until he ran out of adjectives. "Oh please I am full," he had spread his hands on the plate as Abdul offered another chapatti.

"I will have one more. Give me Aakash *bhai's* share," Nadeem said taking the chapatti from Abdul's hands, as he burst into laughter with Aakash.

Aakash drank the buttermilk till its last drop. As the two men ate they kept talking about the general stuff… the non-metallic roads in a village, the erratic power supply, the fresh air, farms, the fields, and etcetera.

As Maulvi *sahab* continued to talk with Aakash and Nadeem, Abdul who was sitting alongside wondered as to why a well-known politician and a big businessman would come to their home. They surely did not come to have breakfast nor were they here to talk about the clean air of villages or the maddening traffic of Delhi. What is it that they want?

Maulvi *sahab* read Abdul's mind and broached the topic.

"Let me know how else can I help you?" Maulvi *sahab* asked Aakash and Nadeem.

Putting down his tea cup Aakash said, "Maulvi *sahab* you know the condition of Muslims is deteriorating with each passing day. They are being persecuted for no rhyme or reason. Every day we see this government implicating Muslims in some or the other fabricated cases. Gross injustice is being meted out to all the followers of Islam. Muslims are denied jobs and equal opportunities in employment. Our party is based on secular ideals and we believe that the minorities must have equal rights in this country. Just because we Hindus are more in number does not and should not mean that we have a licence to persecute you Muslims…"

"…It is for this very reason that my party FPI wants Muslims like you to come forward and do some good for the community. I am aware of all the good work that you have been doing but you have restrained your good work into this tiny village. You should not restrain yourself. Instead, you should think of a larger canvas...," Aakash continued to explain.

He added: "...the Parliamentary and State Assembly elections are around the corner and our party is looking for candidates who can bring a real change in the society and for Muslim community in particular. I cannot think of anybody better than you to fight elections from our party..."

"Oh please Aakash *sahab*. Essentially you want me to enter politics and contest elections? But I am not interested in politics. At all," Maulvi *sahab* had intervened Aakash's talk. And he did not stop with the refusal. He went on, "...and...I do not agree with your contention that Muslims are being routinely and systematically persecuted in this country. On the contrary, I feel an individual who is capable, educated and has the right skills does get his or her due. I do not see religion playing a role. Yes statistically it may be true that Muslims lag behind Hindus but then this data needs to be analysed in the light of the fact that not many Muslims invest in education and skill building as other people do. And this is what I want to change, by educating and by teaching. A child, regardless of his religion, should seek knowledge, education and the right skills and this is true for Muslim children as well. This is what is required and this is what I am doing through imparting modern education in my madrasa. Your offer to contest elections may be tempting for others but I am a simple school teacher and as I said I have absolutely no interest in politics."

"Oh Maulvi *sahab* just hang on for a minute. Contesting elections does not necessarily mean that you shun your lifestyle and adopt something else. And I am not disputing your ideas that children should seek knowledge. On the contrary, your ideas are quite revolutionary. But to implement such big ideas you need to have a larger arena, a bigger canvas. Mere teaching in this village madrasa will not help your case. You may also continue with your simple life but your presence within the legislative set up will mean that you are among the policy makers. You will get adequate avenues to implement your plans into action. There will be people and resources at your command. Your one nod can change things on ground...," Aakash played the hard ball as he tried to win over Maulvi *sahab*. Nadeem smiled and kept nodding his head.

"Hmm okay. I have been running from pillar to post to modernize our village madrasa. We need computers, books and we need to recruit more qualified teachers. You are influential men with big connections. Let us start the scheme of modernisation of all madrasas in this entire region. There are over five hundred madrasas across the adjoining districts," Maulvi *sahab* explained.

"Maulvi *sahab* I feel that you need to think big. What is there in a petty madrasa? Why don't you think that the entire region and the Muslims therein will follow your diktats once you enter the legislative set up?" Nadeem asked leaning forward. Looking straight into the eyes of Maulvi *sahab* he added, "...you will command the entire Muslims of this region. Your word will be law for these people. Your son can be placed at a wonderful position. You will have a big house, big money and wield enormous power," Nadeem dropped the façade and threw the bait directly towards Maulvi *sahab.*

"And why do you think I want all this?" Maulvi *sahab* had abruptly cut him short.

"A…a..a..mmm…I mean everybody in this world wants position. Everybody likes money and everybody wants to enjoy power," Nadeem was stupefied. He had not expected this question from Maulvi *sahab.*

"Nadeem *sahab* it's only the big businessmen and politicians like you who are hungry for power, position and money…"

"Ah come on Maulvi *sahab.* Let's be honest. You don't need to be diplomatic with me. Okay let me elaborate more. You be our party's candidate in the upcoming parliamentary elections. Or if you are not comfortable with the FPI you can choose to be a candidate from the Modern Muslim Party… this will keep your Muslim identity intact. And given the trends, any candidate from our party is sure to win elections this time. This is a lifetime opportunity for you. If I were you I would have grabbed this opportunity with both hands…" Aakash said with a wicked smile looking towards Nadeem for his approval. Nadeem nodded back.

"But you are not me and I am definitely not you. I will not distort the teachings of Islam to suit your wicked ambitions," Maulvi *sahab* said in a calm and cool voice leaning back on the chair.

"Ah you getting us wrong yet again. Who are we to ask somebody as learned like you to distort the teachings of Islam, rather I am trying to explain that if a dim-witted person like *Maulana* Kamran can command such a huge following then imagine the kind of following you will generate if you join hands with us," Nadeem blurted out, rather involuntarily.

"There you nailed it. A dim-witted and scoundrel like Kamran can fall for your evil designs. But you cannot sway me with your charms. I am getting late for the madrasa, please excuse me," Maulvi *sahab* got up, as he understood the real intentions of the two unsolicited guests at his home.

Aakash gave a blank look towards Nadeem. They had thought that Maulvi *sahab* would easily be convinced about coming into their fold and their discussions would centre on the requirement of funds for elections. And once they had Maulvi *sahab* on board, Jamil could easily be kicked out. But Maulvi *sahab* being a man of character did not fall for their evil designs.

"Maulvi *sahab* I respect you a lot. Think about our proposal. We can come again," Aakash said patting on Maulvi *sahab's* shoulders. Nadeem looked bewildered, he had been thinking that an ordinary Maulvi of a madrasa will come running into their lap at this mouthwatering proposal. He was not prepared to hear a 'no' for an answer, and his disappointment was clearly visible on his face.

"Aakash *bhai* I always think hard before arriving at any conclusion. I was being polite in refusing your proposal but I suppose you like blunt answers. So here it is. I am neither interested in you nor your political party. How else do you want me to say no to you?" Maulvi *sahab* looked straight into Aakash's eyes as he asserted his point.

Maulvi *sahab's* gaze somewhat frightened Abdul, who had been passively listening to their conversation.

Aakash went numb for a moment. He quickly gathered his wits, looked towards Nadeem and then towards Maulvi *sahab* and said, "I will still wait for your answer." He swiftly walked towards the gate without looking back, and sped off in his car with Nadeem.

Maulvi *sahab* turned around to put on his slippers. Abdul stood still, tears rolling down his eyes. Begun *sahiba* and Sakina, who had been hearing the conversation from inside the room, had tears in their eyes too. They walked towards Maulvi *sahab*.

"I am proud of you," Begum *sahiba* said holding Maulvi *sahab's* hand as she fought hard not to let tears roll down her cheeks. Sakina was crying too.

"Yes *Abbu*, we are all so proud of you," Abdul said, his eyes moist with tears.

"Thank you Allah for bestowing me with such a wonderful family. I thought that after refusing such a lucrative offer from these Aakash and Nadeem I will have to convince hard to all my near and dear ones. And I will be at pains to explain why I rejected this offer. But the all benevolent Allah is so kind, he is so merciful..."

"We are happy and content with all that is given to us by Allah," Begun *sahiba* said, wiping away her tears.

The family discussion was interrupted by a squeaking sound from the kitchen. Sakina looked towards her mother-in-law, lifting her eyebrows as she tried to figure out the reason for this squeaking noise that was growing every second. It appeared as if water was slowly being poured on fire.

"Allah...," she said running towards the kitchen as she recalled the reason for the squeaking sound. "...I had kept milk to boil on the mud stove."

"Careful. Take it easy daughter, be careful," Begum *sahiba* and Maulvi *sahab* yelled in unison. Begum *sahiba* followed her to the kitchen.

Maulvi *sahab* headed towards the madrasa and Abdul went over to Arjun's place.

19.

Jamil and Afroz were still dozing on the couch, struggling with last night's hangover when Aakash and Nadeem walked in. They quietly sat on the sofa. Nadeem scrolled through the numbers in his phone. Jamil's eyes were still half-open and he asked Bilal to get some tea. He cursed himself for indulging in a drinking spree last night.

"Wake up otherwise it will be too late for us," Nadeem said as he dialled the number on his mobile phone.

"*Assalam-o-Walekum* Usman *bhai*," he said leaning back as he caressed his head with the left hand.

Nadeem's mention of Usman *bhai's* name was like touching Jamil's skin with a hot iron rod. He was jolted from bleariness and made conscious efforts to open his eyes.

"...yes the situation is not good here. The Maulvi has rejected our proposal and we need to think of some other plan... and we need to think fast," Nadeem said as he glued the phone to his ears. He kept nodding to whatever Usman said from the other end, answering only in monosyllables. Five minutes later he put down the phone and turned towards Aakash.

"Come Aakash *bhai*," he pointed towards the other room. The two men remained locked in for several minutes inside the room. The door finally opened and they walked towards the nervous men in the living room.

"What happened? What did Usman *bhai* say? Is he angry?" Nadeem's stream of thoughts were interrupted by the volley of questions from Jamil. Afroz's mouth was wide open as he made efforts to grapple with the whole scenario. Bilal and Anwar stood at one corner, their hands folded behind their backs in expectation of a command from any of the men in the room.

Nadeem explained to Jamil that Maulvi *sahab* was going ahead with his plan to modernize the Basera madrasa, which had angered Usman *bhai*. He added that Maulvi *sahab's* plan with his madrasa had the potential to upset all of their electoral calculations across several constituencies and so Usman *bhai* had sought Aakash *bhai's* help to sort out this mess. Nadeem carefully avoided any mention of their offer to Maulvi *sahab* to fight elections and that Maulvi *sahab* had flatly refused the offer. He also did not tell them that Usman did not trust Jamil to be able to wriggle out of this scenario. He had clearly asked Nadeem that modernisation of madrasa education needed to be stopped as early as possible. "Elections can be won later on as well, but if the madrasa education goes out of our hands then it will be very difficult to tame the Muslim mind," Usman had spelt out in crisp words to Nadeem. In the closed door meeting Nadeem had asked Aakash to take the matters in his hands and help them wriggle out of this precarious situation since the matter had reached the Wahhabi Sheikhs in Saudi Arabia and they wanted a quick resolution to this irritant.

"Aakash *bhai* will be directly in charge of these affairs and you guys will do as he says," Nadeem made a short and crisp announcement. He then left for Delhi.

Aakash turned towards Jamil and Afroz who still appeared disheveled and disoriented. "One hour. You guys have one hour, go take bath and come back to me with a fresh mind. As you have heard, this is a serious issue and I want all of you in an attentive frame of mind," he commanded and without waiting for their answer sat down with his laptop to finish off his party's work.

Jamil and Afroz looked towards each other. The next moment they were scurrying for towels and were inside the bathroom.

Aakash was still engrossed with his laptop when Jamil and Afroz came in. Their hair was now neatly combed and they had put on crisp tees and pants, ready to swing into action on any instruction. They stood like school students hands folded into a cusp in front of their groins. Aakash looked towards them, took a deep breath and ordered them to sit down. They meekly obeyed.

Aakash then turned his head from his laptop towards Afroz and asked if there was any possibility of ousting this Maulvi from the madrasa. Afroz vigorously shook his head and explained that everybody in the madrasa management committee of the Basera village were in consonance with Maulvi. "I am the lone member who speaks against this wretched Maulvi and his plans."

"Aakash *bhai* is this Maulvi, his madrasa and these computers this big a threat for us and our plans?" Afroz asked with a childlike expression. He looked towards Aakash and Jamil for answers. Jamil looked towards Aakash as if endorsing Afroz's question.

Aakash was still engrossed in his thoughts. His discussions with Maulvi *sahab* played like a record player in his mind as he grappled for a solution. Maulvi *sahab's* words still echoed in his mind when Afroz shot his question. Aakash sighed and leaned forward. He waved towards Anwar and Bilal standing near the door to come near and listen to him.

"All of you need to understand certain things very clearly. You win an election only when you are able to occupy the mind space of individuals. The Muslim minorities vote only for those whom they consider as their saviours and who they think would offer some benefits. So, in order to win an election we first create a fear psychosis among the minds of Muslims, and then project ourselves as the saviour of Islam and of Muslims. The Muslims then come and vote en masse ensuring victory for us in every elections. Anybody or anything that has the potential to free Muslims from this fear psychosis is a threat for us..." Aakash explained. He then turned towards Afroz.

"...the answer specifically to your question is a big yes. So, yes this Maulvi is indeed a big threat for us because he is working to occupy the mind space of Muslims in this village and other villages. His plans to introduce computers is the most dangerous as this will make information available to all. We will no longer be able to control the flow of information. An informed person thinks and his thoughts are guided according to the available sources of information... and since we will not control the information-flow, his thoughts will be beyond our control. All our plans to create a fear psychosis amongst the Muslims of this village and other adjoining villages will go haywire and with it our chances to win elections..."

"...this Maulvi and his plans to introduce computers at the madrasa is a deadly spark, and this spark has the potential to graduate into an inferno. It is better and easier to douse a spark than to smother an inferno. Just don't underestimate this Maulvi and his plans," Aakash said in a firm voice as everyone in the room listened to him with earnest attention.

"So what's the solution? What do we do to him?" Anwar asked unfolding his hands. His plain and innocent question unnerved everyone else. Aakash swallowed the lump in his throat, Jamil leaned back on the couch and Afroz looked unnervingly towards Bilal. There was silence for over a minute.

"We are... Well, we are... still trying to think of a solution. But yes, as of now there is no solution in our sights," Aakash fumbled by the plain and to-the-point question asked by Anwar.

Anwar and Bilal were dedicated workers of their political alliance and Aakash was well aware that workers like them need to be kept buoyant for electoral success. Party workers need to believe that their political outfit will win the elections else despondency sets in and that leads to electoral defeat. A seasoned politician that he was, Aakash quickly gathered his wits.

"You know the best thing during elections is confidence of the cadres and the worst thing is their over-confidence," Aakash said standing up. He walked towards Anwar and Bilal and put his hands around Anwar. "The reason I explained so much about this Maulvi's grandiose plans was not to scare you but to ensure that all of us do not take him lightly. We need to work tirelessly and not slacken our efforts. And trust me, I will sort out this Maulvi. It's my promise. We have full support of *Maulana* Kamran so keep your spirits high," Aakash assured. He then looked towards Bilal and said, "Bilal *bhai* can I have a cup of tea?"

"Oh sure Sir. I am extremely sorry I didn't even ask you for tea," Bilal said, visibly embarrassed that Aakash *bhai* had to 'ask' for tea.

The empty tea cup lay on the side table and Aakash lay slump on the couch. He had been constantly thinking about Maulvi *sahab* and his plans but had been unable to find a potent solution. On similar occasions and issues he and Nadeem would come up with a strategy in a jiffy. But Basera's Maulvi proved a tough nut for them to crack.

'This man does not nurture grandiose ambitions, has minuscule requirements and his aspiration is to educate and impart knowledge. How do I deal with such a person? He could not be bought with money. He refused my proposal to hold on to power. His only aspiration is to impart knowledge. Such idealism. Such foolish idealism. How do I deal with this man? If only he was with us we would have easily swept the elections. How I wish this Maulvi had allied with us, instead of this dumb-witted moron Jamil...,' Aakash was deeply engrossed in these thoughts as he sipped tea. He did not realise when he had slumped on the couch and dozed off. He was tired from the early morning long drive from Delhi and despite his best efforts Maulvi *sahab* had refused to be enticed. The thought weighed heavily on his mind.

Aakash had been tossing on the couch, half-asleep, and woke up to the noise of chatter coming in from the adjacent room. He could hear the ongoing discussions. Someone was pestering Jamil for funds. He had turned, closed his eyes making efforts to sleep when he heard someone utter 'Urdu Newspaper'. Almost immediately he was jolted from his slumber. He got up and sat straight. He had his ears to the room from where the conversation emanated. A man was arguing with Jamil and tried hard to make him understand that print costs had risen substantially and that it was getting difficult to run their Urdu newspaper and increase its circulation due to paucity of funds. Jamil argued back that funds were in short supply as they needed more money for other activities.

Aakash walked up to the room.

"What's the matter Jamil?"

"Ah nothing much Aakash *bhai*. He is Zamiluddin, he runs an Urdu newspaper in our locality. He wants to increase the circulation of the newspaper but I feel all these other activities can wait till the elections are over. We can help him later on…"

"*Salam-walekum* Zamiluddin *bhai*. I am Aakash and I head the Federal Party of India," Aakash had abruptly cut short Jamil.

"*Walekum-assalam* Aakash *bhai*"

"Can you tell me more about your newspaper and how do you want to expand it?" Aakash said as he pulled a chair and sat beside Zamiluddin. Jamil and Afroz were bewildered.

Over the next thirty minutes Zamiluddin went on explaining about his Urdu daily. He said that the daily began around six months ago and the current circulation of the newspaper was around two hundred fifty copies that was being distributed in four villages. He added that the response to his newspaper had been very good and it was time to step up the circulation.

"What kind of people read this newspaper?"

"Everybody from the *imams* to the local shopkeepers, farmers, masons, barbers, teachers etc. Anybody who can read Urdu is our reader. Just fifteen days ago I heard that the *imam* of the local mosque in adjoining village was discussing the issues raised by me in our editorial after the Friday prayers…"

"And what was this issue?"

"I had written about Israeli and American forces attacking the Muslim fighters of Hamas in Palestine. The *imam sahab* spoke for almost an hour at the mosque and he kept waiving the newspaper in his hand."

"What are your immediate concerns about this daily?" Aakash said leaning forward.

"Sir, the newsprint costs have gone up and it is getting difficult for us to sustain. We cannot increase our circulation unless we get more money," Zamiluddin sounded desperate, leaning towards Aakash.

For a minute, Aakash did not speak and kept staring at Zamiluddin. Numerous thoughts raced through his mind as he focused his gaze on him. Aakash's gaze was menacing, it unnerved Zamiluddin and he looked towards Jamil and Afroz with guilt for being so forceful in asking for funds.

But Aakash had something else in his mind. He was looking beyond Zamiluddin. Yes, Aakash's eyes were fixated on Zamiluddin's face yet he did not exist for him. In the Urdu newspaper he could see a whip with which to whack and smack Maulvi *sahab's* plans. The answer that had evaded him since morning about how to tackle the idealism and principled approach of Maulvi *sahab* was available right there in front of him.

'Yes, an Urdu newspaper will give us the impetus. A printed word carries much weight. This will offset this wretched Maulvi's idealism. Through this paper we will sell Muslim victimhood and their misery. This Urdu daily will help us win elections,' Aakash smirked as these thoughts raced through his mind. He spoke after several minutes.

"Funds are not a problem, we will take care of everything. You prepare a detailed plan to increase the circulation of your newspaper across this entire region. But there will be a condition. News and views that we send you, should find space in the newspaper under all circumstances….," Aakash had now drifted his gaze towards Zamiluddin, mentally acknowledging his existence.

"Oh don't you worry Sir. I am willing to cede all editorial control to you. If you wish you can appoint your own person who will oversee everything a day before it is published," Zamiluddin was ecstatic to hear Aakash's proposal. In his excitement he slid towards the edge of the seat and held Aakash's hands in his hands. "Thank you so much. I will work out a detailed plan and give you an estimate of the funds required."

"That's good. Prepare a plan and meet me over the next couple of days at my Delhi office. You may go now," Aakash was rather curt. Zamiluddin did not mind and quickly slipped out from the room.

"But Aakash *bhai* why did you agree to this idiot's proposal. And why should we waste our funds on this bugger," Afroz asked Aakash in utter disbelief.

He was confused, as was Jamil for how could Aakash agree to fund a person to run a newspaper who was barely literate and that his 'newspaper' was more of a pamphlet which was used for wrapping stuff by the villagers.

Aakash did not seem to listen to Afroz's question. He knew Afroz and Jamil were puppets in the hands Nadeem *bhai* and none of them had any political vision. Their mandate was to execute whatever plan was sent out to them by Nadeem *bhai* and others sitting pretty at Hyderabad, Mumbai and in Saudi Arabia.

He could immediately visualize the potential and clout of an Urdu newspaper. He understood that acceptance of an Urdu newspaper will be much higher than a newspaper in any other language because a large majority of Muslims still see Urdu as their own language. Urdu words carry larger weight and they can become a powerful tool to spread their version of the interpretations of Islam.

"*Salam-walekum* Nadeem *bhai*. Finally I have some good news," Aakash told Nadeem over phone. He was smiling and he described rather excitedly about Zamiluddin's Urdu newspaper. They spoke for almost twenty minutes and later when Aakash put the phone down he asked Jamil to get Zamiluddin to his Delhi office in the next couple of days.

Jamil looked towards Afroz, the two did not say anything.

"Any problems? Or any questions?" Aakash asked. His authoritative voice clearly meant he did not expect to hear any further questions. Jamil and Afroz nodded like school students. They knew clearly that Nadeem *bhai's* words are final and that their mandate is simply to execute the plans endorsed by him. They were amazed that how could a person like Zamiluddin impress Aakash and Nadeem such that they were willing to splurge funds on him.

Zamiluddin came from a family of tonga pullers. His father and grandfather were both tonga pullers and were illiterates. Nobody in his family had ever been to any school or to a madrasa. Zamiluddin had four brothers and three sisters. He was the fifth child and could barely read and write. But he was fiercely ambitious and had an insatiable lust for money. Sensing his penchant for money-making, his father had trained him in the trade and made him drive his rickety tonga at a fairly young age. Zamiluddin drove his father's tonga for a few years but found this tonga driver's job to be a stifling profession that barely fulfilled his aspirations. He soon quit and tried his hands on several other petty vocations but nothing worked. Over the last couple of years he had been working at a printing press when the idea to start his own newspaper dawned upon him. The owner of this printing press used his connections in government departments to secure bulky government advertisements for his newspaper, thereby raking in huge moolah. A government official had advised Zamiluddin to start a newspaper and run it for few months before applying for government adverts. He had promised to get Zamiluddin a pie from the government's large advertisement budget. Zamiluddin had come over to meet Jamil and literally begged for funds to start his Urdu newspaper. The paper resembled a pamphlet more than a newspaper. It was since been published, albeit intermittently. This was six months ago.

20 .

It was early morning when Arjun reached Abdul's home. A day before, the two friends had finalised the list of books, computers and other material to be brought over for *Khidmat-ul-Islam*, the Basera's madrasa. Today they were to go to Delhi to procure all these stuff. Begum *sahiba* had asked Arjun to have his breakfast at their place. Maulvi *sahab* had blessed and hugged them both before they rode off to Delhi. He stood at the gate along with Begum *sahiba* and Sakina, watching Abdul and Arjun go to Delhi to get computers and books for the madrasa. The three stood at the gate for several minutes even after the dust trail left by auto rickshaw had settled down.

"Today is a historic day for Basera," Maulvi *sahab* uttered. "...after this day this village will not be the same. It will change, and change for better," he said as he walked towards the madrasa across the road with spring in his steps. Begum *sahiba* and Sakina felt ebullient as they returned inside their home.

It was late evening and the mini-truck negotiated narrow curves around the big banyan tree to enter Basera. Abdul and Arjun were sitting alongside the driver on the truck's front seat. The children's crowd running behind the mini-truck was swelling with every passing minute. They were thrilled about the advent of computers at the village madrasa. All of this enthusiastic bunch of youngsters had heard about computers or had seen a computer in a picture but none had ever operated a computer in their life or even seen a computer from close quarters.

The path and culverts in Basera were narrow and the truck's driver was driving slowly. And yet he had no difficulty. A group of children were running ahead of the truck clearing the path and village lanes of squatters and encroachers to let it pass unobstructed. The relatively younger children were running behind the truck shouting, dancing and whistling. Villagers who had been squatting and gossiping after the day's work in the village lanes readily stood up and moved aside to give way to the truck, some started walking behind the truck along with the children, while others broke into an impromptu broad smile hearing that the mini-truck brought in computers.

Mini-truck looked like the groom's vehicle in a marriage procession wherein computers in brown boxes were the groom and children the groom's friends who merrily danced their way to the bride's home, the Basera madrasa.

Jamil was talking over phone as his driver stood waiting to drive him to Delhi. Rashid was still panting as he stood beside him. Rashid had been lazing at his home through the day to beat the hangover of last night's drinking. He was dragging up to the makeshift washroom of his thatched hut when he overheard the buzz about computers being brought into Maulvi *sahab's* madrasa. He peered through the mud wall of his house and saw children running around with excitement.

"*Salam Walekum* Rashid *bhai*. Maulvi *sahab* has got computers for the village madrasa. Come let's see how it looks," a villager greeted him as he walked past his house.

Rashid stepped back stunned. His head was still heavy due to the effect of alcohol and the news of computers into Basera's madrasa made his head go into a tizzy. His own children were joyous and Rukhsana was all smiles as she talked to her mother. Other days Rashid would have been livid and could have shouted his lungs out on Rukhsana but today was different. He had to rush to Jamil *bhai* and tell him that Maulvi *sahab* had put Muslims of Basera village in danger and they needed to do something quick and fast.

He darted out of his house and sprinted towards Jamil's bungalow. Due to the hangover his feet swayed as he ran, yet Rashid was unmindful. He was running to save the believers, the Muslims, from falling into Satan's lap and he thought the only one who could save Muslims was his Jamil *bhai*. He almost fell on Jamil as he came to his bungalow. Grasping for breath he could only utter 'computers in Basera'. Instantly, Jamil understood that Maulvi *sahab* had got computers for the madrasa.

Without waiting for a cue and without batting an eyelid, Rashid went on to explain how Maulvi and his son Abdul were putting Muslims on the sinful path by introducing computers in the madrasa. He described how madrasas were meant only for Islamic teaching and that it was a big sin to even think of American computers inside an Islamic madrasa. Rashid was speaking non-stop, as if he were possessed. Jamil gave a patient ear to Rashid.

"Keep a close eye on the madrasa activities and inform Chacha about every detail. I will tell you what to do next," Jamil said, reluctantly putting his hand on Rashid's shoulders. He then sat in his car and shut the car's door. As the driver sped away Jamil asked for a wet paper napkin. He vociferously wiped away Rashid's sweat that had stuck to his palm when he had put his hand on Rashid's shoulder. His face contorted in disgust as he wiped away the sweat.

Maulvi *sahab* and Aftab *sahab* were eagerly waiting at the madrasa gate when the truck stopped. They burst into a broad grin. Abdul and Arjun climbed down from the mini-truck and hugged them. Maqbool *bhai* and Naseem *bhai* embraced them in a huddle. By now almost everybody had known that computers had come in at the madrasa. Eager children, men and women had flocked around the truck at the madrasa's gate.

"*Aapaa*, what's this noise about?" Heena asked as she kneaded the dough. Heena and Fawzia had to pick up odd jobs in the village households during day. The sisters were working in one of the village homes when the truck had whizzed past to the madrasa.

"Maulvi *sahab* has brought in computers at his madrasa. The children are super-excited about this and so are merrily dancing around the truck," *Aapaa* said craning her head above the short boundary wall of her house that overlooked the madrasa.

"Do you know what is a computer?" *Aapaa* asked, standing up on the charpoy she had craned her neck to get a better view of the melee near the madrasa. Heena and Fawzia blankly looked towards her.

Fawzia who was busy scrubbing the iron pan at a corner of the patio reminisced her childhood when she went to a school in the ghettoes of Dhaka in Bangladesh. One fine day, a team of foreign researchers had come to their school. They had several exotic devices, camera with long lenses that looked like a bird's beak, the triangle shaped tripod which the students thought was a gun with three barrels. But Fawzia was enamoured by the tiny briefcase that had English alphabets stuck in a jumbled fashion. There were numerals, alphabets and other small buttons stuck at the black base-pad. She was enthralled by this sleek but arcane device and continued to stare at it without blinking her eyes. The researcher was impressed by her curiosity.

"This is a computer. A laptop computer," he had explained. He then had made Fawzia and other children type their names on it. The children were thrilled to see their names appear on the computer's bright monitor that they had thought was a briefcase cover. The researchers had promised to come yet again the other day with their laptop computers.

Fawzia was unable to sleep that night. She was thrilled about computers and was desperately waiting for dawn so that she could rush to school and tap her fingers on the computer's keyboard. She had later confided about her dreams to Heena that she would study computers in her college. Heena had hugged her sister and patted on her back. Fawzia's dreams had come crashing down when a few years later she along with her sister Heena were packed off with a Kerala businessman and were forced into harlotry.

Heena looked towards Fawzia who was now scrubbing the iron cauldron. She could gauge her feelings.

"*Aapaa* we are almost done. Can we go to the madrasa to have a look at the computers?" Heena asked mopping the concrete patio.

Aapaa turned around and sat on the charpoy, her neck strained due to the continuous craning towards the madrasa.

"Oh yes. Maulvi *sahab* is a gentleman. He wants everybody in this village to read, gain knowledge and learn new things. He will be happy to tell you girls about a computer. Finish off your work and go," *Aapaa* said, gently massaging her neck and shoulders to rid of the strain in her neck.

Fawzia was smiling. Heena looked at her sister, who probably had smiled after several months.

The revelry had not yet died down when Heena and Fawzia reached madrasa. Children continued to jump around the madrasa ground. A few sat atop the truck, while others whistled and danced. The big brown boxes of computers and the box of books were being offloaded from the mini-truck. Arjun and Abdul along with a few other men carried the computers inside. A couple of other village members had climbed up the truck to lend a helping hand.

Sakina was standing near the truck's rear overseeing the boxes being offloaded when she spotted Fawzia and Heena looking wistfully at the computer boxes.

"*Salam walekum*, I am Sakina. These are computers," Sakina said pointing towards the boxes being taken inside the madrasa.

"*Walekum salam*, yes, yes I know, I know," Fawzia said excitedly as she came closer to Sakina, "...you know I had seen a computer when I was a child. It was my dream....," Fawzia stopped without completing the sentence. She muzzled her voice.

"Go ahead, why did you stop. What was your dream? You can tell me. My name is Sakina and I am Abdul's begum and Maulvi *sahab's* daughter-in-law," Sakina goaded Fawzia to speak up.

"No nothing *aapaa*. We are new to this village and live in a shanty near Chacha's tea shop. We eke out our living through working as maids in village households. Fawzia is my younger sister. We were working at Maqbool *bhai's* home when we heard this noise about a truck coming in at the madrasa. So Fawzia said let's go and have a look. We are getting late…so….yeah…*adaab*," Heena explained in a jiffy and held Fawzia's hand to leave.

"Oh it's completely fine. Don't worry. Come on I will take you inside the madrasa," Sakina held the hands of Fawzia and Heena and walked inside the madrasa.

It was after several years that Fawzia and Heena had stepped inside a madrasa. Sakina led them through the black gates and walking past the grassy stretch the three women walked up to Maulvi *sahab* and Aftab *sahab* who stood at the porch. Sakina introduced the two sisters and led them inside the madrasa. Fawzia lovingly ran her fingers through the engraved patterns, squares and triangles on the madrasa's motif as she followed Sakina. She looked at the white-coloured ceiling and the green coloured carpets laid in the rooms. Unlike her elder sister she had completely forgotten herself and basked in the serene aura of the madrasa.

Heena, on her part, was terrified as she walked along. Fawzia was an idealist and Heena was rational. She knew her present situation was akin to walking a tight rope and that she had lied to Sakina that they worked as domestic help and maids. Heena felt guilty of having lied about herself and her sister and about hiding the truth that they were treated as cheap molls by the likes of Jamil and his men. Yes, Heena too yearned for freedom and like her sister Fawzia desperately wanted to break free of her present and erase her scary past. But her similarity with Fawzia ended at this point. Heena could only believe what she saw around her, and all that she could see was deceit, lust and exploitation.

Fawzia was a dreamer and idealist. Oftentimes she would wander in her thoughts, and dream of a beautiful life. Walking through the madrasa corridors she floated into her own dream-world. Fawzia was ebullient and chirpy as she saw the computers being installed and the books being unpacked. Heena was burdened by the thoughts of what lay ahead for her later in the evening. The sisters were jerked back into the present when someone called their name.

"…Heena and Fawzia, they are sisters." It was Sakina's voice. She was introducing them to her husband Abdul and to Arjun who were busy tallying the consignment with the bills.

The sisters' lives had been through so much turmoil in recent times and they had been through such severe exploitation that they were terrified by the normal behaviour of Sakina.

"*Aapaa* it was so nice for you to let us tour the madrasa. It's already very dark outside and we are getting late. We will take your leave now," Heena said looking outside the window. Before Sakina could say anything she pulled Fawzia's hand and turned around to go. Fawzia agreed reluctantly. Like the kids jumping around with joy in the madrasa she could not remove her eyes from the computer monitors. Sakina could sniff the passion in her.

"We live just across the road. Come anytime during day. Ask for Maulvi *sahab's* home and anyone in the village will guide you to our place," Sakina yelled at the sisters as she waved them goodbye. Fawzia turned around and smiled, and then walked off hurriedly with Heena.

The news of computers arriving at the Basera madrasa had spread like wild fire across several adjoining villages of the region. That evening it was the sole topic of discussions at tea stalls, snack corners, barber shops and all such gatherings.

Rashid walked in to Chacha's tea stall to an intense discussion about computers at Maulvi *sahab's* madrasa in Basera village. As he parked his motorbike aside he could hear the labourers and daily wagers engrossed in a discussion about the merits and demerits of modern education.

"How can an Islamic madrasa have American computers? This Maulvi is hell-bent upon destroying the faith of us Muslims," Rashid thundered as he twirled the chair and sat on it.

Chacha who was stirring tea in the sauté pan, bent his head a little, raised his eyebrows and looked at Rashid from the corner of his eye. He passed on a tea glass to the attendant and raised his eyebrows in a sign to give the glass to Rashid. The steaming hot tea worked up to further stir up Rashid's passions. He was livid. Over the next few minutes, the entire course of discussion at Chacha's tea shack had changed. While earlier the labourers and daily wage earners were discussing about the merits of teaching computers and other subjects at the madrasa, after Rashid's tirade, everyone silently nodded to the notion that computers are actually an assault on the foundations of Islam. The discussions went on for almost an hour.

Chacha, as usual, silently listened to the discussion keeping a keen eye on everyone involved. It was getting darker and almost every customer had left. Slowly, he picked up the phone and called Jamil and apprised him about the ongoing discussions at his tea stall. Chacha was now winding up his tea stall. Rashid walked up to him and asked if he would like to have a drink. The two then went over to the highway liquor shop. As they finished the last peg, Chacha wanted to walk over to Heena and Fawzia's place. Minutes later, the two drunk men were banging on their doors.

The sisters were halfway into their supper when Rashid and Chacha barged in. Fawzia was talking to her sister about computers, about how she was mesmerized with that sleek machine and how that gadget has her heart and soul, when they heard the loud bang on the doors. The sisters begged the two men to leave them for today but they simply elbowed their way inside. It was not that Heena and Fawzia did not know that their primary task was indeed to lie down for the likes of Rashid and Chacha or for anyone else who would be sent by Jamil and Afroz, but today was another day. After a long time Heena could see her younger sister smile and talk about her dreams and so she thought that she would beg Rashid and Chacha to leave them alone, at least for that moment. The girls were grossly mistaken. Rashid pounced upon Fawzia, cursing under his breath as he kicked her food plate aside. The plate with half eaten rice-curry flung to the room's corner and fell down with a bang. The curry made a distinct yellow mark on the walls. Heena cowed down and curled with fear as Chacha came for her.

Abdul woke up quite early in the morning. Today was going to be a hectic day. Last evening they had unpacked all the computers and neatly arranged them on wooden tables in the madrasa's corner room. Arjun had called an engineer who till late at night was busy networking the computers. Sakina pasted, on the doors of this corner room, a paper with 'Computer Room' inscribed aesthetically. Everyone had worked till late in the evening yet loads of work remained.

The books needed to be stacked in the library's cupboards. Computers needed to be connected with the Internet. Printer was to be installed. The course content had to be developed.

Abdul's day was cut out. He hurriedly finished his breakfast and rushed to the madrasa. Arjun and Maulvi *sahab* would join him in an hour.

He was pleasantly surprised to find Rustam and Razzak sitting on their hunches outside the madrasa gate along with their father. Rustam and Razzak were brothers and were quite fond of books. They had an inquisitive mind and were ecstatic when it was announced that the madrasa would soon get computers. They were jumping with joy when last evening the mini-truck came in with the computers and books.

"*Salam walekum bhai jaan,*" Rustam and Razzak said in unison as they sprang on their feet seeing Abdul come to the madrasa.

"*Walekum Assalam,*" Abdul returned their greetings.

"The kids are so excited that they hardly slept last night," Rustam and Razzak's father said with a broad smile.

"Yes I can understand. Thank you so much for bringing the kids so early in the morning to the madrasa. There's so much work and I too need a helping hand"

"Is that so? You can count Rustam's father as well, to help you out," he said and followed Abdul inside the madrasa.

Over the next couple of hours Abdul was joined by several other kids from the neighbourhood who were excited about computers at their madrasa and in their zest had come over to help Abdul.

The madrasa was soon buzzing with activity. New books were being placed on the bookshelves, chairs being laid in front of the computer tables, the printer was installed, and a round table was placed at the centre of the computer room for discussions and short lectures. The enthusiasm of kids was infectious and everybody was busy with something. Those who felt lost in the world of computers and books busied themselves with collecting the packaging thermocol, empty cartons, kraft paper, clamshell packs, bubble wraps, slings etcetera. Each kid and the parent had a desire to belong to the madrasa and it reflected in their actions.

Maulvi *sahab* was pleased to see the enthusiasm among villagers and their kids about education. Happily he stood watching the passion with which the kids, his son Abdul, his daughter-in-law Sakina, Arjun and other villagers were busy with books and computers. Everything was on auto-pilot. He basked in the blissful thought that finally his efforts were paying off and the villagers were realising the importance of modern education.

Later in the morning Aftab *sahab* came along with Maqbool *bhai*. A few of their friends had also come along. Maulvi *sahab* greeted the guests and led them to the newly furbished computer room and the library. Aftab *sahab* had spring in his steps. He used a walking stick for support, but today the stick followed his steps. His eyes gleamed with delight.

"Haider, I think you've made a mistake," Aftab *sahab* said, making a solemn face as he suddenly turned around towards Maulvi *sahab*. He called Maulvi *sahab* by his first name only under special circumstances. Maulvi *sahab* understood there must be something important to which Aftab *sahab* had pointed. He leaned over attentively to hear him out.

"Where are the sweets for these children? You have brought computers and books but where are the sweets and the sherbet? Did you plan for the celebrations?" he fired a salvo of questions as he burst into a wide grin. Maulvi *sahab* and all others burst into a loud laughter.

In the afternoon, there were Eid like celebrations at the madrasa *Khidmat-ul-Islam*. Children had put on their best dresses for the occasion. Maulvi *sahab* arranged a small feast for students inside the madrasa. The cook roasted sausages, the sweet aroma of *jalebis* had filled the air, colourful *barfi, rasgulla* were brought in, and samosas were being fried. Sakina, Begum *sahiba* and a few other women from the neighbourhood were arranging eatables in small paper plates. Abdul, Arjun and other children had decorated the computer room and library with rose flowers.

The madrasa gates were wide open for every villager. Parents had come over with their children to get a glimpse of computers. A number of children who were not students of this madrasa or studied somewhere else had also came over. Parents could be heard discussing that their kids will now be able to receive modern education. There was bliss in the air.

Among the numerous visitors to Basera, were the management committee members of other madrasas. These were the fence sitters who had remained quiet during the grand congregation of madrasas and had been listening to arguments of both sides. Several of these men were seeing a computer for the first time in their lives. The monitor displaying text, images and videos at the command of a keyboard or by click of the mouse appeared divine and outlandish to several onlookers. Hitherto, a computer for this motley crowd was an arcane and highly sophisticated machine that required some super human abilities to operate. That a computer was well within their reach and their own children could learn about it within their village was nothing short of a revelation to the villagers.

Everybody wanted to break the shackles of poverty and wished their children to lead a prosperous life. A lot of those who had come over to the Basera madrasa had to struggle to eke out a living and dreamt of prosperity and peace. But, with hardly any specific skill set they found it difficult to bag worthy employment opportunities. Even those who had farm lands resorted to archaic agricultural practices. The artisans, marginal farmers and landless labourers who had only their physical labour to bank upon were the most vulnerable lot, both financially and religiously. A lot of these villagers had created a mental block for themselves that their children will have to continue in a similar kind of profession. Studying, learning and acquiring knowledge about something like computers was seen as a super-human activity which only the rich can pursue, they had thought.

Computers sitting pretty on wooden tables at the Basera madrasa had a rather liberating experience for both the children and their parents. While the children were excited about being in the proximity to computers, their fathers saw computers as a conduit that could ultimately raise living standards of the entire family when their kids bag a lucrative job in the mighty cyber world.

Today, Aftab *sahab* led the *namaz* at the mosque adjacent to madrasa. After the *namaz* children headed towards the madrasa's computer room. The entire madrasa was buzzing with activity. Sweets were being distributed and sherbet was served. On other days it would have been a tough job to keep children away from the delicious sweets but today was different. It were the computers that had occupied children's minds. They were rushing towards the computer room where Abdul was to demonstrate basic functions of a computer. Arjun had organised children into small batches to enter inside the computer room. Children coming out of the computer room after operating the computer had a swag in their steps. Several of them could be seen detailing other kids, still waiting for their turn outside the computer room about the powers of a computer.

Sakina had been busy distributing sweets to the children and elders who had accompanied them. She was about to step outside the madrasa when she saw Fawzia leaning against the madrasa gate. Gates were wide open but she stood there in a corner, staring blankly inside the madrasa.

"*Salaam-walekum* Fawzia, come inside. Why are you standing at the gate?" Sakina called, keeping the white coloured *barfi* in the paper plate. Fawzia did not respond and continued to stare blankly inside the madrasa. Sakina walked up to her.

"Fawzia? Are you alright?" she asked gently shaking her by the shoulder. Sakina's gentle shake broke Fawzia's stupor. That same moment Heena who was sitting beside on her hunches stood up seeing Sakina.

"Nothing *Aapaa*. Fawzia is not well but she insisted to come over to the madrasa," Heena said hesitatingly, forcing a smile as she tried hard to conceal their last night's traumatic pounding at the hands of Rashid and Chacha. Fawzia's *dupatta* slid sideways with a whiff of air, exposing the big reddish scar below her ear at the back of her cheeks. The fresh scar on

Fawzia's face was Rashid's gift to her last night, when he had run his hands on her face during his intense bouts of passion.

"*Yaa* Allah, how did this happen? Just come to my home and I will apply an ointment," Sakina had held Fawzia's hands and dragged her across the street to her home. She did not wait for an explanation. Fawzia followed her meekly, like a lamb. Heena tried to explain in a timid voice that her sister would be fine and there was nothing to be worried, but by the time she finished her sentence they had already crossed the narrow street and were walking inside Maulvi *sahab's* home.

Bilal was passing by and saw the sisters Fawzia and Heena tagging along with Sakina inside Maulvi *sahab's* home. He paused for a moment, slowed down his cycle but the next moment his foot pressed on the cycle's pedals and he rode away.

Sakina cleaned Fawzia's wounds and applied an antiseptic lotion. Begum *sahiba* was still at the madrasa, helping the students and lending a helping hand. Heena looked visibly nervous and made several excuses to leave. Fawzia was relatively calm and wanted to stay there for a while. She wanted to cry on Sakina's shoulders, tell about her life, speak about the several men who had reduced her to a lump of meat, raise her voice against the regular assaults at the hands of Jamil's men. She desperately wanted to cry her heart out, but stopped. She and her sister had been violated by everyone, their own family had sold them and it could be too early to trust a stranger. Yes, Sakina was still a stranger. They had met just a day before. Fawzia decided to wait for some other day to tell her story.

"*Aapaa* let us know if you require some kind of help in the household. We earn our living by working as domestic help in the village. Cleaning, cooking, milking the cattle, cutting cattle fodder...you name it and we will do it for you," Fawzia blurted out without batting an eyelid. She wanted to come again and again to Sakina, and what better way to come over as a domestic help. Sakina smiled and the sisters left in a jiffy saying they were getting late for their work in other households.

21.

It was dark when Rashid reached Jamil's bungalow. Tension was palpable at the bungalow and he could feel it. Maulvi *sahab* had successfully brought in computers at the madrasa and the only talk in the village was about computers. And there was something unusual about this day.

Rashid did not have to wait endlessly in the lobby to get an audience with Jamil, rather, and to his utter surprise, he found that Bilal was waiting for him. This ordinarily happened only when Jamil had some work cut out for Rashid.

The whole day Rashid had been sitting idle at Chacha's tea stall. He was enraged and had wanted to smash the computer to pieces but Jamil had conveyed to all his men to keep quiet. He had strictly asked the hothead Rashid to stay calm. Aakash had reached Basera during the day and had been conducting a flurry of meetings since then.

Bilal ushered Rashid to the bungalow's first floor. Jamil was sitting with Aakash and Afroz. Rashid stood at the door with his head bowed down. Jamil raised his right hand in a gesture for Rashid to come inside, making him feel important, at least for that moment. On other occasions, when Jamil and Afroz were with other guests Rashid waited endlessly for the meetings to get over to speak to Jamil. He was also required to serve whiskey, wine or rum to the guests. Nothing of this happened today. When Jamil called him inside the room, Rashid felt probably for the first time in years, as a part of the meeting.

"Aakash *bhai* he is Rashid," Jamil said as he flipped his fingers towards Rashid waving him to sit down. Rashid sat on the floor. Jamil looked down on him and asked him to sit on the sofa besides him. Rashid meekly obeyed and hesitantly sat on the sofa besides Jamil.

Aakash bent over to pick up the cigarette packet. He plucked a cigarette from the packet and tucked it in between his lips. He then lit it up using the cigarette lighter and exhaled a thick smoke as he took a deep puff. Slowly he turned his head towards Rashid.

"Oh I am so sorry. Please…" he turned towards Rashid with the cigarette pack, offering him a cigarette. Rashid was flustered by Aakash's mannerism. He was a petty labourer and Aakash was a famous politician, a big man. On other days Rashid would bring cigarette packets, ash tray and liquor bottles for him and would stand outside the room during meetings to offer any other kind of help, but today? Today Jamil had made him sit on the sofa alongside Aakash and he was offering him a cigarette. Rashid didn't understand a thing but his nervousness was evident on his face, which had now turned pale.

Aakash understood his feelings.

"Take it as an honour," he said as he gently shook the cigarette packet in an effort to shake off Rashid from his stupor. Rashid was hesitant, but he lit up a cigarette, albeit reluctantly.

Aakash asked about his family.

"How old are your daughters and what does your son do?"

"Rukhsana is twenty and Tabassum is twelve years old. Akhtar is nine. I have one wife who picks up some odd jobs in the village…" Rashid said hurriedly.

"One wife? And what about the girls Heena and Fawzia with whom you….," Afroz had interrupted Rashid and winked at him dropping innuendoes about the sisters Heena and Fawzia.

"Oh come on Afroz. You don't need to embarrass the poor chap," Jamil castigated Afroz.

Aakash merely smiled, keenly hearing the conversation. Rashid's nerves had calmed down a bit. He felt at ease and had slid back on the sofa, resting comfortably on the sofa's backrest.

Aakash took a long puff from his cigarette and let out a thick smoke. "Do you know why we all respect you so much?" he asked leaning forward, the remnants of inhaled cigarette smoke still pouring from his nostrils and lips.

"It's because you are a Ghazi," he answered without waiting for Rashid's response. "…do you know who is a Ghazi?…a Ghazi is the true soldier of Islam…a crusader who takes it upon himself to defend Islam from the *kufrs* and the apostates and the heretics…all your life you have been working to protect Islam and its teachings…," Aakash had begun his sweet-talk.

Rashid stayed for about an hour and half at Jamil's bungalow, the longest meeting he ever had with Aakash and Jamil. He was all charged up when he left. There was a dramatic change in his body language. He held his head high, shoulders were taut, and he walked with confidence as the Ghazi—the crusader who has to defend Islam. Just when he was walking out of the bungalow, Bilal gave him a small bag and a few hundred rupees. The bag had a bottle of whiskey. Bilal winked at Rashid. He smiled, took the bottle of whiskey and the money and briskly walked away.

The sky, the stars and the moon danced and incandescent bulbs looked like football running all around in the sky. Rashid tried to concentrate but everything around him seemed to dance. Sitting behind Chacha's tea stall Rashid had been drinking the whiskey which Bilal gave him. He had come straight to Chacha's tea stall but he was not present. The lure of exotic whiskey could not hold him, and over the next hour he had gulped the whole bottle and was now completely sloshed.

He could not walk straight and swayed wildly. He whistled and shrieked in ecstasy. He felt he had arrived in life. After years of service Jamil *bhai,* 'the Jamil *bhai'*, who was the richest man in Basera, had finally recognised his loyalty and had made him sit beside him on the couch. Earlier he was relegated to the floor, ate leftover food and had to remain content with the cheap rum that burned his windpipe when he swallowed it. But this exotic whiskey brand was a trophy for Rashid's loyalty, it tasted like fruit juice. It had gelled with his euphoria and gave him a good high. Today was a day for celebrations and Chacha was nowhere to be seen. Rashid blurt out a volley of expletives for his closest aide and companion, Chacha.

Suddenly he turned towards Fawzia's shanty. The sisters lived nearby and Rashid cursed himself for not having thought about the girls earlier. "At least I would have had company while drinking…," he said to himself as an involuntary smile escaped his lips at the thought of Fawzia. "I like Fawzia more than I do Heena. Both the sisters are good but I like Fawzia more and I think Fawzia likes me too," Rashid mumbled as he banged on their door. He kept banging on the wobbly door for several minutes but there was no answer. He had stepped backwards to kick the door and break it open, when he saw a big lock hanging on the door. Fawzia and Heena were not at home. Rashid kept staring at the lock, cursing and abusing the sisters for not being at home to welcome him. After yelling and howling for several minutes he turned around to go, but fell down. After several minutes and several failed attempts later he managed to get up. His steps wobbled as he walked.

Chacha had been sitting with Fawzia and Heena in the living room of Jamil's bungalow when Bilal handed over the bag containing whiskey bottle to Rashid. Chacha had seen Rashid walking outside the bungalow from behind the curtains. He knew that Rashid would go to his tea stall, still he made no efforts to call Rashid and let him know that he was at Jamil's place. Instead, he smiled, a treacherous smile indeed. Bilal carefully closed the entrance gate behind Rashid and walked up to Fawzia and Heena in the living room. The next minute they were in the room with Aakash, Jamil and Afroz.

"Aakash *bhai* the sisters Heena and Fawzia that Nadeem *bhai* had talked about," Jamil said, lighting up a cigarette. Chacha, Bilal and Anwar walked across the room and occupied the chairs besides Afroz. Heena and Fawzia stood like terrified lambs in the middle of the room with a dozen hungry eyes ogling at them. The next moment Jamil curled his lips and thrust the cigarette smoke with his tongue towards the sisters. Heena held back her breath but Fawzia got into a coughing spasm. Heena wrapped her hands around her sister and caressed her back, gently.

"Oh what have you done to this poor little girl," Afroz admonished Jamil as he stood up. He stepped closer to the girls and feigning concern wrapped his hands around Fawzia. Afroz openly felt her up. Tears rolled down from Fawzia's eyes as Heena stood dumbfounded. The next minute Anwar walked up to Heena and began fondling her.

"Enough. Get back both of you," Aakash said firmly. Anwar and Afroz stepped behind and as ordered by Aakash got back to their seats.

"*Salaam-Walekum* Nadeem *bhai*," Aakash had dialled Nadeem. "...yes they are here, standing right in front of me...hmm Heena and Fawzia...yes okay...hmm...okay...yeah fine," Aakash kept nodding to the instructions from Nadeem. They talked for several minutes before Aakash put his phone down.

Aakash kept staring at Heena and Fawzia, turned towards Bilal and asked him to get chairs for them. "Get them some cold water," he asked Chacha. Heena and Fawzia settled on the chair and hurriedly gulped the cold water.

"Look towards me," Aakash ordered. "I hope you remember Nadeem *bhai*?" he asked the sisters and waited for an answer. The girls said "yes" in a meek voice.

"Good. Nadeem *bhai* has told me everything about you and why have you been sent here. I hope you know that he has every bit of information about you both and your family," Aakash said in a stern voice. "Do you both remember what are you supposed to do in this village?"

The girls sat with their heads down. In a feeble voice they said "yes".

"So what is your mandate?" Aakash asked getting slightly closer to them.

"It is to work as domestic help and as maids in village homes," Heena said in a gentle voice.

"And?"

"...to satisfy all of you whenever you so desire." It was Fawzia who spoke this time. She swallowed the venomous disgust for the men around her as she uttered those words. She wanted to spank and whack and thrash each one of the men in the room. Instead, Fawzia had to swallow her fury and utter those submissive words. The emotional upheaval caused a sharp pain in her abdomen and she could almost feel her intestines churning within her. The ambience and air inside the room suffocated her. Her outburst came because she wanted her cross-examination to end quickly. She was mistaken.

"And?" Aakash was not impressed by Fawzia's straight talk and he did not show much interest in her readiness to lie down for men, either.

Heena and Fawzia looked at each other, flustered as to what else they were supposed to do.

Aakash sighed, leaned back on the sofa and rotated his head sideways.

"Your primary purpose is to elicit information and inform us," Aakash said. The sisters looked towards Aakash. They still looked ruffled.

"Okay. Let me explain," Aakash leaned forward and began his glib talk. "...see we are in the middle of this fight for the dominance of believers like us. It's a big battle for the sake of Islam and maintaining Islamic supremacy. It's the battle for Allah. It is Islamic jihad. And in this jihad everybody has a specific role to play. Your job is to keep a close eye on activities in the village, hear the discussions in the households and inform us. This is the basic objective of making you work as domestic help. And you should not worry about the daily expenses... that will be taken care by us. But all this needs to be done discreetly. Nobody in this village should know that you are working for us," Aakash was polite as he spoke.

He then went on to explain how Basera's madrasa was being used by that wretched Maulvi to promote his vested interests. "He nurtures political ambitions. And there's nothing wrong in his having political ambitions. I am a politician, Jamil and Afroz fight elections, but we do so within the ambit of Islamic values. We have never used a madrasa or a mosque in our political battles. But this wicked Maulvi does not shy away from using a madrasa for his own selfish motives," Aakash went on. "...you did well in picking up work at his house. So, what are their future plans with the madrasa?" he asked leaning forward.

Fawzia and Heena were astonished as to how Aakash could know about their visit to Sakina's home. Heena was dumbfounded. She could feel her hands and feet getting cold with fear. Fawzia was terrified too. The sisters could understand that their activities have been under observation. And that they could not bluff them. Fawzia gathered her wits and said softly that it has been just a couple of days since they met and befriended Sakina and her family.

Aakash leaned back and looked towards Bilal and Anwar, the two muggers entrusted with the task of keeping an eye on the activities of Heena and Fawzia. Bilal nodded in their support.

Aakash got up, walked across the room, turned around and came closer to the girls. He could sense that the girls were terrified. He decided to give some pep talk to them to lift up their spirits.

"You girls are doing a great job. And you are doing it for Allah, the all merciful and benevolent. All your actions are for Allah, you must remember. These boys around you... they are giving their life for Islam. They are Ghazis. After a tough day where do they find solace and comfort? They find it with you girls. You have been chosen to comfort these soldiers of Islam," Aakash said smilingly, looking around the men in the room.

"It's good that you had the presence of mind to befriend Maulvi's daughter-in-law. Now try to make her speak about their plans. Also try to enamour his young son Abdul...use your charm to seduce him...try to bed him...indulge in sweet talk with him. The more he gets involved with you the more he will be useful for us...," Aakash's pupils constricted as he detailed the modus operandi for Heena and Fawzia. He further detailed about how the girls should also try and sneak into the homes of Maulvi *sahab's* friends such as Aftab *sahab*, Maqbool *bhai* and Nadeem *bhai*. "Abdul and his friends are young and they are the most vulnerable. These young boys are most likely to fall for your charms. Trap Abdul, cast your spell on him and you will do a great service to Allah," Aakash explained as he slinked off his chair towards the girls.

It had been an hour since the girls came in and were being grilled. Heena was still overwhelmed and terrified but Fawzia had calmed down.

"May I ask you a question?" Fawzia had mustered some courage and decided to bell the cat.

Aakash was pleasantly surprised. He remained quiet. 'Even Jamil and Afroz never have the nerve to ask any question to me and this cheap whore has the audacity to question me, the general secretary of FPI,' he said to himself. Yet, on second thoughts he decided to hear her out.

"Okay go ahead," he said, leaning back on the soft cushion of the chair.

"You are a Hindu, a *kafir* in the Wahhabi parlance. So how can you talk of Islamic jihad and our fight for Islam? How can you expect us to trust you and....?

"Bitch. How dare you talk to Aakash *bhai* like that?" It was Jamil who had lost his control and slapped Fawzia. Shouting his filthiest abuses he was about to hit another blow when Aakash held his hand. Afroz, Bilal and Anwar were enraged too. All were cursing. Heena broke into loud sobs. Fawzia was terrified too, but she maintained her composure.

An astute politician that Aakash was, he was quick to gauge that Fawzia had raised a genuine question. Indeed, he was the only one in the room who was not a Muslim and yet he was calling the shots. 'Today it's Fawzia, tomorrow it may be Jamil or Afroz or anyone. This issue needs to be settled once and for all. I need to nip it in the bud,' he thought and held back Jamil's hand.

"Calm down my friend. The lady has a question and you've hit her. Have some decency while speaking to women," Aakash said lighting up a cigarette. He took several puffs and waved his palm to Jamil and Afroz to calm down.

There was an uneasy clam but the tension had abated. He faced Fawzia.

"Yes you are right Fawzia that I am a Hindu. But you are wrong that I am a *kafir*. I am not. I follow Islam, and in fact I am more Muslim than all of you 'Muslims' in this room put together," Aakash said curling his lips to blow the cigarette smoke from his mouth. "...my name Aakash is just a cover. It's a cover to fool the Hindus into believing that I am a Hindu when in reality I am not. I am a Muslim. I may not be a regular to the mosque or offer *namaz* in the mosque but at the heart I am a Muslim. Nadeem *bhai*, *Maulana* Kamran and several other Muslim clerics in Saudi Arabia know about it. As a strategy I have decided to stick with my name and Hindu identity and yet work for Islamic jihad. And this is exactly what we expect from you both. All your needs...physical, material or monetary are to be met by us. Yet you have to take the cover of a domestic help and elicit information for us. This is your role in Islamic jihad," Aakash said resting his back on the chair. He gave a measured and calculated reply to Fawzia, feeling elated that he could ward off her bait. Aakash had successfully managed to stave off her effort to create a wedge amongst them.

Fawzia was checkmated, at least for now. It was now Aakash's turn to prove that he was boss and the driver of the ship. He took a last puff from his cigarette, crushed its stub in the ash tray and looked towards the girls.

"I hope you don't have any more doubts," Aakash said running his fingers on his lips. His tone suggested that he did not expect any further questions. "Your work is cut out. Get going and get the information for us. And yes Nadeem *bhai* has every information about everyone. So...," he let out a veiled threat by not finishing the sentence on purpose.

The implied meaning of Aakash's words were not lost on the girls and they could very well understand that all these men had the wherewithal to prove to the world that they were cheap whores and that they could do whatever they wanted to them. Heena and Fawzia were subjugated and felt browbeaten. But Aakash was not done. Governance and polity are run by ruling the individual's mind and Aakash wanted to give a final blow to the girls before they left. He winked towards Afroz as he bent over to light another cigarette.

Afroz got up slowly, came closer to Fawzia and with a jerk lifted her in his arms. Before she could understand anything he had carried her inside the side room and slammed the door behind him. A terrified Heena closed her eyes. The next moment she could feel a bunch of hands dragging her. She meekly followed. Anwar, Bilal and Chacha took her to another room. The men brutally assaulted the hapless sisters. As sounds of Fawzia's shrieks and wailings and pleadings filled the air, Aakash was filled with a sense of victory and accomplishment of having vanquished an enemy. He enjoyed every moment of it. He relaxed with his legs on the chair, his left arm wrapped behind his head and cigarette dangling from the right hand.

Jamil brought glasses and a bottle of whiskey. Except for him and Aakash, all were busy assaulting the hapless sisters.

"Keep a close eye on these girls," Aakash said chugging down the whiskey peg. Jamil nodded obediently.

An hour later Fawzia and Heena came out of their rooms, badly bruised and battered. Aakash and Jamil were gone. They were on their way to Delhi. There were other important issues to be sorted out.

Rashid almost fell on the rusty iron gate of his dilapidated house. He banged his head to knock at the iron-gate. Using his hands to knock the gate seemed too taxing.

Rukhsana was sweeping the house's dusty floor when she heard the loud bang. The floor's poorly laid concrete was peeling off from every nook and corner leaving gaping holes in the ground. These holes were filled with clay, brick pieces and concrete slabs giving a patchy look to the floor. Clay and brick pieces did fill in the holes on the floor but generated loads of dust that needed to be mopped every few hours. The kids and their mother had just finished their supper of chapatti and lentils. Rukhsana's mother had asked her to clean the floor and lay down the mat so that they could sleep.

Rukhsana had picked up the broom and had barely begun when she heard the bang on the gate. She knew it was her father, Rashid. She called for her mother and rushed towards the gate. The trademark bang on their gate was now quite familiar, which meant that Rashid had come home drunk.

Rashid's wife had now resigned herself to fate and made no efforts to convince her husband to mend his ways. Rashid, on his part, felt all his actions were justified since his efforts were for the betterment of believers and against the *kafirs*. 'I am a Mujahedeen. I am no ordinary man. Allah has ordained me to work towards saving Muslims from the evil influence of *kafirs*,' he had told his wife umpteen times.

Rukhsana rushed to the gate to find Rashid leaning on it in a sloppy position. She yelled to call upon her mother. Rashid had a heavy built up and when drunk he was much too heavy for anyone in the family to carry him all alone. His wife, Rukhsana, the second daughter Tabassum and son Akhtar supported him so that he could drag himself and lie on the cot. Leaning on his wife and kids, Rashid cursed under his breath.

Rashid's coming home drunk meant that the family's ordeal was to begin. Oftentimes he would throw up and then blurt out the choicest of expletives to everybody in the house. Rukhsana would then clean up the pungent smelling barf without uttering a word. She had used up all her tears and not a speck of water would show up in her eyes. Today was no different. Rashid was cursing as he dragged along holding his wife's shoulders. A couple of steps inside the house, he threw up.

It was almost afternoon when Rashid reached Chacha's tea stall.

He had woken up quite late and felt tizzy due to an overdose of last night's whiskey. Rukhsana and her mother had left early morning to work in neighbouring homes. It was their job to clean utensils, cook food, care for the cattle at other's homes. This was the only reliable source of income for the family. Rashid hardly brought any money home. He came home drunk, ate and slept. In the mornings he shouted for food, ate to his content and left. Rukhsana, twelve-year old Tabassum, nine-year old Akhtar and their mother maintained a stoic silence when Rashid was at home. They had resigned themselves to the fact that this was part of their life and there was hardly anything that they could do about it.

Rashid was least concerned about his wife and children. And rather than being ashamed to elude his responsibilities he took pride in his acts. He firmly believed that since he had devoted his life to the larger cause of Islam so he need not be bothered about petty issues like earning for his family.

He woke up hurling abuses at Rukhsana and asked for tea. His younger daughter Tabassum and Akhtar, who were at home, informed that Rukhsana and mother were out working in the neighbouring households. Rashid demanded tea from the twelve year old Tabassum. The little girl somehow managed and served tea to her father.

After tea, Rashid took a cold water bath to beat last night's hangover and then stepped out for Chacha's tea stall. He grinned thinking about his last night's meeting with Aakash *bhai*. He had proclaimed Rashid as a Ghazi. And he had celebrated his anointment with the whiskey gifted by Bilal.

It was late afternoon and Chacha's tea stall was buzzing with customers. There were animated discussions about how computers can help change an individual's fortunes. Chacha, as usual, remained a spectator keeping a fox like eye on the discussions. He spoke only occasionally whenever he felt that the talks and discussions were dying down. His words worked to add a fresh piece of charcoal to the dying fiery discussions at the shack.

A wry smile burst through Chacha's lips, which looked wicked through his unkempt beard, when he saw Rashid coming towards his stall. Rashid was getting charged up as he overheard the ongoing animated discussions at the tea stall.

"…this is going to be a game changer for us. Unless and until our children get modern education who will employ them and until we find ways to increase our income how will our living standards improve," said Maqsood, the rickshaw puller to other labourers, who listened attentively.

"And what are you going to say to Allah? That you have fallen for the tricks of the Satan. You are straying away from the path of Islam," Rashid thundered as he stepped inside the tea stall, blurting a volley of expletives on Maulvi *sahab*.

"This wretched Maulvi is leading all Muslims on the path of apostasy," Rashid continued cursing Maulvi *sahab*.

"Why are you so upset Rashid *bhai*? We need to understand that whatever Maulvi *sahab* and his son are doing will, in effect, help us lead a decent and prosperous life…," Maqsood made a vain attempt to calm down Rashid. But he cut him short.

"What is this decency and prosperity that you talk about? The only goal of believers is to walk on the path laid down by Allah. This should be our only aim," Rashid roared. His gaze was so intense that it unnerved other rickshaw pullers and labourers who had till now found a valid point in Maqsood's argument. Rashid was infamous for his temper. He often picked up fights over frivolous issues. That he was closer to Jamil and worked for him meant villagers saw him as a walking dynamite waiting to explode at the slightest provocation. None liked to mess with a hothead like him.

Today was different. Maqsood was in no mood to relent, today. He decided to confront him.

"Allah has said in the Holy Quran that it should be the goal of believers to acquire knowledge. Now what is a computer? Well, it is a machine that will help our children gain knowledge so that they can acquire necessary skills and get a good job. You know why people like me pull a rickshaw for living? It's simply because I am not literate nor do I have any special skill set. I do not want my son to pull a rickshaw like me, rather I want him to get a good job and the best way to find a decent job is to seek good education. Maulvi *sahab* understands that computers will enable our children in their education that is why he has introduced computers at the Basera madrasa. Rashid *bhai* you should also send your children to Maulvi *sahab's* madrasa. Your son Akhtar wants to study why don't you send him to Maulvi *sahab's* madrasa? Maulvi *sahab* is a generous man he will forgive you for your misgivings and…."

"And? What do you think that I will send my son to that *kafir*? Enough of your non-sense talks," Rashid had chugged the steaming hot tea in a single gulp. He got up and held Maqsood by his neck, pressing it hard. Maqsood was a frail man and in physical strength he was absolutely no match to Rashid.

Everybody at the tea stall ran towards Rashid and pulled his hand to dissuade him from strangling Maqsood. Rashid loosened his grip over Maqsood's neck and he broke out into violent coughing. Rashid felt a sense of power and pleasure in the way everyone ran towards him pulling his hand and pleading to leave Maqsood. Rashid's freeing Maqsood's neck was like the indulgence of power play by the hawk that gives up on a dove in a mark of confidence that it can pounce back anytime, whenever it wills and whenever it has the mood.

"I am not going to loosen my grip the next time," Rashid warned Maqsood in a flat tone. He was unusually calm as he spoke. There was stunned silence at the tea stall and all discussions had stopped abruptly. Maqsood quietly left the place and all others silently followed him.

Rashid sniffed victory as they left. He got up, paced towards the counter where packets of potato chips dangled from a thin sling. He tore a packet of the potato chips and thrust it into his big mouth.

"Chacha I am hungry," he said.

Chacha didn't say a word. But served him tea, boiled eggs, omelette, fried *pakoras* and other packed eatables. On usual days he would have prepared omelette and bread for Rashid, but today he asked him to step inside the stall's kitchen. He asked the help to get a table and chair for Rashid.

"Have some mutton and rice. Eat it to your heart's content," Chacha said as he let out a wicked smile. Rashid mixed the gravy with rice and started tearing the mutton pieces with his teeth. He gave out a loud burp after he was through. He left his plate on the table and simply walked out without saying a single word to anyone. Chacha picked up his mobile phone to dial Jamil's number.

22 .

Aakash had been talking to Nadeem about the developments at Basera village. Nadeem expressed his displeasure that despite Afroz's presence in the management committee of Basera madrasa, Maulvi *sahab* was able to get computers. A day earlier the Wahhabi Sheikhs had phoned Nadeem and castigated him for not being able to handle the matter.

"Don't think that it's just the question of one village, or one madrasa and its Maulvi. The issue is about maintaining our grip over Muslim minds. If this grip slacks at one madrasa or one mosque then within no time we will loose our clutch on every single Muslim mind across the world that we have been holding on for centuries," the burly Wahhabi cleric had told Nadeem over phone. He had ordered for an early resolution of this issue.

Computers on their own were not much of a concern for the Wahhabis, rather their concern was about its potential use. A computer opens new vistas of knowledge, connects an individual to the whole world, breaks boundaries, informs and educates. The source and flow of information is democratised as no one has the monopoly over information. It was this that had irked the Wahhabi clerics, Sheikhs and financiers sitting in Saudi Arabia. The very foundation of myths that these Wahhabis had assiduously built over the years seemed threatened by this humble machine with a monitor and keyboard.

The more than enthusiastic response with which other villages had received computers added to their concern. Several other madrasas, which till a few weeks back, were undecided about the introduction of computers were now actively conducting a feasibility analysis to introduce computers for their students.

And not just computers, Maulvi *sahab* had introduced history textbooks as well. Over the years a narrative had been built among Muslims of the Indian sub-continent that they have descended upon this land from the hot Arabian deserts and that they have come here to rule the native population. This narrative of Muslims being the direct descendants from Saudi Arabia has further ramifications. Anything pertaining to Arab and Saudi Arabia in particular is branded as Allah's own ordinance and fatwas and diktats of a cleric who come from Saudi Arabia are hailed upon as binding on all Muslims. A thug Kamran is anointed as *Maulana* from Saudi Arabia and no one dares to ask a question. A sense of alienation is created and false sense of victimhood is carved out. All this goes on because of the fabricated falsities being taught about the origin of Muslims in Indian sub-continent.

Maulvi *sahab's* plan to teach history threatened to upset everything. With history teaching it would dawn upon the Muslims that they did not arrive in droves from the hot desert lands of Arabia rather they are the religious converts whose forefathers died fighting the marauding armies from Arab and Central Asia. With this realisation they would refuse to buy the argument of Muslim victimisation. They would demand answers about fatwas and edicts. They would start thinking. They would question. And this will mark the beginning of the end of the politics of Muslim victimisation. The likes of Aakash and Jamil whose entire political careers rested on feeding upon the narrative of Muslim victimisation were worried about this juggernaut and wanted it to be stopped. Nadeem, Usman and scores of financiers sitting pretty in Delhi, Mumbai, Hyderabad and in Saudi Arabia knew that if the narrative of Muslim victimisation is diluted then pushing of the Wahhabi agenda would become impossible. And with this the billions of petrodollars that flowed in every year from Saudi Arabia's Wahhabis in the form of grants and project contracts will be lost forever.

Aakash and Nadeem had been in touch over phone, devising strategies. Nadeem's higher up Usman had given clear instructions to douse the fire before it could turn into a firestorm. The Wahhabi strategists were rattled by Maulvi *sahab's* plans. Though there was no clear strategy about how to tackle Maulvi *sahab,* yet there was a near consensus that he needed to be sorted out.

It had been two days since Jamil came to Delhi along with Aakash. The news from Basera continued to depress them. Enthusiasm across several adjoining villages had been building about modern subjects and computer teaching at their madrasas. Fawzia and Heena who had begun to work at Maulvi *sahab's* home had informed last evening that a team of management committee members from five different madrasas were due to meet Maulvi *sahab* in the coming days. These five madrasas were far off from Basera and were located in different electoral constituencies.

"I am reaching Delhi by evening. Let's re-think our strategy," Nadeem told Aakash over phone. He had been to Mumbai for a meeting with Usman. The anxiety in his voice was palpable. Aakash understood. He could hardly wait for the evening. The churn was faster than he had thought.

Nadeem de-boarded the flight and reached FPI office. He walked straight to Aakash's room. Aakash had been anxiously waiting for him. The situation was slowly but steadily slipping out of their hands. They needed to act fast.

Their closed door meeting lasted for a little over two hours.

Aakash was speaking on phone when Anjali stepped in his office room. She had been waiting patiently for the meeting to get over. She often sought favours from Aakash for her friends. Aakash had obliged her, till now. A minute ago Nadeem had stepped out and left the party office. Anjali walked in, the next minute.

"Yes, you need to come over tomorrow and bring him along. Don't dilly-dally, treat this as your first priority," he hung up and stared at the computer monitor kept at his desk, unmindful and unaware of Anjali, who was sitting across the table.

"You look worried. All's okay?"

"Ah no ... I mean yes. Yeah good that you came in. I was about to call you."

"How's the situation on ground? How's our support this time?"

"We might lose support if this continues. We have to think of a strategy and this has to come fast"

"What's happened?"

"There's a village called Basera and the village's Maulvi has got computers in the madrasa. He plans to teach Mathematics, Science, History and Economics. And the villagers are ebullient about learning computers, Maths, History..."

"So this is good. Isn't it?

"Anjali don't act like a fool. Do you even understand the larger political implications of computers being taught at a village madrasa? There are reports that other adjoining Muslim majority villages are planning to introduce computers in their madrasas. If this happens it will be a catastrophe for us."

"Computers in madrasa is a progressive move. How can you call it a catastrophe?"

"Because not every Muslim can be allowed to learn and read and think. If that happens they will develop their own narrative and no one will believe our narratives that we propagate for the Muslims"

"Narratives that 'We' propagate? There is only one narrative that we fight for and that's the narrative based on truth and facts. What are you trying to prove?"

"Anjali this is not college. This is realpolitik. You need to keep your idealism aside. You are naïve. Now please excuse me, we can debate these issues some other time. Jamil is scheduled to meet me tomorrow early morning and I need to prepare for tomorrow's meet. There is some important project that we are working upon. I want you to take charge of it," Aakash turned his head sideways as he adjusted his glasses.

"Jamil, that creep. And you need to 'prepare' for a meeting with this person. Good luck. I am not getting involved into anything where this Jamil is involved," Anjali said, crossing her hands.

"Anjali you're still a kid. You don't understand realpolitik. You don't have to report to Jamil. You will continue to be associated with the FPI," Aakash said with nonchalance as he adjusted papers on his desk.

Anjali stood up, swung her head sideways in frustration. She wanted to debate and discuss this issue, but Aakash was not in a mood to talk. She felt if there was merit in Aakash's argument then why was he shying away from discussing the finer details? She turned around to leave when she remembered the work that she came in for.

"One of my friend banged his motor bike into a car last night and the police has confiscated his bike. He has been calling me for help…"

"How many boyfriends do you have?" Aakash winked at her.

"Oh…please shut up. He is just a friend. Nothing more, nothing less," Anjali protested.

"I was just kidding," Aakash smiled and scribbled a phone number on a paper. "…call him up, say I have asked to help. He will sort it out for you. "

Anjali thanked for the help and stepped out of the room. Aakash continued to ogle at Anjali as she closed the door behind her. He let out a cold sigh and then got busy with his computer.

The next morning Jamil and Zamiluddin were finalising finer details of the Urdu newspaper at Aakash's office. Zamiluddin was only concerned about the money he makes from the venture while Aakash wanted the Urdu newspaper to cement the radical Wahhabi Islamic ideology across the region among the Muslim electorate. The meeting ended in an hour after

Aakash committed a steady supply of money for Zamiluddin, and in return retained complete editorial control. Nadeem had already roped in *Maulana* Kamran and his ilk for a regular stream of articles for the Urdu newspaper. Aakash gave a week's time to Zamiluddin to sort out formalities of paper designing and printing. Jamil was to use his network across villages to build hype for the refurbished Urdu newspaper and ensure a wide circulation. The paper was named *"Allah-e-Niyamat"*.

Niyamat is nourishment and prosperity from almighty and the strategy was to project the words published in this Urdu newspaper as diktats from the heavens above. *Allah-e-Niyamat* was to be branded as the newspaper, which is in Urdu the language of an average Muslim and which is the votary of social upheaval. The articles in *Allah-e-Niyamat* were to be written in a way that feeds into the victimhood of Muslims and yet opposes any kind of social reform for them. It had to present a world view where whimsical fatwas could rule the roost and fear of persecution could be ensconced in the Muslim hearts.

Aakash briefed Anjali about their Urdu newspaper. Her job was to coordinate and supervise things for *Allah-e-Niyamat* in Delhi. Over the next two days office space was leased in Delhi for *Allah-e-Niyamat*, computers and furniture were bought. Printing and distribution network were sorted out and people were hired. Aakash constituted a separate team of researchers whose main job was to scan each day's news events and spin them in a way for *Allah-e-Niyamat* such that the gullible reader feels Muslims are being persecuted for no fault of theirs. Articles based on interpretation of Islamic texts were to be given by *Maulana* Kamran and his associates. Jamil was to ensure that *Allah-e-Niyamat* reached as many homes as possible across villages. Afroz's task was to ensure that Muslims across all villages read and talk about the issues raised in their newspaper. He had ensured that all tea shacks, barber shops, eating outlets, provision stores get free copies of *Allah-e-Niyamat* across the region.

Nadeem had loosened his purse strings for the entire venture. Zamiluddin, was anointed as the editor-in-chief but he was actually a glorified manager whose main job was to ensure that every morning copies of *Allah-e-Niyamat* reach the bus stop on time for speedy delivery across villages.

Anjali remained a mute spectator during these preparations. She was still unable to fathom where did she fit in an Urdu newspaper. She did not understand the language nor was able to read or write Urdu. Why on earth, Aakash would choose me to lead this venture, she asked herself. When she asked this question to Aakash he had merely smiled and said, 'Just do as I say. I have some big plans for you.'

Anjali was pursuing Ph.D. from Delhi's prestigious Jawaharlal Nehru University, the JNU. She was a strong votary of equality and had vehemently opposed religious fundamentalism since her college days. Aakash spotted her during a debate at JNU where she was defending the rights of women in repressed societies. Initially it was Anjali's beauty that had caught Aakash's eye. She was wearing a tight tee and Aakash could not move his eyes from her bosom. He was smitten by her charm. After the debate, Anjali approached Aakash and explained to him that she was a great admirer of the ideals that FPI stood for. She asked if she could join the party as an apprentice. Aakash had found it difficult to suppress his excitement over her proposal. Almost immediately, he accepted Anjali into his party. He had held her hand a wee bit longer when the two shook hands. This was a year ago.

Allah-e-Niyamat was a big project that was being directly monitored by Aakash. In fact, Anjali had no role to play in *Allah-e-Niyamat* but it was Aakash's shrewd way of handing out a lollypop to the beautiful girls he had his eyes on. Even earlier he had put Anjali only on projects that were directly monitored by him. It did cause heartburn among the older and more experienced party cadres, but they never spoke out in open due to Aakash's stature within the party. Anjali believed it was her merit that made her Aakash's favourite. It never crossed her mind that a middle aged man could be interested in her.

A week had passed since Jamil and Zamiluddin met Aakash and the plans to roll out *Allah-e-Niyamat* were finalised. Things were unfolding at a breakneck speed and Anjali was still at her wit's end. She could not understand the undue rush to bring out an Urdu newspaper with a nincompoop Zamiluddin as its editor.

Anjali finished her lunch that afternoon and had bent over on the table for a quick nap. A rude vibration of the smartphone woke her up from the siesta.

"Anjali be ready. I am sending a car to pick you. This is really important and I want you to come," Aakash announced and slammed the phone. He did not wait for an answer.

'Probably it is urgent and must be really important,' Anjali said to herself giving Aakash the benefit of doubt. Aakash was usually very sweet to her and this was the first time that he sounded blunt.

In less than ten minutes a black sedan pulled over inside the Party Office and its driver asked the security guard to get Anjali. The driver sported a thick beard minus the moustache, and looked like a menacing ape. His demeanour made Anjali nervous and just before she was to step inside the car she called Anil, her colleague at the party office to accompany her. The driver winced and twirled his upper lip in disapproval but Anjali said confidently that Aakash had asked the two of them to come along.

After about fifteen minutes' drive, Anjali and Anil found themselves in the lobby of a five star hotel. The driver ushered them to the suite. Inside were Nadeem and Aakash.

Aakash was grinning from ear to ear as he saw Anjali enter the room. His chuckle turned into a frown when he saw Anil behind her.

"How come you are here?" Aakash was curt, as he asked Anil. He had made no efforts to hide his annoyance. Anil did not speak and looked askance towards Anjali.

"I asked him to accompany me. He was reluctant to come along but I dragged him?"

"Dragged him? But why?"

214

"Because you had sent that ape-looking beast to pick me up and I felt quite nervous sitting alone in the car with him," Anjali quipped.

"Oh my young lady, Bashir is a deeply religious man and he can never hurt any of my guests. And more so when my guest is a beautiful young woman." It was Nadeem who unabashedly leered at Anjali, his eyes following each of her curves.

Anjali cursed under her breath as she straightened her clothes.

"What will you have? Some fruit juice or something hard," Nadeem asked alluding if she was interested in having a peg of whiskey.

"No nothing. Thank you," she said with a straight face and looked towards Aakash.

Aakash stood up and pulled up a black bag from the closet. He bent towards Anjali and rolled down the bag's zip to reveal stacks of rupees stuffed inside.

"Take this bag with you. Jamil will reach Party Office by evening. Hand this bag to him and say Nadeem *bhai* has sent it. Anil please ensure that other than you no one else knows about it. These are crucial election times. You understand what I mean to say," Aakash explained. He was blunt, his eyes focussed and his tone harsh.

Anjali picked up the bag and was about to leave when Nadeem called her.

"Here take this. It's for you," he had pulled out a wad of notes from his coat.

"And may I ask you, what's this for?" Anjali asked with a rather stern face.

"Oh come on young lady. This is a small gift for the beautiful girl," Nadeem looked lecherously at Anjali's bosom as he licked his lips.

"Disgusting," Anjali cursed in a hushed tone, she turned around and walked out with brisk steps. She had expected Aakash to come to her defence but he stood smiling as Nadeem openly flirted with her.

She had wanted to take an auto rickshaw but Anil advised against the idea.

He argued that they were carrying a bag full of cash and it was not wise to travel in an auto rickshaw or any other public transport. Once again, she was forced to sit in that ape-faced Bashir's car who drove them to the Party Office. Bashir was Nadeem's trusted man who doubled up as a driver or as a watchman. He was the one who was entrusted with the task of keeping an eye on Heena and Fawzia at their guesthouse and had later on raped the sisters.

Jamil, Zamiluddin and Afroz came late in the afternoon at the FPI office. They simply barged into the room where Anjali was sipping tea with other party workers.

"Anjali come here," Jamil announced as he entered the room. Anjali frowned at the undue authority in Jamil's voice. She looked around at the party cadres for support but they merely giggled and made suggestive gestures. She decided to confront Jamil and was about to lecture him on some basic mannerisms when Anil stepped inside.

"*Salam-walekum* Jamil *bhai* I was waiting for you. Come, we are already late for our project," Anil said smiling at Jamil, and almost pulled him outside. He deftly prevented what looked like a possible showdown of words. They walked over to Aakash's room.

Inside Aakash's room Anil opened the locker and handed over the bag to Jamil. Jamil unzipped the bag to check the cash inside it. The next moment his phone rang. It was Aakash. The two men talked in monosyllables. Jamil hung up, picked the bag and waved at Zamiluddin and Afroz to follow him. He winked at Anjali before leaving. Anjali remained silent, she felt disgusted by the double-speak and lecherous attitude of all these men around her.

Over the next few days elaborate preparations were made to bring out the first edition of *Allah-e-Niyamat*. The design was finalised, articles were being written, dummy print-runs were done and circulation issues were discussed. Big hoardings and posters were put up across several villages about the launch of a pious Islamic newspaper that would be sharia compliant, raise genuine issues that concern Muslims and would educate people about pious

Islamic doctrines.

The inaugural edition of *Allah-e-Niyamat* came out on Friday. Almost the entire edition harped upon the victimhood of Muslims. There was an article about how Muslims were being persecuted for practicing their faith by the non-believer *kafirs*. Another talked about the American atrocities on Muslims across the world. A column talked about Israel's illegal occupation of Palestine. Even the local happenings were written with a twist which gave an impression to the readers that administration and the existing political leadership have given a raw deal to Muslim interests. The underlying tone of *Allah-e-Niyamat* was to present that the Muslims have been wronged against and are the worst sufferers. Very subtly a few articles argued that the path to redemption for Muslims is to follow the path of Islam.

The first copy of *Allah-e-Niyamat* was well received. It was the first Urdu newspaper to be brought out for the villagers which gave them a perspective that globally Muslims were being victimised. This had a far reaching effect on the impressionable minds. An ordinary village Muslim now felt that his fight was not alone. He was now being told that their Muslim brethren in far-off pious lands have been at the receiving end, and it is the common fight that will see them through.

Over next few days the tone and tenor of *Allah-e-Niyamat* was to cement the narrative about Muslim victimhood. The guided discussions by Jamil's men at tea stalls, barber shops and other such places further fuelled the indoctrination of vulnerable minds. Besides establishing the narrative about Muslim being a victim the paper graduated towards unleashing the Wahhabi ideology. Gradually, articles and columns started appearing which emphasised that only when each Muslim follows the righteous path of Islam, will the condition of Muslims improve. *Maulana* Kamran through several articles advocated and exhorted each of the righteous Muslim to castigate, admonish and discipline fellow Muslims who were found to be deviating from the path of righteous Islam. And this righteous path was the Wahhabi ideology that he ordained through his columns in *Allah-e-Niyamat*. And then there were a series of articles that slammed the study of computers for true and pious Muslims. Computerisation was dubbed as an American conspiracy to snatch employment opportunities from poor

Muslims and gradually push them towards apostasy. Internet was proclaimed as the devil's tool that brought in *haraam* stuff to Muslims.

"...it's the duty of Muslims to stay away from all that is *haraam* and forbidden in Islam...computers and internet are among the things that Allah has forbidden for Muslims...," screamed one of the articles in *Allah-e-Niyamat*.

These articles and columns did have an impact. Several madrasas that had begun the process to introduce computer education for their students had now postponed their decisions fearing social sanctions against them.

It had been almost a month since *Allah-e-Niyamat* was launched. The response had been good, at least for now. The paper's circulation had nearly tripled to around three lakh copies in this short time frame. Most of these were distributed free to the shops and village homes but Nadeem and Aakash were happy. They had found a whip to rein in Maulvi *sahab* and his grandiose ideals. Jamil and Afroz felt relaxed as ground reports suggested they were gaining ground. Heena and Fawzia had been reporting that *Allah-e-Niyamat* was read with veneration in several households of Basera.

After much efforts, things were getting back on track for Aakash and Jamil, or so it seemed. Articles and columns arrived from the Wahhabi preachers in Saudi Arabia and were being published in *Allah-e-Niyamat*. Jamil and Afroz had been given clear instructions to inform each and every development across the region on a real time basis. Aakash was now busy with developments in other constituencies of the country and other party work. Nadeem was busy with his business. The Wahhabi clerics in Saudi were now relatively relaxed.

Maulvi *sahab* had stepped out to buy groceries that afternoon.

"*Salam-walekum* Maulvi *sahab*," Amina greeted Maulvi *sahab* as she walked over to Majid's grocery store. Even before Maulvi *sahab* could return her greetings with a *walekum-assalam*, Majid rebuked Amina.

"How come you've stepped out uncovered?" Majid castigated Amina in a terse voice. Amina was in her late thirties and mother of three children. She was wearing full sleeved, loosely fitted clothes that fully covered her body. Perplexed she looked towards Maulvi *sahab*. Majid was merely a village shopkeeper, he was not even remotely related to her and he had no business making comments on her dress.

"...don't you know that our Islamic rules mandate that a woman put on a *burqa* or a hijab before stepping out of her house? Don't you know of this?" Majid howled at her. His tone was laced with a snobbish tinge that he knew much more about Islam and sharia laws than anybody else.

"Where is this written and where have you read this?" Maulvi *sahab's* voice was polite but firm.

"*Allah-e-Niyamat*. I read it in the *Allah-e-Niyamat*," Majid said confidently.

"And how do you know that *Allah-e-Niyamat* gives you the correct interpretation of Islam," Maulvi *sahab* retorted.

Majid argued back that because *Allah-e-Niyamat* was an Urdu newspaper that was being run by Muslims and all those who write in it are Muslim scholars so whatever it says must be true.

"Does having a Muslim-sounding name makes someone a Muslim? And have you enquired where have these 'Muslim scholars' of *Allah-e-Niyamat* studied and what makes them qualified to talk authoritatively about the Islamic jurisprudence?" Maulvi *sahab* had shot a volley of questions. By now a small crowd had gathered outside Majid's shop. Several bystanders overheard the conversation and gathered around.

Majid kept quiet. He had no answer. Maulvi *sahab* had not raised his voice or threatened him, but his sharp and pointed questions made Majid helpless. He found himself completely ill-equipped to deal with Maulvi *sahab's* logical questioning.

"...meaning of a veil or a *burqa* in Islam means that one should put a veil over one's ego, not boast about the good deeds rather continue to do them selflessly. Whoever argues that *burqa* means incarcerating woman into black tents has not understood the spirit of Islam, rather they are propagating a parochial interpretation of Islamic teachings for their own political benefits. Forcing Muslim women to wear a *burqa* or a hijab is dirty politics. It is recommended by selfish people who want to forcefully subjugate a Muslim woman into submission. The Holy Quran does not say that woman should be relegated into black tents rather it insists on equal participation of woman in a society," Maulvi *sahab* explained to the motley crowd that had gathered outside Majid's shop.

Among the bystanders were Fawzia and Heena who were passing by and had stopped over to listen to the arguments. Also present were Abdul and Sakina, beaming with pride at Maulvi *sahab's* knowledge and perseverance to clear doubts about Islam among fellow villagers.

Argument can only be beaten by counter arguments and logic, Abdul thought. He felt piqued at the grand madrasa congregation for having denied permission to video-record discussions on Islamic teachings and show them on the madrasa computers.

Abdul had been extremely busy since computers were installed last month at the madrasa. Initial teething troubles after computer installations that ranged from networking issues, internet connections, devising course content for students, preparation of notes and then meeting with members of other madrasa committees had kept him tied up. Ditto for Maulvi *sahab*. Initially they also felt excited about the launch of an Urdu newspaper *Allah-e-Niyamat* but when they came to know that Jamil and his band were behind it, they became sceptical. When Maulvi *sahab* saw Kamran's article with his photograph on the front page of the paper he had discarded it without even bothering to read it further. He had said it was a waste of time to read the thoughts of a crook. Maulvi *sahab* and his family had been busy with teachings at the madrasa, having dismissed *Allah-e-Niyamat* as another stunt that will fizzle out. They were wrong. Just like termites that slowly and steadily eats up wood from within, *Allah-e-Niyamat* had begun gnawing the mind space of Muslims across the entire region. The Wahhabis had steadily clawed back and strengthened their vice-like grip on the thoughts of Muslims.

"Why would Allah want us women to be covered in these uncomfortable black tents? Isn't what Maulvi *sahab* explained about *burqa* makes better sense?" Fawzia asked Heena as they walked away from Majid's shop.

"Why do you want to invite trouble for yourself? Just keep quiet and do as is required of us. We are just maids and we do not understand the political dynamics... plus we don't even know if Maulvi *sahab* is an Islamic scholar..."

"Maulvi *sahab* is revered as an Islamic scholar not only in Basera but in several adjoining villages," a woman said interrupting Heena. She turned around.

"*Salam-walekum.* I am Rukhsana. I was walking behind you and heard you discuss about Maulvi *sahab* so..."

"*Walekum-assalam* Rukhsana. I am Fawzia and she is my sister Heena. We are new to this village and work as domestic help," Fawzia was rather quick to introduce herself and her sister.

The three girls then walked along, chatting among themselves. Rukhsana told them she had been living in Basera since her childhood. Fawzia was happy that she could find another soulmate with whom she could spend some easy moments. From that day onwards they usually met and talked. The girls found it easy to bond together. Fawzia told Rukhsana about how she was duped into a marriage and then she landed by chance to this village along with her sister. Rukhsana told them about her family, her younger brother and sister, her mother and the drunkard father. None of them talked about the dark secrets of their lives. So Fawzia and Heena did not talk about their real role as an informer to Jamil and to satisfy the carnal desires of his men and Rukhsana never revealed that the name of her drunkard father was Rashid. The girls were just getting to know each other and had shared only a few aspects of their lives. Fawzia wanted to reveal everything to Rukhsana and think of a possible solution but wanted to wait for an opportune time. But she knew little of the new storm that was looming in the background.

23 .

Abdul was sitting at Arjun's home discussing about his dream to start that tomato ketchup unit at Basera. The friends had been to the bank in the morning to enquire about the status of their loan application. They were informed that the loan amount would be sanctioned very soon. Arjun was quite happy for Abdul. He knew Abdul had a natural acumen for business and that his venture would be a great success. Nobody, except Arjun, knew how much the tomato ketchup unit meant for Abdul. He had been discussing this idea since his college days. And now bank manager had put faith in his vision and the project.

But Abdul was relatively quiet today. He should have been ebullient and jumping with joy but he gazed blankly as he sipped his chai.

"Abdul what's the matter? You don't seem to be happy today?" Arjun asked.

"Yeah...I mean no, I am fine"

"No you are not. What's the matter?" Arjun asked, wrapping his arm around Abdul's shoulder.

Abdul then went on to explain about how Jamil and his gang's Urdu newspaper had begun to sow poison into the minds of village Muslims.

"If this continues then our efforts at the madrasa to teach maths, science computers and other subjects will have no meaning. Already Afroz is against teaching of computers at the madrasa. I am sure he will come up with some other strategy in the next management committee meeting," Abdul rued.

"And what about your plan to video-record the discussions on Islamic teachings…"

"That's been stalled Arjun. Try to understand. Afroz has his men planted all across… this Jamil and his accomplice Afroz are flush with funds, plus these 'Maulana Kamran' types," Abdul cursed under his breath. "This battle is not as easy as it had appeared to me," he added, taking a deep breath. He leaned forward and put down the chai cup on table.

Arjun understood the situation's gravity. He was at his wit's end. The friends were quietly nibbling the biscuits without saying anything. They were thinking and thinking hard. No solution appeared in sight. And then Arjun jumped up.

"Let's catch the bull by its horns. Yes it's true that they are resource-rich and are flush with funds. But it's a battle of wits and we are better off than these rascals," Arjun said as he detailed the plan. Abdul had several doubts.

"Abdul, my friend, please try to understand that it's better to fight the battle with a knife in hand rather than wait for the sword to arrive. At least we can stop the enemy in its tracks and prevent it from surging ahead," Arjun explained.

Abdul smiled, which was the first time since morning. He turned around to go.

"Where?" Arjun asked.

"To make preparations. I need to chalk out a strategy and get it rolling. Come to my home in the evening. I will need your help," Abdul roared as he kick-started his motorbike and rode off.

Arjun had argued that if illogical, irrational and devious arguments being given out in an Urdu newspaper is influencing the mind space of gullible villagers then Abdul needs to bring out his own Urdu newspaper which could refute the devious stuff doled out by *Allah-e-Niyamat* and explain the Islamic scriptures in their correct perspective.

Maulvi *sahab* was at home, reading a book when Abdul came rushing to him. He apprised his *Abbu* about the plans to start their own Urdu newspaper.

"Your enthusiasm makes me happy and sad," Maulvi *sahab* said, as he gently closed the book and kept it on his lap.

"…happy because I can see the enthusiasm in you to do something better, the eagerness to fight the wrongs in the society and gusto to devote your time for a social cause. Yet, I feel sad for you because this is a rough path and it's extremely unlikely that you will receive support from any quarter. The people whom we are fighting are quite powerful. They have the money and the muscle power, while you are short on both. How are you going to sustain my son? Of course, I am there for you but this will be a protracted battle and you will need several warriors to stand by your side. But, what will happen when I am gone?"

"Don't worry *Abbu*. As long as you trust me I do not care for anything. I will fight with whatever resources I have at hand. You have taught me that it's better to take small steps towards the righteous path rather than stand still and not move at all. Let me take those small steps. Just be with me on my side and I promise that I will make a difference," Abdul said. His voice was earnest and he believed in what he said.

Maulvi *sahab* lifted his head and looked at his son. He did not utter a word, but raised his hand and gently caressed Abdul's head. There were no further questions.

Maulvi sahab's thoughts wandered on how to help his son. He knew there was merit in the idea but he did not have the necessary funds to help out his son. At his age he did not want to approach any of his wealthy friends for money. But if he, Abdul's father, would not arrange funds for his son for a pious effort then what use are his contacts? He remained engrossed in his thoughts.

Maulvi *sahab* finished his lunch without uttering a single word. He got up, washed his hands and went inside his room. Begum *sahiba*, unaware of these talks was busy cleaning up the kitchen. Fawzia and Heena were cleaning the courtyard.

Abdul's thoughts wandered too. He was well aware of the fact that starting a newspaper was no joke. It involved huge costs and especially after the recent renovation of the madrasa how will he arrange for fresh funds to start off a newspaper. He was blankly staring at his plate when Sakina came over to put some rice in it. Abdul held her hand. "I am done," he said and walked with brisk steps to his room. Perplexed at his behaviour, Sakina followed him.

"Do you endorse my decision?" Abdul asked Sakina, rather bluntly. She looked puzzled, trying to make sense of what her husband meant. Abdul held her hand and drew her closer.

"I do not have funds nor do I have other resources, yet I am planning to start an Urdu newspaper. I am doing this because I do not want to sit idle and allow the likes of Jamil to ruin my village. I cannot be a mute spectator and…"

"I am with you in all your decisions," Sakina said before Abdul could finish. She gently pressed his hand. "I know your intentions are right and I am with you in all your decisions."

Abdul looked in her eyes, came closer and gently hugged her. She wrapped her arms around him and the two remained in an embrace. She could feel Abdul's warm breath on her neck.

An hour later, Abdul lay on his back as Sakina rested her head on his bare chest. Gently, she asked: "What's the name of our newspaper?" Abdul lifted his head by a notch, looked towards her, curled his lips and said he hadn't given it a thought.

"Mudaakhilat, how's this name?" Sakina lifted her head for a moment, looked at Abdul and before he could say anything she explained further.

"...I have a very simple point. Since our newspaper will intervene and correct the erroneous discourse being established by Jamil and his band of crooks it's good to have this word on the masthead. Let's announce our intention and take these monsters head on," Sakina explained.

"Mudaakhilat, which means intervention. Yes the name is apt," Abdul smiled as he looked on.

"So when is the first edition of *Mudaakhilat* scheduled to be published?"

"I don't know. Maybe sometime next week or next month. From tomorrow I have to start the preparations..."

"Why not tomorrow. The publication of *Mudaakhilat* should begin from tomorrow itself"

"Tomorrow? Are you crazy?"

"No I am not. Please understand, we do not have big funds and so we need to think out-of-the box and also make the best of whatever we have." Sakina then went on to explain that they should publish *Mudaakhilat* on ordinary paper using madrasa's computer and printer. "So, *Mudaakhilat* will look like an ordinary printout but then our purpose is to propagate the correct interpretation of Islamic thoughts, which an ordinary printed paper will serve...We will take a hundred printouts and ask a few of our friends to get it photocopied and distribute the copies of *Mudaakhilat* further in their neighbourhood. This can have a multiplier effect and..."

"Yes this is it. You are brilliant Sakina, you are absolutely brilliant," Abdul almost jumped out from his bed. His eyes were gleaming.

"Let's begin our work. Let's begin it right now," Abdul got a pen and paper and asked Sakina to write about the ways a *burqa* stifles woman's movement and goes against all ethos of equality. That donning a *burqa* essentially means covering ones good deeds and not boasting about it.

Abdul himself began writing about the need of modern education for a Muslim youth. He penned down his thoughts and experiences of studying in an English-medium school at Delhi and how it has opened several career avenues for him. He talked about the need for Muslim children and youth to acquire new skill sets and seek knowledge.

It was still very early in the morning as Abdul fumbled for keys in the courtyard to unlock the front gate. Maulvi *sahab* had milked the buffalo and unleashed the young calf to play with her mother. He looked over his shoulder to see Abdul unlock the front gate. The wrinkles on his forehead deepened as he curled his eyebrows and walked towards Abdul. "Where are you going so early in the morning?"

Abdul explained that he was going to the madrasa to type the two articles written by him and Sakina. He then briefly explained how their Urdu newspaper will be published as printouts and then photocopied by friends to be distributed further.

As the father and son talked, the newspaper vendor flung in a copy of *Allah-e-Niyamat.* The headline of lead story caught Maulvi *sahab's* eye.

His face was red with anger as he read through the news story. He turned around and ambled inside his room. "This is what I had feared about their intentions. In their lust for power they just want to introduce archaic laws," Maulvi *sahab* mumbled as he walked inside.

Abdul read the lead opinion column. It was written by *Maulana* Kamran who had claimed that Muslims in the entire region were slowly but steadily drifting towards *kufr*. He had argued that various political forces have influenced the lifestyle and aspirations of Muslims which are against the sharia laws. The only way to redeem Islamic pride was to introduce sharia laws, Kamran had argued in his column. "Muslims need to be aware of this conspiracy. The only way a Muslim can guard himself from such satanic forces is through following the sharia laws. Being devout Muslims we have taken upon ourselves to shield our Muslim brethren from such wily thoughts. Muslims should resolve all their problems, difficulties and issues only according to the sharia laws. The Sharia laws are Allah's own laws and if a Muslim follows Allah's laws he need not bother about the laws made by man. So 'We' will interpret Islamic sharia laws for the benefit of our Muslim brothers," Kamran had opined.

"*Abbu* will you not do anything to counter this vicious propaganda?" Abdul asked earnestly. Maulvi *sahab* gave a lazy look. His head swung sideways as if in deep thought.

"*Abbu* you have to write. We have to give an antidote to this poison. The only person in this village who can counter them with facts is you and the best way to counter this malicious propaganda is to start a separate newspaper. Today is our first edition of *Mudaakhilat,*" Abdul explained, his tone earnest as he begged his father to write.

"The first edition of *Mudaakhilat* will come out today and in tune with its name we have to intervene what the likes of Kamran are spreading in the name of Islam. *Abbu* they may have the money and muscle but with our passion and commitment we can beat them," Abdul was not ready to give up. He was relentlessly pursuing his father, Maulvi *sahab*, to write.

Maulvi *sahab* did not say a word. He got up and looked for his slippers under the cot, put them on and turned around.

"Come my son. Let's go. The first edition of *Mudaakhilat* should come out on time."

Abdul gave out a broad grin.

Maulvi *sahab* wrote his article in the next couple of hours. He argued that imposing regressive practices and thoughts on Muslims, in the name of sharia law is actually un-Islamic. "...today anybody claiming to be an Islamic cleric stands up and denounces all progressive moves for Muslims in the name of sharia law. Will these self-proclaimed custodians of Islam bother to explain the origins of sharia? Apart from the Holy Quran several man-made sources have been used to derive the sharia laws. So, the local customs, archaic laws and cultural instances have also sneaked into sharia which is now being touted as Allah's laws. A lot of things that are passed upon in the name of sharia are actually man-made laws that have been incorporated into sharia to get a vice-like grip on the Muslim mind that eventually turns them into zombies. The right way ahead is to have a detailed discussion of the sharia laws and their origins and not be blind in following the diktats of some Maulana or a Mufti..."

"...Muslims need to be aware of these vicious clerics and mullahs who are hell-bent upon introducing some archaic laws in the name of Islam. They want you to have a closed mind so that they can rule upon you. Do you think Allah mandated a Muslim to confine himself in the darkness of ignorance or come to the elixir of knowledge? Think my Muslim brethren, Think." Maulvi *sahab* wrote a scathing response to Kamran's vicious propaganda. Without naming Kamran, Maulvi *sahab* had 'intervened' through the first edition of *Mudaakhilat*.

Sakina typed the matter and took one hundred printouts of the first edition of *Mudaakhilat*. She stapled the sheets neatly as Abdul got ready to distribute the copies in the neighbourhood. Arjun had come over on his motorbike to help Abdul roam around the village and distribute the copies of *Mudaakhilat*.

On their way they saw Rashid walking towards Chacha's tea stall. Abdul walked towards him and quietly handed over a copy of *Mudaakhilat* with a word to pass it around after he was done reading. He did not wait for Rashid's response.

Rashid had a look at the contents. He was barely able to read yet he could make out that Maulvi *sahab* had written something that criticised *Maulana* Kamran's opinion of the sharia law in *Allah-e-Niyamat*. He was livid with the audacious attempt to undermine *Maulana* Kamran's views on sharia laws who was an authority on Islam, or so he thought. On impulse, he held *Mudaakhilat* between his hands to shred it apart but then held it back at the last moment. He folded the sheet and kept it in his pocket to be able to show it to Jamil.

Abdul reached Aftab *sahab's* home, gave him a copy of *Mudaakhilat* and urged him to get it photocopied so as to distribute further. Aftab *sahab* quite liked the idea and even promised to rope in a few benevolent Muslims who he thought could provide funds for *Mudaakhilat*. "I will also write an article for tomorrow's edition of *Mudaakhilat*," he told Abdul, as he read through.

It was an interesting scene at Chacha's tea stall, that evening. There were heated discussions about sharia and its relevance. A group armed with the reasoning of *Maulana* Kamran advocated imposition of sharia while the other relatively smaller set quoted Maulvi *sahab's* ideas on sharia. Afroz had come over for the evening cuppa and was quite amazed at the audacity with which a few cycle rickshaw pullers argued and quoted *Mudaakhilat.*

Maulvi *sahab* commanded a lot of respect among the Muslims of that region. His words and now his writings provided the much needed intellectual fodder to the barely literate people in the village. Rashid frustratingly looked and heard the arguments. He wanted to yell and screech and to thrash the guts out of the labourers who dared to question *Maulana* Kamran's words in *Allah-e-Niyamat*, but Afroz held him back. He wanted to see the extent of *Mudaakhilat's* impact.

Later that evening, Afroz apprised Jamil about the newly launched Urdu newspaper by Maulvi *sahab* and his son Abdul. Rashid had collected a few copies of *Mudaakhilat* and placed it on the table for Jamil to have a look. Jamil turned his head sideways as he picked up the copy of *Mudaakhilat,* his pupils contracted and lips pursed as he looked at the computer printouts stapled together. He stared at it for a minute, rolled his head to the other side and then burst into a hysterical laughter.

"This is what is bothering you fellows. Huh. Look at this… does it even look like a newspaper? This appears like an ordinary and cheap printout. It's crap, it's a piece of shit," Jamil held it loosely in his hand and showed it towards Afroz, Rashid and Bilal.

"This is what a newspaper looks like," Jamil said picking up a copy of *Allah-e-Niyamat* from the side table and held it tautly in his hand.

Afroz picked the pages of *Mudaakhilat* from the ground and tried to explain to Jamil that Maulvi *sahab* and Abdul have urged people to pass 'this sheet of paper' after reading to their neighbours. "A couple of enterprising villagers had clicked the photographs of *Mudaakhilat* from their smartphones and shared it with others," he explained.

Jamil raised his hand, palm facing towards Afroz as he gestured to hear him out before coming to a conclusion.

"This is a sign of their frustration. How long can they fight with us. This is going to fizzle out over the next couple of days. We should not bother too much about these beggars."

"But, Jamil *bhai* don't you think that we should…"

"Afroz *bhai,* you worry too much about frivolous things. Jamil snapped before Afroz could finish off. "…can stapled sheets of printouts be passed upon as a newspaper? That this Maulvi has to resort to such mannerism shows that he has conceded defeat. And moreover we have bigger things to worry about. There are hundreds of villages in my constituency. They can merely distribute this sheet in Basera and a few of their friends may further circulate it within their circle, but what about other villages? How will they reach other places? And who will listen to these beggars?" Jamil spoke in a contemptuous tone. "…it's better if you step up your efforts to further increase the circulation of *Allah-e-Niyamat.* Ensure that each and every home, shops and social gathering points get a copy of it…." he went on with his pep-talk for several minutes to lift up the spirits of his team.

"Keep your heads high and chin up. Don't let your spirits be bogged down with these frivolous stuff. Come on, let's have some drinks," Jamil exhorted everyone in the room. Rest of the evening was then spent in celebrations of the huge success of *Allah-e-Niyamat.*

24 .

Jamil asked Zamiluddin to print extra copies of *Allah-e-Niyamat*. The paper's circulation now touched around four lakh copies every day. He had already ordered Afroz to ensure that their paper reached each and every Muslim home in the city. Over the next fortnight a massive branding campaign was unleashed for *Allah-e-Niyamat* in a major marketing push. On the editorial front, the shrillness of Wahhabi interpretation of Islamic scriptures in the paper was continuously on the rise.

The money being pumped in was showing its impact. The copies of *Allah-e-Niyamat* could be seen at almost all public places in the city. Nadeem and Aakash had specifically instructed that all places where people sit idle and gossip must necessarily have the copies of their newspaper. So, chai stalls, barber shops, grocery shops, vegetable markets, provision stores, mosques, madrasas, *panchayats* were getting free copies of *Allah-e-Niyamat*.

Aakash was busy sorting out things at other electoral constituencies, but had given clear instructions to Jamil to update him with ground reports. He and Nadeem had plans to hold another mega-Islamic congregation by *Maulana* Kamran in a month's time.

They had to execute the next stage of their plan. While in the first stage one

Maulana Kamran was branded and established as a pious Islamic cleric, trained and educated in Saudi Arabia, the second stage was to further cement his position through the written words of an Urdu newspaper. The third stage would entail a series of Islamic congregations where he would pronounce the ways to be a true and pious Muslim. Anyone who disagreed with his interpretation of Islam, which in essence was the Wahhabi ideology, would be branded as a heretic and an apostate. With full control of the Muslim mind the next step would be to endorse and issue fatwas in favour of candidates propped up by them. This would ensure that Muslims vote en masse in the name of sharia and Islam.

Maulana Kamran's rally was just round the corner and Jamil had pressed his entire team into action. He personally took inputs from each of them on a daily basis. Even Fawzia and Heena were asked to come to his bungalow every day and brief about the buzz among villagers.

That evening everybody had been to Jamil's place with their briefs except Rashid. Jamil had sent him to the adjoining district to get response to their newspaper. He was keenly waiting to hear from him. He phoned Afroz, who was nearby Rashid's house to go and get him.

Afroz got off from his motorbike and barged inside Rashid's home. He did not bother to knock at the rusty iron-gate or call for Rashid. He walked briskly through the narrow veranda and barged across the rickety wooden door of the room. There was no one inside. He could hear the sound of water being splashed in a corner and turned towards that way. At the other end of veranda was a makeshift bathroom covered with a tin roof. A thick cloth dangled from this tin roof that doubled as the veil and the door. It was more a bath-place rather than a bathroom. The gurgling sound of water clearly indicated that someone inside was bathing. Instead of calling for Rashid or making any noise Afroz tip-toed to the bath-place and with a swipe slid the cloth piece aside. He was stunned and felt an immediate gush of blood within. Rukhsana was bathing. Seeing the intruder she quickly pulled her clothes but that could barely cover her properly. Afroz stood there gazing her with lustful eyes. He would have pounced upon her the next minute if Rukhsana's mother had not stepped in.

It was evening and Rukhsana's younger brother and sister were playing in the streets. Her mother was out for cleaning jobs where she worked as maid. Rashid had not yet returned home. Rukhsana had been working all day and had returned home. Feeling tired and sweaty she went for a quick bath when Afroz had barged inside.

"*Salam Afroz mian…*," Rukhsana's mother almost yelled at Afroz as she ran from the gate towards the bath place. She had always talked to Afroz with her head bowed down, but not today. She saw Afroz standing near the bath-place and could understand his intentions. And came running for her daughter. Afroz stepped back, disappointed like the wolf whose prey had slipped out of its teeth.

"*Walekum-o-assalam.* There's some urgency and I came looking for Rashid *bhai*. I believe he is not at home. Please tell him that Afroz *bhai* had come looking for him," he babbled, turning his head sideways to hide his disappointment of letting go Rukhsana. He was still in a daze as he stepped out, and took several minutes to kick start his bike.

He reached Jamil's bungalow to find Heena and Fawzia talking to Jamil.

"Jamil *bhai*, I need to talk to you urgently. Please come aside," Afroz dragged him to the adjacent room.

"Jamil *bhai* do something for me. I want Rukhsana. I just want to take her, anyhow," Afroz pleaded with Jamil, blinded in his lust for Rukhsana.

"Who is this Rukhsana? And how come all of a sudden you are asking me to arrange for her?" Jamil asked with a frown.

Afroz then went on to explain how he had barged into Rashid's home and then to the bath place where he saw his daughter, Rukhsana. "I just saw her nude…and…," he babbled, running the tongue on his lips. Jamil let out a wicked smile. He promised Afroz that he will plan out something to get Rukhsana for him.

"Right now I have Heena and Fawzia. Pick the one you like"

Afroz burst into a smile and called for Fawzia.

Rashid arrived an hour later at Jamil's bungalow. He had come straight from the nearby city where Jamil had sent him to meet the circulation manager of *Allah-e-Niyamat*. Rashid walked with spring in his steps as he came in with good news about the increasing circulation of their newspaper.

Jamil was ready with his own story for him.

"Jamil *bhai* I have good news for you...."

"But Rashid *bhai* I have an even better news for you. Listen to me first," Jamil interrupted Rashid. He then went on to describe the story he had cooked up. He told Rashid that a rich businessman from Saudi Arabia had come to meet him in the morning. "He saw your daughter Rukhsana and has proposed to marry her and take her with him. What do you say?" Jamil tossed the question. Rashid did not react.

Jamil walked up and sat beside Rashid. Wrapping his arm around Rashid's shoulder he said, "...he is a rich man and you will be lucky to have him as your son-in-law. I will make him pay you a few thousand rupees as well," Jamil winked as he threw the bait.

Rashid smiled. He could imagine himself setting up a business in Saudi Arabia with help from his son-in-law. He was now getting old and was tired of running around the likes of Jamil and Afroz. He was a Ghazi, who had dedicated his whole life for Islam and so he deserved to live like a king. And what better way for a Ghazi like him to settle down than to have a flourishing business in the pious lands of Saudi Arabia. Instead of him being the servant he would have black slaves at his command and probably some sex slaves as well. Rashid burst into a slight smile as he delved into his fantasies.

Jamil saw him smiling and patted his back. There were no further discussions.

As Rashid got up to leave, Bilal gave him a bottle of whiskey and a few hundred rupees. With a bottle of whiskey in his hand Rashid walked straight to Chacha's place.

It was late night when Rukhsana heard the familiar thud on the gate. She understood that Rashid, her father, had come home drunk. He somehow dragged inside and announced in a loud voice that he has fixed Rukhsana's marriage to a wealthy businessman from Saudi Arabia. And then dozed off.

Rukhsana's mother had been waiting for him to return so that she could apprise him of the indecent behaviour of Afroz, about how he had barged inside the home and was leering at Rukhsana. She had expected that the incident would jolt Rashid into seeing the reality around him. She felt her husband and the father of her children could possibly develop some self-respect. But Rashid was babbling something else. She told Rukhsana that they will discuss everything the next morning when her father was in his senses.

Rashid woke up the next morning with a severe headache and shouted for a cup of tea. As Rukhsana prepared tea, her mother sat beside Rashid, her husband, to talk about last evening's incident. Rashid heard her wife as he sipped hot tea. He kept sitting with his head down for several minutes thereafter. Suddenly in a sharp jibe he hit her with his fist and shouted some of the filthiest abuses on her. He kept hitting her till his three children came to rescue their mother.

Rashid created a ruckus outside his home and announced publicly that Jamil *bhai* and he have arranged Rukhsana's marriage with a wealthy businessman from Saudi Arabia. That same evening Rukhsana was married off to a bearded man who had arrived at Jamil's place in the afternoon. During their nikah Afroz wore a wicked smile on his face. The bearded man gave ten thousand rupees to Rashid and said he will be flying off to Saudi Arabia the next morning. Everything happened in a jiffy. Rukhsana's mother was inconsolable and begged everyone around her house to stop Rashid, but nobody came forward. After all Rashid was Rukhsana's father. When Rukhsana protested for the marriage, Rashid gave her two options, either to marry the man he had chosen for her or he would sell her to some cheap brothel. That sealed the matter. Rukhsana's mother cried and wailed but could do nothing. She thought of running to Maulvi *sahab* but held herself back. Rukhsana's sister Tabassum and her brother Akhtar had been crying hoarse but Rashid was blinded by his dreams of setting up some business in Saudi Arabia and then leading a luxurious life.

The marriage was solemnised at Jamil's bungalow. Nobody from Basera had been invited and the only people present during the nikah were usual accomplices of Jamil plus a *qazi* and that bearded man who married Rukhsana. Afroz had arranged for a sequined dress which was handed over to Rukhsana as her wedding outfit. Rukhsana's mother and her two children continued to wail quietly in a corner of the bungalow.

It was still late in the evening and Rukhsana had just been married to some bearded man called Adil. Rashid, her mother and her younger sister and brother had returned back from the bungalow. Bilal ushered her to the top floor of the bungalow. The room, though air conditioned, had no windows. Rukhsana was asked to be in the room. Ten minutes later, Adil with whom she was married announced that he was rushing to Delhi for some important work and would be back next morning.

Rukhsana lay down on the bed. The soft white pillow was soaked with tears flowing from her eyes. The more she tried to hold back her tears the more they flowed with intensity. Tired from wailing and crying and cursing her fate she fell asleep.

Rukhsana woke up to a loud knock on the door. It was late in the night and she cowed with fear. Before she could react, someone unlocked the door from outside. The door opened and Afroz stood there grinning. He shut the door in a jiffy and pounced upon her. Over the next four hours every one at Jamil's bungalow had been to her room leaving her shattered and violated. She was badly bruised with scratch marks at several places on her body. She was wailing loudly, cursing her fate at being raped on her wedding night.

After several minutes Chacha came in. Rukhsana was still sobbing when she saw him at the door of her room. Chacha had been coming to Rashid's house for several years and she had known him since her childhood. Rukhsana called her *Chachu*. She burst into wild sobs seeing her *Chachu* inside, thinking he would now save her from the beasts. She lifted her head hearing a click sound. Chacha, her *Chachu*, her uncle, had closed the door from inside. Rukhsana saw the same wicked smile on Chacha's face.

Fawzia came to know the next morning that Rukhsana had been married off hurriedly to a 'wealthy' businessman from Saudi Arabia. She held her sister Heena and wept inconsolably. At that very instant she had understood Rukhsana's fate. She cursed herself for holding on to her story and not sharing it with Rukhsana. "Probably she could have run away and not been trapped in hell like me. I should have told her," she said as she wept and hugged her sister tightly. Heena gently caressed her back and buried her head into Fawzia's shoulders and sobbed.

25 .

It had been a month since the first copy of *Mudaakhilat* was published. Maulvi *sahab's* incisive analysis and interpretation of Islamic teachings were being highly appreciated. While Jamil's *Allah-e-Niyamat* had the brand power and was thrust upon the villagers, Abdul's *Mudaakhilat* was gaining ground though personal references and spreading rapidly through word of mouth.

Each day the essays in *Mudaakhilat* dissected the vitriol spread through the articles of *Allah-e-Niyamat*, offering a correct interpretation of Islamic texts and their teachings. While *Allah-e-Niyamat* preached and instructed, *Mudaakhilat* encouraged independent thinking among Muslims. It asked them to question, discuss and debate before forming an opinion. Jamil's paper harped on Muslim victimisation and exclusion, Abdul's paper talked of development and inclusion. Kamran's style of writing was "…this is right because I am telling you so" but Maulvi *sahab* wrote "…okay so these are facts and here are my thoughts on the issue, do think over it".

Abdul had convinced Aftab *sahab*, Maqbool *bhai* and Naseem *bhai* to write for *Mudaakhilat*. They, on their part, had roped in several other intellectuals and writers for the paper. The two-sheet printout had now graduated to four sheets and volunteers who photocopied *Mudaakhilat* for further distribution and circulation had also almost doubled. Abdul printed three hundred copies of the newspaper every day, volunteers added yet another two hundred through photocopies. This was still a miniscule number when compared to the four lakh fifty thousand copies of *Allah-e-Niyamat* being distributed every day. And yet *Mudaakhilat* had managed to dent the impact that *Allah-e-Niyamat* could have possibly done if it were the lone Urdu newspaper in circulation. The readers of *Mudaakhilat* included villagers who had some kind of education and who could appreciate that there could be two or more ways of interpretations. These were the technicians, small businessmen, office workers and legal practitioners, among others. They were the people who commanded some respect within their neighbourhood. So, during casual discussions when they gave informed arguments, the other relatively lesser educated readers who had been fed on a daily dose of Wahhabi indoctrination from *Allah-e-Niyamat,* found themselves grossly inadequate to deal with the reasoned onslaught of those fed on *Mudaakhilat* thoughts.

It was early morning and Jamil was in a deep slumber, his head buried between the naked bosoms of the escort girl who lay in bed, besides him. On a high from last night's drinking spree Jamil hugged his playmate tighter as he tried to ignore the phone, but the caller was unwilling to give up and kept calling relentlessly. He woke up bleary eyed, lit up a cigarette and let out a volley of abuses to the caller. He stumbled as he tried to fish out his smartphone that lay on the couch where he had made out with the escort girl last night. The smartphone glowed beneath her shimmering scarf. With a wild swipe of his hand Jamil dug his phone from underneath the scarf. Making huge effort he lifted his head and opened his eyes to look at the caller.

Jamil felt a lightning strike his head as he saw Nadeem's name.

"*A..a..Asalaam-Walekum* Nadeem *bhai*,"

"*Walekum-Asalaam.* My sincere apologies to disturb you during your rest," Nadeem *bhai* sounded caustic, unnerving Jamil further. Jamil stammered and explained that election preparations keep him awake till late in the night.

"I am on my toes all the time Nadeem *bhai*. I am doing whatever you have instructed me to do and I will do whatever else you want me to do," Jamil said in a single breath without batting an eyelid.

For almost a minute there was a pause on the other side, which were like eons for Jamil.

"I want you to come over to Delhi immediately. Put the phone down, put on your pants, sit in your car and drive to Delhi. Right now, do not delay. Do you understand what am I saying? Put the phone down, put on your undies and come to Delhi. Right now. Do you hear me?" Nadeem's voice had a sense of authority and Jamil could barely nod in a 'yes'.

Jamil put the phone down and reached out for his trousers.

The conversation had woken up the escort girl. She dragged towards Jamil and tried to embrace him from behind. Jamil shoved her hand in a sharp jibe, turned around and slapped her hard.

"Get off Bitch," he said and walked off from the room. The stunned woman covered her bare bosom with one hand while the other hand rested on her cheek that had borne the onslaught of Jamil's hand.

Jamil shouted for Bilal and Afroz as he reached for the car keys. Almost on the top of his voice he said that Nadeem *bhai* had called him to Delhi for an urgent meeting and that he was rushing to meet him.

"Something urgent. Inform everyone. I will call and let you know," he shouted to the half-awake Bilal and Afroz. Before they could respond, Jamil had pressed the car's accelerator and sped away.

Rukhsana remained confined to the air conditioned room on the top floor of Jamil's bungalow. The room had an attached bath. And she remained locked inside. Afroz had given clear instructions to keep her locked inside but to provide her with all kinds of food whenever she wanted. In return Afroz and others at the bungalow sexually assaulted her at their whim. Rukhsana was their sex slave. She never said a word. She ate her food and lay on her bed as a lump of meat for the wolves to arrive and feed on her.

She felt disgusted with herself and her life, more than once she had tried to commit suicide. But every time she proceeded, the thought of her younger sister Tabassum held her back. Tabassum was a teenager now and it was just a matter of time when that rascal Rashid would sell her off too, Rukhsana's inner voice would tell her and then she would stop. Rashid had ceased to exist as her father. 'Rascal', 'wretched man', 'scoundrel' were some of the adjectives by which she addressed Rashid in her thoughts. She was now waiting to break away from the incarceration at Jamil's den.

Jamil stopped his car on the porch of Aatif's bungalow, he had driven non-stop from Basera to this bungalow in Delhi. He spotted Aakash's car parked in the side alley. It was eight in the morning and if Aakash *bhai* is here this early then there must be something urgent, he thought.

Aatif was Nadeem's cousin and he was a big meat exporter to the gulf region. Oftentimes Nadeem stayed at his bungalow.

Aatif *bhai's* domestic help was waiting on the bungalow's porch for Jamil and immediately ushered him inside the living room.

The mood inside was glum. Nadeem was pacing restlessly while Aakash was discussing something with Aatif when Jamil walked in.

"*Asalaam-o-walekum* Jamil *bhai*. Please take a seat. We are honoured to have you today," Nadeem *bhai's* tone was acidic. Jamil could get the irony and sarcasm in his tone. He meekly replied with a *walekum-salaam* and sat down on the edge of the majestic sofa. He had clasped his palm together and buried it between his knees. Jamil's mannerisms were like a timid emaciated street dog that shoves its tail between its legs in fear and on sight of a well-fed robust Alsatian dog stepping out unleashed from the bungalow.

His mind raced nervously to figure out what could be the reason for this urgent meeting.

Nadeem, Aakash and Aatif looked towards each other. Jamil could sense the prevailing tension. There was an eerie silence.

A minute later, Aakash broke the silence.

"Jamil... I had told you categorically that elections are just around the corner and we have to keep an eye on each and every activity across the region. And yet you have been so neck deep into women and booze that you don't even care to report things that are happening right under your nose," Aakash admonished him curtly.

Jamil raised his eyebrows, his facial muscles twitched as he still could not fathom the 'grave error' by him that was being talked about.

"This is your problem. You spend all your energy in selecting which woman to sleep with but neglect the most important things in your constituency," Aakash said, his tone agitated and pitch raised. "...look at this," Aakash handed over his smartphone to Jamil.

Jamil rubbed his forehead and saw the picture of *Mudaakhilat*. He looked up perplexed, still unable to gauge what's the fuss was all about.

"I told you this man does not have brains. He is a bloody pimp. All he can do is arrange for the whores, and that's it. He is a fucking pimp," Nadeem was livid at Jamil's ineptitude to understand the danger that *Mudaakhilat* posed for their prospects in the region. He was shouting his lungs out.

Aakash took a deep breath and then went on to explain to Jamil that *Mudaakhilat* may have a miniscule circulation when compared to *Allah-e-Niyamat* but then with its sharp writings it was fast grabbing the eye balls and its screen shots were being shared all across on the social media networks. Maulvi *sahab* and his son Abdul have been slowly but steadily gaining ground and have occupied the mind space of Muslims in the region such that people have begun questioning *Maulana* Kamran's interpretations.

"It's been almost a month now and *Mudaakhilat* has gained a loyal fan following. What started as an ordinary 'computer-printout' edition could possibly be converted into a full-fledged Urdu newspaper that will now challenge *Allah-e-Niyamat*. A Shia has approached Abdul to publish this on newsprint and help increase its circulation," Aakash explained.

"Abdul and Maulvi are not Shias. Are they?" Jamil asked making an innocent face.

"That's not the point. I don't care if this wretched Maulvi and his son are

Shia or a Sunni. The basic point is that their newspaper needs to be shut down right now. Do you understand?" Nadeem was shouting on top of his voice. "...and if you had some sense you could have informed us about this computer-generated Urdu printout kind of newspaper when it was first published and it would had been much easier to deal with it then, than it is now," Nadeem's face had turned red with anger. He was still shouting, and he had his reasons.

A series of articles written by Maulvi *sahab* and Aftab *sahab* had denounced Wahhabism and its school of thought. Maulvi *sahab* had even put a question mark on Wahhabism's authenticity and had termed it as un-Islamic. He had explained the origins of Wahhabism as a tool into the hands of power hungry monarchs of Saudi Arabia during the eighteenth century and how this has been continuing till this day. He had warned the Muslims to stay away from the Wahhabi influencers. Written in chaste Urdu it was being widely shared on social media networks. Several of such articles were translated into Arabic and re-posted on social media networks that had reached the Wahhabi clerics in Saudi Arabia. Late last evening the burly Wahhabi cleric from Saudi Arabia had called Nadeem.

"Why do you think we pump in billions of dollars every year in the name of Islam? Why do you think we suckle and feed businessmen like you?" the Wahhabi cleric had asked Nadeem. Without waiting for Nadeem's response the cleric had himself answered, "...it's only to cement our ideology in the Muslim minds. The billions of dollars continue to pour in only to erase all other competing versions and interpretations of Islam for Muslims, and for the rest of the world. These funds are put into the laps of shady businessmen like you so that you expunge all other interpretations and establish that Wahhabism is the only version of Islam. And yet you have allowed a petty village Maulvi and his madrasa to continue to rant against Wahhabism? And this has been happening right under your nose? Please remember Nadeem Khan that we are under no obligation to continue to fund your businesses...if need be we can replace you with somebody more efficient," the Wahhabi cleric had said firmly. He did not shout, neither did he raise his voice but his cold and calculated words sent shivers down the spine of Nadeem. He felt weak in his knees and had meekly asked for a few days' time to be able to set things right.

244

"Do whatever you feel like but sort out this issue once and for all," the Wahhabi cleric had said before slamming down the phone.

Nadeem had then called up Aakash and they had been devising strategies, finalising things for the rest of the night. It was still very early in the morning when Nadeem finally called Jamil and summoned him to Delhi.

Jamil had dug deeper into the soft cushion of the sofa, lowered his head and buried his face within his palms. A minute later he raised his head.

"I will do as you say. I apologize for not being able to read into the gravity of the situation but give me a chance to correct my wrongs," Jamil said, his head still bowed down.

"Yes this is what I want to hear," Aatif broke his silence for the first time. "Now, you will do as I say," he added, his voice and tone authoritative. Jamil merely nodded like a kid.

Abdul had returned home after delivering the copies of *Mudaakhilat*. He felt elated. At several places he was greeted by eager villagers who were waiting for the latest copy of *Mudaakhilat*. He broke the news that very soon *Mudaakhilat* will be printed on a newsprint that will give it a look and feel of a newspaper.

Hussein Ali, a rich businessman, had reached out to Maulvi *sahab* and was willing to join hands and help in the publication of *Mudaakhilat*. He was Aftab *sahab's* friend and had come over to meet Maulvi *sahab* and Abdul. Abdul's enthusiasm impressed him and he had voluntarily offered to help.

Abdul was thrilled that his work was being noticed and good people were coming on board. He had diligently prepared a plan to get designers, computers and necessary software required to publish *Mudaakhilat* on the newsprint.

Ali had begun negotiations with the printers in Delhi to print *Mudaakhilat* on newsprint and to get it delivered at Basera and other adjoining villages.

Maulvi *sahab* and Abdul were oblivious that *Mudaakhilat* had unnerved big power brokers in Delhi and the Wahhabi gangsters in Saudi Arabia. They were far too busy in their madrasa and the newly launched Urdu paper.

The new subjects and computers that had been introduced at the madrasa and now a full-fledged Urdu newspaper kept them busy the whole day. During day Maulvi *sahab* and Abdul remained busy with students, planning academic lessons and conducting classes. Afternoon onwards, after the madrasa classes, they busied themselves with *Mudaakhilat,* coordinating and planning about topics that needed to be written about, keying the text and then printing. Reader acceptance had helped *Mudaakhilat* metamorphose from a two sheet to four sheet newspaper. But, this had also meant double work for everyone.

At the meeting with Ali, Abdul suggested that they should hire fresh people, get more computers, buy software, get designers on board and other staff. Ali had agreed to all of this and had asked Abdul to prepare a detailed business plan.

Ali was into textile business. He owned several looms on the outskirts of Delhi where he sew clothes for some of the big textile brands. Allah had been kind on him and his business was prospering. He was distantly related to Aftab *sahab* and when, during a family function, Aftab *sahab* discussed about their new Urdu newspaper Ali immediately liked the idea and had offered to help.

It was late afternoon that day. Since morning Abdul had been busy taking computer classes at the madrasa. He had a quick lunch and had logged in to the computer to write an article for the next day's edition when his phone rang.

"Hello is this Abdul?"

The call was from the bank. The caller informed that his loan application to set up a tomato ketchup unit at Basera had been approved.

"Congratulations," the bank officer said. He asked Abdul to come over in a couple of days to complete the necessary formalities.

Abdul felt numb with happiness. He ran to his home and broke the news, hugging his *Abbu* and *Ammi*. Sakina ran inside the kitchen to get some sweets. It was celebration time for the family and for the neighbourhood. Abdul called up Arjun to give him the good news. Arjun was in Delhi for some meetings. Arjun's father, Aftab *sahab* and several people from the neighbourhood came in to congratulate and give their best wishes to Abdul. Fawzia and Heena were sheepishly lobbying with Sakina to give them some job at the ketchup unit. Sakina had smilingly assured the sisters of a job at their ketchup plant. The revelries continued till late in the evening. After dinner, Abdul tip-toed to his *Ammi's* room and quietly sat on his hunches besides her chair to say something.

"*Ya* Allah! Look at this boy…What is he saying to me?" Begum *sahiba* exclaimed and called her husband. "Your son is requesting me to let him and his wife go for a sight-seeing trip to Delhi. And he is seeking our permission," Begum *sahiba* made a grim face as she explained her husband. Maulvi *sahab* made a solemn face and picked up a stool to sit upon. But the next moment he burst into laughter.

"Oh I cannot hold it like you. I am not an actor," Maulvi *sahab* was laughing. He added, "Sakina is your wife and you two should go out often and see the world." Begum *sahiba* was smiling, she lovingly touched her son's forehead drew him closer and kissed on his forehead. Abdul wanted his parents to accompany him but they politely refused, saying the newly-weds should go.

26 .

Abdul and Sakina reached the bus stand early in the morning. This was their first trip since marriage and the couple were pretty excited about it. Sakina was bubbling with enthusiasm, and no sooner the bus for Delhi docked at its stand she jumped inside to take the window seat. Abdul bought some *jhalmudi* and roasted groundnuts, placed in the cone-shaped paper envelopes to munch through during their ride to Delhi. The couple were happily munching and chirping as the bus sped on the highway. After a while Sakina rolled over on Abdul's shoulder for a nap.

A rude jerk woke her up. The bus had stopped at the toll plaza and was about to enter Delhi. Sakina rubbed her eyes and looked outside the window. She was visiting Delhi for the first time. The bus had crossed the toll gate and was now in Delhi. A white car had crossed the bus at that instance, but Abdul and Sakina were too busy among themselves to take note of it. Hundreds of cars had crossed past their bus since they started off from Basera and this car was no special, at least it did not appear to be so.

But this car was special indeed.

Inside this car was Jamil, who was returning to the village after receiving an early morning thrashing from Nadeem and Aakash. He had to reach Basera to implement the plan that they had suggested. Jamil had had an elaborate discussion at Aatif's house about Maulvi *sahab's* madrasa, the computers and his Urdu newspaper *Mudaakhilat*. The solution that Aatif suggested had taken him off his feet. He had been a rogue element all his life and yet this kind was a first for him. He was deeply engrossed in his thoughts and paid no attention to the cheerful face of Sakina and Abdul perched on a rickety bus that crossed his car. Abdul and Sakina were too jubilant to spend an off-day together and did not notice the threat that was driving to their village.

Anjali finished her lunch and had lied down on the bed for a quick siesta. She had just come in from *Allah-e-Niyamat's* office. It had been several weeks since she had been managing the office affairs. It was a plush office and Anjali had her own glass cabin. Yes it was an affluent office, by any standards. Yet, every minute that she spent inside the office, Anjali could feel as if something was amiss, that something was not right, that what this newspaper claimed and what it actually stood for were diametrically opposite. The newspaper was in Urdu and she could neither read nor understand a single word that got printed every day, right under her nose. She could barely trust anyone at her office to talk about her concerns. Her sixth sense said that things were not right around her, but she could not comprehend what was it.

Anjali had barely closed her eyes when a loud and rude knock woke her up. She was piqued by the uncouth intrusion. 'It must be the drycleaner. This guy has a knack of disturbing me in the middle of my afternoon nap,' Anjali murmured, as she got up to open the door.

She unlatched the door and felt a sudden push from outside. Before she could react Anil had elbowed inside and shut the door behind him. Anjali was too startled to even say a word.

Anil held her shoulder and almost dragged her to the chair and made her sit. He pulled a stool from the corner and sat right in front of her.

"Anil what's this nonsense? Are you drunk?" Anjali was visibly annoyed by

Anil's rather strange behaviour and abrupt intrusion inside a girl's room, unannounced.

Anil did not mind Anjali's annoyance. He had no time for this. His face was twitched, lips quivered and he looked extremely worried.

Anil was from Kerala, who was introduced to the FPI's ideology while pursuing his Ph.D. from the JNU. He too was offered an apprenticeship at the FPI like Anjali and later on became a full time member and cadre of the party. Over the last several years since his association at the FPI Anil had come to realise that all ideals, ideology and beliefs that the party preached in public were openly flouted in practice. Its leaders talked of the rights of peasants and labourers but struck deals with the industrialists to grab their lands. In the name of women empowerment they promoted a culture of sexual promiscuity. They said religion was the opium of masses but openly sided with the Wahhabis to use Islam for their political benefits. This difference between the preaching and practices of FPI was suffocating for Anil. Over the last couple of years he had severely curtailed his activities within the party. Oftentimes he thought of discussing his quandary with other party cadres but held it back. Of late he had been talking to Anjali and could gauge that she too felt the same kind of suffocation. It helped that just like him, she too was a Ph.D. scholar from JNU. And then both had together been a witness to the blatant manner in which Aakash collaborated with Nadeem to start the Urdu newspaper *Allah-e-Niyamat*. Today, when he could no longer bear to handle it all alone he came running to Anjali.

"Anjali we must do something before it's too late. They are going to slay the poor man. I heard it with my own ears. Aakash has given clear instructions to finish this issue once and for all," Anil was grasping for breath as he told Anjali.

"Hang on, hang on for a minute…whom has Aakash instructed to finish off?"

"Do you remember Jamil…and his talks with Aakash about a madrasa and its Maulvi at a village called Basera?

"Oh yeah. That lecherous Jamil. I remember that creep"

"I overheard Aakash giving clear instructions to torch the madrasa and…"

"And what?"

"He has instructed to eliminate the Maulvi." Anil went on to elaborate that the Maulvi had recently introduced computers at his madrasa and started an Urdu newspaper that has been gaining ground and had upset FPI's main financiers.

Anil added that he had earlier enquired about this Maulvi from some locals and they had confirmed to him that he is a respected man across several villages of that region. He propagates peace and harmony in his madrasa and through his Urdu newspaper *Mudaakhilat*. Aakash had offered him to fight this elections on the Party's ticket but he had refused. This testifies that the Maulvi has a high integrity, Anil elaborated in a single breath making a desperate attempt to convince Anjali.

"We need to do something. I know Aakash and his coterie very well. He can go to any extent to win an election and this time the elections are very crucial for him. I cannot trust anyone else at the FPI office. I know you do not like Aakash's mannerisms and so I came running to you"

"What should we do? Let's go and inform the police"

"Are you crazy? Don't you know Aakash and the FPI policy? They must have planned it to the last man. Police will abet these rascals. We have to immediately inform the Maulvi and ask him to move to a safe place with his family. But the issue is how do we contact him?"

"What about your local contact in the region? Have you tried to reach out to him?"

"His number is not reachable. And I cannot discuss this issue with anybody else at the FPI"

Anjali nodded. She leaned back and crossed her hands. Her mind raced fast on how they should reach out to the Basera's Maulvi. She could not think of anyone in that town or region. And then her eyes sparkled with an idea.

"Anil, you remember when Jamil had first come over to discuss the issue of this Maulvi he had mentioned that his son was an alumnus of the prestigious Model school of Delhi. Every school maintains an address book replete with phone numbers of its students. I am sure they would know the contact details of this student from Basera village," Anjali said leaning forward, rotating her hands furiously, thinking and speaking simultaneously.

"Yes, let's call them."

Anil dialled the school's number and asked for the phone number of their student from Basera village. The receptionist asked them to submit a written request along with the reason for seeking contact details of their former student.

"Your request needs to be vetted by the school principal and only then can we provide you with contact details," the receptionist said in a cold voice and slammed down the phone.

Anil shook his head in despair.

"Wait a minute," Anjali was not willing to give up. She was pacing down the narrow space between her bed and study table as she tried hard to think of another idea. A minute later she slammed her fist on the table and said, "Yes. Got it. One of my friend's brother was a student of this Model School. Probably he could help us."

Anjali quickly dialled her friend's number and explained everything. He promised to call back in ten minutes.

The next few minutes seemed like years for Anil and Anjali. Both were pacing through the room but their eyes were fixed on the phone. They were waiting desperately for the phone to ring.

And it rang. It was Anjali's friend. He described that his brother is the secretary of alumni association so it was quite easy for him to dig out the contacts.

"There were two students from this Basera village one is Arjun and the other is Abdul. And yeah note down their contact numbers," he gave out the numbers. Anjali jotted down, hung up quickly and dialled Abdul's mobile number, all in a single swipe.

Abdul, Sakina and Arjun were at a restaurant and were enjoying their lunch when Abdul's smartphone rang.

"Hello," Sakina answered the call.

"Hi, I am Anjali. Isn't this Abdul's number. I need to speak to him urgently," Anjali said holding her breath.

"And this is in regards to?" Sakina's eyebrows had curled into a frown as she tried to camouflage her suspicion with curiosity. She had stopped chewing the food morsel in her mouth and tried hard to figure out who could be this girl and why was she calling her husband. Sitting across the table Abdul and Arjun were busy enjoying the sumptuous lunch.

"Please try to understand. My name is Anjali and I am a political activist. I work for FPI and the Urdu newspaper *Allah-e-Niyamat*. There's an urgency and I need to speak to Abdul immediately. His father's life is in danger and probably his family is also in danger," Anjali blurted out as quickly as she could. Amidst the buzzing noise of restaurant Sakina could barely understand that a woman said their life was in danger. She remained nonplussed yet understood that there was something serious that the woman on the other side of the phone wanted to talk about. Without further delay she handed over the phone to Abdul.

Abdul wiped his hands in the paper towel and took the call.

Anjali explained to him quickly that some people have been assigned to slay his father for his initiatives at the Basera madrasa and the Urdu newspaper that he was publishing.

Abdul somehow managed to gulp down the food morsel in his mouth and asked, "Who are you and how do you know all this?"

"I am, rather I was, a member of the Federal Party of India. I am also the General Manager of *Allah-e-Niyamat*. I will tell you the remaining story later on. But right now you must hurry up and take your father and all your family members to some secure place outside the village. Please try to understand this is a serious issue…"

"…but I am in Delhi with my wife," Abdul retorted, interrupting Anjali.

"Oh my God. Where exactly are you in Delhi"

"I am at the Connaught Place in a restaurant"

Anjali paused, took a deep breath and asked Abdul to reach the Barakhamba Road Metro Station in ten minutes. "Please leave everything and rush to the metro station. I will meet you over there," she said and hung up the phone.

Abdul told Sakina about the death threat that Anjali talked about. Sakina could not understand what have they done for someone to want to kill her family. She gulped some cold water and asked Abdul to contact *Abbu*.

Abdul dialled the number as he glued the phone to his ear. In a few seconds, instead of his *Abbu's* soft voice the recorded voice responded that the number was not reachable. He dialled the number several times but every time he received that the number was not reachable. None of the numbers in his village were reachable. His heart was pounding and drops of sweat appeared on his forehead. Arjun too tried to contact his father, but in vain.

Abdul looked nervously towards Sakina and gestured her to leave. They hurriedly paid their bills, left their lunch mid-way and rushed towards the Barakhamba Metro Station.

Anjali put down the phone and rushed downstairs. She and Anil jumped through the stairs to reach to the car. The next minute Anil was out on Delhi roads, as a nervous Anjali looked through the car's windscreen glass, praying silently. On usual days Anil drove cautiously but today was not a usual day, he cut through the Delhi traffic to save a couple of minutes that were precious. They were still a couple of kilometres away when Anjali's phone rang. It was Abdul.

"Yes, we are almost there," Anjali said as she looked helplessly towards the heavy traffic. Anil was honking restlessly.

Abdul and Arjun were desperately trying to reach out to their homes but none of the numbers were reachable. Abdul tried to contact Aftab *sahab*, Maqbool *bhai*. Nobody's number was reachable. Even the landline phones were not working. He looked towards Sakina. She held his hand in assurance and looked around in the sea of people near the Metro Station. Abdul was wiping the sweat droplets on his forehead when a car screeched to halt near him.

"Are you Abdul?" Anjali had almost jumped out of the car.

"Yes I am Abdul. Please tell me what's this going on? I am unable to speak to anyone in the village. Who wants to hurt my father? Who are you and how do you know about all this?" Abdul fired a salvo of questions.

Anjali took a deep breath and explained very briefly that she was an FPI member and the Party's General Secretary Aakash has connived with some Muslim leaders to destroy the madrasa and eliminate Maulvi *sahab*. Anil explained that a person, Jamil from the Basera village has been entrusted with this task.

Abdul swallowed the lump in his throat. He could understand and connect the dots about what Anil and Anjali were talking about.

"What should we do? Please save *Abbu*. Please do something," Sakina burst into tears.

Anjali hugged her and looked towards Anil for an answer.

"How far is your village from Delhi?" Anil asked.

"It's around two hundred kilometres," Arjun replied.

"Okay then it's not very far. If we start immediately we can reach your village by dusk. They must have planned their activities for night. C'mon, let's go," Anil urged as he switched on the car's ignition. Anjali jumped in the car.

Arjun, Abdul and Sakina were hesitant. They barely knew Anjali and Anil.

"Oh please get in. We are here to help you. Trust us," Anjali pleaded.

The next moment Anil had pressed the car's accelerator with Arjun, Abdul and Sakina inside his car.

It was early afternoon when Jamil reached Basera village. On Jamil's instructions, Bilal had already asked Afroz, Rashid and Chacha to reach the bungalow. There was anticipation of a major shake-up.

Jamil veered his car straight inside the bungalow. Bilal had been waiting in the porch. Jamil stepped out along with two other men, and briskly walked inside the living room. He asked about all the people who were present in the bungalow. Bilal took the names of Afroz, Chacha, Rashid and Anwar.

"What about the domestic help and other such people," Jamil asked gesturing towards the gardener who was busy pruning the rose plants.

"Yes, there's this gardener, the maid, a janitor and two other domestic helps," Bilal replied.

"Ask all of them to leave immediately," Jamil said sitting on the sofa. He turned around, raised his finger and swiped it outward. Bilal understood that there was something serious and Jamil wanted the bungalow to be emptied of everyone except his trusted *sepoys*.

He called the gardener, asked him to leave immediately and rushed inside to ask all other housekeepers to go. Over the next minute Bilal had cleared the bungalow of all helps. He did not bother to count Rukhsana, who lay enslaved in an isolated room of the top floor. Rukhsana was completely oblivious of the developments on the bungalow's ground floor, she was least bothered about the happenings downstairs.

Jamil stood up to close the door and turned around to sit on the edge of the ostentatious chair kept in the living room. He was flanked by Afroz and Chacha on either sides. Bilal, Anwar and Rashid hunched on the ground. Jamil looked up towards Bilal with raised eyebrows.

"Yes Jamil *bhai*. Everybody has left. We are the only ones who are left in the bungalow," Bilal said.

Jamil ordered Bilal to cross-check if all doors and main gate of the bungalow were closed. Afroz was bewildered, he wondered what was the issue and why this secrecy.

Bilal returned in a jiffy, shut the doors of the room and announced that all other doors of the bungalow have been shut tight.

"Okay, let me first introduce the friends who have come with me from Delhi, they are Ikrar and Muzammil," Jamil said pointing towards the two men sitting on the sofa. "...all of us need to clearly understand that this is serious...very serious indeed," Jamil went on to explain that Nadeem *bhai* is livid with the way things were developing at Basera.

"We need to understand that Nadeem *bhai* is a Ghazi and a true soldier of Islam. He can tolerate anything but blasphemy. This Maulvi and his son have crossed all limits. First they tried to introduce un-Islamic things at the madrasa and now they have started an Urdu newspaper to push the Muslims of our region towards apostasy. All this needs to stop and we need to stop it now. We are fortunate that a Ghazi like Nadeem *bhai* has chosen us for this pious mission. We will soon get instructions as to what exactly we are supposed to do," Jamil went on with his pep talk when his phone rang.

The caller was Aatif. He informed that *Maulana* Kamran has issued a fatwa against Basera Maulvi and called him an apostate.

"It will be a great service to Allah to behead this man," Aatif said. There was a momentary pause and he added, "...let me know if you need any help and I will be happy to oblige."

Jamil put the phone down, his face had turned sombre. He explained about the fatwa against Maulvi and his being branded as an apostate by *Maulana* Kamran.

Rashid immediately jumped up. His face was seething with anger. "I will slaughter this apostate. I had known all these years that this wretched Maulvi is the biggest enemy of Islam. I beg of you Jamil *bhai* to please let me perform this halal job," Rashid pleaded.

Rashid's plea elated Jamil. He had thought that Rashid would require some kind of cajoling, enticements and incentives before he could be forced into this job but Rashid had picked up the gauntlet by himself.

"Rashid *bhai* you want to go for this? I am worried about your safety," Jamil tried to feign a concern for Rashid.

"Please don't worry about me Jamil *bhai*. It will be an honour for me if I can make myself available in this jihad against that apostate Maulvi," Rashid urged.

Chacha turned towards Jamil and winked. "Rashid *bhai* is a Ghazi and he should be given this honour," Chacha urged as he turned his back towards Rashid so that he could not see the glee on Chacha's face. He turned around only when he was able to gain control over his reflexes and could make a sombre face.

"Okay so it's settled Jamil *bhai*. Let Rashid take charge," Afroz spoke, his pupils constricted as he thought of the forthcoming action in the village.

Jamil dialled Aatif's number. "Our Ghazi is Rashid *bhai*," he told Aatif as a beaming Rashid looked on. Aatif went on explaining several things to which Jamil merely nodded and answered only in monosyllables. He put the phone down, turned towards Rashid and explained that Aatif *bhai's* men, Ikrar and Muzammil are armed with automatic pistols and they would help him in his jihad.

"I don't need a pistol Jamil *bhai*. I will behead this wretched Maulvi with my hatchet," Rashid thundered.

"Yes we know that you alone are capable of executing the Maulvi but we have to go according to the plans of Aatif *bhai*. He is closely monitoring each and every activity at Basera which in turn is being reported to Nadeem *bhai* and Aakash *bhai*," Jamil explained as he tried to calm down Rashid and make him realise that he needs to keep his head cool so that the plan was executed properly.

Jamil asked Bilal to get a pen and paper. He began jotting down the things that they needed to do before Rashid and Aatif's men set the Basera madrasa on fire and behead Maulvi *sahab*.

The first to leave Jamil's bungalow was Chacha. He reached his tea shack and announced to all those having tea that *Maulana* Kamran had declared Maulvi *sahab* an apostate and the Basera madrasa as propagating un-Islamic values. Chacha even distributed copies of *Maulana* Kamran's fatwa written in Urdu and in Arabic. The news about *Maulana* Kamran's fatwa started seeping through the village.

At Jamil's bungalow intense discussions went on about how to execute their plan. Aatif had a reason to send Muzammil and Ikrar to set things right at Basera. Muzammil was a qualified telecom engineer and was an accused in several murder cases. He was out on bail. Ikrar had five rape cases against him and had been involved in numerous robberies and a murder. He too was out on parole. They were the trusted henchmen of Aatif and would do anything for the right price. Jamil assigned Afroz to brand them as warriors of Islam in Basera so that they get the required religious sanction and face minimal resistance from villagers.

Afroz made quick phone calls from his mobile and asked all his associates to come over at Chacha's tea shack.

Rashid led Muzammil to the two mobile phone towers in their locality. Muzammil pulled out the plugs on the two towers that blacked out all mobile phone signals at Basera and nearby villages. He then snapped the overhead telecom wires killing all signals of mobile and landline phones.

Afroz's henchmen created a ruckus at Chacha's shack and created a scene about Kamran's fatwa against Maulvi *sahab*. The news about Kamran's fatwa was now spreading like wild fire.

Aftab *sahab's* domestic help told him that her husband had heard about a fatwa against Maulvi *sahab* being discussed at the barber shop. Aftab *sahab* immediately dialled Maulvi *sahab's* phone number. They were still discussing when Muzammil had pulled the plug of the mobile tower and all mobile phones in the region went out of telecom coverage. Even the internet services had come to a halt, rendering Basera as an island of sorts with hardly any contact with the outside world.

It was dusk when Muzammil came back to Jamil's bungalow and enquired about the emotional overtones of *Maulana* Kamran's fatwa in the village. Ikrar had already filled five big pitchers with kerosene oil. Chacha, Anwar and Afroz were out in the streets mustering support for Kamran's fatwa, inflaming passions that Maulvi *sahab's* work and writings and his teachings were against the spirit of Islam that were propelling Muslims towards apostasy. Phones were not working and so rumours started floating around thick and fast.

Aftab *sahab* was getting concerned about Maulvi *sahab's* safety. It had been an hour since he tried to call him and the phones went dead. His son was away and so he decided to walk down to Maulvi *sahab's* home. Usually, he walked slowly due to his age, but today he had to walk briskly.

Muzammil checked the pistol. It was loaded. Like a pro, he tucked it at the back of his trousers beneath the shirt. Ikrar felt for his pistol stuck at his waist and tightened the canister's lids. They were cool and calm and carried on the process like a routine affair. Rashid was impressed by their mannerisms. His heart was pounding like a sledgehammer. Though he had been involved in petty fights yet this was the first time in his life that he was actually going to kill a human being. Rashid picked up the bottle of an expensive whiskey from the shelf and gulped it neat, finishing almost half of it in an effort to cool his nerves. He would have emptied the bottle if Muzammil had not rushed in to take a quick gulp. Muzammil passed on the bottle to Ikrar who finished it to the last drop.

"*Allah-hu-Akbar*," Muzammil said, belching aloud. "*Allah-hu-Akbar*," replied Rashid as he tried to calm his frayed nerves. Ikrar wore the white skull cap, Muzammil and Rashid followed suit. It was dark and they had to step out on their mission.

The local muezzin called over the loudspeakers for the evening *namaz* when the three men were stepping inside the car. Rashid paused, he thought maybe they should offer *namaz* and then go on for jihad. But Jamil waved his hand and asked Rashid to go ahead. Muzammil pressed the accelerator of the car even as the muezzin chanted the evening prayers in Arabic. Jamil looked at the goblet in his hands and emptied the drink in one shot. Bilal and Anwar had set out on foot as they needed to gather a crowd of like-minded jihadis to give corollary support to Rashid and the two criminals that accompanied him. They headed straight to Chacha's tea stall where Afroz and Chacha had managed to assemble around two hundred people. Bilal shouted *"Allah-hu-Akbar"*. The crowd shouted back *"Allah-hu-Akbar"*.

Almost instantaneously Afroz climbed up on the table and gave a clarion call for the extermination of the un-Islamic Basera madrasa. He read out the fatwa issued by *Maulana* Kamran. His men, among the crowd, started shouting *"Allah-hu-Akbar"* to raise tempers and arouse emotions. In a matter of minutes the fence sitters had converted and had been convinced that the Basera madrasa, Maulvi *sahab* and his Urdu newspaper *Mudaakhilat* were un-Islamic and their presence was besmirching Islamic values and that they were working to push Muslims towards apostasy.

Heena and Fawzia who lived in the shack near Chacha's tea stall had sneaked into a corner, terrified by the loud shouts of *"Allah-hu Akbar"*. The chants were growing louder by the minute as the crowd bade for Maulvi *sahab's* blood. It was Fawzia who mustered courage and glanced through a peep-hole to understand the situation. She could see Afroz standing on the wooden table as he incited the crowd against Maulvi *sahab*. She could feel her heart pounding against the rickety iron door as she peered through the gaping hole in it. She climbed down.

"Let's go," she told Heena and put on her slippers. Heena pulled her down, still terrified by the blood thirsty crowd that had gathered outside. "Come on quickly. We need to reach Sakina *aapi's* home. Let us inform them about everything," Fawzia urged Heena.

Heena, her elder sister, was shaking like a leaf, too terrified to even speak. She held on to Fawzia pulling her back. "No please don't go. We will stay indoors. These men....these men will kill us. Please don't go...please," Heena was hysterically pleading with her younger sister Fawzia to stay back. Fawzia untangled herself from Heena's grip, turned around and gave her a tight slap.

"Kill us? Who will kill us? These wolves who are shouting *Allah-hu-Akbar*?

And are we alive? Listen carefully…we are already dead. Yes we are dead. Both of us. Everyday these vultures come to tear our bodies. We die every day, every moment. What else is left for us? Let us die one last time," Fawzia shot back at her sister. Her eyes were red with anger, pupils dilated, nostrils widened and lips pursed with the determination to play her part in this battle. Fawzia had decided to not remain a mute spectator anymore. She reached for the door and turned around. "Are you coming with me or you want to lie down naked and wait for these vultures," Fawzia asked her elder sister. Heena was still hesitant. Fawzia bent forward, jabbed at her hand and simply pulled her to get up. Heena put on her slippers. The next moment the sisters were running towards Maulvi *sahab's* home.

Muzammil parked the car under a tree and stepped out. Maulvi *sahab's* home and the madrasa were hardly a kilometre away from that spot. Rashid and Ikrar took the kerosene oil canisters. Muzammil pulled out another canister and the three started walking towards Maulvi *sahab's* home.

"Remember we have to first smash all the computers at the madrasa, douse kerosene oil on the books and the library and set them on fire. Rashid you take care of Maulvi," Muzammil explained in a calm voice. He was composed and so was Ikrar. They were seasoned offenders and this was not their first time. Rashid had been involved in petty skirmishes but getting involved in a planned violence was a first time for him. Hailing from Basera, he was familiar with the village's narrow alleys, lanes and the backstreet paths.

His heart was still beating fast and the whiskey had made things worse for him. He was sweating heavily and felt weak at his knees. His vision blurred. He was well aware of the locality and so was supposed to lead the two men. Almost suddenly, his knees locked together and he stumbled. He would have fell flat on his face, if Muzammil had not held his hand at the last second. Muzammil patted on his back to assure him, and the next moment they heard loud chants of "*Allah-hu-Akbar*". Afroz and Chacha were leading a crowd that had gathered at the tea stall towards the madrasa. The crowd walked through a narrow lane that opened into the alley through which Rashid, Ikrar and Muzammil were walking on. The murderous eyes of the crowd instilled a sense of vigour, albeit false, into Rashid's demeanour. He shook off the stupor, raised the hatchet held in his right hand high up in the air, looked towards the crowd and shouted back *Allah-hu-Akbar*. The crowd was now behind them. At this moment, Afroz silently broke ranks and slipped away from the crowd.

Rashid felt like a Ghazi leading the crowd shouting *Allah-hu-Akbar*. The weakness in his knees had vanished and there was spring in his steps. The sloganeering grew louder and louder as the crowd approached the madrasa.

The onlookers and bystanders were terrified at the sight of a murderous procession marching through the narrow lanes of Basera. They ran inside their homes terrified and shut the doors, children sneaked in and hid behind their parents. A few bystanders remained mute spectators, peering from the safe confines of their veranda and craning their neck over the boundary walls of their homes they looked upon the crowd marching ahead baying for Maulvi *sahab*'s blood. A few others were gossiping about what lay in store for Maulvi *sahab* and his family.

Maulvi *sahab* had changed into his white *kurta* and pyjama. Arjun's father was coming over for the evening cuppa. A big publisher of school textbooks was his friend and Maulvi *sahab* had requested to get some books at concessional rates for the madrasa students. Arjun's father had a word with his publisher-friend and convinced him about Maulvi *sahab's* good work at the madrasa. The books were expected to come in a week's time.

Arjun's father lived across the huge canal that passed through Basera village and was unaware of *Maulana* Kamran's fatwa and the devious plans to eliminate Maulvi *sahab* and tear apart his madrasa. He was on his motorbike, and as he crossed Chacha's tea stall he could hear the large crowd shouting "*Allah-hu-Akbar*". He spotted Afroz and thought of the motley crowd as some kind of an election meeting.

The two friends were sipping chai and discussing about ways to further improve upon the madrasa, when there was a loud bang on the front gate. Before Maulvi *sahab* could react, Aftab *sahab* pried the gates and squeezed inside. He almost tripped over as he hurriedly rushed towards Maulvi *sahab*. The chai cup nearly slipped from Maulvi *sahab's* hands as he hastily put it down on the table. Along with Arjun's father he too rushed to hold Aftab *sahab,* who was panting heavily and could barely hold his breath. He raised his finger to the faint sound of the mob shouting slogans as he tried to catch his breath. The sound was growing louder with each passing moment. Arjun's father held Aftab *sahab* by his shoulder, made him sit on the chair and offered a glass of water.

"Haider, my brother…my beloved brother…this is a cruel world. Just leave this place and go away. These people do not deserve your goodness," Aftab *sahab* said as he held Maulvi *sahab's* hands and looked earnestly in his eyes. Maulvi *sahab* was baffled, unable to understand the reason for Aftab *sahab's* rather strange behaviour and why was he asking him to leave. And where should he leave and why.

Aftab *sahab* could sense his confusion. "Kamran has issued a fatwa against you and declared you an apostate. They are coming to settle scores with you," he said as his eyes welled with tears. Maulvi *sahab* didn't say a word.

"Afroz and Jamil have managed to stir up the passion of some fools. Just hear this sloganeering by the crowd," Aftab *sahab* pointed towards the direction of the slogans. Maulvi *sahab* turned his head in the direction of the noise and tilted it back again. He did not say a word.

"For heaven's sake Haider, try to understand. They are coming to slaughter you. Please make him realise the situation," Aftab *sahab* pleaded Arjun's father, tears flowing from his eyes. Begum *sahiba* had also come running out of her room. The sloganeering was growing louder. Arjun's father looked worried. He picked up his mobile phone to make calls but without the telecom signal it remained a useless gadget in his hand.

In a minute, Fazlu, the local barber, came rushing in. He announced that the crowd had swelled and the sloganeering had become more targeted. Several people were now raising slogans to raze the madrasa and were shouting that Maulvi *sahab* be publicly hanged. Fazlu leapt and took out Maulvi *sahab's* slippers from under the cot and put them before him.

"Come Maulvi *sahab* let's go," he held Maulvi *sahab's* hands. Maulvi *sahab* patted on his shoulder and asked, "Where would I go and why should I go? What wrong have I done?"

"Maulvi *sahab* we can debate these issues later on. At the moment our priority is to save your life. Those people who are shouting slogans and brandishing hatchets and knives are out there to slit your throat. Let's go. All these discussions can be had later on," Arjun's father urged. Begum *sahiba* started sobbing and nodded in their favour that this was no time for discussions. The next moment, the black gate opened with a loud bang. Fawzia and Heena who had come running had slipped at the gate. The sisters rushed inside and closed the gate behind them.

"Maulvi *sahab*…Maulvi *sahab*…they are…" Fawzia was panting heavily and tried to catch her breath. In a minute, the sisters were also pleading with Maulvi *sahab* to leave this place and run for his life.

Maulvi *sahab* looked around in frustration. The buffaloes were chewing cud in their shed unaware of the impending firestorm, the table where a few minutes ago he was having chai with Arjun's father had tea cups and biscuits, a cot was lying at the other end of the courtyard, Abdul's bike stood in one corner. Everything in the house stood as they were. He took a deep breath and asked Fazlu, "Is every single villager from Basera wants me to abandon this madrasa and shut down *Mudaakhilat?*"

"Absolutely not. There are a few like Jamil, Afroz, Kamran and others whom these people have made to believe that this is what Islam is all about," Fazlu said. His eyes were still fixed on the gate and he looked nervous as he spoke.

"This is precisely my point. Are these bunch of thugs going to decide what is Islam and who is a true Muslim? Will the likes of Rashid carrying a hatchet or the cronies of Jamil decide what should a Maulvi teach his students at the madrasa? If this self-proclaimed Islamic scholar *Maulana* Kamran thinks that I am distorting Islamic values and teachings then why doesn't he come over to have an open debate with me? You know why? Because these people know very well that what they are doing is wrong," Maulvi *sahab* said in a calm voice. His face was serene and showed no signs of intimidation.

He continued, "Does everyone in Basera want the madrasa to be shut down, tell me honestly. Or does each villager think that I have been writing and propagating un-Islamic values through *Mudaakhilat?* Tell me Aftab *sahab*? Fazlu?"

"Haider…" Aftab *sahab* tried hard to conceal his exasperation. He was at his wit's end to convince his favourite pupil, his friend and brother that this was not a time for intellectual discussion rather a tactical retreat, which meant that they need to get into a hiding as quickly as possible.

Maulvi *sahab* could well understand Aftab *sahab's* quandary. He appreciated everyone's concern for his well-being but was unable to comprehend as to why everybody was advising him to run away. He explained that he had nurtured the madrasa like his own child and no father would leave his child in times of distress.

"…and this Urdu newspaper *Mudaakhilat* is Abdul's child. This paper is published from the madrasa. So how can you expect me to leave my child and grandchild alone in front of these barbarians?" Maulvi *sahab* asked earnestly, his eyes seeking an answer.

"But we surely cannot sit back and wait for these barbarians to rip apart our world? Can we?" Arjun's father asked.

"Of course not. That's exactly what I am trying to explain," Maulvi *sahab* said with confidence. "If everybody in this village does not accept Kamran's fatwa and believes that what Jamil is doing is wrong then why aren't they coming out to defend the madrasa? Is it not the place where their children study, the place that will help build their child's future? If Rashid and a bunch of brutes can shout slogans and think of torching the madrasa can't those whose children study in this madrasa and those who do not subscribe to this barbaric thought come out to defend against these thugs?"

"…these savages are not coming to destroy Maulvi *sahab's* madrasa rather they are coming in to demolish the dreams that Muslim children have been nurturing, they are coming to slaughter the dreams and aspirations of these poor villagers. More than the madrasa's Maulvi it is the ordinary and common Muslim who will be a loser…" Maulvi *sahab* went on with his explanations.

Arjun's father stood up. He wanted to go out and seek support from the neighbours. But Aftab *sahab* held his hand. He understood that at this juncture open advocacy by Arjun's father could take this entire issue on a different tangent. "I deeply respect your sentiments and your love for Maulvi *sahab*. You are his true friend. But your active involvement will give a communal colour to this whole issue," Aftab *sahab* urged.

Maulvi *sahab* agreed and added that this was a battle for Islamic reformation. "...there are certain wars which an individual, a community or a religion has to fight on its own. And this is the battle for Islamic reformation, it's the battle of ideas and ideals, which we Muslims need to fight on our own. It's the fight to know and understand our Islam. It is our battle. This battle was long overdue. I am happy that finally it has begun. It's time for the Muslims to reclaim our Islam from the clutches of these *Maulana* Kamrans and these Wahhabis who maintain a vice-like grip on the minds of us Muslims. It's time for Muslims to know about the history of Islam. Let the Muslims of Basera decide what version of Islam they want to follow. If they think that this Haider, their madrasa's Maulvi whom they lovingly call Maulvi *sahab* is right and who has been advocating the spirit of Islam then they need to come out and defend me against these Wahhabi thugs. All Muslims of Basera and other villages who believe in me and my teachings need to stand up to these Wahhabi thugs who are hell bent upon propagating the most virulent interpretation of Islamic teachings. The Islam which I follow and which I propagate strongly believes in standing up to the adversaries of Islam. A true Muslim will never turn his back when there is a need to protect Islam. I am a true Muslim and these criminals are not coming to destroy this madrasa or a petty Maulvi, they are here to destroy Islam, they are here to slay a true Muslim. I am a true Muslim and I will face them and I will protect my Islam. I will not turn my back or run away. It's for the Muslims of Basera to decide what they want to do." Maulvi *sahab* said with a determined look in his eyes. Despite hysterical sloganeering of the crowd that was inching towards his house and the madrasa *Khidmat-ul-Islam,* he knew no fear.

Aftab *sahab* looked up. His eyes were still moist with tears, but they were now gleaming with courage. He looked towards Fazlu, who was now charged up. He turned around and vanished in a jiffy. Fawzia ran outside too, to inform all those homes where she had been working, goading them to come out in support of Maulvi *sahab*. Heena the most docile of them was also charged up. She stepped out, determined to fight the wolves till her last breath. Begum *sahiba* stood firmly along with her beloved husband, showing grit as she wiped away her tears.

Anil was driving his car feverishly. He wanted to reach as early as possible to Basera. All these years with Aakash and at FPI he had been a party to all kinds of misconduct but today was his day of redemption. The car had now turned from highway to the non-metallic road and Arjun was guiding him on the route. Sakina was sobbing loudly as a disturbed Anjali consoled her. The sun had set but they were still a few kilometres away from Basera. Anil was honking incessantly, leaving behind a whirling cloud of mud and dust that followed the car as he drove on. The non-metallic roads of the semi-urban area had slowed down Anil's speed and he kept honking to keep away the jaywalkers and stray animals from the road.

Aftab *sahab* stepped out to gather support from the neighbours. He had barely reached the gate when a stone hit him on his chest. The crowd had started throwing stones at Maulvi *sahab's* home. The madrasa was just across the road and so the crowd had divided into two halves. The more aggressive of them led by the trio of Muzammil, Ikrar and Rashid were trying to jump inside madrasa while the relatively passive ones were throwing stones at Maulvi *sahab's* home.

Aftab *sahab* made a quick retreat, holding his chest with his left hand. The stone that hit him was small and the pain was bearable. "Haider, these rascals are here. But don't you worry. I will do whatever I can to stop them," he said and then turned around waving his stick as he charged towards the mob, all alone. The men who were throwing stones at Maulvi *sahab's* home were shocked to see a frail old man charging towards them, waving his stick. They stopped pelting stones and looked at each other.

Maulvi *sahab* had also stepped out of the gate. Before he could say anything, another round of sloganeering began. But, the tone and tenor was different. There were some familiar voices. Fazlu, the barber had returned with around fifteen people. They got into an argument with Muzammil and Ikrar. Mudassir, the blacksmith, asked if they were from Basera village and under what authority have they come over to raze the village's madrasa.

Mudassir was joined by Maqbool *bhai* and Naseem *bhai* who had come running in after Fawzia cajoled them to face the crowd that had gathered outside the madrasa.

Begun *sahiba* closely followed her husband on his heels. She had been walking behind him holding his shoulders. Maulvi *sahab* could gauge from his wife's touch that she was anxious and frightened. He turned around, put his hand on her hand in reassurance.

Muzammil waved the paper with *Maulana* Kamran's fatwa written on it. Rashid, already on a high under the effect of alcohol punched Mudassir hard on his face. Mudassir started bleeding. Maulvi *sahab*, flanked by Aftab *sahab* and Arjun's father walked up to the spot. He still believed that he can talk things through.

"Rashid what have you come here to destroy? Do you think this is a madrasa? This is your future my child, it's the future of Muslim children. Why have you become so blind? If you have an issue you should talk. Destruction is not the solution," Maulvi *sahab* had walked right up to Rashid and stood in front of him looking straight in his eyes.

Rashid blinked. Maulvi *sahab's* gaze was gentle yet intense. He carried no weapon but he was confident. He was old and yet he had high dreams. Rashid was high on alcohol but Maulvi *sahab* was high on conviction. His conviction was to seek and spread knowledge, which is the basic tenet of Islam. Rashid chased a mirage and was worried that it would vanish if he did not protect it. This was the difference between the two men who stood facing each other. There was no match between Maulvi *sahab* and Rashid and everybody in the melee knew about it.

Muzammil sensed that if the standoff continued for one extra minute then it would give Maulvi *sahab* an opportunity to debate and discuss and that would take out the zing from their planned assault. He was a hardened criminal who made cold and calculated moves. He was not moved by emotions nor had any liking for scholarly discussions. A paid criminal that he was, he could expect his money only when the task was done.

"This man is a *kafir* and this is *Kafir's Den*. What are we waiting for? The all-powerful Allah has given us an opportunity to wage *jihad* against the infidels. Raze this down O' Believers," Muzammil let out a battle cry. His voice had a stimulating effect. All those who were stupefied by Maulvi *sahab's* presence sprang into action. Ikrar banged and pushed at the madrasa gate but apart from a loud noise the gate did not budge an inch. He flung his hand at the madrasa walls and jumped inside. The gate was locked from inside as well. The attendant had showed some presence of mind and locked the gate from inside. Ikrar thrashed and kicked and smashed at the gate's lock but it did not give way. He took a brick lying along the wall and started banging on the lock.

Naseem *bhai* and Fazlu held Muzammil by his shirt's collar and slapped him. Maulvi *sahab* continued to engage Rashid into his discussions, when they heard some shrill and loud voices. A group of women with Fawzia and Heena were running towards them. In the group were children who were students of the madrasa *Khidmat-ul-Islam*. The sisters had run to several homes informing them of the impending danger on Maulvi *sahab* and the village madrasa. Several men armed with hatchets, axes and knives came along with them.

Muzammil and Rashid who had thought that they would walk up to the madrasa shouting slogans, raze it down and behead Maulvi *sahab* now suddenly found themselves encircled by villagers. Rashid felt weak in his knees. He wanted to step aside from Maulvi *sahab's* intense gaze but could not do so. His feet were glued to the ground. The crowd that moments ago was solidly behind Muzammil and Rashid showed signs of meting away.

Muzammil understood that the situation was fast slipping out of his hands. He had to act fast and act now. He jerked Naseem *bhai* and Fazlu and freed himself. In a jiffy he climbed the madrasa wall.

"*Allah-hu-Akbar*. O' Believers we have been directed by none other than the pious *Maulana* Kamran to destroy this Satan's Palace. This is our *jihad*. If we fail then what will we answer to Allah in the heaven? These are Satan's men and women. Rise O' Believers…rise to the occasion. This is our moment of *Jihad*. Wage *Jihad*. Come on and burn this Satan's Den," Muzammil shouted on top of his lungs, his voice shrill and sharp. It shook Rashid from his stupor. He pushed Maulvi *sahab* and shouted back *Allah-hu-Akbar*. The crowd that had walked along with them once again started shouting the slogans.

Muzammil had jumped inside the madrasa. He picked another brick and jabbed at the gate's lock with all his might. The already battered lock gave way. Ikrar kicked and flung it wide open. "Come on O' Believers. Allah is with us. Come inside and burn this Satan's Den," Muzammil had once again let out the battle cry.

Maulvi *sahab* stood stupefied, his mouth wide open, hands slung as if devoid of any life.

Rashid smiled and ran past him, inside the madrasa. He was followed by Chacha, Bilal, Anwar and dozens of others who had come along with them.

Everyone along with Maulvi *sahab* were stunned for a minute. They could see the thugs running amok inside the madrasa, sullying every corner of it that had been the citadel of learning for poor Muslim children. Aftab *sahab*, Arjun's father, Nadeem *bhai*, Fazlu, everyone were numbed.

The crowd of thugs and criminals were smashing and hitting at the wooden doors with axes and swords, they tumbled and tossed the wooden desks and pulled out the green carpets. It was a race of ferociousness in the melee.

Maulvi *sahab* looked towards Aftab *sahab* and Arjun's father. Nobody said a word. They all felt helpless.

A shrill voice broke their inertia. It was Fawzia who was running inside the madrasa yelling *Allah-hu-Akbar* with a wooden stick in her hands. She hit Bilal with that stick. Fawzia had charged alone, she knew no fear, she had lost everything and she had nothing more to lose. Yet she was determined to do whatever she could to stop these criminal thugs. This was Fawzia's *jihad*. Bleeding profusely, Bilal shouted for help. Two people from among his side of the crowd had to rush to help him. Fawzia hit another man on his head felling him as she jumped ahead. Fawzia's courage spurred others into action. She galvanised them into action, breaking their numbness. Everyone was now running inside with a sole objective to stop the bunch of delinquents from vilifying their madrasa. They did not want to remain mute spectators.

The next moment, a cesspool of dust whiffed past the street as a car stopped few yards from the madrasa gate. Abdul jumped out from the car. Befuddled he looked at his father and the crowd inside the madrasa. He asked Sakina to take care of Maulvi *sahab* and his *Ammi* while he himself ran inside the madrasa. Anil, Anjali and Arjun ran close on his heels.

Abdul was running wildly behind anyone and everyone. He was unable to comprehend anything amidst this ruckus. One moment he was running after Rashid who was smashing the cupboards but the next moment he tried to catch hold of Muzammil who was kicking and dismembering the computers. The ferociousness was just too much for Abdul. He felt helpless as Ikrar and Anwar smashed the computer monitors with glee and tore away the books stashed neatly into the cupboard.

The villagers who wanted to protect the madrasa, its books and computers were hopelessly outnumbered. But they were unwilling to give up. In sheer desperation they tried to hold the hands of those who were tearing away the books only to be shoved and kicked back.

It was Fawzia who was hitting the Wahhabi thugs with a wooden stick. The far end of stick's outer bark had ruptured due to Fawzia's numerous blows on the heads of these brutes running amok inside the madrasa. The stick's whitish pulp had patches of red due to several blood spots on it.

Arjun saw Ikrar running with kerosene oil canisters. He leapt on him, snatched the canisters and threw it on the ground below. The kerosene oil soaked in the mud. Villagers snatched other kerosene oil canisters from Rashid and threw them in the drains. Muzammil was left with the last kerosene oil canister. Being stoutly built he managed to evade Abdul and other villagers and sprinkled kerosene oil in the computer room before anyone could stop him. Chacha set it on fire in a jiffy. The computers that had kindled the hopes of thousands of poor Muslims and their children across the region were up in flames. The printer that till morning had been busy printing copies of *Mudaakhilat* was now ruined and burning.

Maulvi *sahab* and all around him wept in silence as they saw their dreams go up in flames.

Arjun and Anil came running with the peeled off green carpets and threw it on the flames. Other villagers also started throwing mud, sand and water to douse the fire before it engulfed other rooms of the madrasa. After several minutes they succeeded in dousing the fire. All the computers were destroyed but the fire was tamed, and it could no longer engulf other rooms of the madrasa.

Rashid was livid. He looked towards Chacha and Muzammil. They had expected the fire to turn into an inferno so that everything within the madrasa could be burnt to ashes. Yes the computers were destroyed and books torn but that was far from enough.

"The devil has begun its games. The *jihadis* are losing," Ikrar mumbled into Rashid's ear. Chacha too whispered in his ears that the *jihadis* will lose if he didn't do anything fast. Rashid could see villagers dousing the fire and there were no kerosene oil canister left with them to start the fire once again.

"Get up you Ghazi. It is the final battle. It is your *Jihad*," Muzammil yelled looking at Rashid.

Rashid felt a rush of adrenaline and he took out his hatchet to behead Maulvi *sahab*.

Maulvi *sahab* was standing several steps away from Rashid, watching helplessly as the villagers sopped the fire in computer room. Rashid bellowed *Allah-hu-Akbar* as he leapt towards Maulvi *sahab*, his arms up in the air with the hatchet. Almost a dozen people sprung towards Rashid to stop him. Aftab *sahab* and Arjun's father formed a protective sheath around Maulvi *sahab*. Abdul along with Arjun, Anil and other villagers pounced upon Rashid, snatched his hatchet and threw it away. Nobody knew that Rashid was also armed with a pistol. He immediately pulled out his pistol tucked behind his back and fired two shots at close range. Both hit Abdul. He fell down bleeding profusely.

Muzammil and Ikrar were the first to run after the shots were fired. Seeing them flee other accomplices also started to escape. Fawzia, the warrior, came around and with her stick she hit a severe blow on Rashid's head. His pistol flung to the computer room's corner and for a second he was blinded, a stream of blood gushed through his head and he fell down. Rashid wriggled in pain but since all his accomplices were running away so somehow he got up and fled.

Anil, Fazlu and Arjun carried Abdul to the car and sped away to the district hospital. All this happened in a jiffy that left Sakina in a daze. She was so bewildered at the sight of her husband's bleeding chest that she could not speak. It was Anjali who shook her to senses. Maulvi *sahab* and Begum *sahiba* felt a buzzing sound in their head. They could hear people's lips move but they did not hear any sound.

The news of firing and ransacking of the Basera madrasa had by now spread across several villages of the region. People who were content being the bystanders came out of their homes on the streets. Several people ran after Anil's car that carried a wounded Abdul to the district hospital. Sakina had Abdul's head in her lap as she sat on the rear seat of the car. She had kept her *dupatta* on Abdul's wound to stop the bleeding but blood kept gushing out. She felt for Abdul's pulse. It was weak but there was life.

Maulvi sahab sat pillion on the motorbike with Arjun's father. He was stupefied and terrified. Villagers rushed to the district hospital on whatever vehicle they could manage to sit.

The dilapidated district hospital, around three kilometres from Basera, was unequipped to deal with medical exigencies of any kind. The bullet wounds required immediate surgery and the doctors referred Abdul to a bigger hospital in Delhi. The doctors did give some preliminary medication that arrested the blood loss and arranged for an ambulance. A paramedic and a doctor accompanied Abdul in the ambulance till the Delhi hospital.

V. Takeover

27 .

It had been two hours since Abdul was shifted into the intensive care unit after the second surgery. Abdul was lucky that the bullets did not puncture his heart yet they had severely damaged his internal organs. The second surgery was needed to stop the internal bleeding. The duty doctors said his condition continued to be critical.

Abdul lay motionless on the large bed. The white bandage wrapped around his chest had small and bright-red blood spots. A giant monitor above his head made a beep sound every time a wave initiated at its left. A tube brought in oxygen to his nostrils to ease the breathing pressure on his lungs that had been pricked by bullet wounds. The duty nurse meticulously noted all his vitals in a giant chart to help the doctors decipher his condition.

The security guard asked all family members to wait in the lounge and not crowd the entrance of the intensive care unit. Maulvi *sahab*, Begum *sahiba* and Sakina were inconsolable. Begum *sahiba* had been reciting *Quranic* verses non-stop since the time Abdul was rushed to the district hospital. Anjali, Heena and Fawzia tried hard to console Sakina, as they fought away with their own tears. Arjun, Anil, Fazlu and other younger men were running around bringing medicines, donating blood and completing hospital's formalities. Aftab *sahab*, Arjun's father, Maqbool *bhai*, Naseem *bhai* and several other villagers had encircled Maulvi *sahab* in an effort to give him confidence and courage. Every now and then someone would hug Maulvi *sahab* or pat and caress his back and say that Allah is kind and merciful and that Abdul would soon be alright.

No amount of cajoling or pep talk by his friends could cheer up Maulvi *sahab,* he felt that life was gradually ebbing away from him. Unable to stand, he felt weak in his knees and slumped on the waiting lounge's chair. His eyes were closed and he thought of the time when after several years of marriage he was blessed with a son only after he and his wife sought blessings from the mausoleum of Saint Nizamuddin Auliya.

After a while, he heard the faint sound of *qawwali* being sung at the Nizamuddin Auliya mausoleum. Maulvi *sahab* gradually opened his eyes, thinking it to be his hallucination which would recede after he opened his eyes. The Nizamuddin *dargah* was a few kilometres from the hospital and there was no way he could have heard the *qawwali* being sung at the sepulchre. Yet the mystic sounds of *qawwali* grew louder by the minute, in his ears.

Before he could think further, Maulvi *sahab* was walking out of the hospital. Aftab *sahab* and Arjun's father were sleeping on the benches of the waiting lounge while all others were in the hospital canteen to take a quick bite. Nobody saw Maulvi *sahab* walking out of the hospital. He did not care that he was bare footed and was walking past the heavy traffic amidst the blaring noise and horns of thousands of cars and buses and motorbikes. His beard was wet from the steady stream of tears flowing from his eyes. Maulvi *sahab* was not familiar with Delhi roads yet he walked through as if he knew his destination. He could feel as if someone was leading his way and he walked along. After walking for quite some time, he reached a narrow alley with confectioners on both sides who were busy frying *jalebis* and *namkeen* in large iron cauldrons. His shoulders rubbed against others and the shopkeepers solicited him to come over for a quick snack. Maulvi *sahab* was still in a trance and could see all the hustling around him, he saw their lips move but the only sound he could hear was that of the *qawwali*. He was walking like a zombie.

Yes he could now hear the words of *qawwali* quite clearly. He walked past the flower shops into a very narrow lane with high walls on both sides. Several men, women and children were sitting on the sides of this narrow lane, their arms spread up in the air and accepting food and eatables from other people. Maulvi *sahab* walked past this narrow lane and reached the wide space with *qawwals* singing in devotion to the revered Saint Nizamuddin Auliya. His sepulchre lay right in front of the *qawwals*.

Maulvi *sahab* broke into intense sobs, he screeched and shrieked in pain as he lay there, his head touching the revered saint's sepulchre. The thoughts of Abdul, words of doctors and the sounds of *qawwali* formed a cocktail in his head. Abdul's voice echoed in his ears. He could hear him writhe in pain and cry aloud.

His beard had been soaked with incessant tears flowing from his eyes and appeared as if water was sprinkled upon it. A soft touch and caress of a hand made him lift his head. He looked up and saw an elderly man with a soft and reassuring smile on his face.

"Surrender yourself and your problems to the Saint. Accept his verdict, whatever it is, and you will find peace," the elderly said in a soft voice. Maulvi *sahab* nodded. The words worked like a balm on Maulvi *sahab's* soul. He wiped his tears, touched the Saint's feet and hurried back to the hospital. Unlike his slow and trance-like steps when he came inside the mausoleum, he was now running back to the hospital. And he didn't quite understand why the hurry.

Maulvi *sahab* was panting heavily when he reached the hospital's waiting lounge. Aftab *sahab* was sitting with his head down, crying. Maulvi sahab walked up to him. Between sobs Aftab *sahab* told him that Abdul's condition had deteriorated and the doctors were taking him for a third surgery. Maulvi *sahab* ran towards the operation room.

Begum *sahiba* and Sakina were vociferously chanting verses from the Holy Quran. Everyone else were crying silently.

The paramedics came pushing a stretcher shouting at everyone to clear the alleyway. Nurses were running behind the large stretcher on which Abdul lay still, motionless.

Maulvi *sahab* ran along the stretcher till the doors of the operation theatre. He felt helpless. The paramedics announced in a loud voice to the doctors inside that they had brought the patient for surgery.

'Patient', the word pierced Maulvi *sahab's* heart like a sharp pointed arrow. His son was hale, hearty and healthy. He was capable of moving mountains but today he lay motionless on the hospital stretcher and was being referred to as a 'patient'. He felt a pang of guilt. It was he who was responsible for this condition of his son. As the duty nurse led him inside the operation room, he looked at his beloved Abdul. He kept looking at him for several seconds. He stood there motionless, his eyes fixed on his son. This was probably the last time he would see his Abdul. He could hear no voice, no sound, he felt no sensation. The duty nurse had to shake him of his stupor.

Maulvi *sahab* came into the lobby. He did not speak. Nobody asked him anything, they just looked at him and his body language-- the drooping eyes, sagged shoulders and his dragging feet. Maulvi *sahab* stood motionless for a minute. He raised his head, looked around, and slowly walked up to Begum *sahiba* and pulled out the cloth sheet from her bag. He walked to a corner and spread it on the ground.

The only option that he could now think of was to pray to Allah and offer *namaz*. Yet again he could hear the faint sounds of *qawwali* from the Nizamuddin *Dargah*. He offered the *namaz*. Even after it was over, he kept sitting on his hunches, his hand spread out, palms joint at their base and at the little fingers. The fingers quivered as he prayed.

'*Ya Allah*, the Almighty, if ever in my life I have done one good deed and you feel that I should be rewarded for it then I need it tonight. O' merciful, all knowledgeable please give my son back. He has done no harm, he has not hurt anyone, and he will never hurt anyone. I have lived my life, I am willing to give my life for my beloved Abdul. I am past, Abdul is the future. O' merciful Allah I never asked for anything in my life but today I beg for Abdul's life. I offer myself to you… but please….please O' merciful Allah let my beloved Abdul live. I offer my life in return…' Maulvi *sahab's* lips shivered like dry leaves, his hands shook violently and a stream of tears flew from his eyes. He kept sitting in this posture.

Begum *sahiba* looked at Maulvi *sahab*, her husband. Oftentimes he would sit a bit longer than usual after the *namaz*. These were the days when he would silently pray. Yes, today it was understandable that Maulvi *sahab* is praying for Abdul's well-being. Yet, he was sitting motionless.

Begum *sahiba* looked at her husband. Maulvi *sahab's* head had drooped in the front. The neck bone, at the base of his shoulder, pointed like the sharp tip of an arrow. His hands rested softly on the cloth sheet spread on the ground. She continued to stare at her husband, her view dazed by the tears in her eyes.

Sakina had her ears on the movement within the operation theatre. A paramedic had come out and waved to her that Abdul was showing signs of improvement. The next moment a nurse came out and announced that probably the third surgery will not be required as Abdul's condition had improved dramatically. Begum *sahiba* felt a wave of emotions hitting her. She felt elated and concerned. Elated that her son was now recovering and concerned about some unknown fear for her husband who was still on his hunches at the cloth mat after offering *namaz*. She continued to stare at her husband. Through the mist of tears in her eyes she saw a stream of saliva pour from Maulvi *sahab's* mouth and trickle down like a sharp stream on the cloth sheet.

At that moment Begum *sahiba* knew, and understood. Maulvi *sahab,* her husband, was no more. She did not move but her careening body hit the wall with a thud as she loosened herself and fell back. She slid along the wall on the floor.

Inside the operation room doctors were pleasantly surprised by the dramatic recovery of Abdul. His condition improved with every passing minute. The limp waves on the instruments that monitored Abdul's vitals became animated as a sign of life clawing back to him. And doctors finally decided that the third surgery was not needed. The duty nurse came out to communicate about Abdul's improvement.

Begun *sahiba* heard about her son's recovery, she felt herself shorn into two pieces. One wept at her husband's demise while the other part was elated that her son was now safe and alive.

Abdul was in the intensive care unit when his fingers quivered and his lips moved. *"Abbu,"* he said, slowly opening his eyes. A drop of tear rolled down from the corners of his eye. And he did not know the reason. He was soon shifted to the hospital's private room. As everyone took turns to visit Abdul, his father Maulvi *sahab* was being laid on the stretcher, a white cloth covered him from head to toe. The hospital doctor had already proclaimed Maulvi *sahab* as dead. Everyone, who went over to Abdul, made sure their tears did not show up. They talked about the madrasa, the Urdu newspaper *Mudaakhilat* and everything else. Nothing mattered for Abdul. He kept asking, "Where is *Abbu*?" When Sakina could not take it longer she hugged Begum *sahiba* and burst into sobs. Abdul had been fearing about this news. His eyes welled with tears and he began sobbing wildly. The doctors intervened and asked everyone to stop wailing. Abdul's wounds were raw and violent sobbing threatened to shear his wounds.

28 .

The news of Maulvi *sahab's* demise had reached Basera. The already morose villagers felt a pall of gloom descend on them. Maulvi *sahab* had never demanded respect, rather he commanded respect from old, young and the children of Basera and several adjoining villages. His departure brought tears to all.

Jamil and his gang were ecstatic. They were so heavily drunk in their revelry that none of them were able to stand straight. During the party, Jamil embraced Afroz and they swaggered together on a raunchy song at the bungalow. Nadeem and Aakash felt relaxed, they informed the Wahhabi clerics and financiers in Saudi Arabia about the turn of events. The Wahhabi clerics asked Nadeem and Usman to seize the opportunity and cement their position.

A day after vandalism and shootout at Basera's madrasa the *Allah-e-Niyamat* had justified the act as a great service to Islam. The paper had carried a veiled threat that anybody or any institution that was found to be working against the interests of Islam should be exterminated in the larger good of Islam. Yet again they defined Islam through the lens of Wahhabi school of thought. Aakash had telephoned Jamil. He was planning a series of Islamic congregations across the region with Kamran and several other such "*Maulanas*" and "*Muftis*".

They needed to reinforce their advances with new fatwas in order to sail through in the coming elections.

Rashid parked his motorbike outside his house. He was coming to his house after a fortnight. A white bandage was wrapped around his head, the deep cut on his scalp had to be sutured due to the severe blow of Fawzia's wooden club on his head. Jamil had made arrangements for him to stay at a far off garage along with Muzammil and Ikrar. They had to stay in the hiding till the issue settled down. It was Aakash's back-end management with the police that doused the embers at a very early stage about madrasa arson and the shoot-out.

It was evening when Rashid opened the rickety iron gate of his house and walked inside. His wife was preparing *bajra* chapattis at the mud stove and Tabassum and Akhtar were sitting on the charpoy. Rashid walked across the short veranda but everyone in his family continued to carry on. They had refused to acknowledge his presence. Rashid was enraged. Jamil and Afroz had hailed him for his efforts and had anointed him as the Ghazi, showered him with gifts, and his own family was giving him a cold reception.

"Give me a glass of water and prepare tea for me," Rashid thundered at his wife.

"Pitcher's in that corner, go help yourself with a glass of water. And there's nothing in the house to prepare tea for you. Go and ask your Jamil *bhai* and Afroz *bhai* to prepare tea for you," his wife turned around and said in caustic tone. This was probably the first time in her life that she had opened her mouth to counter Rashid.

And she had her reasons. After the arson and shoot-out at the madrasa and subsequent demise of Maulvi *sahab,* the villagers had ostracised Rashid's family. All homes where Rashid's wife worked as a maid had asked her to quit, children refused to play with Tabassum and Akhtar. There was hardly any money to buy ration and the family was left with only *bajra* flour and buffaloes' milk. Akhtar was specifically livid with his father's behaviour. He had always wanted to study and learn new things but Rashid never bothered to send him to the madrasa. He used to laze around with other kids who studied at the madrasa. Quite often, Akhtar brought home their old books, pens and pencils. Along with Tabassum and Rukhsana he enjoyed reading and writing. Rashid was hardly home so these secretive studies could go on for the kids. Akhtar and Tabassum were incensed when Rashid had forcefully married their elder sister against everyone's wishes. This time after Rashid's active involvement in the madrasa vandalism and the family's subsequent ostracism all the village children had refused to play with them. Akhtar and Tabassum had been doing the rounds of the village and around the banyan tree, but no child came over to play with them. Whenever Akhtar tried to actively join an ongoing game the boys would retreat calling him 'murderer's son'. There were several people in Basera who directly blamed Rashid for Maulvi *sahab's* death and the madrasa's arson. Akhtar felt enraged about this. He was a nine year old boy and he felt ashamed to be Rashid's son.

Rashid was furious with the way her wife talked to him when he asked for tea. "How dare you talk to a Ghazi like that? I will teach you a lesson that you will remember for life," Rashid blurted out, picking up the bamboo stick from the corner. He swiped the stick at his wife's back and the poor woman fell aside due to the massive impact. She cried aloud writhing in pain. Rashid knew no mercy. He raised the bamboo stick for another jab but felt that the stick had suddenly gone heavier. He pulled harder but the stick did not budge. Astonished, he turned around to see Akhtar holding it with both hands.

"You son of bitch. How dare you…" Rashid cursed his son, turned around and kicked him hard. Akhtar fell down but he had managed to pull the bamboo stick from his father's hands. He wriggled in pain, yet jumped up and with all his might hit the bamboo stick on Rashid's head. The severe blow opened his raw wound and blood started oozing out from his head. Akhtar hit another blow, this time on his back and then another. His mother and Tabassum ran ahead sobbing incessantly and held his hands.

"Go tell your Jamil and Afroz that Abdul *bhai* is rebuilding the madrasa. New computers will be brought in very soon and I along with Tabassum will study in the madrasa," Akhtar said, his lips pursed and pupils constricted. Akhtar's anger that was pent up for years had now burst out.

Rashid got up. He could feel hundreds of needles piercing his skull as blood oozed out from the wound. He wanted to thrash Akhtar for hitting his father. He was angry and surprised by his conduct. Yet he had no time to waste. That Abdul was revamping the madrasa and getting new computers was a serious issue.

"Abdul is bringing new computers to the madrasa?" he asked Akhtar, limping ahead.

"Yes. He is getting new computers. Go see for yourself," Akhtar said wailing with his mother and sister. Rashid's wife covered her son behind her back lest Rashid hit him.

But Rashid was a Ghazi, or so he thought. He had far more important mission in his life than to correct his errant son.

He ran out, started his motorbike in a jiffy and drove frantically towards the madrasa. Akhtar was right. Villagers were cleaning up the debris, charred desks, chairs, tables and books were lying outside the madrasa. The lights were on and several people could be seen inside tidying up things.

"*Ya* Allah. Akhtar is right, they are getting new computers. I need to tell Jamil *bhai* about all of this immediately," he mumbled and turned his motorbike towards Jamil's bungalow.

It was already dark when he reached Jamil's bungalow. The main gate was locked from inside. Rashid knocked, knocked again and then again, he also rang the bell several times but there was no answer. He waited for several minutes but there was no response.

Rashid collected bricks and stones from outside the bungalow, from the pathway and then made a makeshift pedestal alongside the bungalow's wall.

'The matter is serious. Jamil *bhai* and Aakash *bhai* have said these are election times and all of us have to be on our toes. And then I am a Ghazi. How can I relax?' Rashid gave a small pep-talk to himself as he stepped on the makeshift brick pedestal and jumped inside the bungalow.

He crossed the porch and came to the alley. There was nobody in the living room but he could hear some voices from the meeting room at the far end of the bungalow.

'Probably everybody is busy partying,' he said softly. He walked a few steps ahead and could clearly hear the talks inside the room.

The next moment his blood froze.

"….we need to have a couple of more fuckers like this Rashid. Throw some crumbs for these beggars, inundate them with whiskey and drugs, get them some cheap whores and then anoint them as a Ghazi... and…and…and then win elections," Afroz said, his voice wavering as he burst into a hysterical laughter. Jamil had got marijuana and heroin to celebrate. And everybody inside was heavily intoxicated. Chacha, Bilal, Anwar, Afroz and Jamil were snorting and were smoking weed and this was why nobody heard the knocks or the sounds of doorbell.

"Oh yes, Rashid the Ghazi. He was Chacha's discovery, I remember very well," it was Jamil who was giggling as he spoke. "Oh come on, Jamil *bhai*. You are out of your senses. Rashid was my discovery. I brought him to meet you. How can you forget this," Afroz said laughing out loud.

"Yeah sorry, I stand corrected. And hey this man got his daughter Rukhsana as well. Afroz you are a real bastard. You have kept Rashid--the Ghazi's daughter, as a sex slave. Huh…," Jamil burst into a hysterical laughter. He added "...and look at this Kamran. The *Maulana* Kamran. This phenomenon is Aakash *bhai's* discovery. This fucker is busy with sluts and whores at night and pronounces *fatwas* during the day. Oh yeah... he will be coming for a series of Islamic congregations during the coming weeks. So we need to ensure a steady supply of hookers for this man..." Jamil said laughing out feverishly.

"Hey Chacha where are the girls for tonight. What man what are your arrangements?" Afroz asked belching out loudly.

"I just had a word with the pimp. He said the hookers are on their way and will reach in an hour," Chacha replied.

"Ah one hour, that's fucking too long. Call your Heena and Fawzia till then," Afroz said sounding desperate.

"Heena and Fawzia…the two sluts have ditched us." It was Bilal who explained, caressing the wound on his head. "…oh yeah I remember. Don't worry we will sort them out. Just wait for a couple of weeks," Afroz said, grinding his teeth.

"You guys are worthless. What am I going to do for an hour? Go get Rukhsana from the top floor. Anwar put on some music…," Jamil urged.

"Oh yeah I had forgotten about Rukhsana. Go get her, she will do some belly dancing and entertain all of us," Afroz said laughing out loudly.

Rashid's head was spinning by now. He could feel his intestines churning rapidly and felt an acute pain in his abdomen. He felt giddy and sat down. The dream-castle that he had assiduously built over the last several years had come crashing down. He had pawned his daughter Rukhsana, fired bullets at Maulvi *sahab's* son, set the madrasa on fire, all the while thinking that all these acts were a service to Islam, but they were not. He had thought of himself as a Ghazi all these years and had dreamt of a luxurious life in Saudi Arabia with scores of sex slaves under his command. But his own daughter was a sex-slave of the men he worked for. The mirage that he had been chasing had vanished. Rashid remembered the moment when he had thrashed Rukhsana and dragged her like a sheep to be slaughtered by these butchers. He understood that all these while he had been used as a doormat. He felt proud for his nine-year old son Akhtar who at his early age was able to recognise righteous people.

All these years while Rashid thought that he was fighting for Islam and was a Ghazi the likes of Jamil and Afroz thought of ways to sliver his mind, body and soul. They did not even spare his family. He was fooled into giving away his daughter Rukhsana as a sex-slave.

He lifted his hands and held his head with both hands. A sharp pain shot through his spine and his hands soaked in the blood exuding from his wound. The pain shook him from the stupor. Rashid then made a quick decision. "Yes I am a Ghazi," he told himself and stood up. Jamil had said that Rukhsana was on the top floor room of the bungalow.

Rashid came towards the back of the bungalow. He knew there was another staircase at the bungalow's rear that led up to the roof. He tip-toed to these stairs and picked up the axe kept at the stair's curve. Bilal had reached the top floor using the front stairs and was dragging Rukhsana from her room.

Rashid could hear Rukhsana's shrieks as she resisted Bilal. He jumped through the flight of stairs and without uttering a word struck with the axe on Bilal's neck. His neck broke with sharp click sound and a stream of blood gushed out. Rukhsana was petrified. She looked at the man who was her father. Rashid's eye were filled with guilt but Rukhsana was still not in a mood to forgive him.

"Come with me. I know you will never forgive me but this is no time to discuss...please come with me," Rashid crossed Bilal's limp and restless body, held Rukhsana's hands and walked down the front stairs. He held the axe in his right hand, blood dripped from its blade as he climbed down. Rukhsana didn't say a word. Rashid stayed a few steps behind Rukhsana as they came downstairs. Sighting Rukhsana at the stairs Afroz came out of the room to drag her inside.

"Oh my queen. Come on in. You know I am your admirer since the day I saw you naked in your hut. That fucker Rashid kept this beauty in that hut but see your beloved has arranged an air conditioned room for you in this grand bungalow...come on in my queen...," Afroz was babbling under the influence of drugs. He stepped ahead to touch Rukhsana.

"Oh..ahhh....." Afroz could only moan in pain.

Rashid had leapt forward and struck a powerful blow digging the axe deep inside Afroz's chest. He put his feet on Afroz's abdomen and pulled out the axe with full might. Rukhsana shrieked seeing the gush of blood and stepped back crying loudly. Rashid hit two more blows on Afroz's chest killing him, instantly. Hearing the loud noise Anwar, Jamil and Chacha rushed outside. They were all on a high due to drugs and slipped at the door in the pool of Afroz's blood. None of them were in a position to offer much resistance. Jamil made a desperate effort to rebuke Rashid and make him fall in line.

"What's this Rashid? Are you out of your mind? Do you know who am I and what have you done? Do you even under..stand..?" Jamil muttered but his voice was silenced. In a straight and clean jab of the axe Rashid had beheaded Jamil. "Yes I have understood who you are...and I have understood your games...," Rashid huffed as he swung his axe. He kicked Jamil's headless torso and then turned around.

Anwar was lying down in the pool of blood. Rashid bent over and pulled him up by his hair. With a powerful thrust he flung Anwar to the side wall. There was a loud noise as Anwar's skull hit the wall. Rashid picked up his axe and hit him on his head. The axe broke open Anwar's skull and slid inside his head.

Rukhsana was screaming and screeching with terror as she saw Rashid cutting across men. Streams of blood flew all around. She was too terrified to open her eyes and continued to shriek as she sat on the edge of stairs, burying her face within her palms.

Rashid was unusually calm, his heart beat was normal, he was not sweating and felt in control of his body. He did not feel weak in his knees. Today was his day of redemption. He had lived his life in a fool's paradise but this was his moment of reckoning. He knew that he will never be able to get back all that he had lost but at least he should correct the wrongs to whatever extent he can.

With Bilal, Anwar, Afroz and Jamil lying dead Rashid's eyes were searching for Chacha. He was the only one alive. Suddenly he heard the gate's opening sound. Chacha had run away.

Rashid then walked over to Jamil's bedroom and broke open the locker with the axe. He emptied a bag and stuffed as many wads of currency notes as he could and came over to Rukhsana. He held her hand firmly and dragged her with him.

"Please see if you may forgive me someday. I know that I am the one who is responsible for all this...I will surrender to the police...I will tell them everything," Rashid babbled to Rukhsana, driving the motorbike towards the village. There were vast expanse of sugarcane fields on both sides of the muddy lane, it was dark and the only source of light was his motorbike's headlight. In this shimmering light he saw the visage of a man running inside the sugarcane fields. He knew it was Chacha. He felt for his axe, but it wasn't there. He parked his bike aside, handed the bag full of currency notes to Rukhsana and asked her to run to their home that was now a few furlong away.

Chacha was high on marijuana and was unable to run fast. Yet he had managed to call Nadeem after he ran out of the bungalow. Nadeem, in turn, had informed Aakash. Chacha knew Rashid would come after him and so he had tried to take cover of the darkness and hide in the fields. But it was his bad luck or Rukhsana's curse that Rashid saw him in the fields and was now running to get him.

Rashid did not face much difficulty in catching Chacha in that dim moonlight night. Chacha was high on drugs, his steps wobbled and he was unable to run. Rashid kicked him hard on his back and Chacha fell on his face, bleeding profusely through his nose. He turned around and said, "Rashid *bh...ai....sss*"

Rashid was already on his chest and had strangulated him. He stood up and then bent down to feel Chacha's heart beat and pulse. He wanted to verify his kill. Chacha was dead. Rashid got up, bent again and wiped his hands of Chacha's saliva, blood and sputum in his shirt and came back to his motorbike. Rukhsana was not there. He drove the bike to his home.

Rukhsana, Akhtar, Tabassum and their mother were weeping loudly. They had formed a huddle and were holding each other tightly. Rashid parked his motorbike and walked in.

"Where's the bag?" He asked Rukhsana in a calm voice. She signaled to a corner. Rashid picked the bag, held his wife's hand and dragged her and the children inside the room. Showing them the money he said, "...keep this and use them judiciously. This is for you and the children. I am going to surrender to the police. I will tell them the truth. I will tell them the reality of this Kamran and Nadeem, and this Jamil and Afroz...," Rashid was explaining to his wife when there was a loud bang on his gate. He cut short his words and stepped out of the room.

Aakash had informed his 'sources' in police and they had landed up at his place. "Yes, I am coming," Rashid yelled from inside the room and jumped out. A police jeep was standing outside his gate with two policemen pointing the rifle towards him. Rashid raised his hands above his head in an indication of his willingness to surrender to the policemen as he started walking towards the gate. He was smiling when he reached the gate. He expected the policemen to come ahead and arrest him. He turned around to look towards his family, they were bundled together into a huddle in the veranda, several feet behind.

At that moment, a bike with two policemen stopped across the lane. The police officer pulled out his pistol and aimed for Rashid's head. Rashid was standing right in front of him, at the rusty and rickety iron-gate, his hands were raised up and folded behind his head. He was a sitting duck for the bike-borne police officer. The policeman pulled the trigger of his pistol. The bullet pierced Rashid's head, spilling blood on the iron-gate, the mud wall and the dilapidated ground beneath. Rashid fell on the iron-gate with a thud sound, the last time in his life.

29 .

It had been two months since Maulvi *sahab* passed away. He lay peacefully at the Basera cemetery. Every morning Abdul walked up to his beloved *Abbu* before starting his day, he would caress Maulvi *sahab's* body, lovingly press his feet, kissed on his forehead and hugged him tight. So what if Maulvi *sahab* lay asleep several feet below the ground and a heavy concrete slab rested on his chest, Abdul still sought his guidance before he could start his day.

Abdul's wounds had healed, and the doctors had removed the rib brace a day ago. He was walking briskly towards the madrasa. After the unfortunate arson and shoot out, the madrasa had now been revamped. Instead of the earlier five computers, there were twenty computers at the madrasa. It now boasted of a fully furnished library with all modern books, new furniture, fresh paint and dozens of new students. *Mudaakhilat,* the Urdu newspaper was now being re-published, after a brief hiatus. Instead of a computer print-out *Mudaakhilat* was now published on newsprint and was a broadsheet. Dedicated staff worked on separate computers within the madrasa under the able guidance of Aftab *sahab* and Abdul. Basera's madrasa was everything that Maulvi *sahab* had dreamt of, except that he was no longer alive to feel and witness this whiff of fresh air.

But last two months had been extremely difficult for everyone at Basera.

Hundreds of people from Basera and other adjoining villages had converged for Maulvi *sahab's* burial. Everyone had come in to pay their obeisance and attend his last journey. Abdul limped as he walked, his movement restricted due to the rib-brace and the sling that hung from his right shoulder. There was a sea of people in the tiny village, there were Sunnis, Shias, *Ismailis, Bohras, Ahmadiyyas* and the Hindus.

Amongst this mass was Hussein Ali, the textile mill owner and Aftab *sahab's* distant relative who had earlier been in talks to invest in *Mudaakhilat*. At Maulvi *sahab's* funeral he had the opportunity to interact with villagers and get first-hand information about their issues. Ali being a learned and progressive man, had quietly promised Aftab *sahab* to provide funds for the madrasa and *Mudaakhilat*.

The next morning, a few enthusiastic students had begun cleaning up the madrasa of charred wood, books and computers. These kids were joined by Fawzia, Heena, Anjali, Anil and Arjun. Seeing their enthusiasm Abdul, Sakina and Begum *sahiba* had come out of their home. With tears in their eyes they too began clearing up the mess and were soon joined by several other villagers. It was then that Akhtar, Rashid's son, had come over to the madrasa and begged other children to be a part of the team. Nobody had wanted Rashid's son to come and be a part of the madrasa and it was Begum *sahiba* who had come forward to hug the nine-year old Akhtar.

Later that evening when Akhtar stood up to Rashid, his abusive father, he had blurted out that he would soon be studying at the madrasa and that the villagers are busy revamping and renovating the madrasa. This seemed terrible news to Rashid and he had rushed to tell his Jamil *bhai* about it.

Rashid did not know that Jamil and Afroz had been keeping a close eye on all these developments. Even Aakash and Nadeem had every information about the ongoing activities at madrasa. Nadeem and Aakash had already dismissed the revamping plans of Basera madrasa as a minor issue. Aakash had confidently told Jamil that with Maulvi *sahab's* death, the madrasa did not pose any immediate threat to their plans.

"This is just an emotional upheaval of the villagers. All this will fizzle out in a few days. With that Maulvi gone, we are now safe. Stop worrying about them and concentrate on planning and organizing *Maulana* Kamran's Islamic congregations. We need to cement our place now," Aakash had told Jamil. He was not even bothered about the deserters Anil, Anjali, Heena and Fawzia. "...these are all foot soldiers, we don't need to worry too much about them. I will crush each one of them when the time comes. Think and plan about Kamran's *majlis*," Aakash had said, his tone exuding over-confidence. Nadeem had also cheered up Jamil's efforts, the Wahhabi clerics in Saudi Arabia were elated that Maulvi *sahab* had been decimated. Wahhabis were confident that with the death of learned Maulvi *sahab* the introduction of modern subjects and computers cannot become a movement across madrasas and that they would continue to retain their grip over Muslim minds.

Jamil had broken these news to his team who were now ecstatic. Afroz wanted some special revelry to celebrate Maulvi *sahab's* conquest. He had asked his men to get marijuana and heroin to spice up the celebrations.

Rashid was in hiding due to his head injury, completely cut off from these discussions and oblivious of the drug party at Jamil's bungalow. When his nine-year old son confronted him and told about the ongoing activities to resurrect the madrasa, he lost his cool. In his naivety, Rashid had rushed to Jamil's bungalow to apprise him about the resurrection of 'devil's den' only to find that Jamil was the real devil and his bungalow and was the actual devil's den. As he eavesdropped into Jamil's talks the reality dawned upon him that he had been used as a tool for their devious political games. It was then that Rashid hacked each one of them. Things could have been different if Chacha had not escaped from the bungalow before Rashid strangulated him in the fields. Chacha had telephoned Nadeem and Aakash about Rashid. A shrewd politician that he was, Aakash had immediately called up his accomplices in police and had clearly instructed to kill Rashid.

"Do whatever you have to, but don't take this man into custody. Just finish him off. He should not be allowed to give any statement to the police or to the media," Aakash had given clear instructions to the police officer. It was due to Aakash's connections that two police inspectors arrived on a motorbike and had shot at Rashid's head even when he was unarmed and stood with his hands up in the air, to surrender. The police inspectors had clear instructions to kill Rashid. And they did kill him.

The publication of *Allah-e-Niyamat* was abruptly stopped that evening, there was no edition the next morning and thereafter. The village Muslims never knew what *Allah-e-Niyamat's* regular columnist and the 'revered cleric' *Maulana* Kamran had to say about the spate of killings at the bungalow.

However, the mainstream newspapers and news channels had extensive coverage of the massacre. Rashid was dubbed as the dangerous terrorist who could be neutralised only after he had slaughtered 'social workers Jamil and Afroz' at a 'sleepy village that was just two hundred kilometres from Delhi'.

These newspapers, magazines and news channels maintained an eerie silence about the arson and shooting at the *Khidmat-ul-Islam* madrasa at Basera, and there was hardly any coverage of this mayhem.

Aftab *sahab* had been reading and following all the news. That morning he had picked up the newspaper when his eyes rested on a news item about his Basera village. The newspaper had reported that the police inspector who had fired and killed Rashid was being recommended for a bravery medal. Aftab *sahab* folded the newspaper and switched off the television news channel, without saying a word. He put on his shoes. He had better things to do. He had to reach the madrasa.

Aakash and Nadeem were in a daze. With the death of Jamil and Afroz their election calculations had gone haywire. They had begun screening new electoral candidates. The spate of killings aside they were still under tremendous pressure from the Wahhabi financiers in Saudi Arabia to win the upcoming elections.

"This man Jamil was not up to the mark, his inability to bridle that illiterate Rashid could cost us these elections," Nadeem said with a morose face, as Aakash and Kamran looked on. He had been receiving flak from the Wahhabi sheikhs and clerics who were unrelenting and castigated him for mishandling the situation.

"Don't worry Nadeem *bhai*. The Wahhabi *fatwas* still rule over Muslim minds and their thoughts. There are hundreds and thousands of Rashids living in penury who may sleep on empty stomach but will pick up a gun in the name of Islam. And it's just a matter of time that we find out another Jamil," Kamran said with a smug face, gulping down the whiskey. Aakash remained silent. He knew all these were easier said than done. "It takes time and effort to rule someone's mind. It's not going to be easy," he said sipping the whiskey, gazing into a blank.

Kamran stood and walked up to Aakash. He kept his hands on his shoulders and shook him. "We have been doing this for the last several years. We will do it once again," Kamran said, his mouth and eye wide open, his beard shook vigorously as he nodded to Aakash.

Aakash and Nadeem broke into a smile, an impish smile indeed.

Fawzia and Rukhsana were typing at the computers when Abdul arrived. The girls came very early in the morning to practice what they had learnt the previous day about computers. During day they typed the hand-written articles that came in for publication in *Mudaakhilat*. Heena was in-charge of the madrasa library.

Fawzia and Heena had now shifted to Rukhsana's hut. Rukhsana's mother was generous enough to welcome the sisters into their home. She had bought a sewing machine and two buffaloes that brought a steady income. Akhtar and Tabassum were now regular students at the madrasa.

Sakina was handling the project to set up the tomato ketchup plant at Basera. Of course Abdul guided her, but it was Sakina who was now spearheading the project. Arjun got busy in his father's sugar-mill and extended all possible help to Sakina and Abdul to set up the tomato ketchup plant at their village. They had ordered for the machinery and construction of the plant was in full swing.

Anjali and Anil had formally quit FPI. Anjali had joined a news magazine and Anil took up the job of research associate at a think tank. They came over quite often at Basera to meet Abdul and Sakina.

"*Salam-walekum bhai jaan*," Fawzia and Rukhsana said in unison. They were working on the computers when Abdul walked inside the madrasa.

"*Walekum-salam*," Abdul replied, walking slowly towards the classes. The class was in full attendance when he walked in.

Since childhood he had heard Maulvi *sahab*, his father, say that the greatest sin in Allah's eyes is to sit idle and do nothing. "…yes the devil will play his games, there is no doubt about it…but all good people should ask themselves what have they done to stop this devil in its tracks… Have you done enough to stop devil's designs? Ask this question to yourself…and if you hear a loud 'No' to this question…. then spruce up your efforts…," Maulvi *sahab* had taught Abdul since his childhood.

Abdul had understood that Jamil, Afroz and all his cronies were mere pawns in the larger geo-political game of the Wahhabis. The real architects of the game were sitting pretty in Saudi Arabia and their proxies had taken a tactical retreat. They were busy identifying and grooming the next set of pawns who will soon come to occupy the haunted bungalow of Jamil and the defunct Chacha's tea stall.

But then Maulvi *sahab* had always said, '…this is a battle of ideas and for the mind space. A bunch of thugs cannot and should not dictate about what is Islam. These ruffians are able to occupy the mind space of a Muslim and establish the interpretations given by the likes of *'Maulana'* Kamran only because the enlightened Muslims never bother to educate others about the true spirit of Islam.'

Abdul was on the path to change all this. He knew it was just a matter of time when a new Jamil and a newer Afroz would come to his Basera. Yet, he knew that this time the villagers will not be ill-prepared. He will educate them, he will empower them with knowledge and he will enlighten them about Islam.

'They want to turn Muslims into a mass of zombies, but I will turn them into enlightened humans,' Abdul told himself as he walked on.

"*Salam-walekum* Maulvi *sahab*," the kids cheerfully greeted Abdul as he entered the classroom.

"Walekum-salam," Abdul replied, sitting on the chair.

"...the first and foremost thing a pious and true Muslim should do is to open up his mind. Let thoughts and ideas come from all sides... never try to close your mind. And for this to happen, you need to question and you should think and think hard...about yourself, your surroundings, and your country and of course about Islam....," Abdul said as the children listened in rapt attention. "...let's start from the beginning."

Yes, Abdul had picked up his father's mantle. He had initiated the process to modernise madrasa education into a mass movement. This would be the first line of defence against impending Wahhabi firestorm. The battle for Islamic reformation had begun.

ABOUT THE AUTHOR

Vivek Sinha is a New Delhi-based Journalist, Columnist and Film Maker. He has been writing news commentaries for over a decade and over the last several years he has written news reports for leading publications of India such as The Times of India, Hindustan Times, Deccan Chronicle and The Asian Age. He now writes Opinion Columns at several news portals and blogs for The Times of India. Apart from writing, Vivek is also passionate about films. He has made several short-films and documentaries. His recent Documentary "Muzaffarnagar—*aakhir kyon?*" that details the 2013 communal riots at Muzaffarnagar was highly appreciated and has been extremely popular.

Chip in the Madrasa is Vivek's first book.

Printed in Great Britain
by Amazon